M[...]

Thanks for coming.
I hope you enjoy
the book.

Leaving Lisa

Michael McMullen

Michael McMullen

 FriesenPress

One Printers Way
Altona, MB R0G 0B0
Canada

www.friesenpress.com

Copyright © 2025 by Michael McMullen
First Edition — 2025

ISBN
978-1-03-916712-4 (Hardcover)
978-1-03-916711-7 (Paperback)
978-1-03-916713-1 (eBook)

1. FIC027020 FICTION, ROMANCE, CONTEMPORARY

Distributed to the trade by The Ingram Book Company

AUTHOR'S NOTES

Leaving Lisa originated from a conversation I overheard at a diner well over 20 years ago. Years later my wife Deb told me about a book, The Dinner, written by Herman Koch. He was inspired by conversations at a dinner with friends and the book almost immediately formed in his head. My instant reply to Deb was that I believe I had the perfect opening sentence for a book. Upon hearing the sentence Deb disagreed that it was 'perfect'. (We will let you, the reader, judge that.) The difference between Koch and myself was his story formed almost immediately, whereas I didn't have anything but the opening line. Just a snippet of a conversation that became a personal brain worm.

That sentence and the diner setting was the genesis for *Leaving Lisa*. I always felt that sentence was laden with surprise, sensuality, some consternation and a world of possibilities for storytelling.

At the diner I was in fact eating alone, as often was my preference on business trips. The diner was humble but resonated with a sense of vibrancy and offered comfort food that you could count on. Anecdotally when travelling in new places the classic club sandwich was always my go to. The club sandwich is hard to screw up. On occasion, if the atmosphere was right, and the waitress recommended I would go with meatloaf, a meal that both my late mother and Deb have perfected. I am digressing, back to the story creation.

I had a good starting point. I realized that was all I had and faced the daunting challenge of creating with only spare change in my writing wallet. The setting was simple, and the four characters were there. A couple, a waitress and an eavesdropper. Could I develop a story line that weaved the four characters together? How would or could I write in the respective voices of these four disparate characters? Who were these people? These questions and many others I posed to myself at the outset of *Leaving Lisa*, even before I had a name for the book. This led to a very enjoyable and challenging writing process. Hopefully Leaving Lisa will be an enjoyable reading experience for you. After all I am asking you to check your wallets, purses or whatever means you use for payment to eavesdrop on their conversations at GoHo's diner.

The first draft of Leaving Lisa was completed in late summer 2020 at the same time as I finished writing 'Garbage Boy - The High Bar of Low Expectations.' We decided to bring *Garbage Boy* to daylight first as that tale was the sequel to *Scarred*, my first book. That decision, while natural, was also very prudent. *Leaving Lisa* was not in good shape. There were lots of strong elements, but the characters were underdeveloped, and their interactions weren't congruent with their individual journeys. I was fighting to build relationships between the characters that were believable and not convoluted. This led to 'editing' out some relationship bridges that just didn't work and were unnecessary to the story telling.

The second draft changed the structure of the chapters and delineated the characters perspectives and their separate lives. The third draft built the back stories of the characters and created an interesting juxtaposition of those backgrounds.

Lisa is a musician. The book contains the lyrics to twelve songs, which are in various forms of production that we hope to bring to market and your ears. My favorites are 'Cut In Half; The Maybe Song: Getting to Good and Doesn't Much Matter'.

So welcome to Leaving Lisa! I hope you enjoy your time spent with Guy, Mo, Lisa and Smackin' Mackin'.

Sincerely, Michael

 Guy

 Mo

 Lisa

 Mackin

 Song

CHAPTER 1

Eavesdropping at the Diner

"Let's just go to the condo and fuck!!"

I was already surreptitiously glancing at her when I heard the words come out.

"Okay." The response carried less enthusiasm than I would have expected.

"Now. Right now."

That was not a question from her but an expression in the imperative form. Strange that the urgency of the command didn't match the tone of her voice, meaning that the seemingly implied immediacy of the need wasn't matched by a blatantly lustful tone. There was a definite lack of eroticism or sensuality in both timbre and pitch.

"Sure."

His responses lacked vigour, enthusiasm, and excitement. They were compliant, almost wallowing in defeat or loss. Fatigue was present and lust absent, so dichotomous the words versus the voices. This was a big man whose immediate fate seemingly lay beyond, well, the lay.

She stretched her arms, cupping the corners of her side of the table, and leaned forward, accentuating her chest. It was a formidable, almost intimidating posture. Her physicality was congruent with the command ringing in my brain, shortened and sanitized to "Let's go screw."

On the other side of their booth, his shoulders were slumped, his hands clasped together, resting on the tabletop in a prayerful mode before they collapsed into his lap. It was the posture of compliance, of going along the path of least resistance.

"Get up, get your coat, and let's go."

She pushed out from behind the table, her raven, shoulder-length hair catching all kinds of illumination and colours from the window and the diner lights. She was about one hundred and thirty-five pounds, five foot five or six, appearing taller because of her knee-high boots and shortish black skirt, topped with a tight white blouse. Curved, she radiated physical strength. She caught me looking, surveyed me with a cursory stare, she dismissed my stare, then waited for his response.

"Yes, coming."

He was six foot three, 215 or 220. Cut, ripped, a specimen. His blue T-shirt displayed firm abs and pecs. Over it he wore a patterned navy flannel shirt open to his waist, blue jeans, dock shoes, and no socks, despite the November cold.

"Put it on my tab."

The waitress nodded, and I reflected on what seemed to be an old, quaint expression. "Put it on my tab." I hadn't said that phrase anywhere for a long time, maybe never when leaving a restaurant.

It was 4:30 on a wet, drizzly Wednesday afternoon. I had decided to have a late lunch and then head home. I never used to eavesdrop. Don't know when that started. Tuning my ears up and outward to the sounds of the lives of others rather than living my own life. I imagined—no, I knew—that before things changed others would listen in on our conversations when we were out and about. We had often been described as a dazzling couple, and people would lean toward our dinner table to hear our conversation whether we were alone or with other couples. People on the outside trying to look in. Now it was me observing and eavesdropping. Maybe I was hoping for a vicarious spark of conversation that would ignite at least a low flame in my life.

After they left, I watched them walk past the window. Her head was up, her eyes forward as she trailed her bare hand with black nails, expecting but not waiting for him to catch hold. He shrugged and leaned forward, hands in his pockets, his posture not hiding his powerful physique but diminishing his strength more than one could imagine was possible. My last glimpse was his hand stretching to catch hers and missing.

Badly, it seemed.

CHAPTER 2

Learning a Little About Lisa

"Hey, Guy. Once you stop staring, would you wanna be placing an order anytime in the near future?"

The words and physical actions I had just witnessed seemed so incongruent that I was digesting them rather than reading the menu. Standing in front of me, the waitress appeared to be a mashup of era, air, and attitude, although she was clearly not from that era. Her outfit was right out of the 1950s, down to the thin paper tiara stuck in her hair. Her demeanour seemed contrived as if to fit some stereotype of a brash, brazen tough waitress in some truck stop or late-night hash house. I found myself thinking about her as a character in a dime store detective novel. I don't know if such a thing ever existed or exists now, but that was how I was thinking.

"What's the daily special?"

She flinched at my words. She was maybe in her early to mid-thirties, short, thick brunette hair, five foot one or two, a bit stocky. Her name tag read "Mo." That seemed to suit her attitude. Mo, as in "in *motion*" and "*Move* it along, buddy. Place your order. It ain't rocket science or advanced algebra, and I hated that math crap anyway. Things to do, people to see, places to go, so place your goddam order." She had an aura of impatience because it was a diner where things moved quickly. "A uniform from the 1950s doesn't mean drive in the slow lane, Grandpa." Even though Mo wasn't from the 1950s, she was playing the part of the waitress expediting the dining experience. Was it her real personality, or was she just playing a role?

"Meatloaf, same as yesterday, and if you look forward to tomorrow, it will be meatloaf again. November is meatloaf month, and weren't you here yesterday?"

Yes, I was, and I was sitting at the same table, in the same seat, at almost the same time. My early workday started at 6:00 a.m.; I put in a long, ten-hour day at minimum, every day, with no breaks, which had me eating lunch/dinner in the late afternoon, often followed by a return to work for a couple more hours. The diner was a convenient spot, halfway between work and my new condo, which was just temporary, until I settled down or got myself under control, as my best friend would say.

3

Mo stared me down, waiting for an answer. She shifted her weight, jutting her right hip out for balance, so she could tap her left foot in a cadence of impatience while drumming with her number 4 HB pencil on her order pad. Mo had "rhythmic attitude aggression syndrome." That new medical diagnosis, which occurred to me at that moment, made me laugh inside and push out a smile.

"The meatloaf, Mo. That'll be fine. Especially in *Mo*vember."

Mo looked perplexed by my words and my tone. I had become unexpectedly pleasant, with a bit of humour and had moved to a first-name basis, all in honour of meatloaf month. Her number 4 HB pencil scratched down the order, which she simply recorded as "MLS."

Mo gave me a thorough once-over and then began her interrogation to document the specifics of the meal.

"Mashed or fries?"

"Fries."

"Gravy?"

"Yes."

"Where? All over or on the side?"

"On the side please."

"Oh, a dipper, eh? And a pleasant dipper at that."

"Yes, a pleasant dipper."

"Isn't that sweet. Anything to drink?"

"Cold, white skimmed milk in a tall glass, if you have that, please."

"You just made a glass of milk sound like some complicated Starbucks order. Good for you. I'll check for the thin white stuff and let you know. MLS, fries, gravy, side, with a tall,

lean cow juice, cold."

Mo turned on her right heel and pivoted to go place the order. Her movement struck me as rhythmic, fluid, and efficient.

That hand reaching out and missing, why did I have to see that? I wasn't sure if I was melancholy, self-absorbed, dazed, or just generally messed up. I was trying to walk in a straight line toward a new normal, but I couldn't shake the love I had for my old normal. My best friend said the way I was living wasn't normal. My life was complacent, compliant, comfortable, and cancerous. He liked words that began with "c," not to mention alliterations. I was a fan too. Had that started with characters who said, "sufferin' succotash" and "wascally wabbit?" Who knows, who cares?

"Hey, Guy, we have no lean moo squeeze. What's your second bet?"

"Chocolate milk. It doesn't have to be skimmed."

"Winner, winner, chicken dinner!"

Pivot, gone.

Melancholy. That's what I decided to go with. A whole lot better than morose, depressed, or anxious. Reflective is a good state of mind, right? I asked myself questions, and I answered. All silently of course, so I didn't disturb others, because I wanted to be polite and well mannered. Professional. I also didn't want to appear to be an addled, stirred, and shaken lost soul speaking gibberish to himself, although I have lost a little of my soul. I chose to go with "comfortable."

I was comfortable and content in my old normal. I thought that was pretty good, maybe not all it could have been but far better than it might have been. I would have scored it eight and a half out of ten, the freaking Eastern-bloc judges pulling my score down for lack of creativity and artistic merit. The lower scores came in at six to six and a half, meaning my performance wasn't terrible and was technically sound, but it was also flat, lacking spontaneity, surprise, and sensuality. Or something like that. Close but no cigar, another appropriate phrase for a 1950s-era diner.

GoHo's itself was a piece of work, an antiquity from the 1950s. The front of the diner faced a major thoroughfare in an area called the "SHED," the Sports, Hospitality, Entertainment District. How clever. The window tables were all double-backed red booths with grey Arborite tabletops. In those booths, patrons couldn't see behind them or over to the next booth. They were designed to encourage patrons to focus on their dining companions. If anyone felt the need to have their back covered, they were blind from the rear. That would cause Mafia types some trepidation. However, people could be seen.

The diner had a small, elevated section at the rear. A couple of steps up were the washrooms, and before that was a landing with one high tabletop for two with high barstools. The spot was elevated above the crowd and had a constant stream of people passing by on their way to, well, pass their own streams.

"Here's the brown stuff. You know most guys have a cold beer with the house special."

Mo was sharing insights into guys living my lifestyle. How comforting to know I was part of a group of melancholy, middle-aged men who chose meatloaf. I'm sure Mo hadn't read me as melancholy yet. By "guys" did she really mean guys my age?

Mo was still standing at my table, waiting for a response. I think she wanted to engage me in conversation. Her comment begged for a response, and to hide my melancholy I should have had some snappy comeback.

"No beer. I'm in training."

"Yep, Guys in training usually go with meatloaf, fries, gravy, and full-weight chocolate milk."

"I got a huge hula hoop tourney coming up, and I need to be more circular to get those babies rotating."

"I should enter. I have the circumference for that."

"Not going there."

"Wise man. Hey, I caught you staring at our resident power couple. Well, mostly gawking at the lovely Lisa."

"Yes, they are striking."

"Stop being so politically correct. She has that boy by the balls, and if I can be so crass, he looks and acts pussy whipped."

"Well, that's not how I would describe him, but he did seem compliant and responsive to her lead."

"Man, you're PC to the T."

"I don't like to surmise or read too much into surface observations or snatches of conversation."

"Do you know who they are? Don't you recognize them?"

"They seem vaguely familiar. She would be hard to forget, but I can't place either of them."

Mo shook her head in a manner that conveyed I had just dropped in from another planet. "That's Lisa from the Fashion Channel show of the same name and her current boyfriend, former CFL all-star Al Mackin."

"Now that you mention it, their names ring a bell."

"You're too young to be senile, so I'm going to say your current life has you fully occupied or that your life has conspired to preoccupy your mind because those two are everywhere in this town."

Pivot, gone. Mo could move! She would probably be dynamic in a hula hoop contest. Yes, I had seen and read about those two, more him than her, as my reading predilection was the sports pages rather than the fashion section. He was a stud linebacker, American, from one of the southern states I think, played a couple of years in the NFL, won Grey Cups, Defensive Player of the Year a couple of times, and was perennial all-star. Used to wear his hair long and was nicknamed "Smackin' Mackin." Resembled Thor and was a god on the field who brought the thunder.

As for her, I remember her on award shows, interviewing celebrities and wannabes on the red carpet. She was certainly striking, and her appearance and get-up indicated she had a fashion sense. Then again, what did I know about fashion? I had mentally referred to her wardrobe or outfit or whatever as her "get-up." I needed help. I needed to get out more and expand my horizons. I planned to Google hula hoop contests that night.

The centre of the diner was a straight row of ten tables for four. The furnishings were all kitchen dining circa the 1950s with grey Arborite tables with chromed grooved trim and matching chrome chairs with red vinyl seats. The things were probably worth a lot on the vintage market. The centre of the diner provided a full vista of the restaurant except not fully into the booths on the front and inside back walls, unless a person was directly across from them, as I was with the recently departed power couple. Later, I learned that the centre part of the diner was called "No Man's Land."

"Here you go, Guy. The house special with fries and gravy on the side. Like some freshly ground pepper with that?"

"Pardon?"

"Freshly ground pepper. Would you like some?"

"Yes, please."

"Good luck with that, unless you brought your own."

"But you asked . . ."

"Sure, I was checking to see if you were still on this particular orbit of our planet. You look a little distant, and my job includes the provision of free reality checks. Part of our patron services here at GoHo's."

"So, you don't serve freshly ground pepper?"

"Serve it? Man, we wouldn't even recognize it. This is GoHo's diner, not the Keg."

"Okay, so you're just pulling my leg."

"Hey guy, watch the sexual overtones! I ain't pulling nothing of yours."

"I meant—"

"Jaysus, boy, relax. I'm just playing with you. You gotta get out more. Lisa and Al, they're the city's current power couple. Looks, money, notoriety, brand profile, and sexy."

"Okay, I just—"

"You should just shut up and tuck in."

Pivot. Gone.

You know, maybe my head is stuck up my ass. I can't respond or even decipher an obvious joke. Freshly ground pepper anyone? The diner's name was Gord Hood's, but the last two letters in Gord and the second O and the D burned out on the neon sign, so the place became GoHo's, according to local legend, which was written on the back page of the menu.

The exterior of the diner was vintage fifties look. It was run down and appeared less than hygienic from the exterior. The diner had the same feel, ambience and look of the cover of Hall & Oates 'Abandoned Luncheonette' album. There was even a pay telephone out front on the side of the telephone pole. Younger folks and hipsters made and received calls from that phone for a vintage, retrospective experience. People of my vintage sometimes made calls from the pay phone for nostalgic reasons.

The meatloaf was excellent, and the fries and gravy were fantastic. The obligatory vegetable was carrots, and they were tender and buttery, with a taste of maple syrup. It was a thoroughly enjoyable meal. What wine did people order with meatloaf? I really did need to get out more. But look at me, being all reflective and mentally complimenting the fine cuisine at GoHo's diner. No melancholy here. You'll find melancholy where they do serve freshly ground pepper. In an unexplainable way, I was feeling good. The meatloaf and Mo's banter had lifted my spirits. I was thinking my spirit bar had to be terribly low, and that thought made me smile.

The diner's back wall was also two steps up. It hosted five curved booths, each of which comfortably sat six or eight people with a little squeeze. The back of the booths was the same type of red velvet or an approximation of velvet that covered the front booths and were about seven feet high. Small people seemed dwarfed when they sat in one of those booths. The tabletop was a dark wood that, in many places, had been worn light. Those were the power booths, commanding the heights of the restaurant. People sat in the centre three booths to be seen. They sat in the two end booths to be discreet, clandestine, or because they were the only booths available. The latter was the most likely scenario, though I do wonder about what type of shenanigans took place in those obscured end booths. Shenanigans? I was locked into a 1950s mindset and vocabulary.

"Enjoying the chew, are we? I caught you grinning. Meatloaf will do that! Anything you need?"

"Freshly ground pepper."

"Listen to you all Mister Funny Man now. Good to see you docking with your earth station."

"I do know about Mr. Mackin but not so much about her."

"So, you are curious and you want the skinny on the lovely Lisa, do you? Well, here's the nickel tour. Former beauty queen of some kind, like the Dairy Butter Princess or something like that. A good singer, her band had a few hits, then she kind of fell off the rails when her manager, who was her first husband, screwed her over on her contracts and royalties. She started over, as rumour has it, after some intense therapy. Issues with her parents were more than a bit of what she had to deal with as well. Apparently, the lovely Lisa always had an eye for fashion. She designs upscale stuff, has her own TV show, and designs exclusive clothing for a roster of upscale clients. Unofficially, she's a ball buster. Dates who she wants when she wants and drops them as she wants. Al there will be getting dropped like a bad fumble sooner than later."

"No offence, Mo, but why do they dine here?"

"None taken. Lisa's beginnings, while not entitled, were somewhat privileged and very different from most women like her. The parents again. She likes the reality and the ambience that GoHo's offers. Seriously."

"Okay. Do they come here often?"

"She has and does come every Monday night for dinner and maybe late one night on the weekend for what she calls 'growl chow.'"

"What does that mean?"

"Late at night, been drinking, tummy is growling. . .that kinda chow."

"Good to know."

"Why? You going to start drinking and coming in late at night after your hula hoop wins?"

"Yeah, something like that."

She smiles. Pivot. Gone.

So, I was mightily intrigued by the lovely Lisa and her current arm candy, Al Mackin. "Smackin' Mackin" was legendary in CFL circles. He was a sportscaster now with his own talk show. It struck me that, even eight to ten years after he'd ended his career on his own terms, it looked like he could play tomorrow.

Mo returned, smiling. "Now you look all contemplative and deep. Where are you now? Venus? The planet of love?"

"This planet, this hemisphere, this country, this city, and apparently, in a certain diner with a brash, intrusive waitress named Mo."

"Nailed it! Two points for keeping it real. Dessert or bill?"

"Bill please."

"Here you go. Pay at the counter. I prefer tips in cash, and feel free to tip extravagantly. You're getting some high-quality banter included with the meatloaf."

"The meatloaf is definitely high quality, the banter iffy, just okay."

"More snappiness and wit. Don't forget the lavish cash tip."

Pivot. Gone. She gave a brief glance back and a smile. Mo had to be highly appreciated by the owners of that place. I would return just for her entertainment value. The bill was $17.13 with taxes. I left a five-dollar bill, which I was surprised I had because I didn't use cash much. At the counter I noticed they don't take credit, just debit and cash. Good to know. I often just carried my small wallet with my licence and credit card.

I paid and then left. The walk home was a quick two blocks to the upscale condo I was staying in for free. One of the senior executive VPs in our firm was in Europe for two years on assignment. He had been paying someone to take care of the place, and although I could afford to pay, he insisted I didn't, so I didn't argue. The condo was on the sixty-fourth floor of a seventy-floor building. He wanted it to be higher. I think mostly he wanted someone occupying the space so his ex-wife couldn't get in and wreak havoc. The divorce was bitter, as she had caught him in an affair with a junior vice president in the investments branch of our firm. The way she caught him was legendary. She found him with his ass pressed against the floor-to-ceiling windows in their bedroom, with the junior VP riding him like bucking bronco. The thought of his extremely fat ass flattened against that window was enough to make me throw up just a little. How the ex-wife came upon the affair has circulated throughout the company as the "fat ass windows incident." The junior VP was transferred to the States in a role that paid more with great upside bonus potential. She wouldn't be returning to Canada, or at least not to head office. Neither would he. Corporate exile but comfortable.

I had been an executive vice president for two years, and at only forty-nine years old, I still had lots of runway. Yippee! I was ascending to a ridiculously lavish, expensively furnished almost penthouse suite where I lived for free. I felt like a university grad who had moved back home, and his parents were letting him live rent free, use the car—the good one—and bring girls home to the basement, except this was no basement. I did take his two expensive cars out for long drives—at his request—to keep them in running shape.

My first internet search was for Al Mackin, primarily to prove to myself that

I wasn't some type of perv for searching lovely Lisa first. His story was much like I remembered. A football career, glory, trophies, and the CFL Hall of Fame. Broadcaster, sports analyst, columnist, radio talk-show gigs, and a sought-after motivational speaker. He also had a line of clothing with Lisa that they were growing and promoting. Her wealthy female clients liked the idea of their hubbies dressed in fashion by Smackin' Mackin, the epitome of "studliness" himself. I imagined most of them would have loved to see his ass up against a floor-to-ceiling window too. The oddly disturbing thing about Smackin' Mackin was that all the commentary pointed to what an extraordinarily good guy he was. At forty-three, he had been running his own charity for almost twenty years, running sports camps for underprivileged youth, donating his time and money. He spent all six weeks of his summer at his summer camps. His campers were awarded scholarships, and even though football wasn't the main focus of the camps, two Smackin' Mackin camp graduates were in the NFL, and eleven had played or were playing in the CFL. His camps were about building character, attitude, and fitness. The guy was too good to be true.

And Lisa had this man of men by the balls, big time. Or so it appeared to the manly me on a stomach full of meatloaf and brown milk.

Lisa turned out to be even more extraordinary. She served on the boards of three publicly traded firms, one private company, and two significant charitable organizations. Plus, she chaired her own foundation, but she didn't have a seat at the Smackin' Mackin Foundation table. Al was nowhere on any of the boards she graced with her presence. It appeared their relationship didn't include overlapping or interlocked boards. Their own business endeavour didn't appear to have a board of any kind.

Lisa kept her hand in music, not to mention a foot and her brain. She owned a production company that had introduced numerous new acts and had several gold records and industry awards. She still wrote songs, and several of her clients had recorded them, including a number of notable chart toppers. Lisa toured with her own "house band" for six weeks in the summer. Her shows sold out. In addition to the TV show, she did numerous guest appearances in all media, wrote for magazines and newspapers and her blog, and had tens of thousands of followers on Facebook, X, and Instagram. Her posts were humorous, opinionated, tactless, direct, and current. I signed up to follow her on X. I didn't participate on Facebook or Instagram for personal and professional reasons.

Lisa was a one-woman wonder. At age forty-seven, she was big and getting bigger. She came from a semi-privileged background. Her parents were serial monogamists. Her father became infamous a few years back for a quote after his fifth divorce. "I meet a woman, fall in love, buy her a house, and it turns out after two, three, or four years, I hate her. By then the feelings are mutual."

When pressed about why he was venturing into his sixth marital sojourn, his answer was equally notorious. "Turns out I'm an optimist, I believe if at first you don't succeed, try, try, try again. Besides, my lawyer has really improved at pre-nups." Mrs. Upcoming Number Six must have been very happy to read that!

Lisa's mother was trailing in marital failures by one, currently working on number five. Her claim to fame was her ability to move up the food chain with each marriage. She had the extraordinary ability to marry someone much richer every time. Apparently, her lawyer was also excellent at pre-nups, her wealth having grown by leaps and bounds.

My conjecture was that Lisa's one failed marriage and apparent lack of pre-nup and disadvantageous services contact had soured her on the matrimonial state. Lisa had moved through and beyond four significant relationships, Al being number five. She was estimated to have a net worth of fifteen to twenty million.

She was her parents' only child and counted only one half-brother from her father's third marriage. He wouldn't do well in her father's will. Lisa and her mother's charitable interests would inherit that world. Lisa was set. Her birth parents adored her, and she had never built any significant relationships with any of her nine step parents. Nine? It boggled my mind.

Mackin was forty-three, only six years younger than me.

Oh yeah, Lisa owned a condo on the thirty-sixth floor of my current residence where, currently, she was "'shackin' with Smackin." I giggled as I shut down the Lisa and Al show. She had been the Dairy Queen for the whole southwestern region of the province, and she had never milked a cow.

I did look at her photo gallery, which was maintained on her website. A little ego at play there. She had been striking since age fourteen. Was that a huge burden to bear? The curse of the extremely good looking? I had known girls like that in high school, from a distance. I wasn't in their league.

In high school my hand was always trailing and missing badly. Of course, their hands were never extended.

CHAPTER 3

Best Seat in The House

"I work the late shift every Friday and Saturday from six to four in the morning. The cash tips are phenomenal."

"Thanks, Mo. Good to know. I can be verbally abused for ten straight hours on the weekend nights."

"Guy, you're going to have to move from this table."

"Why? Am I sitting at one of your more lucrative tables reserved for your high-rolling patrons?"

"No, but you're outside of my jurisdiction, and I can see you need my wisdom, guidance, and outstanding service, so we're going to move you."

"Where? The place is full."

"Wait in the doorway—I mean foyer—for ten minutes. I'm going to put you in the best seat in the house."

The foyer was the place between the outside glass doors and the inside glass doors. "Foyer" was a bit of an overstep for a description. I was nestled in the so-called foyer with four other GoHo's patrons-to-be. So, at 2:00 on a Saturday night, Sunday morning to be exact, after watching the Leafs perform dismally against the LA Kings in the fifty-fourth year of their Stanley Cup drought and not being able to sleep, I decided to wander down to GoHo's for some growl chow. I hadn't been drinking, not even a beer to soothe the senses of my tattered Leaf emotions. They had last won the Cup five years before I was born. My dad was a lifelong Leafs fan and had first loved the Toronto St. Pat's, who also hadn't won the Cup in a long time. They had a more reasonable excuse, as they no longer existed. These two teams' odds of winning a Cup in my lifetime were both dismally equal, despite the current clamour of "Leaf Nation," as their followers were called. The Leafs currently resided in a playoff position, sparking some ill-born hope and optimism. Mom had converted to the Leafs when Dad passed, although her dearly beloved Blackhawks had won the Cup three times in recent years. She said it was the right thing to do. Personally, I didn't think she had fully converted. She still loved that Blackhawk sweater and the crest.

"Right this way, Guy. Best seat in the house."

Mo took me to a two-seater high-top table with stools at the far back window corner.

"You can see all the entries and exits. Warn me if you see any D and Ds. You know, dine-and-dash characters. All the bars and clubs are down that way, so the traffic flow at this time of night is all coming in your direction. You'll enjoy the show. It's a bit more exotic and erotic in summer, but it's still a good show."

"Thanks, Mo."

"Also, the high top allows a complete view of GoHo's, even into the booths. Let me know if you see any hanky-panky. I'll want to watch too."

"Thanks again, Mo. So, this table comes with security and public decency responsibilities."

"Absolutely, and a twenty-percent cash tip minimum. Go higher if you like, Guy."

"Hey, Mo, you know my name isn't Guy, right? And twenty percent? That worries me. I don't want to force you into a higher tax bracket."

"Thanks for the concern over my relationship with Revenue Canada. If that becomes an issue, I'll tell you to D and D just before my fiscal year end. And okay, if not 'Guy,' what is it?"

"You know what, Mo?"

"No, what?"

"Guy is good enough for now."

"Guy it is. Hey, you're sharper and wittier than usual. In a good mood, are we? Did you get lucky tonight or something? This is the most outgoing I've seen you, and out late at that!"

"No, nothing that fortunate. The Leafs sent me into a spin of madness and anger once again. Just awake and felt like getting out. Feels sort of good."

"Okay, Mr. Frisky. Kicking your heels up at GoHo's. Watch me waitress my way to fortune and as a side benefit, this time of night is great for people watching. And I bet you're hoping to catch a glimpse of Lisa."

"Why would you say that?"

"Because you eat here every Monday for, what, the last two months. You GoHo's with Mo on Mondays because that's our best night of the week?"

"Okay, the thought did cross my mind that Lisa and Al might power down with some growl chow."

"About that, Al's out. In case you didn't notice, Al wasn't here the last four Mondays. Lisa was with her business agent and main seamstress."

"Well, now that you mention it. . ."

"Bullshit. You're fully aware of the change. Don't try to bullshit a bullshitter."

"Mo, I never considered you to be anything less than a hundred percent truthful."

"Nice try, Guy. In this occupation you constantly spin stuff in multiple directions. Creative thinking and positioning are a valuable asset and provide the ability to describe a basic roast beef sandwich six ways to Sunday. After I'm done my sales pitch, even I want one, and I don't eat beef."

"I admit you're a linguistic artist."

"Careful with the sex talk, Guy. Save it for Lisa. Al's out and 'Gee,' the French version of Guy, is moving in."

"Thanks for the vote of confidence, Mo."

"Nothing to be confident of, Guy, but nothing ventured, nothing gained. What are you growling for?"

"BLT on whole wheat, double bacon and fries. I'll wash that down with a tall Stormwatch."

"The college guy surfaces."

Pivot. Gone.

The pedestrian traffic was fascinating. The human status variations from complete sobriety to staggering shit-faced drunk, was, well, staggering. The animation levels were through the roof. The diversity was also impressive from almost all perspectives, encompassing age, ethnicity, sexual orientation, colour, religion, dress, and socio-economic class. The noise outside was at an impressive level and growing. The bars closed at 2:00, and with the way things were trending, Mo would be running for her twenty percent-plus probably all the way till 4:00 a.m.

Mo dropped my beer and a water without a word—a first for her. She was moving. The place was full except for two booths for six. One was Lisa's table.

"Here's your sandwich. Chew slowly. There's a ton of bacon on there. I told the cook to give you the spicy mayo since you're feisty this morning. Trust me; you'll like it. Another beer?"

"Yes, and Mo, I trust you six ways to Sunday. And oh my God, it's Sunday!"

"Your God? Well, I don't know about that but chew slowly. Your *goddess* has an ETA of ten minutes. Enjoy the scenery. Make your move."

Pivot. Gone.

I watched the cash tips in Mo's domain. They left hundred-dollar bills on maybe fifty-five- to sixty-dollar meals. Mo was raking in the dough. She had twelve tables and was never flustered. Her bus kid was exceptional, clearing any finished plate and turning the table in record time. The kid looked to be a fifteen- to sixteen-year-old Asian girl. She was quick, attentive, and relentless.

She helped Mo with refills, bringing out plates, coffee, and anything else. The two were a formidable partnership.

I didn't know why I was awake and out on the town. Out on the town? Come on! I was in a diner two blocks from my home at 2:30 on a Sunday morning. If that was my new night on the town, I had sunk to a despairingly low degree of life vitality and social interaction. Truth be told, I was feeling disconnected from the real world of personal relationships and engagement with others, especially meaningful others. I had gone to bed, but I felt restless, so I got up, got dressed, and wandered down to GoHo's. I didn't wander there aimlessly. My aim was to see Lisa in her "growl chow" phase. Sad but mission driven. Atta boy.

Lisa and her inebriated entourage arrived at 2:35 a.m., five minutes late, not that I was keeping track or anything. Mo greeted her and mock scolded her for being late and tying up Mo's valuable real estate, all in one welcoming outburst. Lisa apologized and hugged Mo. That's what I'm talking about—real human connection. I needed some of that.

Group hug anyone. Anyone?

CHAPTER 4

Glimpsing Lisa

Guy

My new table, the best seat in the house, was the perfect vantage point for all the shenanigans going on outside and inside GoHo's. The foot traffic on the street was moving south to north, and I guess on a compass face I would be spot on the N for "north." I was gawking at the streams of life flowing by and trying to catch words from the animated conversations taking place inside and outside. Inside GoHo's, no one seemed to notice my intense observations. I guess I wasn't any force of true magnetic north, as no one appeared drawn to my gape-mouthed, wide-eyed expression.

I was self-aware enough and of others in general to realize I wasn't an unattractive guy. Maybe the full impression I was creating at that juncture in my life was "Sorry, just looking." That could have been it. I was performing well in a tough, competitive firm and industry. My output and results hadn't slipped one iota since my personal loss. I might even have raised my game. I knew I wasn't still fully in the game—a bit non-committal, so to speak. That's what a deep razor cut of a life change will do. The proverbial poke in the eye with a sharp stick can reduce one's laser-like focus, drive, and intensity. I wasn't the prowling, potent panther of a life force that I once was. The lion wasn't hunting these days. He was lying in the long grasses of the savanna, licking his wounds.

I don't even convince myself with such self-serving, self-pitying prose.

My vantage point gave me a perfect view of Lisa's booth and Lisa. Thank you, Mo. Her booth was just inside the entrance, essentially the southernmost booth, and she was sitting in the middle. Very much the Dairy Queen with slighter but striking girlfriends flanking her, and they looked like models. On the other side of the booth sat a rotund man, affecting a Mr. Clean haircut, with earrings in both ears, multiple piercings, and an intriguing dark-skinned woman who stood under five feet but with her hair in full afro probably reached five six or five seven.

There we were, north and south. I was cold, distant, and self-absorbed, and Lisa was hot, close, and embracing the world. Not equals but probably polar opposites.

Most of my gawking was aimed at Lisa. The height advantage provided by my elevated dining platform allowed me a clear view of her. She didn't notice me.

As I finished my growl chow, Mo deposited a second Stormwatch.

"Thought you needed this. Staring is hard work. You're hardly obvious. But I'll admit it: she's fascinating."

"I didn't order this."

"Drink up. You need the hydration. Drooling is hard, thirsty work. All double entendres intended."

"Am I really that pathetic and obvious?"

"Yes, but luckily you and I are the only serious observers of others here tonight. So, gawk on, Guy boy."

"If you advise and insist."

"I do."

Pivot. Gone.

I picked up the second Stormwatch tall boy. It was ice cold, and I took a long, enjoyable chug. I laughed to myself, thinking about Mo's turn of phrase. "Gawk on. Drooling is hard, thirsty work." The smile was still on my face as I lowered the legendary beer, thinking about Stormwatch back story.

"Breakfast of champions. You gotta be a manly man. BLT, fries, and a tall boy Stormwatch at almost three a.m. Not visibly intoxicated or a beer belly. Impressive, given this calorie load in front of you. Share a swig of beer with a lady?"

Lisa had seemingly appeared out of nowhere and was pointing at my Stormwatch with one hand and picking it up with the other. She took a good swig.

"Great positioning. Strategic, I assume? Everybody must pass you on the way to and from the can."

"Well, I didn't realize that."

"And my, how bloody charming. Thanks for the beer. My skinny-assed girlfriends say I've had enough to drink. See you upon my return."

That was my first meeting with Lisa. Sure enough, just behind my table was the ladies' room. The sign read "No Ho's, Just Gotta Go's" with a Barbie doll silhouette to indicate the women's washroom. Truly the best seat in the house. Lisa certainly had me tongue tied. My casual banter game needed an upgrade. I was still trying to think of something clever to say when she returned, but I had nothing.

"That beer is cold. Made me pee like a Palomino. You, of course, must piss like a racehorse. Isn't that what all guys say?"

"I don't know."

"Not much of a clever retort there, buddy. Maybe you've overeaten and are currently in a food coma. Mind if I have another taste?"

She took another sizable swig. "Thanks. Next time try to be a little more engaging. You can watch my ample ass as I walk away."

Lisa moved with a side swivel, a slow sashay away, southbound.

"Great attitude," I called out.

She half turned. "You talking to me?"

"Yeah. About your ass. It's more attitude than size."

"Clever. Fuckin' weird but interesting."

Side swivel, sashay. Hip movement and wiggle exaggerated. I had noticed a momentary lull in the conversation volume in the diner during our exchange. Our words carried loud and clear into a space that had a ravenous appetite for our dialogue. People looked for a second and then they cranked their own conversations back to full throttle on the new topic of asses with attitudes. Or so it seemed. Then Mo came wheeling in.

"Clever, Guy. In my section your first words spoken aloud are about a woman's ass having attitude?"

"Mo, you got that out of context."

"Ya think that freakin' matters? Anyway, it's good for business. Everybody's buzzing about it and ordering more drinks. A couple even said, "I'll have what he's drinking." You created a mini *When Sally Met Harry* moment all on your own. People are gawking at you now. Enjoy your five minutes of GoHo's fame."

"Only five? Come on, Mo. You and I both know that the 'ass attitude incident' will be legendary. Look at all the tall boy Stormwatch being ordered."

"Gotta hand it to you, Guy. I didn't see that coming. I'm going to make a bundle on tips. The more drinks, the more they all become champions of the world, and thoughts of glory seep into everyone's mindset. Then they tip like crazy."

"Good for you, Mo. I want a split, a commission at least, on the Stormwatch sales."

"No chance of that happening, big boy. Here's your tab. Pay up. Tip generously, and don't let the door hit your ass on the way out!"

Pivot. Gone.

On the back of the bill, Mo had written "TIP like a champion" and had drawn an ass with squiggly lines beside it to symbolize wiggling. It made me smile on the outside.

I sipped my beer for another ten minutes, sneaking glances in Lisa's direction. I was certainly aware of numerous glances directed my way.

A group of university kids left GoHo's and, directly in front of my window seat, turned around and pointed to their behinds and shouted, "How do you like those attitudes?" in a less than perfect chorus. Inside GoHo's, the place erupted with laughter. We had managed to replicate a *Good Will Hunting* scene as well!

That seemed like the moment to take my final curtain call for the evening. It would have been poetic if I could have exited from the rear. Yuk, yuk! I was cracking myself up! Again, there was that juvenile humour. Will Farrell would have been impressed!

I made eye contact with Lisa as I passed her booth. The three on her side of the table were sharing a BLT, fries, and a tall boy Stormwatch. Lisa pointed to the beer as I passed.

"Breakfast of champions. You should work on your pickup lines." They all laughed.

I leaned into her booth, close to her ear. "The lion doesn't roar when he's hunting."

I nodded, smiled, then kept on walking. Then I paid at the counter and exited. Outside I turned north on my way home. Then I stopped and stared through the window at her. She made eye contact.

"Attitude," I said. Then I turned around, pointed to my ass, and walked away.

What the hell had I just done? Why? And to what end? That made me chuckle. End, get it? I was talking and laughing to myself. I was either losing it or loosening up. The Lisa effect maybe or two tall boys? Probably a bit of both.

CHAPTER 5

Mackin On Gettin' a Smackin

Mackin

I remember the first time I heard a sports reporter say, "Mackin took the smackin,'" essentially turning my "nom de field" around on me. The difference between hearing "Smackin' Mackin" to "Mackin smackin'" hurt like hell. I can't rationalize why that would grate so hard. If you don't want your ego bruised, don't play professional football. There's a plethora of smack talk in the game. I've heard far worse in every game I played than any clever turn of a phrase by a reporter. Many derogatory words and expressions line up well with the name Mackin. That phrase coming from someone paid to be clever in that way, creating a turn of a phrase, hit me like a 250-pound fullback going north south at full speed. Not only does that type of hit rock you, but it also flattens you. It wrecks you. And, brother, the next play you're back on your heels. Even if your mindset is grounded, your body is saying, "Whoa! I just got my ass Mac trucked." Your nerve endings are intimidated and telling the rest of your body via your central nervous system that it ain't real clever to get in the way of the next load coming down the highway.

The smack talk in the CFL is an interesting mix of cultures and upbringings. No one should ever doubt for a second that Canadians can talk shit. However, they're subtle in their wit, with a slow build to the punchline. A Canadian can smack talk you or drop a burner on you, and sometimes you don't realize the magnitude of the burn until three or four plays later. Ouch! First-degree burn. American smack talk, on the other hand, is more direct. It lacks subtlety of any kind and often hints at your genealogy being distantly removed from any semblance of aristocratic stock. That was why it was so shocking for American CFLers to hear Troy Westwood, the kicker for the Winnipeg Blue Bombers, refer to Saskatchewan Rough Rider fans as "banjo pickin' inbreds." Then again, Westwood played his university ball in North Dakota, which explained a lot.

For a couple of years, I had a signature move after a big open-field tackle or a sack. I would square up and rock the Hulk Hogan bicep stance. My fists clenched in front of my gut, my biceps flared and quivering as I squeezed my arms into their full glory, then the Mac truck gesture, my right arm making that universal gesture to truckers that kids make from the window of their family car as they pass a big rig. The pulling motion that means, "Tug on that air horn." They estimated I had three to four thousand fans sporting some type of horn at every game, waiting for that move, so they could give the symphonic Mackin salute. I loved that move. It was my favourite of all my signature celebrations. I developed a new one every two to four years, and sometimes I had a special one for playoffs.

When I flattened opponents, the home crowd yelled "Macked Out!" I loved it, and you wouldn't believe the fire it would light in me! Not only in me but in my teammates too. It would pump me almost out of my game gourd, out of the right mind space, the right mental focus and intensity to stay within the lines of my assignments, follow my reads, and not over commit. Sometimes the "Macked Out" cheer would send me into a volcanic eruption of pure mayhem. I would be flying all over the field with pure, freakin', off-the-charts, adrenalized, testosterone-amped fervour and rage. Sometimes that led to brilliance, and sometimes it just froze the opponents, intimidating the crap out of them. They would run everything the other way, away from me. But I was flying. Mackin was trackin' anything that moved, anyone who had the ball. It was a poetic, vibrating chaos.

In university I remained a star on both sides of the ball as a flat-out power-running fullback and a middle linebacker. As I went from freshman to senior, I migrated more fully to the defensive side of the ball, my number would still get called for power dives, especially at the goal line. That was real smashmouth football from the five-yard line to the goal line. Sometimes it took us the full four downs to get the last yard or two. After that sequence of plays, I was gassed and battered. I left university with the record for rushing touchdowns in a career with forty-eight. That record still stands.

Then Lisa "macked me out." That was a real life battering with just as many bruises and aches, except those are the kind of wounds you don't see; you just feel. She simply told me we were over. Goal line push denied.

Our business relationship was based on power. Dressing people for power, imbuing them with the confidence of being fashion forward, trendy, and of the moment. And, brother, it was wildly successful. I loved it. I learned about fashion, fabrics, styles, cuts, touches, lengths, proportions, colours, seams, silhouettes, drape. . .You name it and I knew it! And I could talk it!

Mackin gettin' a smackin'. Did I see it coming? Was it predictable? I was a high-profile companion partner, eye candy, lover number five. I vaguely knew two of the other guys. I was warned, and I'm not stupid. Almost three and a half years together with Lisa. A new record for her. A personal best. I guess I should be flattered.

Companionship was never a problem, nor would it be for me, if I made that decision. I knew I was too old and mature to try to pick up the ball after a relationship turnover, fumble, or whatever football analogy worked and get back in the game.

Lisa is the whole deal, the complete package. Beauty, brains, intensity, drive, creativity, expansive, and real. With little effort she could relate, adjust, touch, reach, engage, and embrace anyone, any type, anywhere, and anytime. Lisa has the ability to connect with anyone. There's a fine line between arrogance and confidence, ego and intellect. Lisa is uncommonly capable of being common. She has a personal touch, and, brother, it is freakin' genuine. I've seen it, felt it, bathed in it, believed it, learned from it, and loved it. Still do. I try to practise that common touch all the time because it's such an authentic way to walk through life. I always had that feel for people and naturally wanted to engage with others in that manner. Maybe I forgot about being decent and relatable for a while amid the trappings of celebrity. Lisa reminded me and showed me how to ground myself in humanity.

Is Lisa perfect? No, but nobody is. Close? Yes and no. Yes, for all the things I've said. At her core, she's a decent human being. Cruel? No, not at all. Even in her whackin' of Mackin, no cruelty was intended, and she showed genuine remorse for any hurt she inflicted.

She knew I would be hurt. Regardless, we were done. Lisa had a limited capacity for love or a limited time frame for love. Apparently, we had exceeded our best-before date. She hit me like a Mack truck in bed and out of bed. We got to my place at about 6:00 p.m. after walking from GoHo's. We went from the foyer to the kitchen counter—because we needed a beer—to a dining room chair to the bed and finally to the shower. I fell asleep or drifted off at about 3:00 a.m.

Now, there were brief interludes in the night, but when she said at GoHo's, "Let's just go to the condo and fuck," that was what we were going do, and it was what we did. Mission accomplished. I looked at the nightstand clock when she woke me with a kiss on the forehead. It was 4:44 a.m. Is there any symbolism to a row of fours? I'll have to look that up. It certainly wasn't the luck of a four-leaf clover. How the mind wanders.

"I'm packed," she said. She kept enough stuff at my place—a nice condo, by the way, not some shack-up shit hole of a fuck-place apartment where you hide to screw. Just needed to put that in there for my own self esteem. "Enough stuff" included two huge suitcases and three wardrobe bags.

"Someone from the office will come by to pick them up at two. They'll leave my key when they're done."

I didn't say a thing. Really, what could I have said?

"See you at that showing for the Ds at four. They could be great new clients."

A nod.

"Love you."

A fucking dagger in my heart and head, but not another word. She turned and was gone. Mackin was out!

We hung out socially and, more importantly, professionally for the next five weeks, fulfilling all the obligations on our calendars. We worked well together in our business. When the break-up became public, and it was postdated, that surprised everyone. That was a testament to us both for keeping our heads screwed on straight and remaining professional and respectful of each other. Lisa carried that off far better than I thought I did. There was no formal announcement, just a slowing down of our public and professional appearances together. Of course, there was gossip and speculation but nothing of substance and nothing truly unkind.

When my football career ended—my sole decision—I felt a significant loss. It was the larger experience that I missed. The locker room, the men, my companions, the camaraderie, the physical and mental preparation, the shared purpose, and the backing up of each other to reach the prize together. To prepare for retirement I talked to good friends who had retired. I watched others fail badly at walking away from the game and more than one failed attempt at a comeback. Few of those comebacks were successful. There was a lot of hanging on, and at that stage a lot of damage occurred both physically and mentally. Players had to exit with a purpose and the best plan they could muster. I had started cultivating an exit strategy years before. My strategy consisted of three parts. First, building up my foundation, including the camp. Second, establishing business interests and connections. Third, developing relations with the CFL media in the area. My transition wasn't without regrets or second guessing, but it was my decision, and like every game I played, I had a plan.

Lisa? The ending of that relationship wasn't part of my plan. I had no plan for that, for my new single reality. That was her sole decision. Mackin out!

The meaning of triple fours? I took the first phrase that popped up in my Google search, avoiding the angelic and biblical references that followed.

"The meaning of 444 is usually that you're on the right path. Whatever you're pursuing in life, you're heading in the right direction. You may also feel that you've been doing something wrong in your life, but that probably isn't true."

I'll take some comfort in this. There was something in my life that I'd been doing wrong for some time, and it had nothing to do with Lisa.

I had another hand that I had been trailing and failing to grip for a *long* time.

CHAPTER 6

Mo-Town

I know my attitude working at GoHo's is flippant and cavalier. Some customers judge me as a little dumb. Okay, maybe not dumb but limited. The good, kinder people don't see me as limited in capability, but they believe I have chosen to either engage in work that is self-limiting or there are things in my life that lead to self-limitations. As easy and outgoing as I am, I don't reveal that much about myself. Some customers probably wonder about me because my approach, attitude, and demeanour radiate a high degree of confidence. This is probably inconsistent with my apparent station in life, background, and appearance. Ah, the mysterious Mo. Incongruence in motion.

Damn, tonight was a good time. Long shift, full ten hours from 6:00 p.m. to 4:00 a.m. Tips, tipapaloosa, tipendous, tiptastic! Yep, a good night working eight, ten, twelve tables. Good turns, few burns. When Guy got the place buzzing with the "attitude of ass" comment, the people went nuts! They were ordering tall boys of Stormwatch, double CC and gingers, and pitchers of Tequila Sunrise. It was a shame we gave last call at 3:00, only an hour past legal serving time. When Goho's is like that, I'm in my element. It's my go-to happy place. It's Mo-Town.

I sense it when a customer sees me as limited. I see it in their eyes, and I kind of get it. Their perspective is that I've reached the correct level, my proper station in life, my high-water mark, that I have no upward Mo-bility. Ha, ha! Screw you, you pissant silver spoon-in-the-mouth assholes. I don't know if they grew up with everything handed to them; it just feels that way. The condescending attitude, the insincere expressions, the lack of interest in making actual eye contact or engagement. Their failure to address me by my name. For fuck's sake, my name tag is pinned just above my decently sized left tit, which, strangely enough, is slightly bigger than my right. Plenty of customers stare at my tits but not my eyes. Especially tonight with sex even more prevalent than usual in the banter, exchanges, glances, nudges, rubs, and open-mouth tongue tangos. Thanks, Guy. Sex sells, and as the libidos rise, so do the tips.

After ten hours at a diner and the required contribution to the tip pool for the non-serving staff, I have $414. My record in a twelve-hour shift is a take home of $527, but that record has an asterisk beside it. You know, like Barry

Bonds' steroid-driven home run totals. That record-setting night, a very drunk pilot grabbed my ass with both hands and told me he would copilot with me in a cockpit any time. Order, decorum, and decency were restored by the rapid placement of a coffee cup upside his right ear. I only needed one hand to stem the pilot's liftoff. Okay, maybe decorum suffered a bit of jetlag. After the blood, the broken mug, and the dust settled, he left two $100 bills. Not only did he forget to eat, but he also forgot to order. It's amazing how a good smack on someone's head with a coffee cup induced generosity from the other patrons as well. Who would have guessed?

Am I limited or self-limiting? Yeah, sorta. I have a daughter. I'm thirty-two, and she's fourteen. Pregnant at eighteen. Now *that* was not a smart move, but man I love her! With the pregnancy I had to make some quick decisions. There I was pregnant, eighteen, and finishing grade twelve at the end of the month.

My family was so messed up. No support or sympathy would be forthcoming. In fact, in their eyes, I had committed an unforgivable sin and would be damned and probably thrown out of the house. Dad was a fucking drunk loser. For a few years, I had to worry about him assaulting my sister and me. My younger sister, Delta, was just over two years younger than me. So, pregnant and finishing grade twelve, I asked for full time at GoHo's and rented an apartment close by. I took Delta with me. I had to. Delta wanted out, so there we went, shifting our lives into the "you're fucked" lane and hoping there was no oncoming traffic. Not a bad lane shift. It was rather timely, in fact, because we were in the "you're going to get fucked anyway lane," but at least now we were doing the driving.

I didn't look for any options other than GoHo's and independence. I knew I could do well at GoHo's, and I took comfort in that. It wasn't like there were a lot of alternatives available.

The father of my child, the man who impregnated me, well, that's all Delta's fault, or so we kid. Delta lived with me until she was twenty-four. She holds two university degrees and is now teaching at a high school outside of North Bay. Her middle name? You guessed it—Dawn. Yep. Delta Dawn, after the song. My parents weren't very inventive or forward looking. By the time she was thirteen, her initials matched her cup size, and Dad started getting real hands-on in his approach to fathering. In some ways getting pregnant was a blessing. It got us out of that house, which was rapidly becoming abusive and dangerous for both of us.

Two years later Dad was out of the house, and two years after that he was dead. A drunk-driving accident. He was drunk and driving. It would seem hard to miss the business end of a snowplow! However, I guess if you're driving the wrong way on the 401 in a snowstorm and smash into the third of four plows heading up a superhighway, you're a little more than liquored up. He swerved to miss the first two plows in their parade of snow removal, so his death wasn't a suicide. Death by snowplow is an interesting and unique way of kicking it. Actually, death by snowplow *and* Smirnov is more like it. Dad was an amazing functioning alcoholic. There are no blessings or accolades to be had in that ability. If we had attended the funeral, I would have enjoyed saying in the eulogy, "My breast-grabbing, child-abusing dad was an amazing functioning alcoholic. I'm not even sure if he was "current" in or with his faith and had some sort of service. I didn't know if Dad was practising his faith. He would have needed to attend some remedial classes for sure.

We weren't invested or even connected at that stage. Delta heard the news on City TV. Nice way to get the death announcement.

So, how did Delta Dawn get me knocked up? She got me to chaperone at a spring sock hop for a ninth- and tenth-grade dance, where a strapping young buck hit on me all night. He said it was okay, that he was sixteen and a little old for those teeny boppers. He was smooth and good looking. He figured we might be the same age because he was old for his grade. I lied and told him I was seventeen. He got me out in a hallway, and we are necking like crazy. I was wet, and he was hard and all hands. He copped a feel, and I loved it. I yanked his hand from under my blouse and turned to go back to the gym. As I turned, I grabbed his dick through his jeans, and three weeks later we were screwing every chance we got. He wasn't my first, but with my first I didn't have a clue.

That guy didn't have a clue either, so once I got him to slow down, and after some hand jobs that caused him to blast off like a rocket ship with loads of exhaust fluid, he seemed content to get jacked off and let me set the pace. After three weeks I let him in. Twenty-one days in, he went off like a twenty-one-gun salute, and so did I. It turns out I love screwing. He lied about his age. He was fifteen, and I was eighteen. I was screwing a minor. We were careful, but it was as much my fault as his. We were practicing safe sex, but apparently, we weren't very good at it. What a great expression! Practicing safe sex. We weren't practicing. We were going at it. Game on, man. Game on. See? Obviously, it's all DD's fault.

I had missed my period for two months, and I knew I was baking something in the oven. I went to the school nurse, and she said I should visit my family doctor and confirm it. Yes, the bun was in the oven. I told my boyfriend two weeks later, the day I rented the apartment. When I told him I had rented an apartment, it was like his dick had a yeast infection. That thing rose instantly, and just as visions of sugar plums and marathon hide-the-salami fests were dancing in his head, I told him we were done. Then I told him I was about three months along. He was still three months short of his sixteenth birthday. I misjudged his character or his horniness or both because in two or three awkward minutes he said, "Thanks, good luck, and stay in touch."

"Right," I replied.

It turns out as quick as a fifteen-year-old dick can rise to the occasion, the opposite is true for any thought of character, concern, or responsibility. He saddled up and got out of town. It was probably for the best. DD and I needed a safe harbour and a place to grow up fast, and we did. She attended high school, and I worked the six-to-two shifts, with one Saturday night off a month, before and after the baby. On those once-a-month Saturday nights, DD and I would kick our shoes off, eat popcorn, and watch movies. We loved it. Our home was normal. No threats or histrionics, just lots of care and love. A very good if not well-appointed environment to bring up my baby girl.

My fifteen-year-old fuck-a-thon wannabe never showed up at our new place. His mother, however, made an appearance that was a noteworthy cameo role in the movie of my life to that stage. She appeared as a battle-scarred veteran of what I assumed was some significant abuse. She threatened me with charges of raping a minor if I brought any trouble to her boy. She was in full rant mode. Saliva flying, hands flapping, and eyes of rage and lord knows what else. I just let her rage on. When she finally calmed down, she asked if I caught her drift.

I had three responses for her. "Ma'am, you look like you've had a hard row to hoe. And, ma'am, you take good care of your child. I'll take good care of mine."

Grace also rises. Maybe that's my yeast. Grace.

I weighed about 133 when I was in my "screw-a-thon" phase, what I like to call my fighting weight. Some people called me stocky, but the weight was distributed proportionately. I always thought I had a good boob-to-ass ratio, meaning my boobs were big enough proportionately to compensate for a slight over-dimensioning of my butt. Delta Dawn and I shared that physical trait. We would laugh sometimes at women who had boob-to-ass ratios that were out of whack and would, by necessity, at least in their own minds, need to under or over play one of those features.

So, back to the big question. Was I limited or self-limiting? Mostly the latter.

People always have some of the former in some areas, and if you don't think you do, that's probably what limits you. That's down-home Mo 101 philosophy right there.

I watched my sister burn through high school and university like a freaking runaway train. She loves to study. She equated success with the ratio of her GPA to the dollars of scholarships and grants she hauled in. She worked at summer camps, teaching language, math, science, English, and history. She picked up a couple of shifts a week at GoHo's, a few more in the summer. She had the odd boyfriend, went on the pill at age sixteen, and stayed on it. We petitioned for me to become her legal guardian.

DD was a good influence on me. I started taking courses at the university through the extension education program. I had to take prerequisite courses first. It turned out I had an aptitude for study as well. I was a "mature" student. By that time my daughter was in grade one and I studied when she was at school. I graduated with an HBA at age thirty-one. My degree is in English with minors in psychology and economics. Take that and stick it up your ass-sumptions! I often felt that thought bubbling up when some self-important snot-bag dick gave me that look of instant dismissal that all waitresses receive.

Self-limiting? So, I have the degree. DD is gone, and my daughter, Lucille, is now in high school. Yeah, you know, "You picked a fine time to leave me, Lucille" by Kenny Rogers, way back in the day before he got his face all streamlined? No, my daughter isn't named Lucille. DD and I used to laugh and pick names from songs. That would be a great name to ruin a kid for life! Her name is Lauren. Simple, sweet, and with a touch of sophistication, just like my baby girl!

So, come on, Mo. Focus for fuck's sake. You would think an English major would use a more sophisticated vocabulary even when she's just mulling things over. Self-limiting, that's the topic du jour. No, not so much self-limiting as waiting. I needed the time and the money. We saved like bandits, but we never did without. We just made do with whatever we could make. I took a lot of food home from the diner. Some of those times were hard.

You know what I want? Where I have self-limited? In the companionship area. I want a man. Yep. I want to fall into someone's arms and be cared for and loved. I'm idealistic as hell because I want him to support me as I launch my career, not support me with money but support me with care, concern, guidance, and warmth and to pick me up when I fall down. You know I need a decent human being. And if he screws like a racehorse, yippee, yay, cowboy!

CHAPTER 7

Figuring it Out

It was a stone-cold bitch slapping.

I couldn't even use an excuse like I was so deeply invested in the love between us that I was totally blindsided. I knew behavioural patterns. I'm not a stupid guy.

We were comfortable. Predictable. In everything. I would also say we were respectable, accountable, and reliable to each other and to everyone and everything else. We were a force, striding through life together, rising up the corporate ladder—promotions, raises, perks. We got MBAs one year apart—me first and then her. Mine from Western and hers from Queens. Mine was regarded more highly, and it still is. She's three years older than me. I swear to God she was sexier, fitter, and smarter at fifty-two, when she finished us, than she was at twenty-four when we first met.

We married when I was thirty-three, the perpetual bachelor brought to heel and heart. For her at thirty-six, her first marriage was six years in her rearview mirror, and she had decided children weren't her forte, calling, or interest. We lived well. We vacationed. We were athletic. I never entertained the idea of cheating on her. Why would I? Not only in my eyes was she gorgeous. What's the old line? "Your good looks are only exceeded by your intelligence." That was her. That was my wife. I mean, that's still her. She's just not my wife anymore.

She's powerful by nature. Just flat out powerful with a mix of intensity, intellect, stridency, rigour, persistence, quickness, and insightfulness. Stamina like a workhorse. Goes all day and night. We both liked to work. We loved being in the game, the challenge. We loved striving. We liked the accolades and recognition of being successful. We had what the sports broadcasters called "a compete level that was off the charts." I was a little subtler and less strident. She wasn't in your face but in your mind. My career ascended at a little faster pace through our thirties and into our mid-forties. Then at age forty-seven she found or gained another gear. The C suite in a decade became her overriding goal and raison d'être. She didn't say it or dream it. She mapped it. Planned it. Timelines, positions, files, projects. Everything laid out, packed, and stacked in an unwavering straight line to the corner suite. CEO, see me go! It looked like she was going to make it early the next year, three or maybe four years ahead of schedule.

When she kicked in the afterburners, I recalibrated my career path and ascendency. I was forty-four at that time. The CEOs in my firm, which was about double the size of my wife's firm, had never been younger than sixty-two. Our firm's succession planning was state of the art, best practice, and perfect. The current CEO, who was sixty-seven, would transition in three years to the anointed king when the successor turned sixty-four. Seventy was the new exit age prevailing in our firm and sector. I had nine years to reach the necessary level on the succession ladder. Why not? I was smart, played well with others, and I had enough independence, innovative capability, insight, and kick-your-ass energy to get her done! No false steps. No false bravado. Confident, not arrogant. Challenging but not reckless. Bottom-line feeder and top-line accelerator. I could do it.

Our first four years on that rocket ship blast went exceedingly well. We fed each other insights, thoughts, and most importantly, confidence.

Maybe I should have noticed we weren't feeding each other *with* each other. I mean, sex wasn't what you would have guessed. It didn't happen by rote when we were tired at the end of the day or only when we were on vacation or mapped it into our planners. It was spontaneous and rippling, even if it wasn't frequent or amorous. It was need based. I should've clued in. She often said something like, "Thanks. I needed that to clear my head" or "Now maybe I can think straight" or "That was good. I was frustrated with my boss."

"Really? You mean you just fucked me because your boss is frustrating you? I think I'll call him and tell him to frustrate the hell out of you when I'm in the mood to get laid."

We both laughed at that.

Again, if I was thinking about us, I might have noticed that she was fucking for the reasons we stereotypically think men fuck for. Had I been emasculated for years?

To sidestep the boss who had been frustrating her, she took on a series of European projects. That had always been part of her plan to build her brand. Gain global experience and international competence and the accompanying network. She just accelerated that specific aspect of her career-ascent phase. And it worked. Her boss was out, and she was in line for the ultimate C suite. One step below her penultimate goal, and only fifty-two and a bit!

I hit a bit of a speed bump. I had figured out the internal competition, but what I hadn't seen coming was the recruitment of an external superstar. He would take over at age sixty and had a ten-year contract with a firm expiry date. It was a state-of-the-art, best-practice process for succession planning.

Okay, I had to wait another four years and was still only going to be fifty-seven. Heinz, 57 varieties. Okay, I can live with that. The previous king-in-waiting had exited, and I inherited a vast swath of his portfolio, along with senior EVP status and a great deal more compensation. The new king was a king, more than a bit of an imperious prick, and he held a rather fine opinion of himself. He had some faults. He wanted to exorcise the firm of the demons that the previous "king-to-be" had carried, nurtured, and loved. He wanted much of the portfolio I was carrying to be annihilated and expunged. The demons, as he saw them, were mostly good, profitable, growing horned devils, and I was good enough to make them even more profitable. This did not please the new king. Although we did extricate a few demons by working together, according to the king, that didn't go far enough. When he reached CEO status, I wasn't dropped from the inner circle, but my seat was at the far end of the table and sometimes out in the hall. Not to worry. His style, ego, and somewhat arrogant approach weren't appreciated by the board and all the "insider baseball" told us he wouldn't make it full term. The prick probably didn't intend to because a forced premature exit would be extremely lucrative for him. A cynic could easily see that he was jettisoning some good business segments at high price-earnings ratios. It was almost a "pump and dump" scenario in a few cases. The stock responded positively. That made his buyout very lucrative, if it was exercised, as it was tied to stock price.

So, my approach was to go with the flow, under-react to his provocations, under-promise, and over-deliver like a prized goose. I kept laying golden eggs in areas the long-serving members of the board, including the past CEO, loved. I didn't get close to the king for another reason. The inner circle was a place people went to get their head chopped off and watch it roll out of the company. Yep, long live the king, until he doesn't!

On the other hand, my ex-wife must have had extreme bouts of frustration while away on her European projects. Apparently, a person can fuck their way out of those. And she did. Now, I don't know if she had more than one willing fellow to help her deal with the stress and the emotional turmoil. I heard rumours later that she cut a swath through the power and penis corridors of international business. If she did, that would hardly make me feel better or vindicated. When she informed me that we were divorcing, she also informed me that she had a British boyfriend who was transferring to Canada, and they would be together.

Our divorce was, if not amicable, straightforward and without fuss. I walked away with more than my fair share of our joint assets. She got the condo, and I got the cottage that she had inherited and hated. We had stopped going there together several years earlier. It was only a couple of hours north of the city. I loved the whole experience, from the manic, white-knuckled, horn-blaring masses driving out of the city to the tranquility of a three-thousand-square-foot log cabin sitting on a small lake with only two other cabins. I went there four times a year for three to five days, usually while working on a deep-dive project. I considered it brilliant divorce negotiations, as the cottage was way undervalued in the settlement documents. As we were signing the documents, she mentioned the market value was at least $500,000 off on the cottage. She knew it but didn't give a fuck and was disappointed I didn't have the decency to point it out. She crushed me with that and then stood up, turned around, and was gone. Her ass had attitude, and clearly expressed, "Kiss my ass, you pissant."

I experienced a couple of problems with that outcome. Okay, more than a couple. First, a Brit? A fuckin' stodgy, Yorkshire-pudding-and-British-bulldog-loving, bad-teeth, pseudo-aristocratic, royal-acting, bangers-and-mash, soccer-playing Brit? Please go fuck an Italian and get some passion or a Frenchman and get some romance. Pick a swarthy, swashbuckling speaker of a love-language swords-man from the south of Spain, someone who's suave, sophisticated, sensual, and sensational, but a fucking Brit? That encouraged me to endeavour to eradicate the monarchy from our country.

That was the minor problem. Alfred, or whatever his name is, will end up being her butler. The major problem, and what a major son-of-a-bitch problem, was I noticed upon her eviction of me from her life that I loved her. I loved us. No, it wasn't some pity party. Remorse brings a recognition of the five stages of grief. It was an epiphany. Doesn't the word "epiphany" sound all sunshine and light and full of possibility, enlightenment, and all things good? Well, this epiphany came with a thunderstorm of hurt. I pulled back and thought about us, thought about her. I loved her drive, ambition, confidence, unwavering belief in herself, her character, and her makeup. Be all you can be. Be all you want to be, all that people said you couldn't be. The Marines would have loved her. She was a poster girl for women in business. She waded right into the myths, the roadblocks, and through the harassment, kicked the door to the old boys' club wide open. Go, girl, go! I admired her and loved her. You had to see her in "full primal mode." Warrior, fierce, or when her head rested on my chest with a burning afterglow aura. Her smile when I entered the room would light me up. She was passionate about everything important, and for a long time, that included us.

I still love her but not in a melancholy, mournful, mopey way. I just love her. She filled a great part of me, and my definition of myself was wrapped around the two us as a team, a pair, a couple. Now I'm trying to figure things out as a solo act. Maybe somewhere down the road I'll find my own way to someone. Someone else.

There won't be a do-over for us.

She didn't leave with her hand trailing.

CHAPTER 8

Lisa Alone

I'm better alone. I'm not as sharp when I'm in a relationship, especially a deep, loving one. I prefer to have some space. I'm the Gretzky of relationships; I like to create time and space to maximize my performance. I wasn't always this way, and I wasn't born this way. I might have gotten a little warped in this direction by the events of life. Some of the harms that were inflicted on me created a craving for time and space.

I feel like I'm "on" all the time. Centre stage. I'm more than reasonably comfortable with that. I'm not a narcissist—really. In fact, collaborating with a band, a group of musicians, is my ideal space, but right now I must be the centre. I have to be my centre. I must see my ice. My time and space.

My God, I loved Mackin. I probably still do. What a man! Humble and gifted, strong and sensible. Perfect teeth too! I started examining up close to find imperfections, but Mackin is like that song; his imperfections are perfect. His knuckles are gnarly. He told me they were always smashed up and cut. He said that was how he knew he was truly in a game, when both of his hands were bleeding. Most players wore gloves, but not Mackin. He loved the rawness of it all, the skin-on-skin contact. I loved skin on skin with Mackin. Skinnin' with Mackin.

I had to cut him loose, though. He was making me too soft, too comfortable, too safe. Taking me out of my centre. Out of my time and space. That's some strange shit. A strange way of thinking. That all that good stuff felt like it was bringing me down from some high. I'm not cut out for comfort. Time and space. For what? To create, to strive, to drive, to be on the edge, unbound, not framed by the couplings of coupledom. To unravel my pain?

Or could it just be my own deep insecurity? Not daring to fully trust or commit? Man, Mackin was the man. Too good to be true. Eventually, I would have let him down and disappointed him. I knew I would. Or was this all just a replay of my parents' serial monogamy? They weren't true serial monogamists. Their eyes and hands wandered way before their current relationship ended. They were continuously flirting. That wasn't me. I cut my relationships clean and put myself into a self-imposed monastery at the end of every sojourn.

Chastity wasn't a vow when I created this time and space. However, it was a significant and meaningful choice. My periods of celibacy were growing longer and seemed more soothing, but then I would get a big desire to fuck and go big-game hunting. I haven't had a one-night stand or a fling in over twenty years. I don't believe in sexual spontaneous combustion, nor do I become uninhibited when drunk. Well, in truth, I do exhibit quite uninhibited behaviour when I'm drunk. My personality becomes tilted toward a "go fuck yourself" encounter without ever thinking about "let's go fuck." I prefer sober sex. No, all I want is sober sex. Sex brings clarity of mind and body. My mind enjoys what my body experiences. I like them both on full alert. Having thought that, I recognize a good screw on chardonnay is more than okay. Getting hot to trot on merlot. Okay, that doesn't rhyme, but I get my own drift.

Mackin will be okay. Company won't be a problem for him if he chooses to seek it. I hurt him, but I never meant to. That always surprises me. At times I felt out of place on his arm, but never when I was on him. My thoughts can be so crude and inferior. I felt at home, comfortable, and good with Mackin, almost wholesome. Those other feelings, my craving for time and space, had nothing to do with him. He treated me like a goddess, as I so richly deserve, ha ha. His eyes sparkled when he looked at me. I was loved.

So, now I have time and space. "Alone again, naturally." Who sang that one? Well, not naturally. I know what I did is unnatural for most normal human beings.

I'm a little scared, but my decision was triggered by a desire to raise my game on several fronts. Mind and body directed fully at other aphrodisiacs. Mackin is a walking, talking, cocking aphrodisiac. So? Hi, ho, off to work I go. And work I will. I just conjured the seven dwarves and Yoda in one thought.

Is this a sign that I'm focused on the short term? That I'm preoccupied with immediate accomplishments in the very short term? Because Mackin, well, he sure felt long term. I'm just not ready for that, so forget about Mackin. They come and go. No, I came and came and came some more with Mackin. Now I've banished him. He's gone, and I would pay the devil to replace him. Now that's definitely Hall and Oates that I'm ripping off in my wandering, plagiaristic thoughts.

I'm just not ready for a serious long-term relationship. I'm forty-seven. I have plenty of runway. Besides, Mackin is only forty-three. I looked foolish hanging out and living with such a young boy. One upside to all of this was moving back into my place, my space. The condo was sparsely and oh so tastefully furnished, a bit eclectic. All the pieces I liked and had purchased myself. The artwork as well. At heart, I'm an artist. At heart? What a quaint old lady phrase. Forty fuckin seven. Roll the dice. Big numbers. Was I freaking out because the big five-O, the 'Oh No' year was just around the corner? No, I have a perfect vision of me at fifty. Top of the charts.

Here's the plan. I needed to dial down the power-couple fashion. Dialling down meant fewer clients, which Mackin was okay with. As we expanded our roster of power couples that we were dressing for success, fewer of the couples we were taking on as new customers were people we liked. Mackin and I both drew the spotlight, and wealthy people love the spotlight! We built our brand through powerful, monied couples. Mackin and I were receiving more frequent suggestions, hints, and inferences as well as two direct invitations to couple with our customer couples. Mackin led the way on the rebuffs. He found a way to let people down gently. We didn't mix business with pleasure, and we were sure it would be a pleasure. Mackin complimented them while denying them. Polite, clear, and firm.

With the pushiest couple, Mackin had a bit more of an edge to him. The client was groping me like a fifteen-year-old on his first beers. Mackin put his arm around the gentleman's shoulders and, in a jocular manner, suggested they go get a scotch together. Mackin steered him into an empty hallway and told the man to look at the back of his, Mackin's, hands. Mackin clenched his fists and said, "Okay." When he clenches his fists together in front of his waist, no matter what he's wearing, the V shape of his upper body becomes prominent, and the tightness of the cloth on his biceps is stretched to popping. Although his version of the 'Hulk' pose was intimidating enough, it was the knuckles. Those gnarly knuckled knockers! They gave the impression that he had knocked down sequoias with his bare hands. Then Mackin spoke in his low, slow voice, which dripped mayhem and hurt. "These hands have smashed a lot of heads, took out more teeth than a dentist, and cobbled a kaleidoscope of craniums. Your hands, on the other hand, have too much liberty on their mind. If your hands take any more liberties with my friend, then my hands will take liberties with your well-being. If I'm not clear, let me put my meaning in unmistakable terms."

Then Mackin moved closer and lowered and slowed his voice even further, holding one fist closer to our client's face. "These knuckles will knock you into next week. Your recovery time would be estimated at a month, give or take a day or two." By then, Mackin was eye to eye with our customer. A little spittle, just for that rabid, mad-dog effect, emerged from the corners of Mackin's mouth, and perhaps a bit of spit was forced airborne from the low rise of his octave level from that subzero coldness, and it landed on the client's cheek. Mackin's intense, violent action itinerary was persuasive. We got a $100,000 cheque the next day to pay for their wardrobe plus a $10,000 check for Mackin's foundation. The headline would have read "Knuckles Net 110K." Of course, that headline only appeared in our heads when in our bed.

Concentrate, Lisa.

Yes, at fifty, on tour with a new record, a new band, in new venues because that part of my life has never felt finished. It was more than somewhat stolen from me by my first love. What an incredible douchebag that boy was! Somehow, I blamed myself for that gargantuan rip-off. The lost royalties, the high management fees, the side skims. Rumours have circulated for decades that my father got some of the take, which wouldn't shock me. Looking back, my lover/manager/husband had sized me up as a big-boobed bimbo. He guessed right that I had purposely and willfully turned all my expensive professional music lessons from the age of five onwards, into a rock 'n' roll revenge pursuit against my constantly fucking for money, ego, and vanity parents.

At the same time, I loved the music. I was accomplished at piano, the instrument my parents had selected for class and sophistication, where the lessons all started. I took voice lessons because my parents said I looked like an angel, so I should sing like one. Guitar, well for the love of God, let her be a kid if the piano and voice lessons continue. I dabbled in the drums surreptitiously, and I could beat some skins, daddio! Then my real love and most challenging and least accomplished instrument, the violin, came along. I love tucking that beautiful piece of art under my chin and playing. Even failing at the violin is breathtaking, inspiring. You instantly know that you missed the perfection the instrument is capable of, and that recognition is wonderful. You, the bow, and the violin know, and you agonize together if you miss, and your face shows it. Ninety-nine percent of your fellow musicians don't hear the miss. If Gretzky were a violinist, he would have heard the miss. The timing or spacing was just off.

For me, the violin and bow were the perfect synchronicity of time and space coming together. Come together over me. Yes, the violin was my instrument of choice for gut, heart, and brain and full-stroke stimulation and mental masturbation. The violin's purity had to be balanced by my impure thoughts and revelations. Right, Church Lady?

Concentrate, Lisa.

So, the three-year plan. The starting point is writing the music and lyrics.

Getting back to the essence of it all. Attending recording sessions. Talking to the artists that I'm producing. Going to concerts, attending band practices, getting the feel of it all. The pace, the rhythm, the vibe, the interplay, the connections. Connections to the audiences, the venues, the musicians, the gear guys, the technicians, the roadies. Sound, light, staging, backdrops, movement.

The instruments. I was going to lay down all the tracks I could. Lots of violin. Lots of energy. Lots of soul-searching stuff. Introspective. I wanted to develop a conceptual album that had Liz Phair, Melissa Ethridge, Aretha Franklin, Alanis Morrisette, Carole King, Heart, Tina Turner, Diana Ross, Jewel, and Marianne Faithful influences. An indelible scope of influencers.

Year one, write and record a standard ten- to twelve-song album. Later that year and into year two, play a Canadian tour and experiment. Year three, release the record and do a full tour. Conquer the world! Initially, I had thoughts of an album release in year one and a full concept, double-album concept for year three. Forty to forty-four songs, including maybe three or four covers. Melissa's "Bring Me Some Water," a completely rogue version of Aretha's "Respect." The cover songs would be done with complete respect and reverence for the original artists but with my own unique musicality and voice.

I started to tingle, thinking about the path. I would need solitude and discomfort for long stretches to create. So, the first step was Mackin out. One question, one nagging doubt. *Will I need someone? Will I want something? Will there be a hollow space the music can't fill?*

CHAPTER 9

Scotch Glasses

As a rule, and it's a hard rule, I don't drink much, and I don't drink at all at events. Alcoholism runs in my family, and it affected my father for quite some time. I'm always leery of social drinking because everything almost every day is, well, social. There seem to be more opportunities to drink than not drink.

When my wife went all in on the British Empire, I went through a period of self-destruction. There was some heavy indulgence and some stupid behaviour but mostly in private, thank goodness. At least I picked something from the Commonwealth with character and a classic lineage to dull the pain.

Scotch is a heavy friend and costly in many ways. Doubles of eighteen-year-old Jack Jacks were seventy-five dollars in my favourite bar close to work. That's a sobering tab when you have two or three pours. My personal best—or worst, depending on your perspective—was six. Four hundred and fifty dollars before the tip! Ouch! What kind of friend is that? A bottle was $120. I bought a case and drank at home. Besides, I preferred my own company. I drink alone. Right, George T., as you and the Destroyers sing!

That was a sad, sloppy, period that lasted nearly three months. My ex-wife pulled me out of the tailspin. We met, unplanned, at a charity event. She was with the Brit and wearing a low-cut, cleavage-enhancing dress. I said something clever. "Nice boob."

"You mean 'boobs'?" she retorted.

"No, boob," I replied, pointing at the Brit. It made me laugh. She lost it, letting me and the nearby attendees know. Even though it was a charitable event, her comments were anything but. I was drunk, vulgar, and sloppy, just like she knew I would become. Before I could muster a clever response, some form of large, tuxedoed security arrived. The ex-told the gorilla that I was inebriated, vulgar, insulting, and should be removed. I left quietly, primarily because I was already too drunk to muster a clever response. The gorilla's formidable stature was also a significant influence on my decision to retreat.

On the short walk home, I started to cry. Yep. Cry. I still loved that woman.

It was time to lie down, sleep it off, and pull myself together.

The interesting thing about scotch, when poured neat into a whisky glass, then sipped slowly and moderately, is it can create a reflective mindset, providing the drinker with a frame of mind to get things in order. Focus and arrange priorities. Technically, the correct term would be expressed as "time to get my shit together."

My scotch wasn't perfectly neat. I poured it over whisky rocks, which I kept in the freezer to lower the temperature of the scotch just a bit. I also love the aesthetics of the stones clinking in the glass. It feels sophisticated.

What did I see through my glasses of scotch? My scotch glasses? They revealed paths. Paths of pity, self-destruction, and self-incrimination. It's okay to explore those paths with only four ounces or less of scotch. More than that can lead down paths that I had already fully explored for three months

Did I feel sorry for myself? Absolutely! Did I deserve better? Certainly! Did that matter a good goddamn? No! So, pity, especially self-pity, was both pathetic and of no value. Pity from others? Please, no. I needed a shower afterward.

Self-destruction has an appeal. We all like a good train wreck. Look at him hitting the booze. That ain't going to end well. That'll leave a mark. What do you think is next? Gambling? No! Hookers? Maybe! Drugs? Hallucinogens only! Yeah, that could end badly. The outside world sees a slow, general deterioration in appearance, performance, and behaviour. Ya, that's the ticket! Booze fueled and under-performance powered. Sober up, you dick head. Don't become what she said she saw you becoming. Don't fulfill her prophecy.

Self-incrimination. The blame game is good. Blame yourself. It's all your fault. Martyr. Alas, for I have sinned. I've screwed the pooch. All my fault. Fuck that. Live and learn. There's nothing to gain there. Move on.

The real paths? The real way? Who knows? Scotch glasses, those rocks clinking. Did you catch the caramel hints in that twelve-year-old? Almost-sober second thought. My own senate. Third thought, fourth thought, another shot? Two things emerged, two thoughts, two crystal-clear epiphanies.

One, start with adversity. This is the biggest adversity I've faced in my life. Loss of my love. Okay, then let the world judge me now. Judge me as I handle adversity. Let's face a sobering truth. Anybody can be good at whatever they are good at when things are going well. You can be great. On our climb up the corporate ladder, I knew I was a great executive, manager, colleague, associate, and every other role in the corporate world. Family role? Sure! Good son, brother, cousin, uncle, and husband. Extended circle? Absolutely. Good friend, teammate, community member, professional associate, and volunteer board member. Yep, all good. Check the boxes. A good man throughout. Check me out now in adversity.

When I've been spat out, rejected, and kicked to the curb. Am I a good man now? Good character? Still a giving, trusted, charitable, caring, engaged, trustworthy, reliable, loving, decent, and capable human being? Not so much for three or four months, okay maybe six and a bit.

So, number one: don't let adversity win. Rise above, get to your core, your best character. Don't just display that character with a stiff upper lip—more British stoic imperial bullshit. You must live it. Become your best and demonstrate it in every action and interaction. Be selfish about that. Yes, selfish! Being your best is a commitment to what you've spent the last fifty-plus years building. Be that person. It's what others expect and what they respect and love you for. Be that. Be your own best of breed. That's forward thinking and something you can do.

So, number one is simple: control what you can control. Be your best. Go all Boy Scout. Number two: no negatives. Yep, she bitch-slapped you, so now what are you going to do? Rail and whine against her cruelty? What good does that do? A few moments of pity? We covered that. Try to pull her down, tarnish her image? Really? How's that going to work for you? How does that elevate you? Strengthen you? How does that help you progress, recover, bounce back? It doesn't. Besides, who wants to listen to that shit? Who wants to live there in that heap of morose dung? You need the forward gears, positive traction. Stay out of the swamp. You can't drain it. There's no traction, and soon enough, your own alligators will be biting your ass.

You loved her. Seventeen years. For most of that time, everything was good. Cherish what you can, if you can, when you can.

That's it. Scotch glasses. A little tilted and filtered but they work. It's been almost a year and a half now. I'm good. Lesson learned. I want someone.

My scotch glasses also helped me see that I prefer to be with someone. The shared voyage, the shared path is my path.

Do you need anybody? Just somebody to love! Can it be anybody? Just somebody to love!

No fuckin' Brits need apply. I conjure up Joe Cocker or the Beatles in song, then reject Brits. That's funny! Now that's scotch glasses at their finest.

CHAPTER 10

Measure Twice, Cut Once

For a Saturday night, we were kind of slow for GoHo's, but it had just turned midnight, so things could still go nuts. Maybe one of my big three would show up. There was Guy. He'd sit at his raised table, order his Stormwatch tall boy, sip it—manly sips, that is—and observe. He told me that he was a scotch drinker, but our top-shelf scotch didn't make his bottom shelf. He'd been coming here for about eight months, and I still didn't know his real name. He was still just "Guy." Now I knew where he worked, even his title, a bit of what he did, where he lived, very la-di-da, and that he was a divorcee. I could lie with Guy. Oh my, some days I thought I would screw a snake if someone held the snake's head for me—and it wasn't venomous, of course! On second thought, that would make things even spicier. *Come on down, rattler. Shake my coils!*

Then there was the lovely Lisa. If she came in at all on a Saturday night, it was typically late. After 1:00, closer to 2:00. She was accompanied not so much by an entourage but by musicians. They'd finished playing, had a drink or two, and then come to GoHo's for some growl chow. They talked about their music. She wasn't with anyone. How could she replace Smackin' Mackin? I would love to mack some time with him. I could hear myself screaming, legs wrapped around his waist. "Mack me! Mack me!"

Lisa had left me tickets to a couple of shows. She sits in with the band, usually playing the violin, sometimes the guitar, and she sang backup vocals. Clearly, she was talented, respected, and interested in the others' playing and performing. Ah, the lovely Lisa. If I were inclined that way, I would have gone for Lisa big time. Hell, forget my inclinations. If Lisa went for me, I'd be crumbling my crackers in her soup.

Then there was big number three, rumbling down the track. The Mack Attack. What a man! Lisa and Mackin had been coming to GoHo's on the first Monday of every month to have a long dinner and a longer business meeting. All professional. They took turns paying the cheque. Great tippers. Mackin, I'm here for you if you're lonely and longing for some carnal knowledge. As if that man, who was a golden, leaping Adonis buck, the king of the jungle, would even consider lowly Mo for a roll. I can't even manage to fantasize decently about him, although I keep trying. I'm no quitter. Al Mackin, the guaranteed "get her wetter better" man.

He also occasionally came into Goho's when the bars were shutting down, usually with a couple of other current or former athletes. They often had just finished broadcasting a late game. Women gawked and draped themselves over their table, but Mackin and his mates politely declined their not-so-subtle advances. On occasion one or two of them took the offered telephone numbers, but they never gave out their own. It was like an unwritten code. Mackin gave me a look when they needed someone to be politely but firmly returned to their seat and stop interrupting their manly discussions. I provided that Mo-mentum.

Mackin seemed sad. I would have loved to brighten his days for him—and his nights. But I only thought he was sad. How would I know what Mackin was feeling? I can say that late on a Saturday night when he was less than completely sober, he appeared somber. He was okay talking with his friends, but he seemed to clam up and withdraw when ladies came to the table. His buddies would order drinks when they come in, but not Mackin. Wary and weary, that's what he was.

When I finally choose a man, I'm going long, going the distance. Not one night, no short time flings or romps. No, none of that horse shit. Okay, maybe once fackin' with Mackin. Guy, I might give him a try. Just kidding. No, I'm not!

I had a plan for my life. When a man came into my life, it had to be right. I'd become so independent, so determined, and so certain of what I could become that the man was going to need to love all of that, get all of that, support all of that, and perhaps even inspire all of that to an even greater degree. I needed a tall man for that. Not tall in stature—well, okay, I'd take that—but tall and long on character, able to go the distance. I had to measure a man really close to figure if he had that length, that height of soul, care, and love. I might even make a false measure or two. That was alright. I'd learn and grow.

CHAPTER 11

The Melancholy Meatloaf Man

My plane was delayed in Chicago. No big surprise there, but the delay came after we pulled back from the gate and were parked on the tarmac. I wasn't in first class or business class, and I wasn't going to order some crap sandwich or snack. I had rushed to the gate in Chicago because my flight arriving from LA was late, and I didn't have a chance to grab some grub between flights. I don't even know how I got booked on a milk run and not direct. It had been four days of late nights, late dinners, early mornings, and more than a few glasses of wine. I stayed away from the scotch, though, and I ran four miles every morning. I also managed to resist a forty-something lawyer from LA with an impressive resume or something impressive. That wasn't easy. She even said, "Some other time perhaps," when she handed me her card with her number and the words "very personal" written in passionate purple ink. I almost swooned because of her proximity, implied meaning, and her scent. Ah, the scent of a woman. Intoxicating, especially to a thirsty man. Do people still even use the word "Swooned?" Swooned? Really? Even thinking that word made me feel old and out of touch. In full dinosaur mode.

Lost her to a fuckin' Brit! What kind of man lets that happen? Maybe you swoon when the blood rushes to your head because when she handed me her card and her breasts brushed my forearm ever so slightly, my dick mobilized. You know, I had some blood-flow issues, which can make a person swoon. Man, I'm so ready and so not ready to be with a woman.

The lawyer's touch got me through the flight. By the time I landed in Toronto, I hadn't eaten in nearly thirteen hours. The second half of the flight I had been lusting for some GoHo's meatloaf. From imagined intimacies of the female kind to lusting for meatloaf. Lust and comfort in both, I guess.

When I got home, I showered, threw on some jeans, a button-down long-sleeve dress shirt, a sports coat, and some boat shoes. No socks. Down sixty-four floors on the elevator to the street. Forward to GoHo's. Only a few tables were open, as it was just before the more raucous night crowd rolled in for the night's grand finale. My big-top table was open and waiting. I was beginning to feel like Norm from *Cheers*, except nobody greeted me when I arrived, except Mo.

Mo was on and as funny as usual. "Look at you, Mr. Sophisticated, all casual and smelling good too. You borrowed your old man's Old Spice again, and now you're out looking for love."

"No, Mo, just meatloaf."

"Meatloaf at two o'clock on a Saturday—excuse me—Sunday morning?"

"I've been travelling all day. Flight delays. No food. Need some comfort."

'Right, with chocolate milk or a tall Stormwatch?'

"Tall Stormwatch, coldest one you got."

"For you, Guy, we fly them in from the Arctic."

Pivot. Gone.

Every time that Mo exited with that quick turn, it called my ex-wife to mind. Not the physical motion but the precision and execution. My ex-wife seemingly turned on a dime and spun my life upside down. The precision and timing of her quick pivot away from me and then she was gone. The British judge gave her a perfect six for technical merit. The Canadian judge, being me, gave her zero for artistic quality. Look at me, the "Melancholy Man" waiting for his meatloaf.

On the bright side, I loved that Mo remembered my order. We hadn't talked much over the last few months. I admired her drive and her accomplishments. I discovered from the other waitresses that Mo raised her daughter, nurtured her sister's growth, and earned a bachelor's degree. I found her motivational. She had lost some weight over the past few months too. She was good looking. I could find comfort there, but she deserved so much more than me. Mo reminded me of a Tom Waits song. I couldn't remember the name, but it was about a waitress and an older man. The song was about finding comfort, a safe harbour, not so much settling. Mo deserved to be celebrated and lifted by a partner. I got that. It made me happy that I understood that. It said something about me, I think. That I was decent, maybe. That I cared.

There I was, thinking about what Mo needed as she put a Stormwatch in front of me.

"Arctic delivery."

Pivot. Gone.

By then, GoHo's was full. What did I need? A woman. That thought called the Todd Rundgren song to mind, "Leroy Boy." Find your friend a woman and then find one for yourself. Maybe I needed a wingman. Thanks, Todd. The soundtrack of my melancholy life featuring Tom Waits and Todd Rundgren. What did I need? I was lonely and a little lost.

Thank goodness for work and ambition. Even not getting together with the LA lawyer was blocked by my ambition. Work was going well. People were stumbling around and above me. The trip to LA wasn't to save a deal but to put salve on some open wounds. Fornicating with a player at the table would have been bad form. The LA meetings were scheduled for two days. I stretched them to three and a half, including Saturday morning. My firm hadn't executed or organized the details of the deal worth a shit, and our follow-up was atrocious. Without once implicating our firm or fixing any blame on any of the other five camps at the table, I directed a path forward that not only dressed the wounds but also created changes in the plan that guaranteed a lot of healing and would resurrect future extended and connected deals. It was a win. When I landed in Chicago, my phone blew up with texts and emails. The CEO and chairman had already heard I was masterful—masterful! The lawyer had emailed and texted numerous times. She would be in Toronto in six weeks and looked forward to connecting.

What did I need? Meatloaf, fries, and gravy on the side. Thanks, Mo.

I didn't want to be sloppy or embarrass myself. And I didn't want to hurt anyone. I sure as hell didn't want to hurt myself. I didn't want to bounce in and out of relationships. I didn't want a one-nighter or a weekend fling. Although my libido hadn't been crushed, my ego had been. I think I still loved her or the thought of us or something.

I wanted to get whatever was next right. What did I want? I just wanted to feel good about someone with me. It wasn't just comfort, security, or safety. It was about feeling right in the middle of the night. Coming back to bed after a 4:00 a.m. piss and anticipating the great feeling of touching someone, putting my arm around her, and feeling so good about us, I would cry a bit out of joy and love.

Fuck, what a dreamer!

"Mo, can a guy get another Stormwatch?"

CHAPTER 12

Going Long

These hombres I was out with were good guys and I didn't have to be careful around them. They had my back. The social gossip columns and TV shows had already reported that Lisa and I were now just professional partners and that our personal relationship had ended amicably without any toxic or bitter outbursts. Though speculation abounded about the cause of the breakup. Who initiated it and why? What was the underlying beef, grief, or need for relief? Neither Lisa nor I provided the media with any fodder to fuel speculation. Some innuendo emerged when Lisa began hanging around the music scene, but nothing stuck, nor was any of it true. So, it was all old news, or lack of news, and it was all in my rearview mirror.

The three amigos I entered GoHo's with were all ex-teammates, all happily married, and all reliable. Unlike some of my other former teammates, these three weren't out chasing skirts. We went to the Leafs game, sat in a corporate box, and mixed well with our host and his friends. We enjoyed their company, told a few gridiron stories, and made people laugh. Destroyed a few myths and fables about our prowess and created a few new ones. All in all, it was a good night. Then for three hours we hung out with a few of the Leafs. We spent most of the time in the players' area talking to a couple of vets who were in their mid to late thirties, on the down slope of their careers. A few of the younger players wandered in, and some asked for our autographs. The Canadian kids said they remembered watching us with their dads. They talked about the games they had been to and how much they respected the toughness of our sport. These kids were nineteen to twenty-three, getting paid double, on entry-level contracts, more than what I had made at the peak of my career. Nice kids still, down to earth, humble, not afraid to be respectful or a little awestruck. The kids drank bottled water while the vets and my guys drank beer, clearly spotlighting a generation gap.

Our business relationship never wavered. Lisa and I still met with clients on a regular basis, worked together with designers, and had monthly planning and review dinners at GoHo's. All business, all the time. Lisa wasn't cut out to backslide on any decision. I had character enough not to grovel or only grudgingly accept her call on ending us. I respected it without fully understanding it. It still hurt, though. In fact, it created a quiet ache.

After our visit with the Leafs, we went to a bar down the street for a drink and then continued to GoHo's. Mo was working, which provided instantaneous relief and comfort. She was skilled at negotiating bothersome patrons away from our table. We ordered big meals for four big guys. No drinks except coffee. This was my sensible crew. The first two women who approached our table were half our age or less. They were certainly good-lookers and dressed for a night of bar hopping and partying. I don't care how old they are or how creepy it might seem, but the vast majority of men can't help but sit up straight and puff their chests out when good-looking women come by. These two deflated our puffery in one sentence. "Can we get your autographs for our dads?" The second sentence was unnecessarily cruel. "They idolized you guys when they were young."

When those two beauties retreated, an awkward silence hung in the air for about half a minute, then the ragging and laughter started. We dug at each other about our respective reactions and the humbling nature of the encounter.

Mo arrived with the food, and as Canadians typically do, no one bothered us during our meals. We were engaged and visually animated with one another. I kept sitting up straight and swelling my chest as a mockery of the svelte three-hundred-pound linemen sitting across from me. My antics included indicating his belly still stuck out farther than his chest. He pleaded his case about losing seventy pounds since our playing days, which he had. He actually looked svelte compared to when I first met him at an NFL camp when he was about 370 pounds. Now he was a very svelte three hundred pounder, as he liked to say. We laughed. We ate. Life was good with those three. I knew and loved their wives and families. I attended graduations and got invited to holiday dinners and one of their offspring's weddings. Good men, good people. I believe that you need to surround yourself with friends who will keep you whole, sane, and on a good path at all times, especially in down times. Those guys wouldn't let me do anything stupid because their wives would kill them. Self-preservation is good motivation.

Their wives did represent a problem, though it's not what you might think. "Now, Mackin," they joked, "you'll be attracting female attention. Your three amigos? Not so much." They trusted their husbands, and they trusted me. The problem with them was their seemingly endless supply of available girlfriends. They kept providing numbers and introductions. I just wasn't ready. I'm still not. That doesn't sound too manly for a former middle linebacker. The toughest, meanest, strongest position in all of sports. Someone else said that, not me. But who am I to argue?

Whatever I did next, I wanted to do it right. I wanted to play the long game, and I'd been thinking that way since the day after the "Lisa and Al era" ended. I had a revelation that I wanted to be a father. So, in my books, that was the long game. Although that night made me feel old, signing autographs for the girls' dads, I had the long game in my heart and in my head. What my three amigos had with their families was what I wanted for me.

Then in came Lisa, and my heart skipped a beat or however you describe that palpitation. Heart skipped a beat! How old am I if that's the phrase that comes to mind? Put the Four Seasons and Frankie Vallie or somebody like that on the jukebox. "Big Boys Don't Cry." Wa, wa freakin' wa.

I recovered, nodded in her direction, then steeled myself to go long.

CHAPTER 13

Solo to Sunlight

The guys were smoking hot that night. Their mixture of original and cover songs allowed me to fit in seamlessly on the violin and accompanying vocals. They worked with me, and I played my first new original song in front of a live audience. It was tentatively called "Cut in Half." It was about the damage done so long ago and what came out of that. I hoped it would become a song of triumph, self-worth, and self-belief. I believe the violin solos expressed hurt and anguish in the intro and soared to sunlight at the end. Soared to sunlight? Is that corny? An odd or old thought or is that okay? It's not a lyric; it's just a thought. No, it's more than that. It expresses what I want the music and the lyrics to accomplish. What I want the song to say: get to sunlight.

There he was in his high booth at the back wall of the diner—Smackin' Mackin. My heart leaped forward. Man, that man still moved me. That was a hard thing I did. I hurt him. He carried it so well, though. He had been so gracious. What a fuckin' ingrate asshole I was. But I had no time for self-loathing, which would only lead to backsliding. Thank God I hadn't had a chardonnay or a swig of whisky with the band because a Mackin smackin' would have felt unbelievable that night. Not only because Mackin was the real deal, but I was on a high from my music. Making my music is an aphrodisiac. Playing it live can be orgasmic.

Oh, Mackin, please believe it's not you, it's me. I need to do this right. It's my soul at play, and it's a singles game. That might be the theme of my next song.

There were seven of us, but we all fit into my regular booth. Mo kept it open for about ten minutes past our ETA. It was good to see her.

She started with her usual banter. "Musicians, eh?"

"Yep, you guessed it."

"You're keeping some bad company with this one." Mo gestured at me.

My bandmates bit at that remark. "'How so?"

"Never picked up a cheque in her life. And when she comes in here solo, she tips like shit."

"Anything else we should know?"

"Yep. Fights. Always mouthing off to someone. Always causing trouble." She pointed at the bass player. "Long hairs like you always have to stand up and hit someone with a guitar pick or a drumstick—wood not turkey—to defend her honour."

"That's enough," I said, then pushed my way out of the middle of the booth and stood eye to eye with that saucy bitch of a waitress. I glared at her name tag. "Waitress—Mo, is it? Give me a hug." When we hugged, the band exploded.

I caught Mackin's eye, and he smiled at our act. Then over Mo's shoulder I saw Guy, "the ass and attitude guy," and I nodded.

Songwriting is a reflective process for me. I don't have a set approach. I don't string some chords together or start with a line or two of thoughts. My music is organic, not planned. I might strum my guitar or write down a phrase that gets caught in my head. Usually, I just amble and ramble until I stumble into something. My music collection would have a theme. I knew what it would be. It was a genesis and a platform. I knew its bookends, but the deep water, the full backstory, needed to be given structure and then flesh and blood. Or was it the other way around? I thought I had the flesh-and-blood part, including the pound or two I extracted from Mackin, but not the structure. The music was a journey of me for me by me.

> Yet I burn still and deep
> For all to see
> And for none to weep

What was that? Where did that fit? Were they good lyrics, or was I riffing off some Shakespearian sonnet?

See what I mean? Amble, ramble, and stumble. The scientific method on acid. Do people still do acid or LSD?

I was in a reflective stage, digging deep within myself. Level-headed, controlled, and vibrant. I felt alive. I was focused on an outcome but not worried about the past as I immersed myself in my own past to address the damage done. I realized I was delving into a pool of cathartic reflection, but I was alright with that. I needed to get things right for me. Please myself, pleasure myself, the journey of self. No copilots required. I think Mackin understood that. As selfish as it was, it was who I needed to be to get it done. Solo to sunlight.

It's surprising, but when I was at GoHo's the next steps on my path tumbled through my mind despite the chaos of the diner. I was able to see things through a lens that was blurred and jostled with all that life and energy circulating, yet somehow my perspective was clear. Primarily my own perspective, but I also had the vantage points of others circling in the mist.

Song #1 "Cut in Half"

Where are you going?
The door slams, and you're out.
When the door closed
Did our light go out?

Down your road
Up my path
Will they cross
Or are we cut in half?

Hope you find who you are
Wished you'd left our door ajar
Can't pray for things that used to be
You get to you, and I'll get to me.

Down your road
Up my path
Will they cross
Or are we cut in half?

You travel on your own
I hang onto my cell phone
My heart is stone
From the nights alone

Down your road
Up my path
Will they cross?
Or are we cut in half

If you find a better you
Maybe there's a better me
Then you got to you
And I got to me

Down your road
Up my path
They won't cross?
Baby, we are cut in half.

CHAPTER 14

Pastrami on Why

Some nights I can't sleep. Sometimes it's good. I'm all fired up about work, a deadline, a project, an opportunity, a problem, a misstep, a high-risk/high-reward scenario. Yeah, I love those! A chance to step up, the need to lead, the need for speed. I feel it.

The need for weight. You feel me, brother. Feel me bearing down.

The need for the kill, the need for the save, the need to bring my "A" game, not *a* game. The big game, my absolute cock-of-the-walk best game.

I can keep myself awake. I don't mind. Because I'm invested. My brain is crawling with live wires. Energy is pulsating through it. I scribble notes on the pad I keep beside my bed. I fire off a few emails to my team for them to think about, research, and build on. I often ask them to counter, turn the side eye up a notch, take a critical view. I ask them to let the thought sink in, let it go deep, don't judge, feel it first. Thoughts are like eggs. They're fragile; handle them gently before you break them and scramble them.

I was wired, so I got out of bed and meandered down to GoHo's. It was 1:40 on a Wednesday morning or late Tuesday night. GoHo's caught an interesting crowd on weekdays that early in the morning. People working the evening shift, men's beer league teams from the ice rink a few blocks over. I loved the members of the late-night mixed-bowling league from the downtown Dominion Bowl. Like GoHo's, it was a neighbourhood institution just a few blocks over from the diner. I don't know if it was just me, but there seemed to be a continual flirtation among the bowlers. I mean, if you're talking about spares, strikes, gutter balls, head pins, and splits all night, I guess it could get sensual.

I couldn't count on Mo being on. I had contemplated calling GoHo's and asking before I wandered over, just to see if Mo was working and getting her to hold my table. I did that every couple of weeks, an after-midnight shuffle to GoHo's. I got a sandwich and a side salad and skinny brown cow juice, if it was available. They started stocking it for me. I was a real regular.

Tomorrow morning, I told myself, *I'll start with a big workout.* At least a three-mile run on the treadmill and half an hour of lifting. Then that night I'd tuck myself into bed before nine. All good in that cycle, which I would repeat at least twice weekly.

My table was open, but no Mo. Oh, well. I headed directly to my spot, but when the waitress arrived, she told me that section was closed.

"But I always sit here," I protested.

"Well, aren't we special!" Her response was a great "Church Lady" impression from *SNL*.

"I like the view."

"Napoleon complex. A need to sit at the high table. Okay, we can deal with that. You might make up for your stature and your short complex with the size of your tip. You know, generous compensation of your waitperson is good for your mental health, self-image, all that stuff."

"Any chance you were trained by—"

"Mo? You betcha! Best in the business. She said you were a sharp fella, despite some Jethro Bodine-like tendencies."

"That Mo. Yep, one of a kind, and the right kind at that."

"What are you having, Guy? We're busy, and I don't have time for idle chit chat."

"Pastrami on rye, coleslaw, skinny chocolate milk."

"Oh, good for me, not too large an order to haul all the way over to your special table."

Her departure lacked Mo's precision, but Patti—I read her name tag—was good at her game.

My sandwich arrived at about the same time as Lisa did, at 2:02 a.m. I checked my Fitbit. I was way ahead on steps for the day and would crush my office weekly challenge pool with my stroll to GoHo's and an early morning run.

Lisa passed by her booth, which was empty, and headed straight toward me. She nodded on her way to the ladies' room. When she returned, she tapped my arm.

"You alone? Hell, you're always alone. What am I thinking? What a dumb-ass question. Might I sit?" She sat down before I had a chance to show any form of consent. I was too busy passing my tongue over my teeth, hoping to remove any bit of pastrami or coleslaw before I opened my mouth.

"Are you like the original lone wolf? That looks good." She pointed at my meal. "I'm wired in case you haven't noticed. I need to spit some words out loud, and you're my apparent victim."

"Glad to serve as your unsolicited spittoon of choice."

"Can I ask what gets you out of bed for a pastrami on rye at two in the morning?"

"The clever answer would be 'You, of course, Lisa.' That would either take your breath away or creep you out enough for you to leave me alone."

She shook her head. "Neither of those scenarios, at least not yet."

"What would a guy actually have to say to trigger either of those reactions?"

"Well, from you, Guy—at least that's what Mo calls you—nothing. Guy isn't your real name, is it?"

"No, it's not, and why wouldn't I trigger either of those reactions?"

"Taking my breath away? That was a clever answer, but you would need a whole series of clever words and phrases to get my breath to catch even a little."

"I see. Worldly, experienced, not easily impressed, and deep."

"Yep, all that and a bag of chips. Plus, I've been in a phase of 'no one takes my breath away' for a bit of a stretch now."

"And the creepy reaction?"

"You're not creepy by any stretch of the imagination. You sit here in your high seat, and you observe the goings on of life. You observe. You seem like a bystander. Besides, Mo vouches for your character, and she's a good judge. And you don't look creepy or act creepy. You only stared at my ass when I told you it was okay to."

We both laughed.

"How do you know I got out of bed to come here?"

"You're dressed in sweats, a T-shirt, and a hoodie. That's not your normal attire."

"You're right."

Patti arrived.

"I'll have the same as Guy," Lisa said.

"Even the brown stuff?"

"Yep, at two in the morning if it's good enough for Guy, it's good enough for me."

"How nice that you two can bond over pastrami and chocolate milk," Patti said. "This feels so high school and malt shop."

"Why am I out at two in the morning?" I said once Patti left. "I couldn't sleep. Let me put a little more precision to that. My head was on fire. We had a bit of a meltdown on a deal, but I see a big play and a huge upside for us. What really fires me up is I missed this possibility so far, and so did everyone else. So, I fired off a half dozen directives to my team, and they'll be all over it in the morning. So, I'm wired and when I get wired, I get the growlies. You know, 'growl chow,' as Mo says you call it."

"Okay, here's my story. Do you know a little about my music and background?"

"Yeah. Not in a creeper way, but Mo told me some things, and of course I knew about you. One of your songs was in the mix at my wedding. I googled you up."

"*My* wedding? Who did you marry, yourself? And you 'googled me up'? Now I feel violated." She laughed at me, and I think with me.

"My wife left me for another man," I explained. "We're divorced. 'Google you up' is a phrase I think I picked up down east somewhere."

"Okay, back to my story. What's your real name? And, yes, I know you're some kind of high-powered financial mergers or investment business type. Without the details, because no one knows your full or real name, so they can't even 'google you up' if they were interested enough to do so. But leave that for later. Eat up and listen to my story."

"Okay, my name is—"

"Don't. That'll unravel your mystery, and then you might turn out not to be interesting enough to share my story with."

"Okay, but you should know that I'm going to listen intently, and I'll be a great audience. So, play on."

"You're sincere, aren't you?"

"One hundred percent, Lisa. Play on."

"Okay, now you made my breath catch, just a little. A man who listens? No, wait a second. It was just an errant piece of coleslaw going down the wrong way, no catching of my breath going on here."

Her food had been delivered, and we were both eating randomly and infrequently. We laughed again, and I'm pretty sure it was with each other.

"So, my real music trajectory got run over by a Mack truck. Oh, that's a bad analogy. Nothing to do with Al Mackin. Way before that. And—"

"Stop. I know the genesis of the backstory. You were royally screwed over in your early twenties."

"Screwed over? Totally fucked over. Blind-sided. Wiped out. Emotionally annihilated. I was scorched-earth residue. Agent-Oranged. Obliterated."

"I get it. Tell me the story forward from the pain."

She gave me a curious look.

"Look, it isn't your distant past that brought you to GoHo's at this time of the morning. It isn't me, and it isn't the pastrami. Okay, maybe the pastrami. So, play it forward."

"Okay, thanks. Here goes. My music was interrupted, and although I continued playing, producing, and recording others, touring for brief summer stints, and recording a bit, I never let my soul go back into my own music with any depth. Do you get that?"

I nodded, not sure if I did get it, but I thought I could relate to being cautious with my soul once it got ripped apart. "So far, I feel your hurt. So far, I can hear that music is in your deepest reaches, your soul. Your soul got ripped apart, and there might be fear of the vulnerability that gets exposed when you're soul mining and diving."

"Okay, you're good. Or at least good enough for me at this moment and more insightful than I could have hoped or imagined, especially in the early morning hours at GoHo's."

"Yeah, look at the rest of this crowd."

"Yep, beer league, bowling teams, night shifters, and misfits. You and I at the high table. Guy, you could be interesting."

"Thank you."

"Now shut up and listen. I have to get this off my ample chest. Just threw the chest bit in to keep your attention. Did it work?"

"Absolutely, and please notice the iron-willed resolve I'm demonstrating to maintain eye contact despite your direct reference to just one of your many features."

"Really? You stick handle a conversation well, but please just shut up and listen." I nodded.

"Good. Here goes. I'm writing some stuff that's delicate and painful. All my music is coming from this well of emotions. Some deep hurt, anger, and grief. I've suppressed a lot of emotions for a long time despite some extensive and expensive therapy. Stuff I haven't talked about with anyone, and we won't look at that tonight. Just keep listening. So, this well, this soul well, I began lifting the lid and peeking inside. I saw that the well was deep and full. Then I started pumping a little up to the surface, just a bucket at a time at first. Now I'm pumping bucket after bucket. The buckets don't hold the same thing, though.

"It's different stuff and different densities of the same stuff. You see, sorrow and sadness come in different weights, sizes, and measures. There's some good, bone-deep sorrow about some things that were good but went away. Those things were once the bearers of joy, love, love of life, and feeling whole and well. They were wonderful, and the sorrow of feeling that loss of wonderful things in life is a good sorrow. To feel sorrow for the loss of that wonder in your life cements how lucky you were to have experienced it in the first place. Because how do you want to remember your life? It's good to embrace the beauty, the beings, and the feelings that, when lost, brought sorrow. Sometimes overwhelming sorrow. Yet here I am. Here we all are. So, that exploration, that uncorking of sorrow can drown you or raise you to ride on waves. I'm choosing to ride the waves of sorrow's wondrous origins. Those waves either crash over you, or you ride them to glory. Guy, I'm glory bound. Shh...shh...Don't talk. I have more to tell you."

Lisa was snatching bites of food as she talked. Patti came by, and Lisa ordered us coffees even though it was almost 3:00 a.m. I said nothing because I was more wired than before I left for GoHo's, and I hadn't so much as glanced at her ample chest. Honest!

"Now, Guy, let me tell you about anger. Anger is a bull-riding, biting, scratching, hair-pulling, eye-gouging, crotch-kicking bitch. She's born seeing red, talking blue, hearing black, smelling putrid, and feeling fucked over. Anger is a bitch. She knows it, she owns it, and she wants you to know it. She asks, 'What the fuck are you pricks going to do about it?' Her best friends are vengeance and payback. This is one bad bunch of hurting bitches looking for targets."

I sat back as Lisa poured forth and tried to manage some distance from the bitches she mentioned.

"I know anger. I am or have been angry. You know, I gouged away at his career. The career of my ex-husband, my ex-manager. Knocked him down bit by bit. Then Jack Daniels and snow did the rest. They buried him at fifty—his career that is, not him. He's still around in a far less malevolent form. Is vengeance truly a dish best served cold? No! That's bullshit! Vengeance tastes like shit. It wears at you, and it doesn't do you any good, at least in my experience. It makes you act low and feel lower. Vengeance doesn't embrace victory. It's a stick in the eye. Blinds you with rage. My anger was so channeled and controlled. I helped others steal or liberate his musicians, the artists he was developing, the promoters he was working with, the recording studios and technicians he was using. I signed up for venues and summer concert series with an unwritten rider that he and his affiliates couldn't play those venues. I iced him out of so many things, but he still managed a modicum of success. The rage he felt at the continual line of professional snubs was fueled by booze, broads, and drugs. Rage and the self-inflicted damage of his mind and body killed his career and chased away the rest of his crew. Those of any real worth, that is. I could have been a better person, Guy. Coulda, shoulda, woulda, but I wasn't. It was so subtle the way I helped him kill his life. I should have been so much better."

"Lisa, considering all the wrongs he did to you both publicly and professionally, your actions pale in comparison."

"That doesn't make them right, Guy. Patti, more caffeine please."

Her yell got the attention of the straggling bowlers and beer leaguers nursing pints way past the legal time. Patti brought more coffee.

"Jesus, Lisa Marie. You could wake Elvis with that bellow, and the king needs his rest."

"Sorry, Patti, Thanks."

"Guy, aren't you a working man? You can't be out to four in the morning with this wide-eyed, sharp-tongued mayhem incarnate of a musician. Be sensible, man. The economy is riding on you and your cohorts."

Patti refilled our coffee as she continued. "This is some solid advice about the company you should be keeping, Guy, given your important fiduciary responsibilities."

"Oh, Patti, back down. I have Guy's ear. His buy-high/sell-low investment chicanery and bullshit can wait."

Patti winked and then departed. She was as crisp as hell considering it was past three in the wee hours of the morning.

"So, Guy, back to the well and the bucket brigade. Sorrow, grief, and loss were the precursors of happiness, joy, love, and passion. Vengeance, anger, payback, devious calculation, and inflicting damage. They all meet up in the sober shafts of daylight with feelings of nausea and some gut-wrenching self-loathing for not being a better person. The big ones: love and hate. The polar opposites that seethe inside. Then the course for redemption, finding one's true north, one's innermost core being coming up to the surface, swimming through the thick muck of melancholy, the bile of bitterness, the saccharin of living on the superficial plane, the antidotes of the artificial to the real essence of myself and expressing that through music. That's my journey.

"That's why I pushed Mackin to the curb. He deserved better, but he was a blocker. Too good, too true, too understanding, too everything. Noble, fair, and decent. You can't dive into your own shit with a guy like that around. He wouldn't, couldn't let anyone wallow, wade, or worry about that shit. I had to cut him loose. I had to."

"Well. . ."

"Shut the fuck up. It's just after four. I want you to come to my place and listen to two of my songs and sip a scotch. I have a fabulous collection."

"Of new songs?"

"No! Well, yes. But I was talking about scotch."

When we got up to leave, Lisa motioned to Patti. "My tab, big tip."

Patti nodded her thanks.

The walk was brisk and silent. The night security man knew us both well, seeing as we lived in the same building, though his eyebrows rose a bit as he nodded and opened the security door to let us in. When he said goodnight, I read in his expression something along the lines of, "Well, he's no Mackin, but at least it isn't a stoned, drunk, weird-looking musician."

She lived on the thirty-sixth floor, a nice place. She motioned for me to sit on a long, purple-leather sofa. She poured me a scotch and said it was an eighteen-year-old, priced at $475 a bottle, with a particularly difficult Mc-something six-syllable name. Just one ceramic rock for minimum cooling of the liquor with about four fingers of eighteen-year-old brownish-orange liquor.

"I'm going to play two songs for you. The first one is full of sorrow and wonder, tentatively called 'Lost and Longing.' It's about four and a half minutes long. I believe the chord progression is quite strong, building to a full, histrionic peak that cascades to a lingering ending where the longing in my voice should hurt your heart. The second song is screaming through bloodshot eyes with an angry, almost biblical, Old Testament theme of fire and brimstone. The song is all about looking at the scorched-earth impact of my chosen actions and finding myself knee deep in self-recrimination, self-loathing, and anger that gets jolted to the side and eventually succumbs to a deeper pain. Then the pain seeks revenge. It's almost seven minutes long. Not a dance tune! The tentative name is 'Immolate.' An uplifting name, wouldn't you say?"

For almost fifteen minutes through tuning, "Lost and Longing," a chord adjustment, then "Immolate," I sat there enthralled and barely breathing. When she was finished, she looked at me, put her guitar down, then got out of her chair, crossed the few feet between us, straddled me, and kissed me deep and hard. She pried my mouth open with the force of her tongue and breathed into me. It seemed like five minutes, but it was probably just one or two. Then she extricated herself.

"We're not fucking," she said. "We're not lovers. That was a cleansing kiss. What did you think of the songs?"

"Give me a second. I'm not you. I'm on sensory overload. Let me explain. In let's say sixteen minutes you have deeply touched all my senses and a good kaleidoscope of my emotions. You hit a core bundle of my soul. I'm vulnerable. Then you kissed me and tore me open and then declared we aren't fucking. I gotta go. I'm too open and too exposed right now to say or do anything. Your songs? I must swallow and digest. Ruminate. Don't say anything else, please. I have one question, though. What's the title of your record?"

I grabbed my jacket, belted down the scotch, and hurried toward the door.

"'Leaving Lisa.'"

I nodded over my shoulder and then walked out. "Deep," I called back over my shoulder. "That's a good title."

I swear I heard her body push against the inside of her closed door as she let out a sigh. A sigh that might have held longing, sorrow, regret, or something else altogether. I sure as hell didn't know. I slumber-walked to the elevator, entered when it answered my call. I pushed number sixty-four, then leaned my head on the meticulously shiny wall of the ascension chamber. I started to cry. *What a pussy*, I thought. *What a wimp*. Then I cried harder.

Song #2 "Longing and Lost"

Desperate, desolate, isolated
Catatonic and naked
Anger, sorrow, pain, and grief
My blood spills but no relief

My cut isn't as deep as yours
The blood stops, pain still pours
Get to my feet, scrub the red stains
Angry at the self-inflicted pains
Trying to grab hold, find myself
I'm longing and lost, sitting on the
bottom shelf.

Shattered, scattered, broken, and tattered
Gone, everything that mattered
Set my sails and catch any breeze
Just to catch something for release

Rise, watch me rise
Rise, rise, rise
Rise, see me lift
Rise, rise, rise
Above longing and lost
Above longing and lost
Rising, rising, rising

Brought low, in the dark
Didn't see it coming, left a mark
Nothing left, barren and stark
For you, a laugh, a lark
Casual business, a walk in the park
Me devastated, nothing, no upward arc

Desperation, desolation, isolation

Catatonic and naked
Anger, sorrow, pain, and grief
Broken by a thief

There is no light of day
Hold myself, try not to fade away
Close the door, hit delay
Don't ask, I'm not okay
Can't come out to play
Inside myself, I hide away

Shattered, scattered, broken, and tattered
Gone, everything that mattered
No safe harbour
Bleeding from the cuts of the
vicious barber

And yet as I drift, I want to be strong
Not think, hope, or dream but belong
Not to you
Never again that fool
The longing endures and persists
The loss makes me consider my wrists

Rise, watch me rise
Rise, rise, rise
Rise, see me lift
Rise, rise, rise
Above longing and lost
Above longing and lost
Rising, rising, rising.

Song #3 "Immolate (Burn, Baby, Burn)"

The burned-out shell
The empty bucket in the well
The sandcastle demolished by the swell
The catatonic response in farewell

Immolate, immolate, immolate

If I could knock you to the ground
If I could bruise your bones
Scorch your skin to earth
Burn you back to birth

Immolate, immolate, immolate

Let loose the hounds of hell
Rip out your heart and tell the tale
Stake you to the ground
On your own blood I'll watch you drown

Immolate, immolate, immolate

There is nothing left for you to desecrate
You are gone and I now wait
Weak and powerless at my own gate
Emptiness is my fate

Immolate, immolate, immolate

Now empty of my hate
I'm a lonely, hollow, haunted landscape
You destroyed me in your cutting wake
You gone, I'm broken, no escape

Immolate, immolate, immolate

CHAPTER 15

Time to Grow a Pair

How long have I been moribund? How long have I been losing on the inside and doing everything to win on the outside? *Duh, since she left you, ya fucking loser!* It's getting close to a year and a half. *Get a fuckin grip, boyo!*

You know, I wish someone had seen me on the elevator. Twenty-eight floors of tears. That would have been revealing. I can just imagine hearing someone say, "You okay, man?" The person who asked that question would have been one hundred percent sincere. And my answer would have been a one hundred percent mash-up of a smorgasbord of anguish, anger, admission, assurance, admonishment, or full-blown ass-holish-ness. I don't know how I would have answered. Pick from that list of "A" words, the emotions embedded in them and go from there. I thought of a few possible responses to what would have been a straightforward, compassionate, and well-intended query.

"No!" followed by deep sobbing.

"What's it look like to you, moron?"

"Perfect. I just have something in my eye."

"Perfect. Crying in elevators was recommended by my therapist."

"Fuck off and mind your own business."

"No, I'm not. You got a minute?" That would have scared most people out of the shiny chamber.

"Like you would understand, you toupee-wearing dip shit!" The CPA guy who lived on the forty-eighth floor had the worst toupee ever.

"No, I'm fine, just fine. Thanks for asking." The sarcasm would be dripping from my tongue.

"My wife just left me for a Brit, so fuck the empire!"

"The vasectomy didn't work. I'm going to be a father, so I'm emotional at the moment."

"Get the fuck out and walk, you fat bastard."

Okay, you get my drift. I was a wreck. Those songs, that kiss. Shaken, stirred, and my soul poured over the rocks. So, yes, I'd been building up a bit of a lust for Lisa before she sang those songs, and that music put me over the top. I just wanted to hold her, comfort her.

Her desolation made mine seem so minor. That type of clawing, self-incriminating blame and devastation that doubles and triples before you see it coming. Then there it is, and it's a tsunami of self-wipeout. Yeah, she sang to my soul, my well of hurt. She dredged it all up, and yet I was only feeling her sorrow or sorrow for her.

Fuck, Lisa, just a hug. Just a shoulder to cry on, not that kiss. I wasn't ready for that. I wanted that kiss but not like that. I poured another four fingers of scotch and sat in my big leather chair. A power chair, a manly chair, a manly man's chair. A good chair to reflect in and go deep in, to be thorough, to assess where I was at, where I wanted to go, and maybe grow a pair. *Get on with life, boy. A full life. Fill that void because you sure as hell feel the void.* Lisa brought it to the surface.

I flipped through my song list on my phone and played Neil Young's "A Man Needs a Maid." Clean up on the aisle of life. Stat. Had that kiss, those songs, jump-started me out of my somnambulant state? Nice word, good four-syllable descriptor, and an even stronger thought. The scotch burned. Neil's pleading voice and the lingering feeling of Lisa's tongue, mouth, lips, and hips. The pressure of her pleasure parts. Pleasure parts? Wow, that was a senior phrase. Many things had been stirred up.

Two fingers into the scotch, I cried again. Neil was singing "Cowgirl in the sand, is this place at your command?" and I was hearing that first line of Lisa's song, "Brought low in the dark." The tears were good. They'd been well earned and were redemptive. At 5:30 in the morning, I could tell myself that and believe it.

I sent my executive assistant an email at exactly 6:00 a.m.

Hey there, at my morning workout I felt nauseous. Think it's a touch of flu or a stomach bug. Be in by noon. Tell Gerard from Finance and Suzette from Legal that thinking of them and our 10:00 meeting made me puke and reschedule it for 6:00 this evening. Neither one of them ever works past 5:00, so I expect them to have multiple bullshit excuses, then offer them the alternative of 7:00 a.m. tomorrow. No, better still, make it 6:30 a.m. or 6 p.m. on Friday evening. Those two will crap their drawers at the mere suggestion of those times for a meeting.

At 6:15 my phone pinged.

"You should have puked earlier! I would have stayed in bed and perfected my beauty sleep, although that's totally unnecessary. Agree? Of course you do. I'll set the appointment for 6:30 a.m. on Friday, the alternative at 6:00 p.m. I'll bullshit them and tell them I checked and know that their calendars were clear for those prime times. I'll also present you as a veritable saint for offering them such exceptional openings for a possible long and fulsome discussion. Ta, ta until noon!"

Georgia and I had been a team for seven years. When she told me almost a year ago that she was retiring in two years at age sixty, all I could say was, "First my wife and now you?"

She didn't miss a beat with her response: "Yep, and I'm going to London to get me a real man." She was one of a few, no, maybe the only person who could get away with that comment.

I had a restless sleep until 11:00. Then I showered, shaved, suited up, and walked in at 12:00 p.m. sharp. Georgia nodded and asked how I was feeling.

"Good thanks. When will I have the pleasure of meeting with Suzette and Gerard?"

"They gladly accepted 6:00 p.m. tomorrow, your gracious alternative time."

"Well played." We high-fived, which was unprofessional and childish, but what the hell? Just about eight hours earlier I'd been bawling my eyes out in an elevator.

"Yes, they apologized for being so difficult, and by the end of the conversations they had forgotten you were the one who cancelled the meeting in the first place." We shared a laugh.

"Georgia, give me to sixty-one, please. I'm still grieving the invasion of the British booty snatchers."

"Piss off. Sixty and I'm out of here. Grow a pair and get yourself a girlfriend. The line of women from our office alone would go around this building, if you would ever enter the market. And if I was staying for anyone it would be you. You know that, right?"

"I know. By the way I think I found my pair last night."

"What? You got lucky? You got off the bench and now you have morning sickness? Or were you completing a walk of shame?"

We fist bumped on that one, and she snorted when we laughed.

"Not quite, but I made a personal commitment to get in the game. Get me invited to every charity or social event the firm has. A seat at the head table is preferable, and I'll speak at any event, just to ensure I'll be noticed."

"My boy is back. If you make a speech, you'll have to screw your way out of the room. Oh, my God, the room will be dripping with charity-giving divorcees who will want you to mount their philanthropic peaks, or something like that."

"Georgia, the mouth on you! I'll endeavour to give generously and donate what I can to their causes."

"My boy, my boy, please get back to living. Seriously, I see the hurt, and I sense the void in you. Please be good to yourself."

"I will. Thank you."

As I headed into my office, Georgia's heart came out on her sleeve and spilled out of her mouth.

"Be kind. Be gentle. Be gracious. Be true to yourself. Be decent. Be better than what happened to you. Be your best person. Be all that for yourself."

"I will. I promise."

"You better because I won't let you be anything less."

I thanked the Lord for Georgia, my conscience, my confidant, and probably my best friend. Then I plunged into work, deciding to figure everything out later, including my re-entry into the world of relationships. It would probably be good to mull it over at the gym while working out. How to man up for myself without being a total ass. Dating? How the hell do people date these days? I knew the charitable and social world of investment banking and the financial sector was a target-rich environment. Hell, twenty to thirty percent of the women at those events were totally unattached. Many had been dropped or divorced and/or traded in for younger models. How crass was my thinking? This wasn't about getting laid. Anybody could get laid, especially in my tax bracket. That was a crass and crude thought, but that truth was out there. I craved female companionship. What a quaint and colloquial way of expressing my needs!

Work was good. No, work was great. It totally absorbed me. I loved what I did, how I interacted, how I thought, how I drove and built. I have a big, heavy pair at work. What did people call it? "Big-dick energy" or "little-dick drive"? Tomato, tomahta.

Now if I could grow a pair in my private life, that would be splendid. How archaic was my thinking in those old manly terms? I had to clean up that part of my thought process.

Lisa? The title of her new work would be *Leaving Lisa*. As for me, I'd be leaving Lisa alone. She could tear me open, and I didn't need that. I needed cosmetic surgery, not a full dissection. I'd be leaving Lisa alone for now, but maybe when I grew a pair. . .

CHAPTER 16

Old Normal Anguish

I don't know why I kissed him. Kissed him? Christ, I almost choked the man! Then I blurted "We're not fucking!" Where did that come from? The look in his eyes. I strummed the last chord of "Immolate" and looked at him. His expression was one of wonder, loss, and complete compassion. His face reflected the soul I had poured into my music. That face got it. That face understood and mirrored my hurt, anger, loss, longing, and love. I loved that look on his face, and I wanted to pour more of myself into that vessel. He looked so vulnerable, all pure and aching, like I felt singing my songs. I wanted that man, a man who let his feelings show on his face, in his eyes. He looked like a gift from God. He heard my inner strings and chords and vibrations and tempo and rhythm. He heard and felt everything, and I believed he could save me from what I needed saving from with just that look. A look of complete understanding that said, "I get you. I got you."

Then I said it. "We're not fucking!"

What did he say as he was leaving? I know the sound of his voice reflected his face. His look was one of bewilderment. He was hurt. Wounded. Perplexed. I had hurt him. I know I hurt him. But how? I was so into myself. What was I thinking? I knew I was going deep with my music, probing the recesses and abscesses of my life. I was dredging up and articulating some deep shit in my songs. The songs had a life to them. My life. They were also beginning to look forward. They were like an ongoing discovery of my true wants and hopes that I had purposely buried. Deep.

Oh, Guy! I didn't mean to hurt, confuse, or damage you! I wondered what he thought I was. A cock tease? A user? A woman with a past, skeletons in her closet, and a scary outlook on life and love? What did he ask me before he left? The name of my album. Once I told him, he probably couldn't wait to escape. That might have been the most unplanned totally appropriate response possible given the circumstances. He must have wanted out of there desperately. "We're not fucking!" That's what I said to that face of understanding? Really?

Eventually, I drifted off to sleep. I left the entire next day clear for writing and recording, with only an evening meeting scheduled. I woke up at about noon, and there waiting for me was my old, normal anguish. I always carried guilt and sorrow when I did something that may have hurt someone else. I "open carried" my anguish like the gun laws in Texas or some other redneck domain, maybe Alberta. My anguish was palatable, clearly visible on my face and in my demeanour for anyone to see. I looked and felt as barbaric and backward facing as the open-carry laws. My mood was in retrograde or some other astrological bullshit phase.

Thinking I had hurt Guy, I let that anguish build throughout the day. I always carried and felt the guilt and tried to compensate and make up for what I had done, no matter how slight. That was how he got me—my husband and manager. He read me and played me. My regular, predictable anguish at the slightest of my actions and behaviours could be played against me in waves that immersed me in self-doubt, self-destruction, self-recrimination, and self-loathing. That was how he overwhelmed and then crushed me and then took everything.

In those moments, I'd tell him I was sorry. His response? "You should be."

I would say I probably should have done something different, and he would say, "Absolutely. What you chose to do was a poor, inferior, weak choice."

I would say a performance was good, and he would agree and then add, "But it wasn't great."

The anguish would build and build and then devastate me. All the while he could see he was eroding my confidence, killing my nerve, diminishing my drive, and most damaging of all, demolishing my belief in myself. I was so demoralized and defeated that it became easy for him to manipulate my career, my business dealings, and my money and leave me with almost nothing. When he "left Lisa," there was almost nothing left for her and very little of her.

Now I was feeling a crack of remorse for kissing Guy. If I was going to feel remorse for anyone, I should at least know his real name.

I felt remorseful about Mackin too, but by the time I'd decided to cut him loose, I had gone through the whole rationalization process. Of course, Mackin handled it with such gallantry and calm. I almost wish he had shown anger. He just showed loss, hurt, and all the understanding he could gather. Gallant, decent Smackin' Mackin. It was good to feel remorse. I felt a little embarrassed too. All this would pass.

I didn't let the flow of anguish build into self-defeating waves like it once did. I was stronger than that now. So, I pushed into my writing and chording. I was working on a song that centred on a bass player who was in my original band. I knew him from my first and, as it turned out, my only year of university. He was laid back, easy going, and constant. His character was like his playing. The steadying rhythmic strength of the bass, always supporting and building up. He was subtle in his guidance. He would say about my husband, our shared manager, "That man is a wild hair. That man is driven and relentless." Those were his warnings about my lover, my manager, my husband. Why didn't he speak the whole truth? My husband was ruthless not relentless, destructive not driven, and wildly self-centered. The bass player was the first musician I called for my new work. He accepted in a second. He never questioned me about time, place, pay, theme, or outcomes. He just said, "Yes." When we met, I told him I expected more directness in his playing and his personal guidance. He asked if I was able to listen to directness.

I bowed my head, and a tear spilled down my cheek. "Yes, I think so."

"Good," he replied. "Let's lay down some awesome shit."

I warned him that there was anguish, pain, bitterness, and a whole lot of cathartic crap coming his way. He stated his truth, his essence. "Never mind. Never worry. The bass has a deep soul. Catharsis begins and ascends from the soul."

My first band member was a great choice. I needed some people who understood where I was at and what had transpired in my life. That knowledge would be beneficial in helping me order and structure my raw emotions into meaningful music. A good "bass," double entendre intended.

Guy, what the fuck is your real name? It should be romantic like Raphael or Michelangelo. I promise not to be disappointed if your name turns out to be Bill, Ted, John, or Mike. If one of those common names is your actual name, I'll call you William, Theodore, Johnathan, or Michael.

"We're not fucking."

The absurdity of that line struck home once again. I started to giggle and then I laughed out loud. Once I was able to extract myself from the moment and stand back a bit, then the scene was more than a bit comical. *Oh, my God! That poor man! What must he be thinking?* I knew what I needed to do, what I needed to say. I had a bit of a logistical problem, though, because I didn't know his real name, first or last, or his number.

I thought about it all day and throughout the evening. My anguish needed to be extinguished. Finally, I phoned GoHo's and asked for Mo. She was working the late shift and took my call, starting the conversation in typical Mo fashion.

"You're burning through my service-oriented time and hence my tip income potential, so make this count!"

"What's Guy's real name? And what's his number?"

"Why? Are you trying to get into Mr. No Name's pants? This guy should work for No Frills! I don't know his real name."

"No, I'm not trying to get into Guy's pants. Well, not yet anyway. I'm not ready. What about a number?"

"Well, Guy needs a good banging, so don't get in my way. Her Mo-ness might want some of that herself." Mo snorted when she laughed at her own joke, and so did I as I echoed her laughter.

"Do you have his number, you wild, horny thing?"

"You know what they say? Once you bang a waitress, you've heard all the sweet music and got all the rhythmic bopping you'll ever need. So, skanky musicians like you don't have a chance after that." That was followed by another round of mutual snorting and laughter.

"Okay, wild thing. Get your mind above your waistline and concentrate. I need a number."

"What for? Ask your concierge or night valet or whatever that doorman is supposed to be. They'll have his number for sure."

"That would be indiscreet."

"Indiscreet? We've been talking about humping the guy, and you're worried about discretion? Hang on. I'm going to check our pickup and delivery register; Guy sometimes orders takeout."

"Good thinking, Mo."

She returned a moment later. "Yep, here it is. I got a number, but he uses the name 'Guy' when he orders. How devastatingly cute of him. So, no name, just his address and a phone number. Got a pen?"

Mo gave me the number. I thanked her, then hung up and dialled before I lost my nerve. The call went straight to his voicemail, and the message didn't include his name. It was just a curt, professional, "Sorry I missed your call, yada, yada, please leave your name, number, and a brief message."

I tripped over my tongue but managed to spit out my number, asked him to call back as soon as possible, and added that it was my personal, private line. I don't know why I added that pretentious bullshit. Maybe I wanted to create a sense of urgency and connection. I called him at exactly 2:07 a.m. That's right, in the morning.

I went back to the song I was working on. It was about finding a good man to be with and defining a good man. Me creating that song? How audacious and pretentious that I thought I had that kind of wisdom. But I needed to write it. I needed to write what I needed, what I felt I needed. I wasn't describing him as perfect. I was reflecting on Neil Young's "A Man Needs a Maid." Not the lyrics or the theme so much as the strong sense of need. That was a good thing to think through and express in my own unique voice. Need. What I needed. Decency, trust, and human—not perfect but human, with imperfections. Not Country and Western imperfections like dirt under his nails and muddy boots but real, relatable flaws like strong opinions, doubts, and emotional blips. Perfection is unrealistic and overrated. It's an ideal, not a state. The posturing of people as if they were in a perfect state, is the ultimate pretension. And self-deception.

The song was simple. "Wanted Man." I'd sing it for Guy someday, but not right away. It would seem like too much of a come-on after my now infamous "We're not fucking" line.

I worked on "Wanted Man" all afternoon and through the evening, changing some chords and refining the lyrics. I also added a refrain. When I sang the refrain, it filled me with full-throttle, inflamed emotions. Then one word came to me and seemed so filled with power—"rising." I sang it over and over. The word described exactly what I wanted to achieve for myself. Rising, rise up. It held so much meaning for me, and yes, I could hear the beginnings of that word were knee deep in that old anguish. It was an anthem for me. I added that refrain to "Lost and Longing" after I finished tooling around with "Wanted Man." Rising. Above the "old, normal anguish." Maybe there was another song in there.

The phone was ringing as I stepped out of the shower. Naked and vulnerable, I wrapped not one but two towels around me. I was hoping it was Guy. It was 6:12 a.m. I couldn't let Guy hear me naked.

"Hello?"

"Hello, Lisa. This is Sean."

"Who?"

"Guy. You know, the guy from the diner."

"Oh, Guy. The guy I told we're not fucking."

"Yes, that Guy."

I couldn't tell if he was angry. He did sound a little cold.

"Can I explain that?"

"No need. You were crystal clear. Although your delivery mechanics could use a little work." He was definitely cold.

"Guy, can you give me a moment here? I mean, Sean, please?"

"Yes, but as I said, you don't need to explain."

"Sean, that was impetuous, selfish, and hurtful."

"It was just a kiss."

"No, Sean, I was trying to devour your soul as well as your face. Thirty seconds longer, and we would have needed something like a crowbar or an exorcism to extract me from you!"

He laughed. "You know how to break the ice."

I laughed too.

"I apologize, but the look on your face after hearing my songs. I know that look, that feel. I live that look. Vulnerable, hurt, sad, and maybe a little lost. Your face was a mirror image of my feelings, my emotions, the part of my soul I put into my songs. You got me. You understood me. I loved that. I had to snatch that. It was a primordial instinct."

"You overwhelmed me, Lisa. You simply overwhelmed me, so much so that you woke me up. Outside of work I've been sleepwalking through life. You know what I did in the elevator last night?"

"No, what?"

"I masturbated. I live twenty-eight floors up from you, and I came on number fifty-seven. I thought that was fast. I still had seven floors to go."

"You did not!"

"Sure, I did. I was vulnerable. It was either cry, find someone to fight, or whack off. I decided to pleasure myself, and why not? I could still feel your tongue, your breasts, and your hips pressing into me. I haven't been that intimate with anyone in eighteen, maybe nineteen months. I rang up Mrs. Palm and her five daughters. Those girls never say no."

"Come on, you didn't."

"Of course not. I did the only thing I could. I cried. And I cried some more into my four fingers of Scotch, which I poured upon my arrival in the relatively safe containment of my sixty-fourth-floor abode."

"You cried?"

"You saw my face. My wife left me for a fuckin' Brit, with the stereotypical bad teeth, bad hair, and a non-athletic build. He isn't even smart, well monied, or royal. I've been devastated and relationship neutered ever since. I pour myself into work and workouts. Your song crushed my pretenses, and your kiss kicked away all my defensive fences."

"Guy, Sean, I'm so sorry."

"Don't be."

"Why shouldn't I be sorry? I hurt you, didn't I?"

"Yes, in a way. But you also opened me to my own mirror image. I've been shut down. My balls disappeared into the void of my personal not-quite-real world. So, this morning at about six a.m., I grew them back. I mentally took my balls out of mothballs. You awoke the absolute necessity for me to get back in the game. I've been moribund, housebound, and given myself no chance at a rebound. You woke me up, Lisa. I should thank you."

"No, Sean. I didn't know all this. I don't really know you at all. I didn't want to hurt someone who was already hurt. You just appear so strong, confident, and decent."

"Well, I am all that, and I'll approach my re-entry with those characteristics intact. I could never be the guy in your songs. Never."

"Good. That's so good to hear. I need to play another song for you. If you'll let me."

"Not right now, Lisa. I need to get firmly on my feet first."

"But this song is totally different. It would mean a lot to me."

"No, Lisa. Not now. It would seem too much like charity, and I know that's not what you intend, so let's leave it be for a while."

"How long is a while?"

"I don't know. Three months? Six months? Whatever I need. You would be too overwhelming at this moment, and this isn't about you; it's about me. I need to be fully me before I get to you. You deserve me, not my shadow. Your songs told me that."

"Oh, Sean, but I feel sadness, what I call my old normal anguish, about this."

"Don't. Finish your album, then let me hear this other song before it goes public. You need that sense of completion. Then you might be really ready, and I might really be me."

"You're wise, gallant, and decent. You make me feel."

"Use those feelings for whatever they're worth when you write. And, Lisa, just two things."

"I will, Sean. What two things?"

"Don't tell Mo my real name but let her know you know. That will drive her bananas!"

"I'm okay with that. That'll be too much fun! And the other thing? I feel like a big shoe is about to drop."

"Well, yes and no. Lisa, we're not fucking." He laughed. "For now!"

I laughed too, then he hung up.

The old, normal anguish felt a little punted to the sidelines. Mackin would like that analogy, maybe not in that context, though.

With Sean, I felt a new type of anguish, an inner lament for something so close but so far. But maybe someday. That anguish was good. The feeling of wanting something. Something coming from a place of goodness.

One of my songs was tentatively titled, "Getting to Good." I knew that song would grow fuller because of this.

Song #4 "Wanted Man"

We have no time for the shallow end
If we go together, we dive deep
We come up for breath
Clearly in over our heads
It's going to be a hard road
But I promise, you're my wanted man

You're not perfect, neither am I
Together we blend and we try
To make our faults slighter and understood
Help me, help you, help us
My wanted man

I can be petty and shallow
You can be hard and closed
We aren't full of poetry and prose
We are piss and vinegar in a leaky jar
But we are what we are
And we can be okay with that,
My wanted man

You're not perfect, neither am I
Together we bend and strive
To make our missteps part of our strides
Help me, help you, help us
My wanted man

Lay beside me, let me watch your chest rise
We have too much of this and not enough
of that
We aren't as graceful or as smart as we hoped
We are speakers of our minds
We mend each other and remain gentle

and kind
And this is more than all right,
My wanted man

You're not perfect, and neither am I
Together we mend and heal from the inside
Makin' our scars heal and not go so deep
Help me, help you, help us
My wanted man

You're the rhythm, the solid bottom line
I harmonize with you and keep time
We play the chords, we sing the tune
We miss the odd note, the occasional word
But we play our songs, we play them
out loud
Us together, I feel whole,
My wanted man

You're not perfect, and neither am I
We knew that from the beginning,
no surprise
We play well together, blend into each other
Help me, help you, help us
My wanted man

Mmm, my wanted man
Be there, I need just you, my wanted man
All of me is for you, my wanted man
All of you is for me please, my wanted man
Bend me, mend me, bend us, my
wanted man
Mmmm, my wanted man.

CHAPTER 17

The Gotto's Mixeteria/Miseria

There were many fascinating aspects about being a waitress. The kaleidoscope of the ever-changing customer landscape, which was absolute theatre. I watched the unfurling of the human condition as people ate. Observed their actions, behaviours, relationships, nuances, all as they processed food and each other. The solitaires were particularly fascinating, ranging from the power performer to the agoraphobic hermit.

The power performers were formerly only males, but lately, women came to put on the "I'm something special" show as well. A new gender-equality scenario. They spread their power tools out over the table. Power phone, maybe two. iPad, tablet, or laptop with stylus to tap the screen with their pure potency as if they're humping their technology. Earbuds embedded. They spread out and took ownership of a four-seater or a booth for six. They were performing. "Look at me—savvy, wise, and so important! My equipment tells you so. Look at my long, swinging technological dick. People need and seek my wisdom constantly. Not even a second of my existence can be wasted. Look at me. I'm a conceited, self-obsessed, narcissistic, king/queen of the fuckin' universe." They talked louder than necessary because they wanted us, the peons in their universe, to hear the rumblings, the machinations, and the intellect that they possessed and spewed.

When we were busy, and sometimes even when we weren't—because I could humble even the most pretentious power performer—I simply didn't serve them. They'd point at the coffee pot and wave their cup in my direction, but I just stood there, staring. When they removed their earbuds—or not, and usually not—without even a minute gesture of politeness or thought of saying please, when they just looked at me, I shook my head.

When they said, "What?" I'd tell them to pack up. "We need to make you comfortable at a smaller table. We need to keep this spot open for larger groups, so we can provide good customer service."

If they protested or responded with attitude, saying "I'm good where I am," I told them they would be far more comfortable and get better Wi-Fi reception at the Starbucks just two blocks down.

Then I exited, exuding the ambience and the definitive "kiss my ass" attitude that they so richly deserved.

"Kiss my ass, Hollywood." That was what my body language screamed at them. Their own loudness had already secured the attention they craved, so everybody was watching their reaction. If they deigned to make eye contact with any of the other patrons, they didn't catch one iota of a supportive glance or nod. What they saw were looks of disdain and some low front-burner anger. If they could interpret those faces and looks, the message would be crystal clear: "Get up and get out, you sanctimonious piece of shit." They seldom survived the open contempt in the air. One guy started shouting for me to come back, yelling, "Can you believe the service in this place?"

"Hey pal, you heard her," one of our regulars said. "Move your ass and shut the fuck up. We're all tired of your voice."

The perpetrator left.

The hermits, on the other hand, had to work up their courage even to surface. The courage to pull their heads out of their shells and come to GoHo's. Some of the hermits were regulars or semi-regulars. If I could, I placed them in a low-traffic, low-visibility spot. The less noticeable, the better. They never came in when GoHo's was busy or the streets were jammed. Accommodating them in a booth was okay. They usually knew what they wanted and ordered right away. They'd made their choice from an old takeout menu that they had stashed at home or from our online menu. When I interacted, I blocked them from the view of the other tables nearby. I made it a small, safe world between me and them. I protected and respected their need to feel comfortable given all the internal stuff they had going on. They were self-limiting and limited, and I could relate to some degree. I would leave a jug of water or a thermos of coffee, so they could serve themselves. I didn't intrude, make small talk, or ask them more than once if everything was good.

A great meal outing for them was obvious. Their shoulders pulled back a little, and their stature became less slumped. They looked around in a slow panorama, taking in GoHo's, the patrons, the staff, the decor, the ambience, everything. They were absorbing and storing, building knowledge and, hopefully, comfort. Their constant, furtive glances and cowering over their meals dissipated a little. Their minds and bodies got a brief break. They made me try to be the best human I could be for them.

Interesting, the "mysteria" of the human condition. GoHo's was a natural "mix-ateri." The characters, ranging from the centre-stage, showboating, self-promoting,

"Hey look at me being all I can be and that you should try to be" were contrasted with the "Don't look at me," "Let me be," "Let me breathe just my own air," "Let me just peek in," "I mean no harm," quiet isolation of the hermit. I fell in love with the bravery of the latter and despised the bullshit bravado of the former.

Lisa sometimes made a grand entrance. She had an overwhelming smile that was only marred by a glint of sadness in her eyes. The smile on Lisa's face, when she asked me her big question, was of the overwhelming variety. "You know Guy's real name, right?" That Mona Lisa smirk told me she knew his name, and she knew I didn't, so I cut to the chase.

"What's his name?"

"You don't know?"

"You know I don't know, so quit jerking me around and tell me."

"What makes you think I know, Mo?"

"Your shit-eating, smart-ass grin, you fashion-forward fuck."

"Mo, Mo, such language. So unbecoming of a sophisticated, well-educated young woman."

"Look, I have my BA, but you're just giving me BS."

"Guy said not to tell anyone, not even you. Actually, especially you."

"More BS. Come on, spit it out."

"Can't. I promised him."

"How did you find out? Did you have your way with him? Some girls on the late shift said you and Guy left together early one morning."

"I didn't fuck it out of him, Mo. I'm a lady."

"Now listen to who has the potty mouth. Was that when he told you? The night you were here late together?"

"No, much later. The next night."

"When he was finally pulling his pants back on?"

"Mo, the innuendos you're making. You're making me blush. No, we didn't get intimate, and he told me he has no plans to even attempt that."

"Please tell me he's not gay."

"Definitely not. He's saving himself."

"For you? Later?"

"I doubt it. He did tell me that if he were ever to approach me in that way for that purpose, it would be at least six months down the road."

"What? Does Guy's cock have an internal clock, a timeline, a date stamp, or something?"

"No, his wife left him over a year and a half ago for a Brit. A Brit he describes as being non-royal, non-athletic, and not rich, with bad hair, worse teeth, and no intellect. He was crushed and just recently decided to get back in the game."

"He told you all of this, and you didn't screw him? That degree of openness and vulnerability makes that man instantly doable."

"He told me over the phone. Would have been difficult to screw him long distance."

"Is that when he told you, his name?"

"Yes."

"Does his name suit him?"

"Didn't think about that, but yes, it does."

"Good. And you better be right about that. In my mind I hear soft sounds that underscore strength."

"You hear that in your mind? Mo, mentally I think you're already doing Guy."

"Oh, yes, I channel Guy through my friend, Vinnie Vibrato, on a regular basis."

We both laughed. A good, shared laugh with a friend over some silly, slightly slutty girl talk.

"How long has it been since you and Smackin' Mackin parted loins—I mean ways?"

"Six months, give or take. And, I haven't been given or taken since."

"Well, good for you, but you're not even trying. I've been celibate for twenty-seven months. Not that I am keeping track or anything."

"What did you get your degree in? Abstinence? Sainthood? Religious studies?"

"None of the above. I just wanted to focus on school, my daughter, saving some money, losing some weight, and getting myself straight for what's next."

"What is next for you, Mo?"

"Really, Lisa? A big success like you wants to know my next move? Worried some mogul-like competition is headed your way?"

"No. Sincerely, you handle people in all situations and all conditions so well. You would be great in a position based on opening and building relationships and partnerships."

"Yeah, Vinnie says that all the time. I make him play so many roles. It's the backbone of our relationship." We shared a giggle, then I continued. "I think I could be very good at managing an enterprise that requires strong relationship building. I have a strength in planning, organizing, and getting things done. And I work well with all types, sizes, and attitudes."

"You know, I believe you could manage a small-scale organization to start. You have a natural affinity for adapting to different personalities and demeanours. You create a good vibe around you. You come off as sincere and genuine, and you have a beautiful sense of humour."

"Can I use you as a reference? That was very kind and beautiful and probably a tad overstated."

"Just a tad, and yes, I'll be a reference. Gladly."

"Thanks. Now, what about you, Lisa? Alone again and absorbed in your work. Are you okay?"

"Ah, you know. Focused. I'm working toward something to get to that next step."

"But you're working through some old pain. Some misery."

"We all work through some degree of pain and misery, don't we, Mo?"

"Yes, but yours was publicized to the nation and is still mentioned frequently even when everything you touch goes splendidly."

"My misery was and is still in the public domain. Therefore, every step I take gets a little more attention and analysis than it deserves."

"Your band friends who are working with on your new material, when they come in, they talk about your writing. Your songs."

"And what do they say, Mo?"

"The cathartic experience of epic proportions with all the elements. Pain, hurt, anger, misery, love, deep emotions, finding a path. They talk about you with admiration. How you carried that devastation and rose above it and now have the strength to address it."

"They are great bandmates and even greater friends."

"Back to the origin of the question, Lisa. How are you handling facing those old miseries?"

"Mo, I think you're helping me craft a song. 'Those Old Miseries.' I feel good and strong. I'm emptying some painful places that have been tucked away. Nicely compartmentalized with a lot of expensive therapeutic help."

"'Old Miseries.' I think I could sing along to that. Maybe with a glass of Old Misery whisky."

"I don't do country songs."

We shared a giggle.

"Those spots you're emptying, I hope you fill them with something good. I gotta get back to work."

"Thanks, Mo. Let me know when you need that letter."

It was that slow time at GoHo's on a Saturday night. After the late-dinner crowd and before the shows got out, between 9:45 and 11:00 p.m., so Lisa and I had been able to chat for a while. That night could be big dollars. There was an NHL game, a major concert, and a couple of box-office winners—plays and movies. *Ooh la la, let the moolah flow!*

I'm building my nest egg to start low on the corporate totem pole and work my way up. My supplemental savings have become quite substantial, not including the money I'm packing away for my daughter's education.

Until I'm ready to launch, which isn't far in the future, I'll watch the mixture of misery and mystery that people bring into GoHo's. The full gamut of human experience on display for my entertainment, enlightenment, and curiosity. GoHo's own combination of "miseria and mixeteria," served up like the Saturday night special.

CHAPTER 18

Thinking While Flying Solo

I strolled into GoHo's solo at 10:45 p.m. on a Saturday night. Not my usual style, but I had nothing to do, and I was feeling a little lethargic toward the social scene. I watched the Leafs game at home. Man, that team deserved a break. The media was relentless and almost asinine in some of their articles about the Leafs' perpetually failed bids for the Stanley Cup. I don't know hockey, but I do know sports, and some of those media guys are so far offside, they couldn't even find the rink, let alone the net. I tossed down a couple of One Great City Stormwatch IPAs, imported all the way from Manitoba, while watching the game, and now I had the need for some growl chow. I slid into my regular booth and ordered immediately when Mo arrived.

"Chicken pot pie, fries and gravy, and some cold water, Mo. No ice please."

"Sure, thing, Big Man."

Mo did her toe pick and scooted away like an inside linebacker reading the fake to the outside, then the slant in of a simple, beautiful tight-end pattern. I loved reading that play. It was all about timing.

The ball was already in the air as the end gave the out juke. Me up on my toes, split-second decision, and the calves, hammies, and glutes were all committed.

Boom! Smack the small of his back as the ball hit his hands and chest. Sometimes the hit was so hard and targeted I could hear the air rushing out of him. One hand came under his arm and up to his chest, and often the ball hit my clenched fist, knocking the football from the tight end's grasp. Sometimes, not often, that fist travelled through and caught the bottom of his chin, which meant his arms were stretching out for the ball, which was not necessary on that type of timing play ninety-nine percent of the time. Arms extended was a rookie mistake from the fear induced by the impending hit. My weight was all forward. The other arm, usually my left, was grabbing something and pulling him down.

I'd be airborne, just six to ten inches. My shoulder trajectory would be in a downward motion, so if he held onto the ball or not, he was still earthbound. I'd be in an open jackknife position, my body weight fully levered into his back, so when he hit the ground, my legs were fully extended. My full body weight would drive through an area of about fourteen to eighteen square inches in the small of his back. If he landed right—or wrong, from his perspective—the air went out of him completely. Sometimes the ball would be positioned, so the tight end's solar plexus was absolutely crushed. I loved the impact, the timing, the science of fully leveraging my body weight and angle, separating the man from the ball.

The art of the game, the nuances of physical mayhem. If I missed on a huge man like that, often times as big as six foot seven or eight and weighing 260 to 270 pounds, and if he was turned up field, legs driving, shoulder lowered, I entered the world of hurt. Seconds and positioning determined who got hit by the truck. Road warrior or roadkill. All determined by our ability, our instinct, our brains, and our brawn.

Brawn is the easiest to acquire. Although saying that, the precision a player develops in the brawn comes from the brain, the desire, the dedication, and the perseverance to become a physical specimen with distinct properties and possibilities.

I got a flood of football memories from the precision of Mo's turn, or more likely I just loved conjuring up the game. I was in a deeply reflective space in my own head. I loved the game. Still do.

I'd been reflective and introspective lately. I felt fortunate and blessed—extremely blessed. I loved the fashion thing, taking "dress for success" to another dimension, another field. We—that is, Lisa and I—were still accomplishing that together. We'd begun to move away from the power-couple focus to what we called "Move, Live, Feel." The MLF products were about comfort, fit, and emotion. Clothing should move to how a person lives and how they feel. There should be a naturalness to their image. There was certainly a large degree of artifice in dressing power couples. Clothing should fit a person's substance, not any pretense. People thought, and still think, the MLF product line was an acronym for "Mackin Lisa Forever." A little wrong on that, folks, at least the "Forever" part.

Emotional hits are harder to overcome than physical hits. Physical hits can be addressed by rehabilitation efforts. Treatments, exercises, steam room, ice tubs, meds, and working with doctors, trainers, masseuses, and physical therapists. Hits to hearts tend to make people lean to some negative paths that are far less healthy and rehabilitating.

Me? I just swallowed really hard. Acted all stoic. You know, tough. Rise above. Macho bullshit stuff. But hurt? Yep. Absolutely crushed. Hollowed out. Blindsided. Didn't see that coming. That was gonna leave a mark. It did, and it still does. I got up, though, and kept going.

I'm extremely glad that now I had the maturity to not pursue negative paths, like drowning my sorrows in alcohol or chasing women for the thrill of the one-night hookups. Drinking and women can be easy paths to pursue and temporary cures for what ails you, but they're also destructive and counter-productive.

Expectations were a bit of a ditch. I couldn't avoid them, and I had to drive through or around them. Everyone, even close friends, expected me to get right back in the saddle. "Smackin' Mackin will have a lineup of women eager to start something up." Maybe so. Maybe not. I couldn't think of women that way. That wasn't the cure. And my mother wouldn't stand for it. After all, the big, tough linebacker was just a mama's boy. Thinking that made me smile.

Introspection is good. Get the sorrow in the right proportion to everything else. Get the perspective on the whole field. Think about what you want, then move forward accordingly. Move, live, feel. MLF.

Lisa leaving was brutal, but it needed to become vital and substantial. Drinking and chasing is superficial and hollow. I was making the right moves for me. Smackin' Mackin was known for not overreacting to the feints, jukes, double, and triple teams. He just stood his ground, figured it out, and then mowed it down. It was funny thinking about me in the third person like that. Drawing analogies from the field to my approach to how I felt and how I chose to act in real life. Football was more than a game to me. The game was and still is a classroom. I wasn't running on empty like some folks say when they suffer a loss. I was filling the tank, getting ready for everything that was next. I was getting to a good place. Good things—no, great things—start from a place of internal strength. I'd get there and then some.

Mo delivered my order. I smiled. She started up a conversation, whether I wanted to talk or not. That's our Mo.

"You look awfully content for a middle-aged man eating a meal his mother might make and all alone on a Saturday night."

"Life is good, Mo. If you know where you want to go and believe in your ability to get there."

"Does the chicken pot pie help with that? If it does, I'm taking the rest home with me for dinner!"

"In a way it does, Mo. There's comfort in comfort food. I am comfortable with where I'm at. And you can drop the middle-age references, as I'm entering the prime of my life."

"Are you over her?" Mo gestured over her shoulder to Lisa's booth.

"In most ways, yes. In some ways, never."

"Sounds like you're torn."

"No, the 'never' part is good. It means it wasn't a waste of time, but a significant period of life and time well lived."

"Mackin, you're deep for a mad-dog linebacker. Eat your comfort food. I'm glad you're good."

"Thanks, Mo."

I had articulated something important there. Not so much for Mo but for me.

CHAPTER 19

Just Goes to Show

Man, that Mackin has his act together. I think there's another country song in his words and thoughts like "Dropped but Didn't Hit the Ground" or better still "Dropped not Broken." I'll have to pass those song titles on to Lisa. Maybe they'll fit with something she's writing.

What did he say? As long as you know where you want to go or end up and believe you can get yourself there, then it's all good? Something like that. I need to remember that.

I'm always amazed at what I can learn about someone and what I can take away from that learning for myself. Like Mackin never regretting or needing to let go of the good parts of his time with Lisa. Him being comfortable despite loss and moving forward. Just goes to show that even a broken-hearted linebacker can recover a fumble in his life if he knows what he wants and maintains a belief in himself. Well, if Mackin can plow forward, this waitress can too. Someday people will say, "Look what Mo made of herself. Just goes to show, you work hard, stay true to yourself, and believe in yourself, and good things happen." They'll be saying that sooner rather than later.

I can see what I want to do, but do I have enough faith in myself? I should look at what I've done so far and check the boxes—success as a single mom, as a scholar, and as a phenomenal waitress. Always moving forward and at a pace and in a place that others would regard as dismal, but this has been all me, or us, going forward and making progress. I'm not sure where I can end up, but I know I haven't made any major or even minor missteps for about fifteen years.

I returned to his table. "Thanks, Mackin. Good talk."

He looked as bewildered as I looked calm.

Song #5 "Old Miseries"

There are times in the night
I pray for morning light
Don't ever make it to dawn
I get up, get doing, till the old miseries are gone

I mean it's silly, it's sad
All these years, still hurts this bad
You haunt me and they follow me around
These old miseries keep bringing me down

Too long to feel this hurt
Wear it like a badge on my shirt
Old miseries, old miseries, so deep, so real
You'll never know the pain that I feel

Tried everything to shake them away
Meds by the hour, liquor all day
Old miseries have roots deeper than trees
Pullin' me down to my worn beggin' knees

Plead to let go, to forget
Your blows never relent
If old miseries were whisky, I would drink some
No need cuz old miseries already leave me numb

Too long to feel this hurt
Wear it like a badge on my shirt
Old miseries, old miseries, so deep, so real
You'll never know the pain that won't heal

Figured it out, you gotta look at 'em straight
They ain't any good, just dead weight
Don't need them, don't want them, they're no good
Old miseries, I'd give them back to you if I could

Old miseries, old miseries, I gave you a long life
You're a hard hold to break, but closing time's in sight
Moving on, moving on, I got me some light
I'm better without you and I'm gonna get right

Too long to wear this hurt,
Puttin' old miseries away like a worn-out shirt
Old miseries, old miseries, gone and forgot
New life, new loves, gotta give it a shot

Old miseries, put down
Old miseries buried deep
New mysteries to lift up
New mysteries to make

Song #6 "Dropped not Broken"

Things end, there is hurt
You can't pretend
You're not that different
You're not that shallow
I didn't see it coming, blindsided

The drop is steep
I can't breathe, I can't sleep
But I'm not broken

This is certain
You're gone, you left
I am wandering, wondering
Shredded and bereft
Not ready, blindsided

The drop is steep
I can't breathe, I can't sleep
Dented, bruised, not broken

This is my new reality
These wounds are open
But they can heal
All a matter of mind
My own will

The drop is steep
I can't breathe, I can't sleep
Healing, not broken

So now I'm up on my feet
Looking ahead
Moving, living, feeling
Without the sharp pain

The drop is steep
I can't breathe, I can't sleep
Living, not broken

You don't know what
You can gain
No need to stay blind
Get up, move forward
I'm not staying down this time

The drop is steep
I can't breathe, I can't sleep
Up and moving, not broken

Up, up to my feet,
I breathe, I sleep
Not broken, not strong
Awoken
Dropped, not broken

Strong, strong,
Stronger, stronger

CHAPTER 20

The Phillip Anguish Society (PAS)

Mackin was long gone before GoHo's turned full gung-ho gong show. At about 2:00 a.m., things really get rolling. Generally, after the shows and the hockey game end, people hit the bars, but a portion of that human tide decides they need to eat to keep the night moving. The real hardcore night surfers start rolling in at about 2:00 a.m., mostly surfing on the crests of their altered states of mind. Some in that crowd already know they're going to wipe out and crash hard, but WTF? Surf's up, and so am I.

That night's crowd was upscale and uplifted. Definitely a positive vibe in the air. (The Leafs won, a change from their recent skid.) Lots of banter between tables. Lots of appetizers and shared meals. Lots of growl chow.

The tips were outrageous. We didn't serve shots, but people were ordering triples straight and pouring their own shots in their drained water glasses. Shots drove the average check and gratuities up substantially. GoHo's was hauling in so much cash that Gordon Junior called us into the kitchen at 3:30 a.m., and we all did a "whisky neat." The whisky was the very best from our very low-level top self. It felt good. The team gathering was what really felt good. The Crown Royal burned and snapped my senses. I loved the Canadian feel of it all. A team with multiple differences gathered to celebrate and with a famous Canadian whisky to boot.

Thirty minutes to official close, I was feeling good and richer, and in walked Guy. He saw his table was open and headed right to it.

"Hey, buddy. This table is reserved for a regular guy named Guy."

"Mo it's me, Guy."

"No! It's not. Apparently, you have a real name. A name that is both masculine and indicates a sensitive nature."

"I do have a real name, but I love that you call me 'Guy.'"

"I call a lot of customers 'Guy.'"

"No, you don't. Maybe you used to. You call most of your customers, even the regulars, names like Buddy, Champ, Kid, and Pal but not Guy. Because I'm your Guy."

"Really? You listen to me that closely?"

"Of course. I hang on your every word, and you don't call anyone else Guy. Never. It makes me feel special."

"You're not special. You're okay. You're alright. Okay, you're slightly above average in the tipping department, but other than that you're just, well, a guy. Seemingly a good guy, modest and unassuming. You seem decent, reasonably intelligent and you're not too hard on the eyes either."

"Like I said, Mo, I'm special. You just described a guy who's a special guy."

"Okay, you're a good guy, but why does Lisa get to know your real name?"

"She choked it out of me."

"What, with her big knockers?"

"No, with her bare hands."

"Tough chick."

"I'll say. Like you."

"Okay, Guy, I understand that if I wait for six months, then you'll reveal your real name. But please, if it's Phillip, don't tell me. That would make me puke!"

Guy looked bewildered and hurt, and his head slumped forward, so I followed up.

"What an impact. Did I guess right? You're a freakin' Phillip?"

"Why did you say 'Phillip'? Who told you? How do you know about him?"

"How do I know what about who? Lisa didn't tell me anything about your name. Who told me what?"

"That name causes me some anguish."

"Well, join the club. That name causes me anguish as well, although it did help produce some major joy."

"What anguish? What joy?"

"Well, since we're members of the same club, the Phillip Anguish Society, why don't you go first?"

"Okay. Phillip is the British prick now married to my ex-wife. They had an intercontinental affair, and she left me for him. I was very much in love, and if that wasn't anguish enough, he's a fuckin Brit with bad teeth, bad hair, bad build, not a fuckin' rock star or a royal and not even on a great career trajectory. If he had been a French romantic or an Italian stallion, it might have been a little more understandable, but a freakin' flabby, gap-toothed Brit? Now that induces real anguish!"

"You gotta come in more often at 3:30 for these true confessions."

"And you, what is it about the name Phillip that causes anguish for the indomitable Mo?"

"Give me your order and let me check my other tables. Details to follow when I deliver your food."

"Double cheeseburger, fries and gravy and tall, cold Stormwatch."

Pivot. Gone.

Well, that was the big reveal, except for my name. At least I held something back. GoHo's was packed with a few tables just beginning to leave. There were drinks on every table, even though legal ordering time stopped at 2:00 a.m. The mood in GoHo's seemed buoyant, ebullient, festive, and full of merry making. My thinking was in quaint, somewhat nostalgic, and definitely happy terms. It had been a good night until I heard that stupid dick weed of a name, Phillip. I had been out on a first date that had gone great. Splendid.

"Double-trouble bypass, boat load of fries, and cold beer here."

"Mo, you brought two cans of beer. I'm not drinking that heavily."

"One is for me, guy with a real name. My true confession requires alcohol."

We look at each other, raise our Stormwatch tall boys, tap the cans together, and take a long pull on our beers.

"I'm ready, Mo. Pour your Phillip anguish on me. Your fellow 'PAS' member is ready for the baring of your pain."

"Here goes. Eat while I talk. And try not to cry on your fries. So, at eighteen I got pregnant."

"Phillip?"

"How intuitive. Phillip was a fifteen-year-old rabbit."

"Aren't all males at that age?"

"Guy, not your real name, shut up and listen. I haven't told many people this tragic story, so just eat and be attentive, if not appreciative. Phillip. He went by Phil."

"My ex's Phillip is a full Phillip. That pretentious British prick wouldn't shorten his name. That would be too common, too crass."

"Again, Guy who has a real name, shut up and eat because, sincerely, I don't know if I can get this out. Interruptions won't help."

Guy nods in acknowledgement and stuffs fries into his mouth to confirm and solidify his silence.

"So, I didn't know he was only fifteen. Phil wasn't truthful about his real age. I gave him an easy out. I said he didn't have to take any responsibility or be involved. I was only half hoping he would take that opportunity for departure, but he grabbed that opening as enthusiastically as he had been grabbing my knockers every chance he got. Then I got really brave. I was already working here and going nowhere in school, so I rented a place, packed up, took my little sister with me, and moved away from the shit and abuse that was our childhood life."

"Really? You were on your own at eighteen?" Guy choked on a big bite of his cheeseburger and followed it with a big swig of beer. I used his interruption as a chance to take a good slug of my own beer.

"Yep. Both tragic and stupid right?"

"I didn't say stupid, Mo. I never would."

"You know something, Guy whose real name isn't Phillip? Thank the Lord you're not that kind of guy."

We tapped our Stormwatch and took a drink.

"Amen to that," Guy said.

"With my little sister in tow, we set up house. We got some furniture from Gordon Junior and his family. Thank the Lord for the good people in the GoHo's family."

We tapped our Stormwatch again and nodded at each other, looked around, then we both smiled.

"About a month into our little home, our wonderful shelter from shit and abuse, we got a visitor."

"Your mom? Your dad?"

"Shut the fuck up! You're spoiling the narrative. If you're going to interject, at least be real. This isn't some fairy-tale conjuring of supposed happy endings. What part of a shit and abusive home life doesn't make sense or resonate with you?"

Guy took another slug of his beer, his expression conveying empathy and understanding. "True confessions are thirsty work, Mo. I may need another Stormwatch."

I nodded. "I may need one too. My throat is getting scratchy just letting this stuff catch air. No, the knock on the door was Phil the rabbit's mother. She didn't have much time for niceties like, 'You've done wonders with the place' or 'You look good' or 'Thank God, is that my grand baby in there?' No, just a blast of bitch venom from the old hag. Her profanity-filled, full-volume narrative went like this: 'You make any trouble or get any notion of receiving support from us or Phil, and I'll have you up on charges of statutory rape. You fucked my son silly, and he didn't even know what was going on.' At that point, we both looked down at my belly before she continued. 'Phil didn't know you were trying to get pregnant to get out of that hell hole of a home of yours,' she continued. 'Hell, that child might be your old man's if half the stories about your old man are true.'"

Guy and I both took deep pulls from our beer.

"Mo, I don't know what to say."

"Then don't say anything. Do you know what surreptitious means?"

"Sure. Why?"

"God, I hope when I find out your real name that it makes you sound and act smarter."

"Gee, Mo, what did I say wrong now?"

"You aren't grasping the concept of 'shut the fuck up' as well as one would hope. Now, surreptitiously go over to Gordon Junior, and get us two more Stormwatch, then surreptitiously get them back here. I need a moment to compose myself."

Guy dutifully made the trek to the counter. I got up and closed off the couple of tables I had left. GoHo's was emptying out quicker than I expected. Gordon Junior hung the "closed" sign on the door. He turned off the neon "open" sign and the faulty GoHo's sign a while ago. My last tips were more than generous. It was well after 4:00 by then.

Guy was already back at the table. He didn't say a word, just raised his fresh Stormwatch. We tapped our cans and took a pull, and we both had something akin to a smile in our eyes. Probably the shared look of recognizing each other as companions in the order of hurt. The beers were cold and good. Guy didn't talk.

"Glad we cleared up that Chatty Cathy bullshit of yours, but enough with the small talk. Pregnant with a thirteen-year-old sister in tow, working multiple shifts, and fiscally responsible for a household. I love saying 'fiscally responsible' instead of 'in debt up to my tits.' One sounds elegant and all ladylike, the other like the gutter-trash reality, which was how Phil's mom made me feel. His mom had a few more nasty things to say, but other than telling her that the baby was one hundred percent her grandchild, I didn't say much. Once she ran out of venom, she left. Never heard anything from that family again, which was good because their social standing was probably one or two notches below my own family's. That equates to all seventy floors and the underground parking levels in your condo building if you want some strong mental imagery of how low we were, how we were living. I threw the condo analogy in there so you can relate, given your fancy abode in a high-rise."

"You know, Mo, fuck you just a little. You have no right supposing my formative years were a bed of roses, and that's what it sounds like you're implying."

Guy's response kind of took me back, and this time I had no smart-ass comment about him interrupting the narrative. His tone and look made it clear that his life had some interesting dimensions. I just nodded in acknowledgement, then raised my Stormwatch to tap his before we both took a drink.

"Sorry, Guy. That shot was uncalled for. Someday—no, some night—maybe we can talk more about our lives. Tonight, I'm just focused on the Shakespearian tragedy portion."

"You know you're right, Mo. A fuckin' flabby Brit with bad teeth, bad hair, mediocre career, everything. Why couldn't she pick someone like Ricardo Montalban with the rich Corinthian leather?"

"So, let's wrap this up. Mo's monstrosity of a tale. I delivered a healthy baby. She is now thirteen, going on twenty-one, smart, and getting ready for high school. My sister, Delta Dawn, now twenty-six, is a university graduate. She earned two degrees and now teaches high school. I just graduated with an honours B.A. via correspondence and night school. I left out a lot of detail."

"You certainly did. Sorry, can I speak or am I still in 'shut the fuck up' mode?"

"Speak when spoken to. Go ahead. What's your name?"

"Nice try, Mo. The Stormwatch haven't made my tongue that loose or my brain that addled."

"Addled. Isn't that a nice English word?"

"Don't be such a bitch with the English references. I haven't tipped you yet."

"Oh, economic sanctions, how very colonial and ruling class of you!"

We both laughed, then tapped our cans and took a drink.

"It was as hard as hell, Guy. My sister—I'll explain her name some other time—worked part-time here, babysat my little girl, and studied. Her scholarships and grant money almost fully paid for university. After a few lean years, we stayed way above the water line. We were so careful, so spartan, so satisfied with our lot in life and our progress. But it was hard to go without things and to miss out on big things like vacation, nice clothes, haircuts, and manicures. Jesus, that could be a long list. We did each other's hair, and we had nail nights. We watched movies and did our nails, and when Delta Dawn was old enough, we drank Rusty Nails on nail nights! It still makes me laugh and cry when I think about that."

"Mo, it's quarter to five."

"Is that Greenwich Mean Time? That's in England, isn't it?"

"Mo, that is a very sad attempt at extracting humour from my humiliation and pain."

We both laughed, tapped cans, and drained our Stormwatch.

"Yep, time to go, Guy O! Our stories to be continued. Deal?"

"Deal."

He put his coat on and smiled. He started to lean in. I hoped he would try to kiss me, but all I got was a stiff, awkward hug. How bloody British and Phillip-like! Then he left.

To be continued? Who knew? I hoped so. Then I realized he hadn't paid! That dine and dash wasn't expected. *That's good,* I thought. *Now I have something to hold over him.* Then I realized, apparently not. When he'd gotten our second set of beers, he'd settled his bill with Gordon Junior and tipped extremely well. How bloody proper of the old chap! Not British proper; that would be cruel. Apologies to the Bare-Naked Ladies and green dresses everywhere.

CHAPTER 21

A Pre-Launch Interlude

I'm a graduate. Mo, the waitressing university graduate. I'm certainly not the first person in this category, and I certainly won't be the last. If whatever comes next doesn't work, I can always waitress. This job has been good to me, and in many ways, it's been good *for* me. GoHo's family of owners, the Gordons, have provided a protective and secure spot, and I thank them daily from the depths of my heart. I went to my graduation, even though I hardly ever went to real classes. I basically corresponded my way to the degree. Corresponding is such an intriguing, old-school word to describe the process of attaining an artium baccalaureus. I graduated with honours, with distinction.

My daughter; my sister; Gordon Junior and his wife, Bolly the cook; Frank the dishwasher, maintenance man, and jack of all trades; and two of my waitress friends attended. I had a freaking entourage. It made me cry. They all brought flowers, which made the little impromptu get-together we had for my grad party at our apartment look like a funeral. I'm pretty sure Frank and Bolly bought the first thing they saw at the florists—wreaths! They might have been more appropriate for a funeral, but those good men spent money to celebrate my life and rising. Their eyes and Gordon Junior's were rimmed with the moistness of fatherly pride. Their humble, heads-down mannerisms at the grad ceremony, as they probably felt as out of place as I did, were contrasted with their fierce, shining pride in their stand-up-straight, Sunday-best clothes and wide-smiling joy.

People don't have to be grand to be glorious. My grad day was like that. People I knew, loved, and had worked alongside for eighteen years and my sister and daughter. It was a glorious day of celebration. No pomp, little ceremony, and lots of pride.

Not to be crude, but my sister mentioned that she thought people were supposed to get laid at grad. We laughed. I didn't, of course—get laid, that is. I would have finished Bolly and Frank off, and I loved them too much to kill them in the heat of my pent-up passion.

I had my degree in hand, my daughter entering high school, a nice amount of coin in the bank, and my sister pledging her help until my daughter graduated from university. The table was set for an adventure, a step forward, a risk. I was taking the summer to think and to plan my next phase, my next line of work.

We were taking a vacation. A two-week vacation. Imagine that! My daughter, my sister, and I rented a small chalet on a lake, a four-hour drive from the city. We didn't know how we would get there, as none of us drove. But we were confident we would work it out. We always did. At the moment, as I pause and ponder, nothing seems insurmountable.

Taking a breather would be a new experience for me. The thought of it struck me as something grand. Something unexpected yet something richly deserved. I didn't need to recharge my batteries or anything like that. I had a full tank and a clear road ahead. I had built my Mo-mentum. But the ability to hit "pause" for a moment was exhilarating and invigorating. Maybe the break would punctuate the point in my life where I launched myself into a new atmosphere, a new realm of me.

Frank volunteered to drive us to the chalet, and Bolly volunteered to pick us up in two weeks and drive us home. My everyday workmates for all these years, once again being kind, decent men.

So, off we went, where the Mo I knew had never dared to go, leaving behind my limits.

CHAPTER 22

Balancing My Act

The three-year contract offer was unexpected. I would have done the colour commentary and analytics of CFL games for free. I love watching the games and diving into the tactics, the faults, the finesse, the adjustments, and the sheer unpredictability of twenty-four men set into motion. Every moment is filled with intricacy, timing, chain reactions, and detailed plans that are performed in an environment of mayhem and moment-to-moment chaos. Individual decisions, adaptations, indecision, and a whole bunch of WTF moments.

The game is visceral, intuitive, instinctive, and arbitrary. The whims of the gods roll over the playing field. Wind, rain, snow, sleet, hail, baking sun, but the mailman is supposed to deliver. And Mackin delivered. More than not! This game neither grants nor tolerates perfection. Hell, the game hates perfection. Twenty-four creatures on a playing field of organized chaos. Nothing is better. Nowhere did I ever feel more alive.

I was waiting to sign the contract. I was balancing my act, thinking long term. The contract created a three-year set of time boundaries and defined constraining parameters. It was also lucrative. More money than I'd made in my playing days. That didn't seem right. I had some star power that had a higher cash value than a perennial all-star linebacker. The MLF brand of clothing and my association with Lisa added more rating power, attracting more women, couples, and a wealthier demographic to the game. Sophisticated power and strength are part of my brand appeal. The appeal to the corporate sector and their egos is high. They can align the game to their corporate credos. They get a vicarious testosterone shot. Their balls get bigger by association. If I told you the number of corporate jack offs who asked me how much I bench pressed or how many push-ups I could do, you'd be floored. I never answer, but they invariably share their own personal bests. How sixteen-year-old-like and fixated are those egos on their glory days and personal bests? With the really obnoxious ones I talk about my black belt and Navy Seal-based training that enables me to kill a man in mere seconds. Then I tell them what great inner strength, power, inner peace, and knowledge rests in my soul with that ability. They usually gulp and walk away. I refrain from saying, "Go in peace, grasshopper."

Yes, I have a black belt. No, I can't kill a man in mere seconds, but sometimes narcissistic, egocentric pricks need a sharp smack to their self-centred asshole core. Ah, Smackin' Mackin saving the world by humbling one narcissist at a time!

The CFL broadcasting contract was a conduit to a line of even more lucrative potential endorsements and contracts. It was a big opportunity that I could fully leverage. But did I want to? Exhibition games started in four months. I had some time. An interlude. Time to feel a little contentment with where I was, what I had done, and who I had become. It felt good.

There was a gap, a big crater, left by Lisa, that needed to be filled. Like the holes that open in the line on a running play, I had to fill that gap. That would come. I wouldn't be over- anxious. Didn't Mo say something about that guy putting himself on hold for eighteen months? I wondered if I should talk to him. If Mo liked him, talked to him, and trusted him, he was probably more than a little bit all right.

I will sign the contract, as the deal fit with my longer-term life plan, which I was still figuring out. Overall, "All good here. Thanks for asking. Oh, by the way, three hundred and sixty-five pounds, you pompous prick."

I would get a handle on that gap. I'd find that balance. I knew what I wanted on that side of the ledger. A trip home was up next. Some time with my mother and some old friends would provide perspective. I could benefit from that.

CHAPTER 23

Take the Shot

The kiss kind of settled the course.

I finished writing the "Maybe" song, "Getting to Good," in a couple of days. The song wasn't inspired by the kiss, and none of the lyrics, thoughts, or rhythms came from that moment. What the kiss and Sean's response did was refresh my thoughts on where maybes and maybe nots could take someone. Okay, that someone being me or hopefully being me. Facing indecision and finally deciding. Going forward, not *maybe* going forward. Leaving behind the stuff that was holding me back. Get that trash outta here!

"Getting to Good" was a love song, a heartbreak song. A Gretzky song, as in a shot not taken can never score, or whatever the Great One said. Please excuse my messed-up attempt at paraphrasing a hockey saying. I dated a football player, not a hockey player. Dated a football player? Sometimes I think in such quaint, old-lady terms. No, I had a full-on love affair with that man. Dated? Not even close to describing our connection, our love, our time together.

I settled in mentally. In my mind I was camped in a creative space, and I wouldn't leave until the record was finished. I cancelled, well, delayed all major projects and deferred and delegated much of my work, including the MLF fall lineup. I had already stamped the line with the major design elements and fashion direction. I had even sketched my own tour wardrobe. That tour line went from cover-girl edginess to urban tart and back. No dresses, no halters, no lace, but edgy and more than a little sexy. The tour clothing line would move, love, feel, and riff off the MLF brand. It would sell. The line was accessible and not made for models only.

I was also considering what to do with my hair. I had worn it long and straight since I was a teen. Maybe that was a stance against my mother who frequently changed her hairstyle to accommodate her marital status or planned shifts in marital status. She went from Sinead O'Connor/Grace Jones bald to full-on, multi-hued Cyndi Lauper, to a striking silver, to a full-on Afro-like look, and a number of other eccentric, eclectic, and/or ethnic leaning styles. She was and is the shapeshifter of hair. She seemed to change hairstyles to match the colour or hue of her current husband or to infuriate Mr. Current as she set her sights on Mr. Next. The hair change was usually the telltale prelude to divorce.

I was thinking a change in hairstyle would also mark my change to me for me. I was styling my hair *for* me, not *against* my mother.

I was taking a full-blown interlude from what I had been running from and progressing by running toward it. If that even makes sense. I think it does. Therapy is good and at times maybe was my salvation. But self-immersion was way better. Clearing out the demons, sweeping the ghosts out of the closets, addressing the ache, and creating my heart sound. Peace was washing in as I discarded all kinds of baggage and crap. I wouldn't have a small summer tour as I usually did. I wouldn't do any production for other musicians either, just work with my band. I set no release date and had no venues booked and no tour planned. I was planning to play my songs to an audience of one, Sean, before the first show, release the record in March, and start the tour at the end of that month. A firmer plan would develop as the record progressed.

For the moment, I would just write, play, sing, rehearse, record, repeat. I was going to dance too. No choreographed stuff, just whatever flowed out. So, I started working out. The show might be laden with melancholy and wallow a bit in loss, lament, and grief, but I swore people were going to come out of that show lifted up and feeling like they could do this, whatever their "this" was. The last stanza of "Lost and Longing," the "Rising" segue into the closing song, was going to bring them to their feet and knock the roof off the place. Even in outdoor venues.

I was going to be whole. Time and space. Right, Wayner? I think they called Gretzky that. Create time and space, and make good things happen. Take the shot, Lisa. Take your shot, Lisa. Take it!

CHAPTER 24

The Dated Dater

I needed to do this right. I mean, the whole concept of dating was strange. It was a learned behaviour. I kept hearing there were rules and even tactics. I didn't want that horse shit. I'd try not to be a cliché by just being me. No rehearsals, no preparation, no lines, no game plan, and certainly no timeline or schedule. My expectations weren't low, but they were definitely modest. Just be. Dating will be my transition back to being real.

So far, I had gone on three dates over a three-week span, then one second date. I liked the woman I had the second date with, no question. She seemed easy-going, but at times she displayed signs of an ache, an old or maybe a recent wound, which manifested as a flicker of anger. She was just being human. She had been traded in for an office bimbo who was taller and leaner. She laughed when she said she missed the memo that breasts and butts, full-figured women in general, were out of fashion. In my mind, she was striking. Striking? Is that a forbidden British term for a ten?

She was also clever. A geology professor. She liked rocks and formations. She loved her field and talked passionately about her work. I liked that passion. I liked that commitment to what she was. So, we went on a third date, this time to the theatre with a drink afterward. When we were deciding on where to go for a drink, she said she was hungry and that she had been too nervous to eat before the date. I told her I was too, and that was the truth. I was more than a little nervous.

We were just around the block from GoHo's. I asked if she would like some non-pretentious comfort food in a down-to-earth setting. She said, "Yes," and then stuff spilled out. She asked if she was trying too hard and never let me answer. She said I was different. No pressure, no lines, no attempt to impress, and no self-inflation. That made me very attractive and different. Then she asked if this was my game, my act, my ruse. Then she said she was sorry and that she shouldn't have asked those questions. Questioned my intent, my nature, or anything. I had given her no reason to question. She said she shouldn't have to think that way, but she couldn't take a few weeks of screwing and then be discarded. She was crying. She said that on the third date, according to some of her girlfriends, she was supposed to screw, so she was more than a little worked up.

Finally, I had my opening. "We're supposed to screw on the third date? Didn't know that. Thanks for the heads up." She laughed. I told her I wasn't ready. I wasn't that type of boy. She laughed again. I had her in the palm of my hand. Then I delivered my killer "get into a girl's panties" line of the century.

"Do you like meatloaf? The food, not the musician."

"Seriously?"

"Yeah, seriously."

"I love meatloaf. I haven't made it in years."

"Then let's go to GoHo's." We set off with our arms locked—after a brief kiss.

On the walk, I said that I felt grateful, then added that I knew it wasn't a romantic or an inspiring phrase, but it was true. By "grateful" I meant extremely happy that she had said "yes" three times already. That meant the world to me.

"Thank you for being you," I said. "Just real, kind, vulnerable, and nervous. One more thing before we enter the inner sanctum of GoHo's, though."

"What's that?" she asked.

"Well, actually, two things. First, they all call me 'Guy' in there. Don't worry. I haven't told them my real name, so play along please. Second, meatloaf is a lousy aphrodisiac."

We giggled as we entered.

It was my real-world comeback, being real and overcoming heartbreak to laugh and just live a little. It was beginning to feel like I hadn't passed my best-before date, my sell-by date, or my expiration date. At least I hoped I hadn't!

CHAPTER 25

Guy Brings a Date

I don't know if my jaw hit the floor or not, but it sure felt that way. It was just about 11:30 p.m. and GoHo's was already shifting into overdrive, a little earlier than usual. It was going to be a lucrative night for a certain lovely, loquacious, laugh-inducing waitress—me, your scintillating, wise-cracking servant goddess, the one and only, her Mo-Ness!

Guy strolled in with a real knockout on his arm. Did I just use a descriptive term from the 1950's or 1960's? I did. I'm taking this diner theme way too literally. Guy wasn't supposed to be with anyone. He was supposed to be there alone as Guy. Guy alone. That was normal.

Or he could have been with me. That would have been okay. No, that would have been great! Sometimes I thought about certain customers that way, and having Guy tucked under my sheets had crossed my mind once or twice. Or one or maybe two hundred times. Tomato, tomahta, potato, potahta, libido, libido! Suddenly, I felt pissed and then absurd. I had no claim on him. Hell, I didn't even have grub stakes. Mining references? Mo, get a freakin' grip!

Guy and the beauty headed to his table. He didn't see me when they came in, probably because he was too busy giggling and staring at her.

He should have been with Lisa. That would have made sense. He was calm, which would have been good for her. But then, Smackin' Mackin was calm and gentle. I told myself to just get over to the table and start my usual banter.

When Guy saw me coming his way, his face broke into a broad grin. That made me feel good and pushed some of my pissed-off-ness away.

"Mo, how are you?"

"Just swell there, Mr. Guy Bon Vivant. Miss, you know that he'll be asking you to split the check and pick up the tip. Guy has never bought anyone a meal here. Never. Just fair warning because we don't like to take gratuities from the uninformed."

She laughed and didn't miss a beat. "Mo, my date has raved about the service and the meatloaf at GoHo's. So, if the meatloaf is anywhere near the quality of your humour, this is going to be splendid. I don't have to tip you for Guy's meal, do I?"

We all laughed.

"So, he's your date, and you don't know his real name either? That must be a bit unnerving."

"No, I think Guy suits him. Somehow it just fits. You know what I mean, Mo? He's kind of plain, a bit simple, incapable of being a master planner or even smart enough to be a little devious."

"You've read him like a book. Glad to meet you. I'm Mo, as you know, and you are?"

"Gina."

"Damn, you look like a Gina, like Gina Lollobrigida or whatever that Italian bombshell's name was, without the Italian part."

She smiled. "I'll take that. Thank you."

"If you two are done, we'd like to order," Guy said, interrupting our little "get to know each other" chat.

"Who are you again? I don't think I know your name."

"Funny, Mo! We're going to have meatloaf, fries, and gravy."

"My God, Gina! Did Guy have you watch home movies tonight and slides of his grade-eight field trip to Niagara Falls?"

"Yep. That just about covers our evening."

"We'll have two tall Stormwatch with our meal," Guy said.

I couldn't help myself. "Gina, for the love of God, you deserve better. Please let me introduce you to some of our classier patrons. Oh, I almost forgot, what's his name here is the cream of this clientele."

As I left their table, their laughter followed in my wake. *Damn I wish that was me with Guy.* I couldn't hold back that thought as I retreated to spike their order and get their beers. I needed a man, a real companion, someone I could joke with like that, whose face lit up when he looked at me. And I needed him soon!

When I served the meatloaf, I had to say something. "Guy, you know meatloaf ain't going to lead to a *Lady and the Tramp* spaghetti moment. Just saying that the meatloaf special doesn't really scream romance."

"Gee, Mo, where I come from, they serve meatloaf at wedding dinners."

"Remind me not to visit your hometown—or your planet! Enjoy!"

Lisa arrived at about 12:15 a.m. She was with her band, and she was wearing a big smile! She shouted my name and hugged me on her way in.

"We laid down two great songs tonight. They're going to be fantastic. We need twelve Stormwatch fast, please."

"There are only six of you," I replied.

"We're thirsty, and we've earned it."

"Your booth awaits."

I caught her eye and nodded toward Guy's table. Her smile broadened, then her eyes lit on fire. Lisa took a half-step turn toward Guy's table, then looked at me. Her expression changed to dismay and disappointment.

"He's got a friend? A lady friend?"

"Apparently, her name is Gina. She's funny and beautiful, but they ordered meatloaf and beer, so they can't be screwing."

Lisa snickered, then her face changed again. What was her face expressing? Loss? Missed opportunity? There was a definite sadness in her eyes.

"Please bring the beer. Fast!" She lowered her head like she didn't dare look in Guy's direction.

I did. He had seen Lisa, and his smile was big and genuine. He waved, but if Lisa saw it, she didn't acknowledge him.

Some gut-wrenching inner turmoil was swirling through GoHo's diner.

The night was picking up. The after-theatre, after-game, after-whatever crowd had come and gone, with just a few stragglers remaining. Now the after-bar, not-getting-laid-at-least-not-right-away crowd was jamming the joint. A loud, drunk bachelorette party was making its way through poutine and milkshakes. Several candidates in that group would need their hair held back for them as they clung to the porcelain throne later that morning.

Several GoHo's regulars were also in the room. The place had a good vibe going. Tips were flowing, and the only clouds on the horizon were of my own making. Guy and his date were casting a bit of a pall, but only on Lisa and me. Whatever Lisa was gathering in her own storm cloud was intermittently stitched on her furrowed brow. She alternated that storm cloud look with joyful expressions that were generated and radiated from the obvious camaraderie at her booth.

The cheer from Lisa's table as I delivered the tall boys was spontaneous and raucous. The whole diner chimed in. Some applauded. Lisa stood up and took a bow, to more applause. They all lifted their Stormwatch in, tapped their cans together, and then snapped the tabs in perfect unison. More applause and cheers from the crowd.

I looked right at Guy's table. Gina and Guy were watching Lisa and her band. They were laughing and tapping their cans in a salute. God damn. At that moment I realized I cared deeply about those two customers. More than I should have. As that thought reverberated through Mo-Town physically, mentally, and emotionally,

I shuddered. Then a cold wave of reality hit me. I wasn't on their playing field. I was "but a bit actor on the stage of life" or some type of ill-fitting bullshit Shakespearean soliloquy echoed in my head. That was some good learning and vocabulary right there. That education of mine was really paying off.

Guy and Gina were taking a leisurely approach to their evening—eating slowly, drinking slowly, and talking a lot. Eye contact was off the charts. When I cleared their plates, they asked for water, not more beer, and they seemed in no hurry to leave. As I turned with their plates in hand, I was already thinking that I would be dashing out of there. In truth, I would be pushing Guy out the door to get him back to his place to screw right away. Then again, I wasn't the gorgeous Gina, who, with her body and brains, didn't have to hurry anything. She struck me as a woman who got what she wanted when she wanted and how she wanted. Confident and cocksure. I'm a vulgar little creature because when I think of Gina and the word "cocksure," I think she is sure she can get cock from the cock store by special order and have it delivered to her as per her specifications with a bow attached. Okay, I'm being a bit vulgar, but I'm also somewhat funny—at least in my own mind.

CHAPTER 26

Forecast Celebratory with a Chance of Cloud

My band was amped up. We knew we were creating something good. There was a tremendous esprit de corps. We were replaying some of the process of how the music and lyrics were progressing and evolving. I loved telling the band what a song should evoke in the listener. I told them about the emotions, the feelings I was trying to get across, and then I played a few chords of how I thought the music could sound before I shared any lyrics. I loved telling them the title of a song, even if it was tentative, and then studying their reaction. When I dropped the title "Wanted Man" or "The Maybe Song," they looked at me really hard, all of them wondering, *what's she thinking?*

They all knew my history. Some of them were there for part of it. My lyrics, my words, were filtered through that lens. I watched the reaction in their eyes. I made eye contact with all of them. A few heads nodded, some soft sighs surfaced, some breaths caught, some chests puffed out, and some sank in. There was silence. The room became a pool of perception, a well of introspection. Their minds travelled through their thoughts of me to their thoughts of themselves. The room was filled with a washing silence in the tumbling drum of individual and collective feelings, emotions, instincts, impressions, and insights.

I had a two-minute rule. When I told the band the title of a song, they weren't allowed to speak for two minutes. Sometimes they asked for five minutes to absorb and reflect before they reacted. They wrote down notes and thoughts. I wanted their immediate thoughts, the gut kick or the heart pull they felt. The triggers pulled in their brains, the nervous tick, the knife cut of pain, the emotional volcano, the tornado impact when it first touched down. Then I played the same chords and maybe added a few.

I had a second two-minute rule. "What does the music sound like to you?" I asked. "Can you connect the sound to the song title? What would you add, subtract, multiply, or divide to the song's basic theme?" No playing, no strumming, just thinking. I asked them how they thought the song would settle in the listeners' ears. Will it nestle, snuggle, pound, vibrate, irritate, stimulate, claw, soothe? What was the auditory sensation? That was round one of our collective creative processes.

We were celebrating two songs brought to fruition, having gone through five or six rounds of creation, development, and evolution to a finality of sorts. It was a celebratory night. So, why was I letting Sean "call me Guy" hang like a dark cloud over my parade? He deserved companionship.

Companionship? How fucking quaint, maternal, antiquated, and ridiculous a description for his date. Was I jealous? Disappointed? I didn't know. That would require some reflection and maybe a song— "The One That Got Away."

But not tonight, Lisa. Stay in the moment. Stay focused on these five souls who are collectively creating a life for your music, your soul, your thoughts, your being.

I looked at them, smiled, raised my drink, and saluted them.

"To you wonderful, beautiful, creative inspirational bad-ass sons and daughters of musical mayhem, genius, and heart, thank you." We tapped cans, cheered, and laughed.

Life is good, I told myself. *Just don't look at Sean.*

After all, he's just a guy.

CHAPTER 27

Fumbling with Focus

I caught Lisa looking my way—our way—a couple of times in a surreptitious manner. Such furtive glances were unlike the brash, confident, and intimidating Lisa I knew. Lisa didn't make or even minimally maintain eye contact. She seemed oblivious to me or maybe oblivious to everything except her band. They were clearly celebrating. I wondered how "Immolate" and "Lost and Longing" sounded now. Had these songs even made the final cut for *Leaving Lisa?*

Suddenly, I felt awkward and more than a bit self-conscious and out of place. Bringing Gina there felt like an invasion of Lisa's space. I was violating a sacred trust, a sacred place, or some form of sanctuary.

Gina was intelligent, articulate, and funny. We continued to chat, but I was distracted.

Focus, man. Stay in the moment. It should be easy because Gina is someone who deserves your focus.

I returned to the moment at hand, to the person across the table, to Gina, and I engaged. The conversation was easy, and it flowed. We turned, laughed, and tapped our Stormwa as Lisa's group erupted in cheers, salutes, and drinks. They were obviously in a celebratory mood. They seemed victorious. They had clearly accomplished something.

At that moment, Gina got up, moved next to me, then wrapped her arms around my neck and kissed me on the cheek. "Sean, you're a beauty."

She got up to go to the washroom, and I couldn't help but turn and watch her walk away. Her movement was magical, the swing of her hips, and I could still feel her lips on my cheek. The brush of that kiss lingered, and I savoured the feeling.

When I turned my head back, Lisa was staring at me. She wagged a finger, pointed at the sign for the ladies' room, then laughed.

I felt conflicted. I shouldn't have been, but I was. I thought my head was clearer than that or at least capable of clarity.

Focus, Grasshopper. You're with Gina, and this could be good, really good, but not if you fumble it. Stay locked in. Stay with what's in front of you. Gina deserves that, and everything you feel wants to give her that. You've gotten past your past, so stay in the moment, and keep moving toward your future.

CHAPTER 28

And Along Comes Mackin

The door swung open wide. It had to. Smackin' Mackin's shoulders needed the full width to enter GoHo's. It was about 12:55 a.m. Trailing Mackin were two equally wide but not as handsome companions. Mackin pointed at me, flashed his panty-removing grin, and in one continuous movement flowed into his centre-stage booth on the inside wall of the diner. The booth was smack-dab in the centre of the diner; it seemed fitting that Mackin and the "Smackins" would sit there. I always referred to Mackin's companions as the "Smackins." I thought it was a clever and funny description of his companions, his brothers-in-arms. So did Mackin.

Those three large, well-built, muscular men would gain attention almost anywhere, but with Mackin in the lead, they were like the king and his court. GoHo's took on a different buzz when they arrived. They were sports celebrities. Men sucked in their guts when Mackin and his crew were around, and women puffed out their chests. Mackin seemed to be totally oblivious to the attention and the reactions. He seemed satisfied, content, and authentic. Apparently, they had just finished televising a west-coast game and were coming to GoHo's to wind down. His entourage was also ex-CFL all-stars, but they didn't have Mackin's charasmatic glow, and the GoHo's crowd knew it.

"Mo, can you understand a quick-snap cadence?" he asked when I got to their table.

"A what?"

"Quick Six SW Frosty."

"Can one of you—hopefully, non-concussed and steroid-free—guys translate?"

"Come on, Mo. I know you're a football freak. We need six cold Stormwatch tall boys, quickly!"

"Oh, will this whole ordeal with you three sides of beef be fully conducted in football jargon? Will I need a translator?"

"No. We'll wind down and talk diner lingo."

"Thanks. Should I head off the invasion of the drunken bachelorette table by saying you're in post-production?"

"Mo, that would be appreciated. However, we're irresistible forces of nature,

116

so concentrate on Quick Six SW Frosty for now."

As I turned and headed to get the beer, I felt a sudden and overwhelming need to be found attractive, so I accentuated my departure with a saucy sway of my hips. I was back in a flash with the six cold beers, and the boys were already scratching football petroglyphs on napkins and were fully engaged in their post-game analytics. People were staring at them, but they were blissfully absorbed in the companionship and camaraderie of deeply shared experiences.

One bachelorette, with a wondrous chest pushed up and out, managed to wobble over to their booth and was given only cursory glances and polite autographs for her younger brother. The napkin with her phone number written on it was integrated into the next formation for a tight-end sweep or maybe a spread-receiver formation. Football terminology can be so sexually stimulating; at least it was in my mind tonight.

"Thanks for the beer, Mo," Mackin said. "We're going to have the extreme nacho platter with chicken, not beef, extra real cheese—not your usual gooey mess—and thirty-six wings, six of all six varieties.

"Good, healthy choices. Will you be needing utensils or just your usual shovels and pitchforks?"

"Hell no, Mo. This is a hands-to-mouth-only operation."

"Good to know. I'll warn the rest of the patrons not to watch and to stand back."

I left to a round of laughter from the incredible Smackins.

CHAPTER 29

Leaning Out

We had such a good broadcast. The game went into overtime. There were as many great plays as broken plays. Typical unpredictable CFL mayhem. We got so into it. This game was a beauty. The walk from the studio to GoHo's had taken about fifteen minutes, and we were still pumped when we arrived. As we walked, we worked on some of our commentary for the following day's live and taped interviews. I didn't notice Lisa until Mo was walking away with our food order. Her profile was striking, and my spirits sank a bit as I gawked for an extra-long second, like a smitten schoolboy. My buddies snapped me back to our napkin analytics, though I still felt an ache. Some residual pain.

Move on, Mackin.

I was like a receiver when the pass was behind them. They stretched back, and they got absolutely pummelled by a hit. They knew the hit was coming, but they still reached back for that ball, leaving themselves completely vulnerable. Yep, that was me, except I was leaning into Lisa when she was leaning out. A hit coming from someone moving in the opposite direction, if unexpected, is a punishing blow. The receiver's hands go out for the ball, and they grasp nothing but air, as the air is knocked out of them.

She dropped you. So, get your head out of your arse, and get in the game. Flanker option. Yeah, that works. Call that freakin' play, Mackin. Plenty of options with your extensive and impressive playbook. Decent looks, health, money, career, and a genuinely nice guy.

I was the decent human being that my mother raised me to be. She wanted to dance with me at my wedding when I found the right girl. She had already picked our song: "Simple Man" by Lynyrd Skynyrd. How cool was that?

I noticed that the "Guy" guy was there. Our table is excellent for scouting a room, just like the middle linebacker positioned in the centre of the field. The linebacker has the perfect field of vision to scout the opposition's formation. So, should I have seen it coming? Good question.

Mo interrupted my wandering mind. "Chew time, big boys. Please don't gnaw off any fingers, especially mine, as our first-aid efforts here at GoHo's are notoriously spotty and slow. Anything else before the food Armageddon begins?"

"A big jug of cold water, Mo, and Quick Three SW Frosty."

"Yeah, Mackin, three beers and water to put out the fire from those nachos."

He nodded. "I see you've been studying the playbook."

Lean out, Mackin, I told myself. I was coming as Lisa was leaving. There was no trailing hand to catch. Nothing but air and a world of hurt.

CHAPTER 30

On Leaving Lisa

Mackin is so striking. I knew it was him from just a glimpse of his shoulders when he and his friends entered GoHo's. I also picked up on the collective sigh of lust from the women throughout the diner. Mackin could own a room with one stride and one smile. I heard one of the models describe him as "scintillatingly sexual." I understood what she meant, but he was so much more than that. If only they knew Mackin like I knew him, but I was glad they didn't. Word on the street was that he was still on his own. Not even rumours of dalliances, brief flings, or one-nighters. And not one negative beep about our relationship ending. Not a whisper. I don't know how graciously I would have handled being the one dropped. Probably not well. What a man. What a decent man.

I had done the right thing to cut him loose. I needed to find me before I could do "fine time" with someone else. I was painfully self-absorbed and perpetually distracted by myself. *Poor, little rich girl, get over yourself! Physician, heal thyself. Do I have a fool for a doctor? Through the music, through the music, heal. And then what? Guy? Mackin?*

The "Sean, call me Guy" option looked like it was going into shutdown mode. Good for him. Mackin round two? That would be cruel to both of us. It would be hard to restart something that I had ended.

Guy deserved warmth and love. So did Mackin. Me? God damn right I did.

Time, Lisa, I told myself. *In your time, the right time.* I needed to leave myself to find myself. I had to stay focused. My band was there, and they embraced me in my search for me.

Through the music. Through the music. I am going to come out the other side of this lengthy, personal creative deep dive and become something whole. Something lovable. At least to myself.

The name of the record was etched onto my being.

Leaving Lisa.

CHAPTER 31

Getting in My Own Way

There I was with Gina. She was a wonderful human being. What would my mom say? Easy on the eye, equal or better of mind, and a real partner. Passionate, authentic, non-compliant, capable of making me better and devoted to do so through love. Like Mom had and what she had given Dad. Was I looking for too much? Then Lisa "we're not fucking" jumped into my brain. Then the fuckin' Brit. I needed to get out of my own way.

"What just happened?" Gina asked. "You went all sullen and solemn on me. Indigestion? Constipation? Perspiration? Third-date weirdness?"

"I'm sorry. Just a momentary blitz of bad karma from my past."

"Why now? What was the trigger?"

She was so good, so straightforward, capable of addressing awkward moments. I needed to answer Gina with nothing but the truth. "I flashed on some hurts at the precise moment I was experiencing some untethered joy with you."

"Well, I like the second part. Press on."

"I still wonder what I'm capable of with someone. You make me wonder because you're someone that anyone would be so lucky, blessed, and fortunate to be with."

"Hang on, Sean. I have some pain in my caboose too. Remember, I was 'exed' by someone too. I'm not the total prize package, so please don't put me on that pedestal."

"I don't want to put anyone on a pedestal. Been there, done that, got the papers. I want to be able to stand together with someone."

She nodded. "We all carry that image with us, but what stops you?"

"I'm not sure if I have it together enough."

"Don't bullshit yourself, Sean. If you're still angry and hurt, maybe the expiration date on those feelings is still a ways off. Do you want a piece of advice?"

"Yes."

"Set the expiration date. Be firm on it, then move forward. That's what I did."

"Anything else?"

"Yes, and this is important, true, and heartfelt."

"What?"

"I hope you call me on that day."

"What do you mean?"

"Call me then and only then, on the expiration date of your hurt and anger and whatever else you're carrying, because I think we could really work. But I'm not settling into any house with ghosts in the closets."

"But, Gina, I'm so close to that expiration date."

"Great. Once you get there, call me. Pay the cheque, then walk me home. Kiss me long and hard and say goodnight. I deserve all of you, and I won't settle for anything less."

I caught Mo's eye and motioned for the cheque. Mo seemingly missed how the mood had turned at the high tabletop, from the heights of great expectations to an incoming low-pleasure atmosphere.

"Meatloaf and beer. You need to tip extra graciously just for forcing me to serve that combo while on a date. You've violated my late-night GoHo's dating standards."

We nod and then exit.

CHAPTER 32

Leaving Behind My Behind

They just smiled politely, no laughter. Guy tipped excessively. They gave me a fleeting smile again on their way out. Guy wasn't getting any that night. Something had gone wrong at the high-top table.

Lisa's crew were on their fourth round of Stormwatch and had worked their way through a couple of rounds of appetizers as well. They were getting ready to go. Lisa tipped excessively too. She got out of the booth and walked over to the counter.

"Mo, what happened at Guy's table? They looked sort of down when they left."

"Don't know. It certainly seemed to be going splendidly from my vantage point as a lowly server. But Guy definitely isn't getting any loving tonight."

"Okay, that's a little sad."

"Or is it good news that he may still be on the market?"

"Maybe, but I'm not currently seeking love. And you?"

"I'd hurt the old guy. My needs are primordial."

We both laughed and then Lisa gave me a goodnight hug. I looked over at the last of the three customers who seemingly meant more to me than they should have, the incredible Mackin. And then it swept over me, out of nowhere.

Mo, what's going on girl? Why am I so close to tears? These three people are getting to you. I need an emotional rescue. Cue the Stones. Mo girl, you gotta leap forward. Move on to your own life. Go, Mo, go. What's in your playbook? Call your own number, Mo. You gotta leap forward. You gotta leave your behind, behind.

CHAPTER 33

À La Mode Therapy a GoHo's

My colleagues dropped twenties on the table and told me I could cover the rest. That was kind of them. They're both good men. Married, responsible, with kids. Professionals. Great to work with. No egos getting in the way. No one-upmanship in the broadcast booth. Surprising for a wide receiver and a quarterback.

Mo sidled up to the table.

"Anything else? Your friends said they left plenty of cash so that you can tip extravagantly."

"Yeah, Mo, apple pie à la mode. A big slice."

"Whoa, a mama's boy order."

"Funny thing is, Mo, I was thinking of my mother right here tonight. Make it a double."

"What are you buying me dessert as well as an extravagant tip?"

"No, I meant—okay, sure join me, but make my portion a double."

"Okay, since you invited me so graciously, I'm in." Mo turned to go place the order and, I assumed, get our dessert.

The place was emptying out, which wasn't surprising at 2:30 a.m. Mo returned quickly with a monster plate of pie and ice cream for me. Her own plate looked empty by comparison.

"Two IC, Pie right on two."

"Great play calling, Mo. Next time I'll invite you to sit with the guys and analyze plays."

"You boys sure looked like you were having fun tonight."

"We sure did. I love working with those two, and we all love what we do. That makes it great."

"They were stud players as well, right?"

"Absolute studs. MVP awards, Grey Cups. Canadian Player of the Year. Perennial all-stars. They both hold more than a few team and league records."

"So, as good as you?"

"Different positions, but yes, as good or better than me, but not as good looking, and they're cheap. They left no money for your tip."

"Funny boy!"

"Mo, can I bend your ear on something?"

"Sure, after I see a decent tip."

"Seriously?"

"Okay, but this is a diner booth, not a therapy couch."

"Are you always this funny or just at work?"

"I'm continuously at work, so I'm always funny."

"Can you be a good listener?"

"Yep."

"Okay, then here goes. I got everything. I'm blessed, lucky, and things are going my way. I've constantly enjoyed success, but I'm staggering forward because I need something that I might not be able to get."

"Me, right? And yep, you have no shot." We both laughed hard, good, and pure, like old friends would and should.

"I want a family, Mo. I'm forty-four, and I want what my two buddies who were here tonight have. A wife, kids, and a real home. If I date younger women, I feel weird, a bit like a pervert. Other professional athletes make us all look stupid with trophy wives who are fifteen to twenty years younger, and they leave their families for that. I think I missed my chance."

"Mackin, you're not a pervert. I've seen other athletes, even some of your buddies, the way they ogle women and chase tail. You're not cut that way."

"Oh, I can ogle and chase."

"I'm sure you can, but your heart isn't in it, and neither is your dick."

"How crude of you, Mo, and how true! My friends worry about me because I've been basically celibate since Lisa."

"Listen, Mackin, you're either celibate or you're not. Celibacy doesn't come with a basic option."

"Okay, almost celibate, not quite ready for the monastery."

"Good. That would be a waste."

"Thanks—I think."

"You want some advice, Mackin? Doesn't matter. I'm giving it anyway."

"Have I tipped you yet?"

"No, but you will, and you'll be generous, or I'll tell your buddies you kept their twenties and pulled a D and D. Here goes. Just move forward. Test the waters. Doesn't matter if she's twenty or eighty. Okay, a little too high on the old end, but you won't settle. Even if you find someone ten, fifteen, or twenty years younger you'll lock onto her for all the right reasons because that's your character. That is in your DNA. That's what and who you are."

"How can you believe that about me?"

"I don't know."

"You don't know who I am, what I'm made of."

She chuckled in response to that. "Mackin, every freakin' shift at this place is a psychology lab. Every table, every customer, especially regulars, reveal who they are. And, my friend, you are the real deal, the genuine article. No facsimiles accepted."

"You're my friend? That's a great thing to hear."

"What else could I be, given the paltry gratuities you leave me? Throwing nickels around like they're manhole covers. I must be your friend, or how else could I stand the pittance I receive in your servitude?"

We both laughed, then lowered our heads after a good moment of eye contact.

"Good pie, Mo. Better talk. Thanks. I need to get out of my own way. I need to stop stoppin' before I start. I have to leave the perceptions of others out of the picture. I need to be hungry in the pursuit of my dreams."

"That's it, Mackin. You've called your own play. Now get in the freakin' game."

"Thanks, Mo. SM power drive on hut."

"Yeah, some shit like that, Mr. Smackin' Mackin. And listen, I gotta charge extra for the therapy."

Once again, we shared a laugh, like good friends.

"Thanks, Mo, sincerely. I needed to hear that. Get that shove. Let me settle up. And, Mo, I'm getting in the game."

"You have someone in mind already, don't you?"

"Yes."

"I saw you looking at Lisa tonight. You know it can't be her, right? She ain't the one for you, Mackin. You can't ask that of her. She isn't cut that way and probably never will be. You know that, right?"

"Right, Mo. I know. Mo, it is my mother who has someone in mind. Not a specific person but definitely a specific type of woman. Cheque please."

"You're a mama's boy. Apple pie and ice cream and listening to Mom. I hope she's not into arranged marriages. That doesn't work so well in this country. Maybe in America where you come from. Are you a Joseph Smith kinda Mormon throwback or into something like that? Never mind; I don't want to know. Listen to your mom. She knows you and loves you and wants the best for you, of that, I am sure."

"You're right about that, Mo, but way off on that Mormon and arranged-marriage angle. Thanks again."

With that, Mo was up and gone. I just sat there for a minute and thought through the therapeutic value of à la mode and Mo.

CHAPTER 34

Salty Thoughts and Tears

I got Gordon Junior to drop the cheque at Mackin's table. I was done. I couldn't look at him anymore. In my mind an incessant chant had arisen.

Pick me! Pick me, Mackin! Pick me! You want me to call a play? How's this scenario work for you? I'm going to tackle your ass to the ground and make plays on you all night. Mo, fornicate, right, centre, left on one, two, three, and so on till exhaustion. Or until time runs out on the clock as we put one more score through the uprights or in the end zone or whatever. Or until you expire in pure ecstasy or something along that line. More likely I'll expire in a blissful afterglow or something they would say in a freakin' Harlequin romance. Maybe I'll read a couple of those books while we're on vacation, just so I can get my sexual comments all politically correct.

Does anyone remember or still think in antiquated terms similar to salty language or risqué behaviour? Is that how people would refer to my thoughts on touching down with Mackin—as salty?

Instead of words, some salty tears leaked down my cheeks.

Fuck you, Guy, I thought. *You bring a date, and all this chaos of emotional highs and lows—mostly lows—rains down.*

Song #7 "Doesn't Much Matter"

Slipped through my hands
Wiggled off my hook
Passed me in the night
Couldn't see in that dim light

You got away, you got away
How doesn't much matter

Didn't use both hands
Failed to set anchor
Took my eye off the road
Didn't listen to what I was told

You got away, you got away
How doesn't much matter

Hole in the bucket
My fingers fumble
Left one screw loose
Forgot to bolt the door

You got away, you got away
How doesn't much matter

Barn door left open
Kicked over the can
Tripped on my shoelace
Fell on my face

You got away, you got away
How doesn't much matter

The price you pay
For being careless with love
The empty space at the end of the day
You were my one

You got away, you got away
How doesn't much matter

CHAPTER 35

Guy's Play

I love the gym. I love listening to my music at the gym. Headphones on, volume cranked. I love the Cult. "She Sells Sanctuary," "Fire Woman." The Hip. "New Orleans Is Sinking," "Wheat Kings," "Bobcaygeon." Led Zeppelin. "When the Levee Breaks," "Kashmir." Springsteen. "Thunder Road," "Meeting 'Cross the River." Not "Glory Days" but just about anything else from the Boss. The Who. "Won't Get Fooled Again," "Baba O'Riley." This is just a partial list of the music I listen to when I work free weights.

The Sunday morning after the Great Gina Meatloaf Massacre, I was up by 6:00 a.m. even though I didn't go to bed until 3:00.

I walked Gina home. She kissed me long and hard. When she finished, she held my face in her hands and looked me square in the eyes with her own blue-eyed clarity. "Sean, pick an expiration date." She paused, but before I could respond or nod my head, she continued. "Pick a date, Sean. Not for me and not because of me. Not because of anyone. Pick it for yourself. Then get back in the game, fully. No, not the game, get back into real life." She kissed me again, softer this time. "You may be worth waiting for. I'll wait for a while to see. Don't ask how long. That wouldn't be fair to either of us. You'll know. If we're to be, we will be. Oops, I went a little Yoda there."

We both laughed. She kissed my cheek, patted my shoulders, and then clenched her fists and hit my chest. "Damn it, Sean." Then she turned and opened the glass doors to her condo foyer. The night security officer watched our entire exchange. I thought Gina was shaking her head at me, but I also thought there were the beginnings of tears in her eyes. I hoped they were tears. I hoped they were tears of care for me, for us, for possibilities temporarily passed. Hopefully, only for the moment, though. I had to get straight. To decide. And Gina was right. I had to do it for me, not anyone else.

I started walking home, alone with my thoughts. The distance was just over three miles, a good five-kilometre run. I felt like running. Would I be running away from something or running to something?

What direction, man? Pick one.

Running away from loss and the rise of the British. Running from the "Phillip the Prick Empire" or running to the "Sunshine State of Sean" and a future? Wow, what a fucking Harlequin romance of an analogy! That's some bad mental imagery.

I needed a drink. So, I kicked my own arse in my mind all the way home, poured four fingers of Jack Jacks over two whisky stones, took out my laptop, and popped up the next month's schedule. No travel except one day trip to Ottawa and an overnighter to Calgary. I banged out a schedule for training and circled a day, forty-four days from then, and labelled it "expiration date." I couldn't help myself! I texted Gina the date, and beside the date I wrote the word "FIRM."

"Having a glass of wine," she texted back. "I imagine you're having a scotch. Good for you! Be firm. Those weren't tears. I had to stop Alice the security guard from going to punch you out. LOL! As I told Alice, I just had something in my eye. It was you. Don't reply."

I didn't.

Six in the morning. Free weights, ten exercises, three sets each, eight to ten reps, a five-to-twenty-pound weight increase for each set. Tried to get to ten reps in each set or to failure.

I like the repetition, the cadence of lifting, the concentration, the intensity, the music, the rhythm. The edge of repeating to failure. Increase the weight and, thereby, upping the challenge. I scheduled twenty-three sessions over the forty-four days, all on odd days, ending on the forty-third and the forty-fourth days with back-to-back lifts. On day forty-four, every set would be extended by a max weight goal. Every even day was a run, no less than three miles and no more than five. Day forty-four would be seven miles. Day forty-four would also be my fifty-first birthday. A good day to end my midlife, lost-wife crisis.

On every lift day and every run day, I let my mind do three things. I was multitasking like a Jedi master. First, there was a mental process of concentration on the physical activity. Perform better. More weight, more reps, better process. Slightly more speed, steadier cadence, fewer walking intervals. The second mental process was in the work realm. A work thing. I would write down a specific nagging element of a task, a project, a hurdle, an issue, or an opportunity. Big or small, something to "mine in my mind" by looking for nuggets of wisdom, searching for gold.

The third mental process was in the realm of Sean. Thinking about me, what I wanted, how I wanted to play this game of life. What, when, who, where and how, all driven by *why*.

The mental processes, one and two, were no problem. I loved a self-challenge.

The one-on-one intensity of my strength against dead weight. *I can lift you one more time, you son of a bitch. You can't weigh me down.* Mind over matter, rep after rep. Lift to failure. Challenge my limits. Incremental gains. Push through.

All these great physical lessons are applicable to work and the rest of life. Run faster, better splits, better times, improve by seconds, not minutes. Incremental gains.

I was also working through the work situation. Rolling over the analytics, the pragmatics, the realities. Standing back and getting a perspective provided by different viewpoints, which could be the competitive view, the internal process, the constraints, the restraints, the market structure, the finances, peoples' competencies and capabilities or the lack thereof, resources, and/or capacity. I looked for the gaps. For the arrangement and structure of things and resources. For blind spots. For leverage. Incremental focus and resource allocation where there were competitive or market gaps that could be widened or exploited. Pragmatics, perspective, and then the real driver. Passion. Why would we have a passion for this? What made it worthy of our care and concern and nurturing? What got us to put another twenty pounds of weight on our workload to lift it? I had to find the passion in it or someone with the passion for it. I loved grinding through my "3P" process—pragmatics, passion, and perspective.

The third mental process, the realm of Sean, wasn't so much fun. I could hide in the first two for long periods with such focus and intensity that the lift or the run was over before I knew it. However, thinking about me, concentrating on self? That was a difficult exercise in staying on point. I seemed to keep looking at myself from an outside perspective. If I trained hard and worked hard, people would see a better me. A sharper, slimmer Sean. The truth is, I loved the exercise routine, but I'd never make it through all forty-four days of training. Most but not all. I'd still have a slight paunch on day forty-four, but I'd feel better. Work? I probably couldn't work harder, but there were always opportunities. As long as I didn't become autocratic or interact with a level of intensity that had me acting like an overbearing asshole.

That was the first revelation. I wasn't going to be the CEO. There were a couple more rungs on the ladder for me. They both would have some vertical lift and horizontal shift. That was okay. So, the first thing I determined was a career line that was way more than just accepting my fate and settling. My chosen career path would still require drive and results. It wasn't midlife settling; it was a mid-career reckoning. That was a good thing. I still had a strong drive to move forward. My mindset was to control what I could and to control it masterfully. Influence what I could influence with skill and effort. No complacency ever.

I had work and career kind of figured out and mapped, subject to vagaries beyond my control and influence, but what about work/life balance? That phrase seemed so trite. I loved to work, and that gave me balance, clarity, purpose, and joy. Joy, damn it!

Joy! The joy of accomplishing, seeing tasks through, and completing projects. Making the plan and working the plan. The ability to shift, change, and evolve. A lot of character and craft was required to adapt to a Plan B mentality. It was too easy to get locked into a plan. Obstinate. Resolute. Refusing to adjust because I'd fallen in love with my original thinking was just so "high school." I needed options that I had thought through in advance. I had to be cognizant and knowledgeable about the options because they would change too. I also needed the courage to change direction and work the options. This ability, this flexibility, would provide momentum. I found great joy in having continuous, adaptive, forward momentum. Work had character, and how I worked defined my character and constantly refined my character traits and enhanced my self-worth even when success wasn't fully achieved. Partial wins were still wins. I decided to take the win, take the joy. I was trying to build a plan for myself. Build the plan. Work the plan.

Life. What did I want? Health? Check. Security? Check. Companionship? *Of course, you stupid dick.* Companionship? That struck me as formal and British, so I had to find a term that had a more personal connection and meaning.

Friends? Yeah, I needed to cultivate a few. *Cultivate? This isn't farming, asshole.*

Family? Yeah, I need to make more of an effort. *Oh, for the love of God, man, grow an emotional set of balls. Show some care, some love, and reach out. Take the first step. Get engaged with them.*

Soulmate? That was still too much of a stretch to contemplate. *It's too early, you romantic dreamer. You're a person, not a Hallmark card.*

Lover? That was more like it, but meaningful intimacy—mind, body, and spirit. *Well, now you're on the right track, dipstick.*

I laughed whenever I made my silent, self-denigrating comments. Dipstick, gonad, dick weed, asshole. *It keeps me grounded, you big dipshit!*

Goals? Check.

Health, security, intimacy, friends, family, and a person of special interest. Yeah, I liked that. A person of special interest. An elevated level of intimacy. Trust. Connection on many levels. That was worth pursuing. I could sense that, feel that. I wasn't going to be perfect at it, but I was a decent-enough guy to be very good at it with someone, that person of special interest.

My first lesson, the first fundamental truth, was to be me. Just be me. That would have to do. I wouldn't allow my work persona to have pretenses, and I couldn't go about my life pushing a false narrative, a pretense. I wasn't smart enough to maintain pretenses, and I wasn't a good actor either.

My second lesson was that I didn't want to get hurt. I had been decimated once, and recovery had been tough and ongoing. So, I needed to be gentle and kind, to go forward with good intent and take my time. It wasn't a race or a workout. I had to be open, not blind.

The third lesson was to worry less about everything. To let it be. To be me. They would be them, and we would see what we could be. It couldn't be a stress test. I had to let it flow. Be spontaneous. Take joy. Love the little things. Love my path. Be easy on myself.

Forty-four days. Not a "best-before date" but a "great-after date." So, forty-four was based on a milestone birth date. Forty-three to go, forty-two, forty-one . . .

No, I couldn't do a countdown or cross out the days on the calendar. I had to just go to it, live through it with focus, intent, and most importantly, self-care. Then the question for our time. Lisa, Gina, or someone altogether different? I wouldn't even allow myself to think of doing a comparative analysis. That would be a totally degrading, a desperate dick-weed move. They deserved a better, fuller consideration than that. I had to think about them softly with a focus on their well-being if I was lucky enough to be with either one of them. How about both? *Both? You naughty boy. Not fair. Not even going to go there. You're not a player, Sean. You're a monogamous mountain. For some reason, that's the way you were cut.*

So, how was I going to work my plan? Was I going to take some steps, make some moves? What was at the top of the list? Calling my mom. I didn't see that coming. I would make the drive to her place that weekend. Go for a walk. How long had it been since Dad passed? How was she doing? I had never talked to her about the royals, a.k.a. the Brit and my ex. I probably should have. My mom did look a lot like the queen mother.

When I thought about Mom, the emotional levee broke. I was at home in the condo, picking up the phone to call her when a bubble of emotion rose up. Before I could catch it, I choked on a whimper, and the bubble burst. The choke produced a tear or two. Then a sob escaped. The sob was woeful, full of lament, and it hurt. I was crying. Losing control and breaking down. I attempted to hold back the sobs by holding my breath. My lungs and chest folded down as I let the air escape until I needed to breathe again. When I tried to breathe, the sobs that escaped were filtered by my attempt to repress them, unleashing a strange, strained wail. The series of attempted restraints capitulated to a wrenching, guttural wail of woe. I was a heaving, sobbing, wailing mess. I hadn't decided to go with the anguish. The anguish was taking me where I needed to go. It was a voyage. I had repressed the hurt, the loss. I loved her so much, and I probably still did. My thoughts were unclear. I'd become a quivering blob of emotional lava. The cap on the walled-up volcano of loss had been blown off. I was erupting. The lost love lava of my life was spilling out. Such serious sadness. I gave up on any attempt to hold it back. My awareness seemed to be clicking back on. I wasn't in a fetal position, but I was damn close. I moved into interval breathing. Hard sobs, followed by a downstream of jagged breathing and tears that teemed, not streamed, from the corners of my eyes. The second part of the interval breathing was the gathering of short breaths in quick succession, moving toward recovering, transitioning to increasingly deeper breaths. My chest was no longer heaving; it became regulated. I was settling down, gaining control.

The word "control" was a trigger. *Control? Fuck control!* Control was a horse shit, motherfucking insult to my hurt, my pain, my loss. The interval phase of anguish blossomed again, full grown and in full colour. *Fuck control!* Then I grew tired, and the regular breathing cycle started.

Control. Erupt. Control. Erupt. Control. Erupt.

I was in the control phase when I felt the onset of nausea. I felt imbalanced throughout this cycle, but then I felt some sort of vertigo. I got up and staggered to the kitchen sink. As I passed the powder room on the way, I had a vision that if I went to my knees at the toilet bowl, I would never rise. Needing to stay on my feet, I headed to the kitchen sink.

My vomit was limited in volume, which was a total mismatch with the power and force of my retching. My gag reflex was doing sets of increasing velocity and power. If this was a cleansing process, then I was being emptied. I clung to the kitchen sink as if it were the sides of a lifeboat that I had to hold onto, so I wouldn't drown. My mental command was, *don't go to your knees. No knees! No knees! No knees please. No to the knees. Head and shoulders, knees and toes. Head and shoulders, knees and toes.* I was getting weak. Trembling. Quaking. At that moment, I would have been a star in a revivalist prayer tent, the southern preacher proclaiming, "The demon is coming out from this sinner. Save his soul,

Lord. Out, demon, out. Your evil venom has been spewed forth. Your liquid of sin has poured from within. Your hold on his heart and soul screamed as it exited, brought forth by the Lord. Thank you, Lord, for this miracle. Thank you for pulling the devil out of this unworthy wretch. Blessed are you, Jesus!"

Hold it! I thought. *Unworthy? Fuck that, you son of a bitch.*

I was snapping back. My total mental and emotional collapse ended with the summoning of a southern preacher saving the wicked in a prayer tent, me being the wicked. It was time to slip back onto *terra firma*. I was still quaking at the sink, but now I was laughing on the inside. Southern preacher? Whoa, I had some seriously suppressed angst.

I couldn't believe I had thrown up. I looked at my watch. Apparently, my collapse had been going on for two hours. It was too late to call Mom.

One could say it was cathartic. I knew the shit wasn't over, but it had certainly gotten real. *Good for you, Sean boy. Good for you.* I had no idea why I was congratulating myself at that moment. It felt good, though, somewhat celebratory. Shaking the demons of doubt and loss? Maybe. A good step, except maybe the puking. That had actually hurt. Feeling that physical hurt and recalling what had just occurred made me snicker at myself and for myself. *That wasn't so bad,* I told myself. *Now get after it. Get after a real life.*

"Will you always hold my hair back?" My wife had just thrown up into our toilet. First time ever. We had been out at a big celebration dinner after she had netted a huge international deal. She was the front person in the negotiations. My company was part of the deal. My team was executing many of the process details—the implementation, protocol, organization, and executing initiatives. We had landed the deal as separate components of the two firms.

She never celebrated with alcohol. She rarely drank. A large glass of pinot grigio followed by a chardonnay with dinner and then two vodka shots during the after-dinner toasts. She never ever did shots! That night was an exception, and what an exception for her! She probably saw it as a major step toward her career trajectory. The win was that huge.

For the first time, we also had front-row seats, watching each other's different but complementary skills and character traits at play. Leadership, strategic moves, tactical platforms, team building, and communication. We saw each other's capabilities and competencies under the spotlight at centre stage. We both loved what we saw and learned about each other.

When we arrived home, she said she felt tipsier than ever. She shed her overcoat and went directly to the bathroom, her heels still on. She weaved her way there, and I followed, entranced by that wonderful being and love of my life. She knelt in front of the bowl with grace and a supine refinement, then rested her arms on the seat. "Please hold my hair back," she said, and I did. I watched her poor excuse of drink-induced vomiting. Somehow, she remained as controlled and as elegant as one could imagine.

Later as I tucked her into bed, she asked if I would please kiss her. She said she was afraid I would never kiss her again because her breath would be terrible forever! Despite our cursory and furtive attempt to brush her teeth, we accomplished little in cleansing her breath. I came close and kissed her on the lips anyway.

"I'll always be here to kiss you no matter what."

"I love you," she replied. "You're brilliant at what you do. We're brilliant together."

"Yes, we are, and I love you too, for always."

"For always?" she asked.

"For always, my love."

"Me too, my love. One more thing."

"What's that?"

"Will you always be there to hold my hair back?"

"Always!" I bent over and kissed her again. She sighed and closed her eyes, and then I started to tiptoe out of the room.

"Honey, I'll always hold your hair back too because I love you," she said. Then she snickered, sighed, and went to sleep. I stood in the doorway, rooted to the spot, a tear of joy running down my cheek.

Six months later she sat across our kitchen table and informed me that we were finished. She placed the legal documents on the table. Then she simply stood up and exited my life.

She wasn't there to hold my hair back at the kitchen sink. The depth of my immediate sorrow was profound. I sought no legal remedy or any other form of remedy, except for three months or more of scotch. I sought no condolences. No counsel. I shunned grief. I chose stoicism. I chose cold. I imagined stoic bravery as my self-portrait. After recalling these painful memories, I wanted to call my mom, but I didn't.

The kitchen sink incident occurred at the exact midpoint to my best-before date. Twenty-two days left. In my mind my path was clear. I knew what and maybe even who I needed.

CHAPTER 36

Mo's Play

I was so done watching life play out in front of me.

The stage at GoHo's featured players whose acts ranged from going about the daily grind to the theatre of the absurd in terms of human interaction and behaviour. Being a waitress provided all the necessary field experience to be a good clinical psychologist.

A symphony of solos played out in front of me every day. The solitaires, the "I eat alone diners." Alone by choice, by default, by loss, by ironically seeking solitude in public, by convenience, by plan, by random. They dined alone with joy, with sadness, with ebullience, with melancholy, with patience, with urgency, with care, with despair, with winning, and with loss. Their faces were etched and full of their story lines. Some mouths were full of paragraphs and fries. Other mouths were empty except for the self-reporting of their own lies. Eyes sparkling, laughing, and content. Eyes bleary, dull, mournful, and full of lament. People struck the poet in me, or at least I thought they did. Mo, the poetess waitress. Maybe that was my new career path.

I tried to read the lone diners and the couples. I tried to gather my observations into a condensed version of who they were and what they were feeling at that "GoHo'sian" moment. I created their story line, the trajectory that had brought them to that point in time. I adjusted my service and approach accordingly but never veered too far from the unabashed brashness of my own Mo-ness.

I tried to define couples. I wasn't as good at that. Lack of experience, I assume. I had no empathy for whining, complaining couples, whether the whining and complaining was directed at each other or toward other things or people. *Be together,* I told them in my mind. *Be focused on the upside, the path forward. For the love of God, take joy from your moments together.* So often I heard them stealing joy from each other. At those moments I often intervened with a "Mo-ism," some witty comment about our menu, their choices, the weather, whatever. I was giving them the gift of a circuit breaker, something to react and respond to that stopped them from hurtling toward sadness and pain. It was me trying to uplift or shift the path of their discussion to lighter fare, unlike our menu choices. "Mo-isms" were well-rehearsed witticisms that had worked countless times. I didn't break out new material on newcomers or those who were obviously in despair.

With most couples it didn't take me long to discern who was hurting or who was inflicting the hurt. For a long time, my view slanted heavily toward viewing all men as bastards. However, as the often-invisible waitress, I had learned our fair sex could hold their own as assholes.

In groups of three or more, I always looked for the relationship scenarios and the alpha diner. I loved figuring out a table of businessmen. Who held the highest rank. Who had the biggest sway, who was full of bullshit. Who covered his or her lack of substance with an amicable presence in their absence of substance. Who was worried about their status and future and most likely to look for GoHo's exit. Who was the quiet corporate assassin. Who truly bore the corporate culture. Who posed as a corporate loyalist. Who was the false prophet. Who was the silent core strength. Who led, who followed, and who needed to get the fuck out of the way. I loved puzzling through this complex weave of interaction, mannerisms, body language, and behaviour. It was my social-psychology field study.

The dynamic changed dramatically when it was a mixed group of businessmen and women. The core characteristics and behaviours and roles remained the same, but the shift in tone, nuances, and innuendoes increased. The old, underlying sexual tension and posturing at work? I guess so. When there was one woman and several men, then the men's posturing toward the woman and their relationship to the other men's behaviour was so different. I saw smart women who understood all the bullshit macho stuff going on around them, and they ended up owning that table. I admired them. I admired the lone she-wolf. Lisa would be the alpha female in a group like that.

I could ramble for hours in my own mind or in talks with my sister about what I observed. How I interpreted the dance of diners—solo, couples, or multiples. Such sojourns into the paths of others wouldn't advance my path, my journey, my quest.

Alas, poor Mo! We knew her not well. At the periphery of our lunch table, she did dwell. Quick of wit and nimble of thought. She seemed to take aim but never take her shot. We are sure her star trajectory was high, but alas, fair Mo never tried for her sky.

Mo the waitress poet. See? It did work! It didn't pay what I was fully worth, but I was comfortable doing what I did well. In the world of waitress poets, there wasn't much competition and no upward mobility. On the plus side, it was pleasant, intellectual self-stimulation. A dildo for the mind to blind me in mental masturbation.

Do something, Mo! I shrieked in silent frustration.

Okay, here we go!

I was proud of what I had achieved. A caregiver since I was eighteen for my sister and then even more so as a single mother. A university degree. A sister with a university degree—two, in fact. That was three degrees above the zero our family had previously accomplished. My daughter was doing well as a teenager. I had money in the bank and a nice start on some savings. I was ready to launch. But how and toward what?

I could manage, respond, and pivot in real time. Customer relations second to none. Quick study of people and things. Quick learner.

Character. Ethical and driven. Overdeveloped degree of empathy. Quick intellect and wit. Straightforward and transparent. Confident.

I knew I could manage GoHo's. I knew what I would change and what areas of the diner to prioritize when making the change. I knew the people to go forward with, the people to let go, and the people to replace. I knew how to tweak the product, the menu, the service, the layout, and the ambiance. I knew how to go from quaint to trendy without losing our core appeal or our current clients. I could work the room like a genius.

I was considering the option of buying in, as Gordon Junior's kids had avoided the place, somewhat at Gordon Junior's urging. The Gordon family owned the building and could sell it for a large capital gain. I knew about that stuff. Gordon Junior loved the place and said he would work there for another fifteen years, until he was sixty. He knew it needed a capital outlay, and he had the money. I was paid an almost ridiculously high wage for a server. I was part of the ambiance and order of GoHo's. I was in the woodwork, or more correctly, the Arborite and velvet, and after nearly eighteen years of service, I was embedded in the soul of this place. Only Gordon Junior and Frank the cook outranked me in terms of seniority. I was the face of the organization, the embodiment of the GoHo's brand experience. I liked that marketing term. I also liked "brand ambassador," so much classier than "waitress," "customer service agent," "wait person," "order taker," or "low-wage earner." I was paid at management wages-plus already. Gordon Junior offered me a management position and title years ago, but it would have cut my income significantly and probably would have negatively impacted his revenues just as much. My exemplary service capabilities were born from the desperate reality of needing to pay the rent, nurture my baby daughter, and get my sister through school. The fact that I genuinely liked interacting with anyone and everyone as well as the pace and the order of GoHo's made work not only necessary but also motivating and stimulating.

I had a tremendous ability to impact my own fortune and enjoyment at every table I served. To be a chameleon in adjusting to the moods, temperament, and needs of every diner. Talk about being centre stage all the time. I loved it. I loved being Mo the waitress!

Gordon Junior and I agreed almost tacitly years ago that I would run the front of the house when I was on shift, managing the cash desks, the bus boys and girls, the waitresses, and waiters—the few waiters we had, that is. The management hierarchy was easy for everyone to understand. Simply put, the law was that Mo was the "go-to." That was rule number one for all front-of-the-house staff, even the security we employed on weekends, busy periods and when crime waves occasionally hit our part of the city. GoHo's had only been held up once. The police response was overwhelming. Police Station House Number 54 was less than half a mile away, but that wasn't what elicited the mass response. GoHo's was the go-to cop stop for shift change and breakfast. The word got out quickly that GoHo's was not someplace where one wanted to commit a crime. That reputation held for late-night behaviour. GoHo's was seen as a safe haven because it was under an informal police umbrella. The police didn't want anyone messing with their own place for comfort food and relaxation before or after shift. For the last couple of decades, GoHo's had few problems or problem customers. Security was just for handling crowds on busy event nights when a few people who had obviously been over served arrived at our door.

The back door of GoHo's was another matter. Gordon Junior followed in his father's footsteps. The back door provided food seven days a week to various shelters and a small number of regular clients. Street people only came when they were really needy. They didn't even tell their friends because they respected what GoHo's did for them and their community through the shelters. GoHo's had the quietly famous "Guys with Ties" program as well. The back story had originated about twenty years ago. Two drunk corporate elites were both puking out back of GoHo's. Almost passing out and blind, stumbling drunk, they migrated down the alley as one of them felt a violent need to regurgitate our famous comfort food, meatloaf. It provided little comfort on the way back up. His buddy, and usually reliable wingman, upon seeing his buddy in the two-thousand-dollar suit puke, decided in an almost involuntary or reflexive manner to retch alongside of him.

As the story goes, it was a cold December night, and the two executive geniuses left their coats in the diner when they thought that the back alley of GoHo's was the best choice available for vomiting.

Their business brilliance devolved into a state of drunken dementia. After they both reverse engineered the eating of their meatloaf, they felt exhausted, especially after they experienced an extended series of dry heaves. The executive-decision-making duo then decided they required a bit of rest as they sat in their meatloaf mess, or maybe no decision was made, the more likely scenario being they just collapsed. The GoHo's staff did a cursory sweep of the streets in front of the restaurant and, not finding the intoxicated titans of finance, they assumed the pair found a taxi, which was well within the scope of their masterful managerial abilities. The staff never thought to do a perimeter sweep and figured that the two gentlemen would mentally retrace their steps the next day and realize where they left their coats.

This is where the story becomes interesting and almost mythical. Just before 3:00 a.m. and with GoHo's already shut down, two homeless folks, a couple, knocked on the front window. They were straining mightily under the weight of the corporate elite. The homeless couple carried and dragged the business boys to the front of GoHo's. Talk about the irony of the downtrodden uplifting the elite.

They knocked on the back door, but nobody was opening the rear entrance after 2:00 a.m. The business boys had been in the back alley for almost an hour and a half by then. Hypothermia hadn't set in, but it was close at hand. It took another hour and a half to bring them around, sober them up a bit, and warm them. The homeless couple stayed with Gordon Senior throughout the recovery period, worried about their boys. They gratefully ate the soup and bread Gordon Senior served up, never taking their eyes off their charges. They said the guys with ties weren't cut out for back-alley shenanigans. That was best left to pros like themselves. They laughed at their own self-deprecating humour.

When the corporate chiefs finally came to their senses and Gordon Senior explained what happened, they mumbled thank-you to the couple. When the homeless couple realized their charges were okay, they laughed off the thanks with "Been there, done that, lived through it, except for one finger and two toes." Then they asked Gordon Senior for coffee and a piece of pie to go. He brewed some fresh coffee and filled a big thermos. Then he handed them two pies, lemon meringue and apple. They smiled, the gaps in their teeth showing, and quipped they didn't have a sweet tooth left between the two of them, so they would prefer two apple pies rather than the lemon meringue, if it wasn't too much trouble.

Legend has it that Gordon Senior asked if they needed forks and napkins. They laughed him off, proudly displaying their own cutlery in the inside pocket of their jackets. As for napkins they said, "That's why God invented sleeves." With that and their pies and thermos of coffee, they slipped out.

As the two business boys surveyed the damage to their suits, which would need to be dry cleaned, reality set in. They might have died in a back alley, which would have been a precipitous fall from their height on the corporate ladder. At that moment, in a panic, they checked for their wallets. They were still there, untouched. Wonder and bewilderment blared into their consciousness. They looked out the door, but their back-alley benefactors were gone. They had left without asking for anything and without taking anything. The business boys' own toxic levels of assumptions toward the homeless were nuked as sobriety and sense seeped back into their brains. *My God, what a miraculous act of kindness that we didn't deserve.* Embarrassment at their state of disrepair evaporated in the light of the humility and the act of grace that they had just received.

Gordon Senior had never seen the homeless couple before, so he couldn't provide any leads to their whereabouts. That all happened on Thursday, December 1. Every year after that "guys with ties" set up an often-chaotic outdoor soup kitchen in the alley behind GoHo's for all thirty-one days of December. Over the years many people tried to gentrify the Guys with Ties event with marketing and campaigns like fifty-dollar bowls of soup with proceeds going to homeless shelters, but the two businessmen would have none of that. If anyone wanted to help, that meant serving soup, bread, coffee, and apple pie in the back alley over night from 1:00 to 5:00 a.m. Never lemon meringue pie!

The rules for participating in the program were simple. People paid for the privilege. They covered the cost of the food served. GoHo's provided the space and did the cooking. Well, the GoHo's staff supervised the volunteers who baked, chopped, stirred, cooked, and served. The two guys eventually allowed GoHo's to collect money in a big soup pot in front of the restaurant. Annual collections topped $50,000 per year. The two guys didn't allow corporate donations. The money had to come from an individual's wallet or purse. No charitable receipts and no tax deductions, just the grace of giving time or cash, preferably both.

Every December 1 at 5:00 p.m., the two guys returned to GoHo's. They had the meatloaf special with Gordon Senior and many of their own family, even their grandchildren—the grandchildren they might never have known except for the grace of that unknown homeless couple, whom they never found.

At the end of their meal, they would sit with Gordon Senior and have a glass of scotch. They always brought their own bottle. Gordon Senior took no offence at that. The guys with ties always referred to their scotch as "drinking with the same girl who took them out to the back alley all those years ago." One of the two would say, "Been there, done that, lived through it, except for one finger and two toes." Then they would open their pockets, show their plastic cutlery, smile, and make a toast to grace, humility, and empathy. They invariably cried in homage to their unknown benefactors.

Every December 1 was sign-up night for the Guys with Ties program. The corporate leaders paraded in with their group and signed up to serve one of the nights in December. The night of December 1, the whole restaurant was filled with business types who had signed up and stayed for the special of the day—soup, bread, apple pie, and coffee, all served with plastic cutlery and no napkins. The price was twelve dollars. After the first couple of years, no one left less than a hundred dollars, another unwritten tradition of Guys with Ties. The evening became a revered ritual for many firms. All the money raised went to homeless shelters and the meals offered by churches in the vicinity of GoHo's.

The working shift started with preparations at 10:00 p.m. Then people served until 5:00 a.m. After the first couple of years, every night in December was taken, except for Christmas Day when GoHo's was closed. The founding fathers of Guys with Ties always worked the December 1 shift with so many of their family members that there wasn't enough room for all of them.

About four or five years ago the mystery of the homeless couple was solved in an unexpected way. A package arrived for "Mr. Senior," which everyone assumed meant Gordon Senior. When he opened the package, all it contained was an old, battered thermos. Etched on the bottom rim was "GoHo's Diner" and the address. Gordon Senior remembered they had some failed promotional giveaway with thermoses a long time ago. A note in the box said, "At the request of the deceased, they have asked us to return this bottle to the proper owner, Mr. Senior."

Gordon Senior opened the thermos and inside was a letter.

Dear Mr. Senior,
If you get this thermos, it means we have both passed away, and your thermos won't be doing us any good anymore. Ha

ha! We never got around to thanking you for the soup, buns, coffee, and them two apple pies. Neither of us ever liked lemon anything much, so the apple pie was mighty, mighty pleasin'. We had enough money to head to Vancouver and left the day after we made friends with those two guys with ties. They seemed like good fellows, if a little fancy for our tastes. Ha ha! We hope they recovered OK and didn't lose anything from the cold. We can tell you from experience that losing toes makes walking and navigation a little tougher, even when we haven't been saucing it up. Ha ha!

We ate them two pies all the way to Vancouver. They were good nourishment and about all the food we had to eat on that damn Greyhound. Mr. Senior, we got a lot of meals at shelters from your kindness and had a couple of late-night meals out your back door. Folks don't think that's much, but to us it was everything. So, sir, here's your thermos. Granted, a little worse for wear, but it was a treasured companion, and every time it got filled, we thanked you for your kindness. And if you see those guys with ties, remind them that God created sleeves, so who needs a damn napkin anyways?

Bless you,
Jim and Donna McGregor

When the "guys with ties" read the letter, they reached out to the McGregors' children and told them how their parents had saved them and asked for nothing in return. The McGregor children had no clue where their parents had been for over twenty years. The guys told them everything they had discovered about their parents. It gave the McGregor family some closure.

Jim and Donna passed away within three months of each other. They had been sober for almost ten years, walked in Stanley Park daily, and lived a hand-to-mouth existence, but to anyone who encountered them, they appeared happy. The flophouse where the McGregors lived was only a few miles from a high-end condo where the eldest son of one of the two "guys with ties" lived. I don't know if that had any meaning, but it resonated with me and made me think about the random nature of some things.

This is why you never get to yourself, Mo. You let your mind wander into long stories about the trajectories of others. Concentrate, woman. Focus.

I wasn't going to let randomness determine who I was or what I became. Nor would I accept fate or some other bullshit excuse. I was going to make things happen.

So, I decided not to buy into GoHo's. It was a good plan with a long runway, but I needed to step out. GoHo's would be too comfortable, even in ownership. It would be Mo comfort food. My world was too insular and isolated. I needed to kick through comfort and into a new space. A scary space. An unknown space. I needed to expand. I wanted a different plane of interaction, of relationships. My world was too narrow. GoHo's would be a viable option for a few years. Not as a fallback but as a go-to when I rounded things out.

I decided to eliminate the service sector—food, retail, hospitality, hotel, and whatever else fell under that swatch of possible industries—from consideration. I needed something where I didn't automatically lean on the strengths of my personality. Something that stretched me. Something that pushed my interaction ability, intellectual capability, and my underdeveloped competitiveness. I need to find out what my extended range really was or could be.

I wanted to manage something a little more complex than GoHo's with more and varied relationships, deals, negotiations, contracts, personalities, technicalities, scope, and scale.

Pretty vague stuff, Mo girl, but I like your thought process.

My first step was to develop a list of customers over the last fifteen-plus years. At the top of the list was the Guys with Ties men, their close contacts, and other long-term customers in the business world. I'd been serving up scintillating conversations alongside sizzling sausages to people across every sector of industry. I would talk to them and get tips, advice, and leads.

Second, I would sit down with Gordon Senior and Junior. I loved those men. One as a father figure, the other as a dear, trusted brother. I knew they would act as ambassadors and advocates in the moon launch of Mo. They would also provide a soft shoulder and attentive ears if I missed or failed, and they would offer safe harbour.

Third, I would study and search. Open up. Find out, explore, believe, attempt, try, fail, kick open doors.

Pursue and persist. Press.

One hundred days. In one hundred days I would launch. I needed to leave GoHo's behind, at least for a while.

This was about me, for me. Of course, I'd always have a safety net. I didn't have that much risk tolerance. I didn't know how my background as a teenage single mom could or would allow that level of risk. Still, I would make it a moon shot. That was what I was going for, a higher, wider orbit around the sun.

As for a relationship, I would let it come, let it arrive naturally, organically, unexpectedly, and untethered. I would let a relationship come in the context of who I was becoming, what I had accomplished, and where I was headed.

Mackin? Guy? I always thought such men were way beyond me. Even with my slimmer figure, I was still more rounded than curved, but I was okay with that. The man who got to me would get me. I couldn't be something I wasn't. He'd find me or I'd find him. It wouldn't be a dedicated search. It would just happen, or it wouldn't. I'd wait and see.

As for Mackin and Guy, they simply didn't or couldn't see me that way. At least I didn't think so. And why would they? I didn't present myself that way. I didn't talk that way or act that way around them. I couldn't. That wasn't me. So, I'd let those two boys down easily and hope they recovered. They had already lost recently at love. Hard losses at that. I hoped that being denied an opportunity with me didn't destroy them. I would be gentle. The fact that they didn't know I was a "no go" didn't mean I needed to be unkind.

References will flow from the Gordons, the guys with ties, and the many sincere clients who had said over the years, "When you're ready, Mo, let me know."

Okay, Teddy, Betty, and Freddy, Mo's ready!

Launch point. I wouldn't settle for anything less than a starting management position. Anyone or any company that viewed me only as a waitress or presented my limited experience as a barrier wouldn't want me. And guess what? I didn't want them. I needed to find a company with a soul, with a belief in people and not in a resume. A firm with a willingness to take a risk based on character and a non-traditional path.

One hundred days. I talked with the Gordons and submitted my formal resignation. They ripped it up. Later that day, Gordon Senior gave me an envelope. He was followed by Gordon Junior, who gave me another envelope. On the outside of the envelopes their handwritten notes read "Open tonight at home with your daughter."

I did exactly that, right after dinner, starting with Gordon Senior's envelope.

It contained a brief note.

Dear Mo,
We love you.

I know that isn't the typical response one might expect after
a long-time employee resigns. However, it's been a very long
time since we ever thought of you as an employee. You're
family. We're so proud of you, raising your sister and your
daughter, achieving your degree.

You're so much like a daughter and a sister for the Hoods.
You're the essential spirit of GoHo's. We will all miss
you deeply.

Having said all this, there are several requirements we must
fulfill with the departure of a long-time team member. Please
check your current payroll direct deposit at your earli-
est convenience.

With love,
Gordon Senior

What the hell did that mean?

I had my daughter read the letter aloud, and both of us were in tears after the
first two paragraphs. The last paragraph by comparison seemed stiff and formal.
I pulled out my laptop, and we checked my bank account. There was a direct
deposit for $50,000. The tears started all over again.

We opened the second letter with trembling fingers and tears rolling down
our faces

Dear Mo

Although we respectfully accept your letter of resignation,
the GoHo's corporate entity and owners must inform you of
the following:

1. Your resignation is accepted. However, your position at GoHo's will be held open for a ten-year period. We will welcome you back at any time in that period.

2. Second, as you transition from GoHo's to another entity, all your benefits will continue until you're fully covered by a new employer.

3. Third, if you do return to GoHo's, your years of service will be fully recognized for seniority, benefit eligibility, and compensation.

4. Last and certainly not least, we will give you the right of first refusal on an equity position at GoHo's over the next ten years if we decide to open that door.

With love,
Gordon Junior

By then we were bawling and melting into puddles of wonder and emotion.

At the bottom of both letters, the Gordons had written "P. S. Launch, Mo, launch!"

That was a safety net. I was ready to launch, but by everything or anything considered holy, their letters were rocket fuel. Kindness and understanding were all I needed or wanted from the Gordons. Then they give me all this! The financial and long-term possibility and security were sensational and overwhelming. They and their family had taken our breath away. I would launch. I wouldn't settle in life, work, or love. I never had before, and there was no way I was going to start.

It was Mo time!

One hundred days started that day. I marked it as the start of a new year. I told my daughter that we would celebrate that date annually. On that day, we wouldn't self-recriminate, chastise, or beat ourselves down. We would take joy, look forward, and project upwards. Upward trajectory was what we planned, wanted, and sought. The path we chose may not seem like much to others, but that didn't concern us. We would rise up with joy and embrace the other people in our lives. My sister, the Gordons, and whoever else was in our orbit of care, kindness, and love. We decided to call that day "MoGo" and celebrate accordingly with raised spirits, high hopes, thanks, and joy.

You're granted the opportunity to fly primarily through your own will, your own drive, from a platform built on hard work and strong love. Your flight training has been brilliant on its own, full of life and love. Occasionally, you have benefactors, and may they be blessed. Hold them dear. Time to fly. Time to go, Mo!

CHAPTER 37

Mackin's Play

First, I had to be honest with myself. I was devastated. Lisa had crushed me. My brave face and my calm, quiet, controlled demeanour was all a crock of shit. But good for me. I manned up with the perfect "water off a duck's back" response.

"That? It's just a scratch. Not even going to leave a mark. Lisa who? Oh, that was primarily a business relationship that led to some infatuation." Okay, maybe a bit more than infatuation, seeing as the relationship lasted a bit over forty-two months. Putting it in perspective, though, it wasn't even half a football field in terms of yards. Of course, the opportunity for a dalliance presented itself. Attending big events and galas, travel and road shows, dinners with fabulous people, drinks till we were almost under the table. Adjacent hotel rooms. It was bound to happen. An extended infatuation, that's all.

Over her? Well, it would be callous and rude to dismiss any relationship as casual or unimportant, but yes, I am so over her.

You big fuckin' liar! Self-delusion isn't sustainable.

Second, devastation went hand in hand with self-evaluation. Was it me? Was it something I did? Something I said? Was I getting too possessive? Was I basking in the shallow superficiality of the celebrity aura of our power coupling and matching eye-candy status rather than diving into our relationship? Was I overly fascinated by the starkness of our contrasts? What had I missed during our time together? What did I do wrong? Did I under-appreciate her? Where did I fail her?

Heaven forbid she sensed I was getting too needy. Did she read my eyes and sense my next move, like a quarterback reading the defense? I can't say I was needy, but I can't say I wasn't. I was there, though, right there at that door. I told my mother I was ready to commit. A ring before the New Year but not on New Year's Eve. That would have been far too much of a cliché for Lisa or me. My mother's eyes didn't sparkle with the news. That should have alerted me. My mother always believed differences were good and should be appreciated, but she also believed that similarities led to stronger core bonds. Her beliefs weren't driven by ethics, creed, or colour but by her core belief about where strength in partnerships existed and thrived.

When my mother expounded on these core strengths, I would jokingly ask

151

her where I was going to find a 240-pound Hall of Fame linebacker to marry. She always laughed and said, "You know what I mean," and I did. Knowing my mother's strengths and the strength of her relationship with dad, I knew exactly what she meant.

In my self-evaluation, I never found my fatal flaw with Lisa or even a reasonable accretive combination of minor flaws. Yet somehow, I wasn't what Lisa needed.

Third, it had to be her. It couldn't be me! So, God damn it, what was the matter with her? I loved her. That was obvious. I was a lovesick puppy dog around the lovely Lisa.

What was her need? Why did she assume I would interfere with her creativity, her search for her music? I wasn't tone deaf. I heard what she needed. I could have parked on the sidelines for a while. I could have ridden the bench. Why did she dump me? Why did she think it was the only answer for her? And it was an unceremonious dumping at that. Well, there was a bit of ceremony. The "let's go back to the condo and screw" ceremony. After that I was put on the waiver wire with no chance for recall. Lisa even organized our business relationships and agreements in a manner that prevented them from being affected by our split. She also shielded us from any opportunity for rash behaviour, which was more likely from me than her. But that just added insult to injury. Well, not really insult, just another layer of pain. Lisa was being clear-headed about the dissolution of our love and worried about me being so emotional that I would do something rash. Man, she had just kicked me in the balls with a sexist role reversal. And here's another truth: she was probably right. Devastation can take a person to some low, ugly places. I'm not saying I would go low, but I sure identified how to go low. Ugly and inescapable thoughts crawl out of the darkest spaces when a person is devastated.

Putting together business documents prior to the breakup? What kind of cold-hearted bitch would do that? That was it! That was the ticket to punch. Lisa was a cold, conniving bitch who had used me to further her brand profile. I had enabled her rise to another level of power players and brand profile. Sports celebrities were a ubiquitous and reliable source of entertainment and attracted the spotlight. Being on the arm of someone who still commanded national attention was good brand building. Cutting me loose was the ultimate expression of power, dominance, independence, and ascendance.

Except, my dear Smackin' Mackin, you know that isn't true. Lisa gave me full disclosure about her life. Her parents' sequential matrimonial nature. Her devastation and anguish from having such a deep love and trust annihilated by her ex-everything and her subsequent relationship failures. Lisa even revealed her lesbian experience to me. She trusted me to hear her soul. *Not her sorrows, you brain-scrambled linebacker, her soul.* That description was so clear, resonating with her truth, her needs, and her wants. *She spoke so honestly, transparently, and trustingly to you, you big man blob.*

"This isn't about you, Mackin; it's about me." Lisa had made that clear, and she had no intent to inflict collateral damage on her way to leaving herself behind to find herself, but there it was. It wasn't intentional, and it wasn't meant to be cruel or painful. She expressed all of this with genuine sorrow and remorse at what she was doing and the impact on me. When Lisa finished her "letting me go" soliloquy, I loved her even more.

There's the rub, Mackin. No A-35, Tiger Balm, or cortisone shot for that stuff, Mackin my boy.

Then there was the other thing, the fourth element. Maybe Lisa would "out me." Out me as the big pussy. That "outing" was the one thing about me that no one had ever written about or even thought to research. I'd never hidden the truth intentionally. It just wasn't obvious enough for anyone to consider.

So, maybe that's the rub, Mr. Smackin' Mackin. If you're ever fully, completely in love, you'll have to reveal all.

That was probably why my mother's eyes didn't sparkle when I told her about my intentions with Lisa. My mother had lived her whole life—unintentionally, as it turned out—without the big reveal. She wanted me to reveal the concealed to whoever I fell in love with. My mother also wanted whoever I fell in love with to share my absolute core traits.

That was a big ask, to reveal a central fact of who I was so late in life was certain to be the subject of praise and attack, likely with a big dish of ridicule on the side. The reveal had to be done in the right way, preferably with the right person at my side. In my mind, Lisa could have been that person, but not in my mother's mind. My mother had a mission for me that I needed to get busy with, and Lisa lacked the core traits for it.

What I learned from Lisa was the necessity of finding myself by leaving myself. Forty-four years of development and becoming who I was without being recognized for what I actually was.

Reverse fields, Mackin. I had perpetuated the misdirection game for long enough. There was a wide opening on the other side of the field that I needed to run through. I needed to run through to that bright daylight of the essential Mackin.

There's a joke that all defensive players secretly want to be on offence. That linebackers, when they pick up a fumble or intercept a pass, have more than a moment of hesitation. Like the dog who finally catches the car. All that barking and tearing after the car while proclaiming what they would do when they caught it. Then what? What do I do now?

Run for the daylight, Mackin. Pick up some blockers on the way.

Lisa would be one, my mother another. I could think of many more, which made me smile.

So, what came out of the devastation from Lisa? I firmly believed my mother was always right. I, Smackin' Mackin, perhaps more than anybody, had to be true to my core truth. Even more so than Lisa herself. Why? Because there simply weren't enough of us who shared my core truth, and it had to be preserved and lifted high. On that path, on that leaving of Lisa, I felt thrilled and frightened at the same time. I was vibrating with self-identification and quiet exhilaration for my path forward.

Thank you, Lisa, for having courage. The courage to find yourself. That comes with a cost and a loss. I know you felt the loss deeply, and I know you're not stone cold. That's what has helped me rise through desolation, the self-blame and blaming you.

What made me come full circle? Well, I took myself back to my pathetic exit from GoHo's. Lisa told me we were over with one final dalliance, if I so chose. I chose the dalliance, but as we sat in GoHo's, I finally digested the full weight of our finality. I was bruised and battered in my head and in my heart. I loved her. Loved everything about her, from her boots to her business acumen. I loved us together. I loved our differences and our similarities. Her inadequacies were too inadequate to register.

I trailed her to the condo, vowing all the way to make love to her with fire, passion, gentleness, and a focus that would shake her to her foundations, causing Lisa to toss away her plans. It worked the other way. She reduced me to a quivering emotional and physical state. Not Mackin the great lion but Mackin the jellyfish. Hear me roar? More like "hear me squish."

I cried when we were done. First in the shower. Long, guttural sobs of anguish and loss, then while getting dressed. Every step in the closure drew water. Buttoning my shirt, zipping my fly, tightening my belt, and tying my shoes. Lisa stood on her toes and kissed me goodbye. There might have been a tear in her eye, but I'm not sure. Tough to see water through water.

As I sat in my empty home, I wrapped myself in manliness. Mentally, I recited all the things I could do in the void that Lisa left behind. But those fleeting images didn't last as even temporary cures. There was no panacea. The appearance of stoic manhood would be my path. No binges, no outrageous partying, no phone calls to old lovers, and no false pretenses except the pretense of stoicism. The linebacker in the middle of the frenetic field, directing traffic and remaining emotionally sober and mentally stable. All things would flow through me. I would be my own captain of control and chaos. I chose control, at least on the surface.

My first plan to keep Lisa was to engage in an unparalleled display of "studliness" and testosterone-fuelled passion, making her succumb to the best she ever had. That game plan didn't even make it to the launching pad.

I looked up the definition of "emasculated." I thought of emasculation as some type of weakness. "To deprive of strength, vigour, or spirit." Well, that certainly felt true on the inside. But that was never Lisa's intent. I had to remember her decision was about her, not me.

I controlled my destiny and my own degree of desolation. One route was up and courageous; the other route was down and dangerous.

My mother's guidance was coming to fruition and in force. Yep. Turns out in the end, that's where the courage lives. My play? The big reveal.

The first stage of my new game plan—a temporary leave of absence from everything. It wasn't a retreat to lick my wounds. It was a full-on forward march to myself and what I was beginning to feel was an overwhelming call to my destiny, to doing the right thing. Not only the right thing for me but also for the people who meant the most to me. I needed one hundred days to do what I needed to get done. The time frame was according to some background research and my mother's guidance.

When I said I would be back in the broadcast booth by mid-season, no one blinked. All my contracts would be held open for me. My employers and comrades respected me that much without my revealing the reason behind my temporary departure. They all wanted to probe, but they held back as much as they could. Many of them assumed that my leave was necessitated by the downstream impact of the Lisa fallout, that I hadn't been able to fully deal with it or wrestle it to the ground. But I assured them that it wasn't about Lisa; it was about me. Their care for me manifested in trusting that my absence was a necessary part of my path. I would let my close friends in on my big reveal on the cusp of it becoming public knowledge.

In reality, I was leaving Lisa for good to follow my own path. One hundred days. It was time to stop yackin' and start being Mackin.

CHAPTER 38

Lisa's Play

The creative process was winding up. We had twelve songs to choose from. I'd decided only ten would make the CD. "Immolate" was necessary to write, but it didn't fit with the rest of the songs. It didn't have the same tone, feel, or message, and it hinted too directly at self-destruction rather than self-discovery. It was off key because it was accurate, but it was too honest. A bit too bone deep for me to put out there at that point in time. But I would release "Immolate" in some form one day. Probably bury it in the double album I envisioned releasing in a couple of years.

It had been good. The luxury of the deep dive into self. I can't say what answers I was looking to find. I was trying to find me, unencumbered by the needs, wants, and thoughts of others. I was hunting demons. Not to kill them but to lay them to rest. I found them, stared at them, turned them around and over. Categorized them into two buckets, demons by and from others were in bucket number one. Those demons had been forced or dumped on me, usually when I was unprepared for their onslaught. Facing them again, I recognized them as the evil pricks they were and how solidly they had gripped and ripped me and, in some cases, how they still had a hold on me. My lover's betrayal, which had led to the destruction of my confidence and then the long-term sidelining of my full capability and ambition. My parents' continual chess or tennis match with my emotions. Love-forty. No love. What love? Facing them now, it was almost comical how they held such power, such sway. I needed to punt bucket number one to the side forever. Creating *Leaving Lisa* was about doing that.

I had one pure moment of vindictive joy in booting demon bucket number one to the curb. I phoned my ex, the man who had rained demons down upon me and unleashed the hounds of hell. He was so pleasant on the phone. He had heard from musicians and people throughout the industry that my upcoming release was going to be fantastic, a creative and likely a phenomenal commercial success. He couldn't resist expressing how maybe, just maybe, I had learned a thing or two from him.

That was the perfect segue.

Yes, yes, I had learned a thing or two. Among other things, I had learned that success could be fleeting and mystifying and often determined by those I surrounded myself with. "Like you," I said. He responded instantly by thanking me, and I could feel his slime-ball smile spreading. The thought of his face and that arrogant look sent toxic tremors through my core.

"I'm not finished," I replied. "When I say, 'like you,' I don't mean in a positive sense like you assumed because of your inflated ego. What I meant is surrounding myself with the right people, which you never were, nor will you ever be. I say this as a matter of fact. In the twenty-five years since you took advantage of me as a young, naïve, trusting, loving neophyte what have you accomplished?"

He started to bluster about his track record, but I stopped him cold. "You've had six number one songs. We had seven in our brief time together. You've been continually falling from that pinnacle, and your descent is accelerating. By the way, if you've been counting—and I know you have—I, on the other hand, have produced twenty-seven number one songs for other artists and seven more for me. Is the scoreboard clear to you? That's thirty-four to six. Also, in case you're not looking in the mirror, you're a bloated degenerate on your fourth wife. You now have the creative, commercial, and sex appeal of a Panamanian tomato slug." (I have no idea why I picked Panama or tomato as a form of slug, but it worked for describing him.) "You're also only a matter of moments from the 'MeToo' movement catching up to you. You know it, I know it, your wife knows it, your agent knows it, the industry knows it, and so does everybody else, including your family. I would tell you that disgrace is going to fall on your back like a ton of shit bricks, but you're already feeling the weight and smelling like it."

Amazingly, he didn't hang up, so I continued. "Since you're listening, get this too. No one will think of you when they hear my songs. You know why? You're mostly irrelevant and forgotten, except when you become notorious, but that stage in your life won't have anything to do with me, thankfully. Unless they ask me to testify. Then I'll be Crown witness number one.

"One last thing. I'm saying this just to be cruel and completely truthful. You were an unbelievably lousy lover. You probably knew that too. Even your ego couldn't hide that truth from yourself. Have a good night!"

Was that vindictive? Yes. Necessary? No. Did it feel good? Absolutely!

What I really purged went into bucket number two. The demons of self-doubt, self-destruction, self-recrimination, and self-loathing. The four demons of degradation. Powerful, axe-wielding assholes that cut and slashed to the bone.

Bucket number two was filled to overflowing by my parents, their endless game playing and manipulation. They inflicted hurt like other parents distributed love. It was like they couldn't help themselves. In their contest against each other, I was the classic game piece, sacrificed and coveted. They made me vulnerable to the manipulation of others, and when that embrace came from a man twelve years older, I was easy pickings. Their tug of war over my emotional loyalty made me think that was how the game of life and love was played. That I was supposed to taunt, chastise, criticize, humiliate, and basically trash my partner. Then, as collateral damage if I didn't align myself with the vindictive outpourings of one parent against the other, the attack shifted to me and my betrayal and hurtful failure to see that their side was right. By the time I reached my late teens, I was so vulnerable that I jumped into his arms, his care, his advice, and his management. When he began to taunt, chastise, criticize, humiliate, and trash me, I just assumed that was how relationships worked. It was my fucked-up version of normal.

Did my parents love me? One always assumes the answer must be "yes," but who knows? They were so busy carving their own story lines that I became a symbol of their own capabilities. They pointed to their successful daughter and humbly accepted the praise for their creation of such a wunderkind. In an offhand and humble manner, they would imply how their role in my upbringing was much more significant than their spouse. "I got her started on the piano. I saw the potential in her voice. I knew the violin would stretch and challenge her musically. Yes, that was my guidance, my love, my support." Back and forth, on and on. It was all about their own capabilities rather than anything shared or accomplished by my ambition, drive, and talent. The continuous maneuvering, the chess-playing bullshit. And I was just a gambit.

Did I love them? No, not particularly. Is that terrible to say? I guess it sounds terrible. It wasn't something I said out loud, except to my therapist. There was no need for me to be publicly toxic.

Besides, if I spouted that truth, the toxicity of their response would be of biblical, catastrophic scope. Suffice it to say they wouldn't be invited to the release party or my first concert. That message to them would be intentional and purposeful, though I doubted either of them would get the meaning. Or even care.

My parents' issues were complicated and hard to figure out, so I stopped trying. My therapist helped me get past that. My Uncle Theodore, on my father's side, probably helped me the most to get beyond my parents. He spun out his version of his brother's truth.

"He's the whitest black man ever. He likes being white. Or at least acting so white he seems to be white even though he's as black as black. He's the original Oreo cookie, black on the outside and creamy white on the inside. Being a black, white man seems to come naturally to him. We used to tell him to stop putting on airs. That was the kindest expression we could use to describe his 'whiteness' in mixed company. We even nicknamed your father 'His Whiteness' for a long time. We tried to steer him back to a simple pride in who we are and where he came from, but that never caught his attention or interest. We figured he was 'blinded by the white lights.' Then we just gave up and let his black ass act white. Except I don't think it's an act anymore. He seems white, at least to the family.

"He plays his dark shade of white to the T for his white friends. My brother's black background makes him incredibly cool and accessible to his white friends. He prefers white company to black. That's why I believe that after your mother, he's married a series of progressively whiter women. The second-last—or was it the third-last? —wife we called 'cream.' We called another one 'a whiter shade of pale.' The family calls his current wife 'ghost,' but I'm partial to referring to her as 'Casperella.'

"Your father loves acting black around his white friends. He turns into a jive-talking black bad ass for their comedic benefit and entertainment. They lap it up. This parody of our race pisses most black folks off. I had to warn him that if he ever pulled out his blackface routine in front of me again, I would demonstrate for him what a bad-ass black man could do. He's never crossed that line again in my presence or around the rest of the family. So, we just kind of shrug our shoulders and let him be the blackest white man ever.

"Your father's career prospered the whiter he became. His corporate and social fit became easier on his way up the ladder. He was rewarded for being an Oreo, with more and more cookies coming his way as the firms he was with wanted to show diversity, and your dad fit the bill. He was head hunted all the way up the ladder to the second in command. Step by step, move by move, to the 2IC slot.

"Now, your mother, on the other hand, is a different colour code altogether. I think your father was attracted to her because she was the whitest black girl available. Not in pigmentation but in orientation. She was raised in an all-white environment, and she thrived. Her parents were wonderful. They broke some colour barriers in humble ways. Where they lived, where they worked, and how they became engaged in the community. They promoted being black by being black in white enclaves. They never lost sight of who they were, though, and they were proud of their race. They were cultural ambassadors before we even thought about that term or what it could mean. They were comfortable in their own skins and never pretended to be anything else, no pretense. They were black in a white world. That's probably why your mother thrived as a child and felt no stigma.

Then your mother married my brother. It took her a few years to realize he was on a mission to become the whitest black man ever. Maybe even a few more to grasp that his attraction to her was largely based on the whiteness of her upbringing and her ease of melding into a predominantly white scenario. When your mother fully understood her husband's ambition, her reaction wasn't what he or anyone else expected.

"She went black. I'm talking *all in*. Your mother launched almost desperately into becoming the blackest black woman ever. She had no background or upbringing in being black, so she swung for the fences and went outlandishly black, almost becoming a parody but not quite. Her fashion, her hairstyle, her diet, her music, her art, her interest in movies, and her reading all went full black.

"Her reading saved her from parody and embarrassment. Your mother became the family teacher of black history. She instilled a lot of pride in us for who we are and how far we've come. She stirred our emotions with the history of our people's suffering on the journey to where we are today. She sparked our awareness of the indignities and the racism that still exist. She made us confront those realities and encouraged us to work against them, which we all have in our own way, all of us inspired and prodded by your mother. She made us all prouder black people. That part of her going all in was beautiful. We had a nickname for her as well, but it was meant with love and admiration. We referred to her as 'Dark Vader.' Children of Africa, I am your mother.

"There she was, married to the whitest black man ever, and he saw her changes as ridiculous and embarrassing. At the very beginning, as newlyweds and into your early teen years, your mother seemed to have little interest or inclination in being black, so her marriage to the whitest black man ever seemed natural. We were wrong about her.

Her drive into her blackness, her deep dive into our culture and historic waters, evolved her into the blackest black woman ever. Your mother and father were diverging on the colour spectrum. Except white and black aren't in the prism; they fall outside that. Your parents fell outside the spectrum and fell rapidly out of any form of love for each other.

"Your mom was successful in that transition. Her drive to blackness made her seem authentically black. At first maybe only to herself but then to bring our family the story of Africa, slavery, and our cultural heritage. It was astounding, informative, and real. She impressed the hell out of us, especially when she was still living with the 'White Shadow' or 'Casper,' as we called your dad.

"However, sometimes your mother went a little too far in her expression of her blackness. There was a time, just before your parents divorced, when your dad was acting so proper, like he was playing a Sydney Poitier role, and your mother was all like Downtown Jackie Brown. It was strange. Your parents had managed to screw up the whole concept of colour and the shades of black and white.

"Then to further mix the colour wheel, when your mother divorced your father, she married men of various shades. She was an equal-opportunity marriage maven. There was the Swede. Now *that* was a real white man, maybe because of the Scandinavian cold or the white fury caused by assembling IKEA furniture. Then the Asian, followed by the Bolivian, then the African, which was her shortest marriage. Now she's with a Greek.

"Your mother also kept climbing the money mountain. Each husband was richer than the one before. Her pre-nuptials were always windfalls of larger takes."

At the end of all this, I asked my uncle where I was on the colour wheel. His answer wasn't helpful.

"You, my dear Lisa, are in a peculiar situation. Your predicament is that you have no true colour spectrum. Your parents were piss-poor role models. Your upbringing was a refracted spectrum of the two non-colours, black and white. And those two colours are about the absence of colour. Then when you try so hard to be a colour you're not or the darkest possible shade of the colour you are, you tend to end up absent of any true colour."

"Does that mean I'm totally fucked?"

"Yes, my dear Lisa, I believe you are, but you'll emerge into your own beautiful colour."

Out of all that, one singular outcome was that for most of my life, I'd been drawn to white men. After my father, my mother pursued every colour possible except black, except for her brief African dalliance. That seemed like a hell of a contradiction when one fully embraced their blackness and ended up with all types of different colours on the wheel of humanity. Somehow, I think she wanted to emphasize her blackness against a full colour wheel in her subsequent marriages. My father pursued whiteness like it was the Holy Grail. Now he and his current wife were unofficially known in the family circles as "Casper" and "Casperella," which was funny.

I was emerging from my cocoon as I eradicated the demons from buckets one and two. I was emerging as a woman of colour, clear in who I was. The creative process was cathartic. Through the process I slew the four diabolical dangers in bucket number two.

I was emergent. The release party would be my coming out, my debutante ball. I believed it would be a demonstration of me being me. With post-production and creative for the covers yet to be done, we had scheduled the release in seventy-five days. The countdown to emergence was on.

The four demons of degradation—how could I forget those bastards? Some of them existed solely as part of me. The demon of self-doubt was something I had a big hand in bringing to life. When I created or stepped in a new direction, the needles of apprehension and worry injected themselves. That was a natural outcome considering my upbringing and life experiences, which created a significant degree of uncertainty. I was uncertain of who I was and what I was capable of accomplishing—of creating. Both my ex and my parents dealt the addictive drug of doubt freely and frequently. My sense of my own capabilities had been battered and bruised. Writing and creating *Leaving Lisa* was finally eliminating a lot of that doubt. I poured myself into the work. My colleagues were people I trusted, both as human beings and as talented musicians. I took all their feedback and criticism as positives. I swam in their input. Through their honesty, they lifted me above the waves of doubt. They inspired me through the doubts I held regarding my talent and vision.

The demon of self-destruction wasn't a full-blown demon. He was on a leash. I knew at my core that I was holding myself back, stopping short of driving my creative strength and being bold as a solo artist. Self-destruction was just a step away, like falling back into an alcohol or cocaine cycle or both. All kinds of behaviours are addictive and have the narcotic effect of covering a person's fears, concerns, and worries. So, we mask them with some behaviour, either physical or mental, and prevent the slide into self-destruction mode. The act of going to my own well of hurt could trigger self-destructive behaviour. I knew that. I needed the strength to deal with that demon on my own. I needed to prove that to myself, for myself, and by myself. Self-destruction was the demon I had to face alone. So, Mackin took the smackin'.

The fear of failure or ridicule held me back and ate away at my soul. I found myself dreaming of myself as a little girl, all balled up with my knees pressed against my chest, my arms clenched around my knees, and my head tucked down, resting on my knees. In my dream, I realized I had wet my pants, and I ran to my room in shame. My father was in the dream, staring down at me. No comfort, cold or otherwise, was emanating from his face, which was framed in an aura of white. What I read in his face was an expression that barked, "No white child would wet themselves at a party."

My mother was in this dream too. Her face emanated an attitude of animosity toward my father. She saw my predicament quite differently. "The girl was jubilant. Her black soul was flowing because she hasn't been allowed to express her blackness with untethered joy, so her body betrayed her when that jolt of emotional authenticity was expressed. Your white tendencies have messed with and menaced her soul."

"So, she pisses her pants?"

"You created the condition of destroying her identity, so, of course, finding a slice of herself—her true self—would be overwhelming."

All I remember from the beginning of that dream is that I was dancing with joy to some sort of boogaloo song and drinking far too much Kool-Aid. I'm not certain if it's a dream or something that really happened.

My father categorized my behaviour as follows: "If she hadn't been jumping around like she was in some travelling minstrel show, which is degrading to our race, this wouldn't have happened."

"So, dancing with joy and freedom is degrading to our race?" my mother countered. "Well, then, yes, Master, let's do some hillbilly line dance with your white friends and restrain our joyful black bladders."

Such dreams or memories have raged within me, leading to the big questions. Who are you? What are you? Walk this line. Walk in circles. Colour inside the lines. Colour outside the lines. Fit in this box. Fuck the box. All these things, my parents' contrary opinions, narratives, machinations, and behaviours created destructive waves, which I let wash me from shore to shore and under the surface.

I decided to attack the waves in my late teens. My attack wasn't subtle. It involved outlandish fashion. Drinking. Drugs. Dubious boys. I graduated from bad boys to worse men. I'm not sure which was more of a problem—drugs and drinking or boys and men—but the combination was devastating. Even when I was having fun getting stoned, drunk, laid, or all three at once, I knew I was careening around on the edge of a chasm of self-obliteration.

My music sobered me. I was talented, maybe even gifted. When I played or sang, I was fully absorbed. Music saved me from the demon of self-destruction.

That demon had to be tethered and put in restraints because he could be very seductive. He was numbing and allowed escape and diversion. When I plunged into those behaviours, there was a wild-ass freneticism to it all. Diving in was always a rush, followed by a blur, a whirlwind, then a crack, boom, bang. That demon was often masked in being so cool, so wild, so notorious, so rock 'n' roll. Sometimes I watched myself as if I were an avatar in a video game of oblivion. "Watch the talented black chick self-immolate."

Then there was him. Twelve years older, so rock 'n' roll, so cool. He was a surprisingly steadying hand back then, at least at first, guiding my talent to productive creation. He drew lines, parameters. Create. Work. Party. Repeat. He was my manager and my funky rhythm guitarist. We got married. I was nineteen. He was thirty-one.

I was signed and wedded. I think he was faithful through our first two records, which took us through six months after our vows. My mother attended the wedding and definitely got her freak on. I think she was with her first Asian husband or maybe the Swede. Dad was a no show. Sent his regards—and his disdain.

My manager/husband managed to ball every backup singer in our band and anybody else who came within his grasp. I'm pretty sure he was swinging both ways because we always had an effeminate keyboard player or percussionist around. He delved into their musicality rather deeply in long, solo sessions.

Three years in, after two smash records and two not so good releases, he declared I was a fucking mess and not living up to my promise. Only when he started divorce proceedings did I realize what a horrendous contract I had signed. I walked away with little money and two years left on a contract that gave him artistic and monetary control over my career. My parents stepped in and battled for me, and maybe they helped a little. But dear old Dad walked away rather quickly, seemingly content after a long session with my ex-husband's lawyer. They could have helped a lot more, but they were too busy battling each other. To say creating *Leaving Lisa* was a cathartic experience is an understatement of magnificent proportions.

Do the four demons of degradation follow some sort of chain of command, some sequential system or order? Who knows? Minor self-recrimination blossoms into major self-doubt. Self-destruction is either the prodigy of self-loathing or the parent. Again, who knows? Maybe those two big swinging dicks, doubt and destruction, are a couple. One begets the other, and the other begets the one. The demons of degradation, the branches of that family tree are intertwined and inbred.

With the demon of self-recrimination, I picked at myself so hard. I would scratch the minor itch of recrimination until it festered into agonizing mental blotches of worry. Simple, everyday things like how I handled a conversation. Did I talk too much or not enough? Was I clear? Coherent? Consistent? Did I show respect for others? Was I attentive enough? Responsive enough? Engaged enough? Did I demonstrate understanding, care, and interest? Did I connect?

This was the trivial nature of my worries, which could bloom from real or imagined, petty, minuscule faux pas I might have made in an inconsequential conversation. I let such petite recriminations digress into voluminous minutiae that grew into continuous and ruinous recriminations about my appearance, my fashion sense, my look, my style, and, oh God, my skin and my hair. I let the drip, drip, drip of minor recriminations continue until they grew into increasingly wide, deep pools. Then the buoyancy of my self-confidence would deflate, and I would sink below the water line, drowning in self-recrimination. Those little pieces of shit kept me awake at night. Then all my energy and capabilities were drained into a circling cesspool of crushing, crippling self-doubt. I second-guessed myself into a stupor, which I eased with self-medication—the gateway to self-destruction. Then occasionally I would pull back from it all in a moment of sobriety or a flash of self-clarity or during rehab or in therapy and say to myself, "What the fuck?" The realization of what I had done to myself was devastating if it wasn't managed and debriefed or constructively walked and talked through in a process guiding me toward the light of understanding and self-acceptance.

If not, then the big demon, the last bastard of the four, who had been standing on the top rope, would jump down and squash me into the mat and mess me up so much that I had zero self-recognition. The demon of self-loathing, in his masked behemoth muscularity, would pile drive me into absolute self-destruction mode. That road was a blinding tornado of self-contempt and self-immolation. My saving grace? Music.

When I emerged from the two years of contractual obligation, I had barely survived my self-destruction. Somehow, I staggered to a friend's house with my guitar and a carry-on bag. She took a long look at my physically and mentally wrecked countenance but never said a word. I hung in the door frame as she put on a jacket, grabbed her purse, sunglasses, cell phone, and car keys. Then she anchored me in the crux of her elbow and ribs, spun me around, and led me to her car.

We drove for two hours. I knew where we were going. She had been there several years ago, and she was still clean. We had no need to talk during the drive. She asked one question as she gestured at the dashboard. "Music?" I shook my head.

About an hour in, I mustered up one word: "Puke."

She careened into the next gas station, and I puked in the parking lot. Then she took me into the washroom and cleaned me up as best as she could. When I peed, my urine was discoloured. A reddish hue. Was it blood?

She got us some water and some Wunderbar chocolate bars. "You can only get this good stuff in Canada, you know," she said as she unwrapped it. I didn't know that, and I attempted a grin. The chocolate bar was good, and the wonder was I held it down. The water was better. I wondered what the "Wunder" in a Wunderbar was intended to be. I wondered if I would last through rehab.

Two weeks in I told them I was ready to sign out. Apparently, I had contracted for a month. I was trying to break the contract. My friend arrived back the next day. She brought Wunderbars and asked if I had figured out what the "Wunder" in a Wunderbar was. I asked what the hell she was talking about. She told me the only words I had uttered on the drive up were "puke" and "thanks," except for one other sentence. I had wondered aloud what the "Wunder" in a Wunderbar is intended to be.

An embarrassed look of woe and hopelessness must have swept over my face because I saw worry and fear in her eyes as she read my vacuous expression and my even emptier eyes. Our crying started simultaneously. She hugged me close and hard. I felt her mixture of love, fear, and concern for me. Emotions are real. They have a physical presence. Maybe that's the wonder in the wonderful love of a friend.

We hugged and cried until I was drained. Then she talked to me about me staying for the whole month. I shushed her and asked her to come with me to the administrator's office. We had an impromptu meeting with the facility leader. I asked to see my contract, scanning it until I found the clause regarding the month-long stay. I asked for a pen and scratched out the month and wrote the day that I wanted to be released.

My friend cried again. What a big baby! I committed for another two and a half months. Everyone smiled.

We went back to my dorm room, and I asked her to stay and listen. I picked up my guitar and strummed some chords. I ran them together into the start of a song with a nice little chorus section. It was the beginning of the "Maybe Song." The "Getting to Good" song started happening at that moment. It took me twenty-five years to get back to it.

Music saved me. It's been my constant lifeline. I never let go of it, but I never fully immersed myself into the comfort and fulfillment of creating my own voice, my own musical expression of who I am. I never went to find myself, to find Lisa in my music.

So, for twenty-five years I flourished at a commitment level to my talent of about sixty to seventy percent. Then it dawned on me that I had to go all the way unencumbered and without a safety net. I started to hear in my head what *Leaving Lisa* might or could sound like. I was starting to feel what I could truly feel about myself and my journey, and I realized I was strong enough to commit to me. Selfish enough to jettison distractions. To put aside love. To drop Mackin.

And so, in I went.

Leaving Lisa, coming to iTunes, online streaming, CDs, radio, and concerts soon.

If I had stayed with Mackin, I knew I would lash out at him during the process. The trip was too personal. No wingman wanted. No passengers on this trip. I had convinced myself I was being cruel to be kind. Mackin and I would never have survived *Leaving Lisa*. He was too kind, and I knew I would feel anger, remorse, and even hatred while confronting my demons.

Cruel to be kind in the right measure, yada, yada. Even though I knew what I did was right, it was still wrong. Right for me but so wrong and undeserved for Mackin.

Was it worth it? Was it repairable? What about Sean? There were two good men out there. The tour was going to be demanding and tempting. The physical grind would be exhausting. I was working out hard to get in shape and build my stamina. I wasn't a big dancer, but I did cover the stage.

On tour I had to control the temptations, and there were always temptations out on the road. I had succumbed to them before, willingly and totally. After every concert if I played and performed well, the feeling was exhilarating and celebratory. I had banned drugs for everyone involved, except for weed. I also hired an athletic trainer who developed a five-week training regimen for all the band and key crew members. She would accompany us on tour, and we would have daily regimens. I hired a good health consultant who designed a full-fledged menu for the tour. I was going to protect and nourish myself and my team—but we would still party.

Ah, but what about the temptations of the flesh? I had succumbed and fallen before. I decided I needed a wingman for the tour.

Song #8 "The Maybe Song (Getting to Good)"

There's a place up ahead
Think I've been there, but I don't quite remember
At one time we might have been there together
It's a hard road to travel and seems a hard place to stay
My memory is faulty, and I don't know the way

Maybe you can help, maybe you can't
Maybe you want to, maybe you don't
Maybe we've been there, maybe we were close
Maybe ain't getting me nowhere and in maybe there's little hope
Maybe there's no place ahead, maybe there's no place that good

In the morning, I tell myself I'm getting to good
I tell myself if you loved me maybe we would
You're the one I need, the one that could
Baby with you I'd be getting to good

Sometimes I might have wanted more than that place up ahead
More is just stuff cluttering your head
Your heart ain't about more, it's about loving
If I could hold you and get held back
The road would be smooth, and I would have nothing to dread

Maybe we can help each other, maybe we can't
Maybe we want to but held each other back
Maybe we can get there, I hope that we can
Maybe it ain't easy, I know that for a fact
But maybe ain't getting us nowhere, so let's take the chance

There ain't no maybe, about who I love
In the morning beside you I'm getting to good
Tell you I love you more than I thought I ever could
Your arms around me, your voice in my ear
No maybes here, we're getting to good.

No maybes, none allowed around here
Voice in my ear, love you, getting to good
Maybes are gone, we're getting to good.

Song #9 "White/Black (The Oreo Song)"

Well, I am the dark
Raised to be the light
The contrast is stark
The black and the white

Oreo, Oreo, Oreo
There she goes
What is she? Oh, oh
Nobody knows

Raised to fit into the white
Put my colour inside those lines
Clenched fists, dark as night
Fighting what my colour defined

Oreo, Oreo, Oreo
There she goes
What is she? Oh, oh
Even she doesn't know

Dad colours himself light
Mom delights in the black
Parents tug me day and night
Always torn and under attack

Oreo, Oreo, Oreo
Where you gonna go
What, what? Oh, oh
Up to you, you know

Black crust layers
White cream players
Strange stuff to chew
Does this taste good to you?

Oreo, Oreo, Oreo
Where you gonna go?
What, what? Oh, oh
Put on a show

You're blinded by the white light
As you rise, dark knight
Stare through their light
Come to your own right

Oreo, Oreo, Oreo
What have you done?
You're the show
The show of what you've become

CHAPTER 39

The Call and Response

The call was unexpected. Could I meet for drinks at the Four Seasons where we used to meet after work at 7:30 p.m.? Yes. Good. See you then. Bye.

Crisp, abrupt, efficient, no nonsense. That was my ex-wife's style. Her operational mode was always that efficient, no nonsense. Decide, make the call, move forward, get to action. Now her tone and approach seemed even crisper, with a sharper edge. She had a strength in her voice that moved me to "yes" quickly. She was always firm, steadfast, and anchored. Those were the central tenets and qualities that she brought to our marriage, and I relied on them. That is, until I couldn't. *Anchors away, me boys!* Even with her curt manner on the phone, I detected a smidgen of mirth and mystery. She enjoyed being an enigma.

I arrived at 7:30 sharp. I mean *major* sharp with my jacket already checked into the cloak room. I was striding, in as manly a fashion as I could muster, to our former usual table. Our table was a high top with high-backed leather stools adjacent to the bar and in a highly visible spot. It was a place people sat to be seen. She loved being seen. When we were together, I must admit, so did I. That night? Not so much. During our joint return to our old stomping grounds, we would be recognized by more than a few. Eyebrows would be raised. We would provide fodder for several conversations. I imagined that one or two of those conversations would include someone mentioning if I had come back to retrieve my balls or something equally derogatory about my manhood. So be it.

In the two days between her call and that night, I had wondered about her purpose, her motive, her expected outcome. I hadn't seen her in almost a year despite the proximity of our offices and the nature of our work. We had nothing in the works between our two firms that would even remotely necessitate a preliminary meeting. I had checked. On an ongoing basis I had Georgia, my loyal administrative assistant, discreetly screen meeting and conference lists to avoid professional contact. My ex-wife had seemingly acquired and seamlessly taken over our previous social and charitable calendar to the degree she wanted, with Phillip at her side—or more correctly, in tow. Although that calendar takeover wasn't a formal part of our dissolution agreement, I understood it was a predetermined outcome. I didn't mind. I had lost the appetite for appearances.

The shock was that she was there before I arrived. That had never happened before. She liked to make a late grand entrance. Showmanship had always been more her forte than mine. She was perched on a long-backed chair at the high table with her legs crossed, wine glass in hand. I saw several surreptitious and some direct glances in her direction from the men and women standing at the bar as I approached the table. I would have been glancing, maybe even full-on gawking at her as well. She was dazzling, looking even better than I remembered. Radiating confidence, she was a formidable presence. A woman clearly comfortable with power and control. And those legs. I thought of the Sharon Stone moments we had shared at that table—exactly four times—and the incredible animalistic sex that followed, once in the cloakroom of that very establishment. To say the least, before the hellos, I was rattled.

She didn't stand up. Instead, she uncrossed her legs and leaned in for a light hug and the "au courant" European double cheek lip brush. It wasn't even a kiss, just a rumour of one. She caught my glance as her legs uncrossed. "Tonight, I have panties on," she said as her lips brushed my cheek and then she laughed. I choked.

My two fingers of scotch with one cube were waiting. She had just started her nine-ounce, upper-shelf cabernet sauvignon. She had me flummoxed, enraptured, and bumbling.

As usual, she led the conversation. "Let me address the elephant in the room."

I wanted to ask which one because I had a whole parade of pachyderms marching through my mind, but away she went.

"I'm leaving the Brit. I needed someone who wouldn't be sharing the spotlight. Sean, many people thought your intellect and professional approach were propping me up and that I was reliant upon you. Many viewed you as a Svengali-type creator of my character. People saw you as the silent assassin stalking in the weeds, guiding the hunt when I closed a deal. They saw our success as a couple, not as individuals. The Brit, on the other hand, wasn't imposing in any way, and there was no threat of him casting a shadow over my abilities or raising doubts about them."

She was already talking about Phillip in the past tense. The lioness hunted, fed, then moved on, leaving the carcass for the hyenas. *Phillip, old boy, welcome to the Hyena Dining Club.*

"I also believed that you would peak at a particular corporate watermark and park there with a full measure of contentment. I, of course, wanted more, and I still do."

As I listened, I sipped my scotch, a very expensive McCallan. I decided she was buying and motioned for a second.

"Now I'm fully solo," she continued. "Empowered, established, experienced, and international with a formidable track record and an obvious launch trajectory."

I nodded. Why the hell not? I was still waiting for more elephants to be addressed.

She continued her cold, analytical dissection of her latest roadkill. "I've been able to fully develop Phillip's introductions and familiarity with international connections, and now I can leverage them, which will be invaluable. You'd probably like Phillip if you got to know him. He has that classic dry British wit, excellent manners, and is a very useful wingman, but he has too much of a subservient aura about him. You know it was never about him?"

I didn't.

"It was always about you, Sean."

My response to that was a silent *WTF?* and raised eyebrows. That set me back a bit, and a second parade of elephants entered the room. I was bracing myself to hear a long list of the faults that I had manifested during our time together, thus driving her away. Then I responded, "I'm sitting down, and I have a good scotch in my hand that you're paying for, so let me hear the long litany of my shortcomings."

She cocked her head back, laughed, and then let a long thrill of cabernet pass her lips before continuing. "That isn't it at all, Sean. I loved our time together. Our lifestyle. Our emergence as a sophisticated rising corporate power couple."

I sensed an elephant-size "if" coming, and she didn't disappoint.

"But I thought we were plateauing and getting too comfortable. Our striving tended to be sedentary. I felt you didn't have the prerequisite drive, ambition, or blood thirst and taste to go for the top shelf."

Well, that was true enough to some degree about the blood sport. She, on the other hand, was acquiring more of all of that. Her battle mode was "Damn the torpedoes! Collateral damage is to be expected. There will be blood, and I will drink your milkshake." Her ambition wasn't blind, but it was blinding to others.

"Sean, you would likely have become collateral damage professionally if we stayed together. You know that my ambition is to reach the C-Suite." Her ambition had always been clear—to be the first woman in our industry at the top, and that likely would have entailed deals across firms where she would have to obliterate anyone blocking her path. I realized I could be in those crosshairs.

"I see myself as a she-wolf, a she-hulk, a she-goddess with an unfettered, unrestrained willingness to go all in. I just felt that we were too linked as a package deal, that we would be judged as competent and capable but oh so comfortable, not champions in the octagon. Not killers. Some might see my decision to jettison you as a mid-life crisis, stemming from my need to have an open-top Mercedes Benz career trajectory. Phillip was but an accoutrement, a trailer, not an anchor or a drag. You, on the other hand, were a partner. A substantial partner. And sometimes partners follow different paths or go in different directions."

I was starting to form a response that would have gone something like "You ignorant, egotistical, narcissistic, self-serving, manipulative bitch," with a "fuck you" or two thrown in for good measure. Before I spit that rant out, though, in my head our two paths became clear. Her holding her hand up as a sign she planned to continue and that I should stay quiet helped prevent my outburst and maintain my mental clarity.

She said that she manipulated the international posting as the first leg in our journey of separation. The second leg was the dissolving of our partnership while simultaneously acquiring Phillip as a tertiary and somewhat complementary accessory, although the Brit was an important bit player in her rise to prominence. She had also studied the careers of the men at the top. International experience was a must, and a second and/or third wife was another notch in the belt of the corporate rock stars. Wives number two and three were subservient and compliant, unlike most first wives. First wives or partners married for who their husband was. Second and third wives married for *what* he was. The first wife bought in for better or worse. First wives were true believers in the wedding vows. Second and third wives were there for glitter and pearls and believed more in the language of the prenuptial agreement than the language of the largely ceremonial oath taking. That was what she had observed. She wasn't far off, although it was a cold, cruel, sweeping generalization.

To her credit, if one can receive credit for such actions, she openly confessed her moves as self-serving, self-centred, and ego based. Her game plan was working. Within six months she would be back to Europe, the continent already conquered or reasonably subdued, ripe for her to plunder the riches and reach new heights of corporate ascension.

They're all going to be pussy whipped over there, I thought.

She wasn't done reciting her plans. "So, now on to Brussels as head of the European group." Her eyes brightened as she riveted her gaze on her target—me. "I could use a solid EVP and a known entity if you're even slightly interested."

Throughout her narrative, I had been flooded with a range of emotions and revelations. Her declaration of a "leave no prisoners" approach to climbing the corporate ladder shook me up more than a little and caused some instantaneous self-reflection. I had been comfortable and content with who we were together and what we were. I also knew that I had measured my own competition level and ambition. I wasn't going to drive to the top. I didn't have the deep ego need or the type of fire that was required. The she-hulk across from me was providing me with a concave window into my own ambition level and comfort zone. At that moment, I believed I had the stuff for a solid number- two or number-three guy in the corporate hierarchy. The stay-at-home defenceman—solid, reliable, stoic. Blocking shots, making hits, and moving the puck up to the gifted scorers, the real playmakers, the finishers. I could also serve as a hell of a plan B in a pinch or in a crisis. Like when the supreme leader or, in this case, the goddess was hit by an errant asteroid or plagued by hemorrhoids. That thought made me smile, and she jumped on it.

"So, Brussels in a year?"

I shook my head.

"Do you think people will see me as a conniving bitch, capable of anything?" She seemed to be genuinely interested in my answer.

I nodded.

Her response should have been a shocker, but it wasn't.

"Some probably do already, maybe most." She snickered before she continued. "That's a legitimate, well-earned perspective. That's okay. I'm good with that. If I were a man, how would I be regarded?" She laughed, full throated, like a neglected, unsatisfied housewife navigating the thrill of her first vibrator. "If I were a man I would be seen as a 'balls to the wall' badass, capable of anything, as competent as hell, and a fierce 'no prisoners, no brides' warrior."

I'm not sure I was following all her metaphors, but she was on point. I asked her if she saw herself as Matilda the Hun.

The vibrator was on full throttle then, and her deep feisty laugh was that of a woman who pleased herself whenever necessary, or just for fun. "That's a good one, Matilda the Hun." She reached across the table and dragged her perfectly manicured nails across the wrist of the hand that was clasping the scotch. "You should come to Brussels. We could have some fun." She had lowered her voice to that husky, erotic, sex-infused level and was almost singing the Dire Straits lyric. "We could have some fun! I'll kick ass and chop heads, and you can bury the bodies."

Her fingers lingered. I had to admit that a power-driven, intellectual, self-confident woman was one hell of an aphrodisiac.

She was reading my mind. I knew that look. "You're thinking about banging me, aren't you?"

I know I flashed a sheepish, "hand in the cookie jar" look, but I answered honestly. "Yes. Yes, I am. Definitely."

"Phillip wasn't much in the sack. He was more of a potato sack." She laughed.

As she did, the word "emasculated" flashed in my brain like a neon sign.

"Phillip is tolerable. He'll do in a pinch." She snickered, her voice husky with sex and laden with intent. "Is that how men talk?"

"They used to, and some still do. Mostly, when they're drunk and not getting laid. At that stage, only their bravado is up, not their dicks. But that's never been my style."

She nodded. "I know. You've always been a gentleman in public and in private. That's one of the many things I loved about you. Always classy. But don't you want to take me right now and bang my brains out? It would be like great revenge sex but not served cold. Served steaming, juicy, and hot as hell. Well, Sean, I'm working myself up." She slid her hand up her thigh and smiled. "Oh, yes. I remember you used to just touch me in a few spots, and I would get so wet, just at your touch."

Although I was more than a little taken back by the turn in our conversation from "come to Brussels" to cumming, I still managed to speak. "I do remember. You weren't wet; you were soaked."

"Drenched," she said, drawing the word out.

"I remember the spots. Just above your left hip, the small of your back, behind your right ear, and the very top of your erotic but not quite erotic spots."

She squirmed. "Sean, you gotta take me. You must want to fuck me silly."

"I do."

"Now. Let's go."

"Let me go to the can first."

"Okay," she said. "But when you get about five steps away, turn around."

My eyes went wide. I knew what was coming next. The *Basic Instinct*, Sharon Stone moment. We had done it four times before, and I remembered them all.

At four steps, I turned back, and she uncrossed and recrossed her legs—slowly. No panties. She had planned this. My lips rose in a smile as my dick stiffened in tribute.

In the can, I had to will my dick down as I pissed. The damn thing was stiffening just from a breath of fresh air and a glimpse of her naughty parts, as the Church Lady from SNL would say. I washed my hands, splashed copious amounts of cold water on my flushed face, and listened to my heart in my chest. I was going to bang her brains out.

I stopped at the coatroom to pick up my jacket and almost asked for hers. I couldn't remember if it was on the back of her chair or not. As I re-entered the dining room, she smiled and motioned for me to slow down as she, once again, uncrossed and crossed her legs. My dick started swelling again. I got to the table with my jacket folded over my arm and covering the lump in my pants. I leaned in until my jacket covered her lap. Then I slipped my hand between her legs and touched her. Her eyes closed as she tilted her head back. She quivered and gasped. "Oh my God."

As my finger stroked her, I whispered behind the centre of her right ear. "Sorry, not tonight. We're not fucking. I have a date. Thanks for the drinks. Good talk. Call me. You have my number."

Then I walked away.

I was maybe ten feet from her table, still semi-erect when I heard her say, "You fuckin' son of a bitch," followed by my glass of McCallan shattering on the floor somewhere behind me. She never had a good throwing motion. She would have to work on that.

As I strode away, Richie Havens singing "Freedom" was echoing in my brain. Perhaps no sex was the best revenge sex, served hot and steamy.

Almost involuntarily, my right hand trailed behind me, and I held it out for her to see, especially my extended index finger.

CHAPTER 40

Call to Faith or Not

I wondered if I should find my faith. Should I even bother? Was I missing it? It wasn't like I woke up every morning and asked, "Where the hell did I put that thing? That thing called faith?"

Because of my humble job in the service industry, many people assumed I wasn't engaged with a faith or a religion. The pious, who were mostly arrogant Caucasian types, at least from what I observed, assumed low-income earners were generally those of little faith.

My faith had to be lying around somewhere in the shaded areas of my mind and heart. Perhaps it had been dispensed to the darker recesses, the rooms where cynicism and non-belief dwelled.

I was almost certain I hadn't missed my faith, but sometimes I wondered. How could I not, seeing as a great many people found solace, comfort, serenity, rapture, forms of conceit, grace, arrogance, superiority, peace, delusion, and safe harbour in their faith? It meant so many things to so many people. Rapture. Bliss. The chosen ones. The true believers who would ascend and inherit the kingdom of their faith. Hell, I had inherited constant aching arches and a wider ass than a person with either a little or a lot of faith would find useful or find solace or comfort from.

I didn't do my famous snap turn, pivot, and gone on my heel and expect to find my faith. I couldn't spike a dinner order and expect faith to be served up, although both of those actions would be handy and expedited paths to faith. Finding faith, I imagined, was more of a rigorous journey.

I loved when people asked if I was practicing my faith. That seemed totally incongruent. I was particularly amused when people told me they were devout practitioners of their faith. To me, faith was faith. No practice required. People either had faith or they didn't. What did they practice? Did they only practice faith when they needed faith? When self-reliance, self-confidence, and self-determination left the building? With or without Elvis? Did the practitioners of faith run into the temple, the mosque, the synagogue, or the church and run plays? Or did they only pull-out faith on game days? On their way to their particular religious shrine, did they get all psyched up for faith and put their game face on? Did they call the plays of faith or was it the "prays" of faith?

Chant #5 "Buddha is the Baddest Ass"

God is Great Flanker Right on hut. As in Jabba the Hut?
Death to the infidels, Suicide Bomber Option Left on one.
Prayer mats out, head down, centre draw, quick snap count.
Bag skate until you find Jesus and your two-hundred-foot game.
Multiple Wives Screen Right, Mormon tight-end formation.

Faith was faith. People didn't lose it or practice it; they just embraced it in their own way.

Leaving our faith behind sure didn't harm my sister and me. In fact, not clinging to our faith, as our mother had fervently recommended when we were young girls, probably saved us.

My father didn't lose his faith entirely, just conveniently. His faith was often drowned in the bottle. That triggered our mother into punting their faith out of her life and then stomping it to death with shrill cries of betrayal. Why had her faith abandoned her?

My father may have dropped his faith publicly at first to fit in, but that didn't work out so well. The adage "to your own self be true" comes to mind. His spirit couldn't survive a split or duality of battling belief and value systems.

My father only applied his faith when it came to my sister and me. Then he taught us the expectations and demands of tight controls, narrow social boundaries, virginal behaviour, and following the commands of faith and our father, which were one and the same as far as we could tell. He preached that there was only one true belief system and corresponding path for us. We tried to follow his rants, as the meek tend to do.

That was until he tried to have intercourse with me, just after my fifteenth birthday. Intercourse. Isn't that such a nice, polite word? Far better than "My old man tried to rape me." Intercourse didn't quite fit the scenario or the reality that he was trying to fuck me, rape me. "Nice, Dad. Good talk. Strong motivational speaking. Really, seriously motivational."

I've heard that Intercourse is a quaint, little Amish village somewhere in Pennsylvania. That Intercourse would be fun to experience, unlike the version of intercourse that Dad wanted me to visit.

I was studying comparative religions as part of my grade-ten elective courses at the time. Although I didn't quite get the Mormons, their book came in handy.

Dear Dad had declared I was an evil temptress. Thirteen to sixteen ounces of Seagram's whisky brings that sort of clarity, wisdom, and pillow talk out in a man.

He shoved me backwards into my bedroom and knocked me to my bed with a roundhouse right. Then he closed the door. My mom was passed out on the couch, and my sister was at a rarely allowed sleepover. Perfect opportunity for some father-daughter bonding. It occurred to me that Dad had some clear premeditation. Get Mom drunk and get his youngest daughter out of the way and then party time.

Well played, Daddy.

As he was undoing his belt and unzipping his pants, he ranted about my sinful acts and disrespectful mouth, which he was about to fill with his salami.

Uh, Dad, we don't eat meat, and we're not Italian.

He was preoccupied with unbuckling, unzipping, and trying to keep his oration on topic, so the justification for his soon-to-be-consummated teaching methods was understood. I had time to wipe the blood from my mouth, slide my hand under my pillow, and grab the Book of Mormon. It was a hardcover edition that Dad had forbidden to enter our house. For that reason, I had hidden it under my pillow, not due to some prurient, sexually enlightened fantasies of Joseph Smith and his multi-wife entourage. Old Joe and the gang didn't get to me in that way. I always hid course materials of a religious nature because my dad, who was about to rape his virgin daughter, had declared that all other religions ranged from aberrant to abhorrent. He defined the Latter-Day Saints as promiscuous devils.

Dad finally managed to free his teaching tool of choice and took one clumsy step forward. His pants were at his knees, and that impediment, along with Mr. Seagram's impact were making his act of sexual predation awkward. Poor Dad.

I, on the other hand, had riveted my whole skeletal structure into a fluid moving machine. Fear and terror will do that. Fight or flight. Flight was not an apparent option. I thought, *Screw flight anyways. This girl is taking the fight route.*

With my feet planted on the floor and my knees bent forward, my torso came up in a solid, abdomen-driven crunch. I rotated through my quads, hips, and shoulders, clasping the Book of Mormon, hardcover version, in both hands in an arching, downward-swinging pendulum on top of Dad's dick. The blow staggered him, and he hit the closed door and bounced forward with his "salami and meatballs" slightly extended and unprotected. I was beginning to get into the Italian theme, despite my vegetarian preferences.

My pendulum reversed direction, and that Mormon testament, hardcover version, caught at least one of Dad's balls and the base of his dick rather nicely on the return swing.

By then he was howling, mostly in fear. It seemed that his rage and anger had fully dissipated. His salami was no longer angry either. It was rather placid, no longer standing and in teaching mode. The Mormons were still angry. *You shouldn't mock or disparage the faith of others, dear Dad.* The Mormons proceeded to pound his face several times.

There was blood. His nose appeared to be broken. He had black—well, actually, multi-hued eyes for the next four weeks. His upper lip required some patchwork, and he nearly bit through the tip of his tongue. Dad's diction was never that clear, so that added infliction to his linguistic ability, effectively silenced him for almost a month. In silence there was reprieve and comfort. Was that part of our faith? If so, that part was a keeper.

I never asked about his salami, and I never saw it again. He never mentioned it either. A conversation we both found no need to expose again, ha ha. He took to locking the bathroom and his bedroom door. Maybe he started those safety measures because he remembered my sweet whispers as he bled onto my bedroom floor. He was cowering, hoping to avoid further lessons from the Book of Mormon, hardcover version, as I whispered in his ear that I would slice his salami clear off if he ever came near me or my sister again.

Take that on faith, Dad.

I constantly worried about him preying on my sister. He worried about the increasingly larger books, hardcover editions, that I was bringing home and the thirty-six-inch steel ruler that I insisted I needed for art. Mostly, I think he worried about the butcher knife that was missing from the kitchen. His worries about the Mormons had diminished. There were other signs of "clear and present danger."

That was why it was so easy to take my sister with me when I got pregnant. On the home front, that decision was never a discussion with our parents. I did leave Dad a softcover version of the Book of Mormon. A parting gift with special father-daughter memories.

By the way, what kind of Indian Muslims named their daughter Delta Dawn, especially after I was named Maurinder Savinder? Jesus, which name was more cruel? Oh, I shouldn't have invoked another faith with that question.

Faith? Was I missing something that might be important to me or to us, to my tight, little circle of Delta Dawn and my daughter?

To reconcile or re-explore my faith was a big question. I had sixty days left on my timeline, and that had become part of my resolve.

CHAPTER 41

Mackin Emerges

My mother was ecstatic. Her joy knew no bounds when I told her of my intentions. I asked her if it would be difficult to set up. Would they even let me in? Accept me?

She was confident of my acceptance, of my being embraced.

She called back in just over an hour. "You're in," she said. "Your immersion starts January first. Your homecoming experience will take about four months, including your journey. You will gain wisdom, culture, and connection. Most importantly, you'll gain yourself. You're young enough to become an important leader to our people. We're different. We were meant to walk the earth differently. You've never even seen our paths, let alone walked them. Most of our people don't follow our path well or fully. You could be someone who illuminates our path, our world, our culture."

"Will I be accepted?" I asked. "Taken in? I've tried to ignore my culture for most of my forty-four years. To be oblivious to my roots. I've exhibited no interest, and worst of all, I've never identified myself as one of our people. Do I even deserve to be accepted?"

"You never denied it, though, and that's very important. You've never spoken falsely about who you are."

"I was never asked. I appear different from our people, and my name isn't of our people. We never lived with our people. So, I was never questioned. You could say I was hiding in plain sight, but that's a bit of a stretch."

"You're one of our people, even though you didn't realize it. The way you conducted yourself, all your actions and all your behaviours mirror the best of our culture. Fierce pride, respect, a focus on group success, giving to others of yourself, carrying yourself with pride and dignity, yet graced with humility and humour. You embody our people's best traits. Now you must discover our ways, immerse yourself in them, become one of our people."

"What if I truly don't belong? What if I can't immerse myself? I don't want to fail you or disappoint our people."

"You won't. You can't, and I won't let you. Less than twenty percent of our people are full blood now, as you are, and that will mean so much to our people. You can become a symbol. Less than ten percent of our people speak our language."

"I don't know if I want to be a symbol."

"Your path will be your path within the grace and wisdom of our people."

"You make it sound mysterious, almost sacred."

"It is a path of connection and sense. Not common sense, because our ways, even within our own people, are not commonly seen, held, or practised. If this is a sacred path, it's sacred because it's steeped in caring. Care for all things and all people. If decency is sacred, then so are our ways."

"Can I truly become one of our people?"

"You already are one of us. You just need to be wrapped in and nurtured by who we are, by our ways, our beliefs, and our history. Come to this simply and openly, my son. Don't overthink it. Let it come into you. Be open."

"There's no naked howling at the full moon at midnight stuff is there?"

We shared a laugh over that. The laughter resonated with warmth and affection and was full of feeling.

"Son, you're humorous. That might be your way. Besides, how good would it feel to be naked at midnight, howling at the full moon? If your spirit is there and your mind is clear, it might be a moment of pure joy, a moment of cleansing, a moment of primal connections and, most importantly, a moment of your own spirit and soul."

"Okay, you're even making being naked at midnight and howling at the moon sound good and almost normal. One condition, though."

"You should have no conditions. This is unconditionally coming to who you are, coming to our people."

"The one condition is this 'naked howling at the moon' stuff can't be a mother-son event."

She responded as I had hoped, with deep laughter and love choking her throat and voice. "I will *definitely* not sign us up for any naked mother-and-son events. Besides, I've already found my path to our people, as will you. To my knowledge, none of our people have chosen a path that included howling at the moon while naked, especially with their mother beside them. But who knows? You might be a first."

"Will you be there?"

"At times, during some ceremonies and prayers. I'll be one of your storytellers. I wish your father was still here to be with us, to be with you."

That choked me up more than a bit. "Did you tell me the stories of our people before? When I was young."

"I told you many stories when you were young. Then your path led you away from our people, guided at that time by your father and me for what we believed were the right reasons. We always intended to bring you home to our culture, our ways, and our people. Your father died before you could return. I chose to remain distant but not spiritually removed from our people to avoid exposing you until you were ready."

"Have you suffered in your separation from our people? You sacrificed that connection for me?"

"I wanted us to go back to our people together. The wait is part of the journey, part of my journey."

"Mother, I love you. We need to talk more about this."

"We will. But let me be the first to say this 'you are Choctaw'. You're a Choctaw brave. You're of Choctaw blood, and in that blood runs Choctaw character and spirit. You're full Choctaw. Past, present, and future. You will find your path to being your true Choctaw self."

"You're making me weep and feel proud of my ancestors even though I know so little about them."

"You'll be proud of your ancestors. You'll become Choctaw in your mind and heart. Choctaw are an ascendant people."

What I learned from my mother about my divergence from our Choctaw Nation came out in long conversations prior to January first. At the age of twelve, I had been scouted by several high schools in the area. I was a football prodigy. My strengths were my relentlessness and my intuition. My size, speed, and strength were all near the top end of the scale. I played hard and fast. A newspaper story said I got to the ball carrier or quarterback "strong, quick, and angry." I also played offence as a running back and was very good in that position as well. Defense was my preference, though, as hitting and outthinking offences was my true football love.

We were living forty miles away from our reserve. Dad was an engineer, and my mother was a lawyer. We were upper middle class. Dad and Mother never denounced their Choctaw status; they just didn't mention it. Back in the 1960s when they were going to the University of Mississippi, being Indian, being a Choctaw, wasn't a good thing. Our tribe had largely lost its way to drugs, alcohol, and the futility of reservation life. Dad was a great track athlete and got scholarships. Mother had some of the best scores in the state in terms of aptitude and entrance testing. She was also the valedictorian of her high school class because of her top grades. Her scholarships were paltry compared to those of lesser white academics and Dad's. A fast Indian was way more valuable than a smart Indian.

Both sets of my grandparents moved off the reserve to escape blinding poverty. They started working menial jobs. All four ended up at supervisory levels. My grandparents reached a lower-middle-income level of housing and success. All four were full-blood Choctaw and had two children. My grandparents never returned to the reserve, both sets had a child who did. My grandparents outlived those two children, as their children couldn't defeat the prevailing demons of reserve life. I lost an aunt and an uncle I never knew. The other two ascended off reserve. Those two, my parents, met as teens and married as sophomores at the U of M.

The original plan was for me to spend summers as a Choctaw on the reserve with cousins when I turned thirteen. Two things prevented that. The year before I was to go, two football players from the reserve were being touted as top five candidates in the statewide recruitment ranking. Jimmy Clawfinger was the top-rated wide out at six feet four inches and 180 pounds. He won silver in the one-hundred and two-hundred-yard races at the state level. With hands like glue, he had a crazy wingspan and was as tough as leather.

Jimmy Bearclaw was a fighter, an actual Golden Gloves heavyweight. At six feet two inches and 235 pounds, he loved putting a "hurt" on anyone who moved on the other side of the line. He was regarded as a man among boys and feared throughout the high school league. They played for the Central Choctaw Chiefs and won state finals for mid-size schools. After all the great recruitment talk, they both received only partial university scholarships, about fifty percent of that received by white kids with far less talent. The tribe matched the scholarship funds, and those two great Indian football players were off to the U of M.

Allegedly, they performed badly on the field, although they never got to start all season. Off the field, they allegedly fit in poorly, behaved terribly, were socially inept, and their grades were horrendous. They were back on the reserve by Christmas. No other schools came calling, not even junior colleges.

The official statistics in the football annual indicated there might have been some talent.

> **Clawfinger, Jimmy**
> Position—Wide Receiver
> Vital Statistics—6'4" 180 lbs.
> Games Played—2, with 22 minutes total playing time

Game Statistics
7 Receptions
132 yards gained
3 touchdowns

Bearclaw, Jimmy
Position—Linebacker
Vital Statistics—6"2" 235 lbs.
Games Played—2, with 29 minutes total playing time

Game Statistics
12.5 tackles, 8 solo tackles
1 interception for a 45 yards TD
2 knockdowns, 3 sacks

The two Jimmys were athletic freaks. They only played in two away games. It wouldn't do to start or even substitute an Indian into a home game at good old U of M. Their teammates, the few who weren't racist or biased against Indians, loved them, and so did the offensive coordinator, who cited the discrimination against the two Jimmys as a primary reason for why he left the school at the end of that season for a head coaching position at a top Division I school in California.

The two Jimmys never had a chance. The head coach didn't want a disruption in his program. The athletic director had forced the recruitment as being good for the school's image.

The two Jimmys received zero academic guidance, personal counselling, or assistance of any kind. They were lost souls. Their initiation and hazing included a mock scalping. Their heads were shaved. Throughout the hazing, their teammates played on plastic tom-toms and wore cheap Indian chief "war bonnets," purchased at the local five-and-ten store.

The second thing that pre-empted my Choctaw indoctrination at age thirteen was a huge drug bust involving roughly $30,000 in weed, hash, and cash that occurred on the edge of the reserve. Four Choctaws were arrested and tried, and they eventually served prison terms ranging from four to seven years.

The same undercover task force scored another drug bust worth almost $1.4 million in weed, meth, heroin, LSD, guns, and cash. Nine white men were charged. Three served time, ranging from one to three years. Ah, Mississippi justice in 1986.

At that point, Dad and Mother decided to keep our Choctaw heritage on the back burner, turned down real low. My grandparents agreed. So, as kids we grew up primarily in white schools with a few blacks and Hispanics mixed in. Our parents were professionals, and the name Mackin excluded any possibility or thought that I could be Indian. My mother's maiden name was Shaw. It had been shortened and changed from "Old Squaw" by a thoughtful Baptist minister a couple of generations back. And after all, Choctaws weren't professional-calibre individuals like my parents.

It worked in terms of getting me a full-ride scholarship, academic guidance, and a starting position as a freshman. It didn't work in terms of me being me, a Choctaw, or my embracing our hereditary cultural pride and dignity. Sacrifices were made. Sacrifices that needed to be righted.

We decided to hold a press conference on January 2. The media release read: "University of Mississippi football alumnus to make major announcement about scholarships and internships at his Canadian sports camp for underprivileged talented local and Choctaw youth athletes."

The big reveal shocked the hell out of everyone, including and especially the current executive director for Choctaw university programs and students. The chief and the Choctaw councillors in attendance knew some of my plans, mostly about the scholarship program. The only Choctaw fully aware of my full immersion into our culture was the elder who had accepted that responsibility. He had been preparing and guiding me along the way.

The board, the athletic director, and all the other folks in attendance—most of them white—were stunned into silence. We live-streamed the event and invited colleagues I had worked with in media across Canada. The Canadian media presence in the room was significant, even though it largely consisted of stringers and full-time sports reporters in the US for college bowl games and NFL playoffs.

We composed individualized emails to arrive in people's mailboxes at 11:57 a.m., three minutes before the press conference, which started precisely at twelve. The recipients had all been notified to check their emails at precisely 11:57 a.m. and to stay quiet until 12:15 p.m.

The shock and awe were off the charts. Exactly what we wanted. I read my press release verbatim.

"Good morning, Chief, university dignitaries, alumni, and friends. I'm here to announce ten annual summer scholarships and ten internships at my 'Mackin It Real' camp on Lake Stanton in Port Stanton, Ontario, Canada. These scholarships and internships will be offered to ten young men from town and the surrounding area and ten young braves from the Choctaw reserve.

"Details on the application and selection process will follow. All twenty young men will be required to be completely substance free for three months prior to the camp, starting on June twenty-fourth. All twenty young men will attend Choctaw culture and language classes. They will spend time learning the local Ojibway culture in Canada as well."

I paused to look around the room and saw the positive impact that the announcement was having. There were smiles and nods of approval. The Choctaw program coordinator gave me an enthusiastic two thumbs-up. I had learned that the man was not Choctaw, and in his four years in the position, he had never once visited the reservation.

"At this time, I would also like to share my heritage with all of you," I continued. "I'm one hundred percent full-blood Choctaw, as is my mother, my deceased father, and all four of my grandparents. My family chose to blend into white society. It was a choice we did not make lightly."

By then the room was a mixture of stunned white faces and proud Choctaw faces. Reporters were scribbling notes, and if they hadn't already been recording, they were turning on recording devices.

"Our family chose a path that would allow us to prosper to a degree far greater than an environment of almost enforced poverty and hopelessness. Our choice was to try to survive, if not thrive, in a climate of bigotry and racist beliefs and behaviours. We succeeded on one front, blending and rising. But we failed on the most important front in not being open and showing pride in our Choctaw blood and heritage. On that front, we will make personal and communal amends."

I paused again to read the room. The whites, especially the higher-ranking university officials, were still reeling with the revelation of my being Choctaw. I saw embarrassment and shock in their eyes, and I hadn't even delivered the big blow yet.

"Details on the scholarship and internship application and camp programs will be distributed along with some Choctaw history and, very importantly, the story of the two Jimmys. At the end of the two Jimmys' story, I've added some of my own experiences here at the university. Those were not pleasant as a Choctaw. Bigotry and racism against the Choctaw and all Indians were rampant, something I heard and witnessed daily. The administration didn't do anything to stop or improve the on-campus experience or accessibility to the university for Choctaws. Please read and distribute the material as you see fit. Please pay attention to the details of the two Jimmys' experience at this university. It explains, but it will never excuse, why my family, as Choctaws, didn't reveal our heritage, our cultural identity. Moving on, we would appreciate your help in recommending young men for 'Mackin it Real'. Personally, I'll be going to our reserve for a four-month immersion into our Choctaw culture, traditions, and language. I come to my people late in life with humility and the hope for forgiveness."

The audience appeared to be spellbound. The university officials were staring at the floor.

"Today I will finish with three points. Fellow U of M alumni, thank you for your attendance today. Your help in providing scholarship funds would be greatly appreciated. This would be a great sign from the U of M community, recognizing a history of discrimination and bias against the Choctaw people and many other creeds, colours, and ethnic groups.

"Second, my mother and I have been consulting elders and have sought their advice, forgiveness, and permission to enter our culture. We thank them for their grace, dignity, and forgiveness.

"Finally, I repeat I am one hundred percent full-blood Choctaw and extremely proud of that. We won't be taking any questions today."

The end of my statement was met with stunned silence. It was more than awkward. Then some staggered applause followed, with intermittent participation, especially by the U of M officials and dignitaries. They had just been called out for their history of failing to address systemic racism by an alumnus who was in their hall of fame.

My mother and I strode from the room with our heads up, making full eye contact. We didn't engage in any handshakes. However, I veered close enough to the executive director of Choctaw programs to whisper a single word: "Resign."

We had recruited four Choctaw students from the university to hand out our material. They knew nothing about the program and hadn't even seen the material, as it was sealed in envelopes. They were as stunned as everyone else. A babble of befuddled exchanges was just starting as the doors of the media room closed behind us.

The Chief came out of the media room first and then circled in front of us. "Holy bat shit, Robin, is this all for real?"

I smiled. "If that's a traditional Choctaw greeting or saying, I'm rather surprised!"

"Mr. Mackin, this is so great. We've spent so much time with this university, trying to be white Indians, and you just blew them out of the water. We fight like hell to get our kids into this university and keep them in." He was smiling, but his eyes were watery.

"Chief, I want to help in that fight, if you'll let me back in to be part of our people."

"A full-blooded warrior will always be embraced and forgiven. Welcome back. You have a lot of learning to do."

"Don't I know it," I said.

"Let's get out of here and get to the reserve," my mother said, taking my arm.

The reporters were just coming through the doors. My mother asked the chief to go back and bring the four students out to the reserve and say nothing to the media. The reporters were circling and asking us questions, but we walked in silence out into the sunlight. An elder was waiting, and my immersion began.

CHAPTER 42

Guy Out, Sean In

First order of business. Following a brief workout, shower, shave, and a fruit smoothie, I called Gina. It was only 6:30 a.m., quite early, before sunrise, still dark. Okay, moving from dark to light. How wonderfully symbolic. But Gina picked up on the first ring.

"You know how to keep a girl waiting. God, this is Sean, isn't it?" Her voice was breathy, full, and vibrant. I smiled into my phone as she giggled. "Say something. Say anything."

I couldn't help myself. I started to sing. "In your eyes. The love, the heat, in your eyes."

"Singing? My goodness! Are you feeling well, or are you expiring on your expiry date?"

"No, I'm thriving. And you?"

"Well, February twenty-eight started about seven hours ago, and I had this romantic idea that you would knock on my door at 12:01."

"I wanted to call, but I didn't dare think of coming over. Alice would have kicked the crap out of me."

"You remembered her name. That's somewhat impressive. I hope you don't think I've been hanging around waiting for my phone to ring for forty-four days. Or are you that sure of yourself?"

"In my mind I continually see you through that glass door in your foyer, with something in your eye and Alice comforting you as she glares at me. It's become an unforgettable moment that's seared into my brain. Forty-four days and you remembered the expiry date. Now *that's* impressive."

"Not really, I just nonchalantly copied it into my appointments app on my phone, and it popped up at midnight."

"Nonchalantly? Okay, if you say so."

I heard her giggling, probably with her hand covering her mouth and hiding her smile but not the flashes in her eyes.

"I'm not going to be nonchalant. On an expiry date, a person needs to act fast and firmly. Boldly, as a Brit might say. Those poor, misunderstood Brits."

"Sympathy for the Brit? That's like sympathy for the devil coming from you. You might not be as expired or as sour as expected. It seems you've turned a corner."

"Yeah, sympathy for the Brit has to do with my Sharon Stone moment, but that's a story for another day."

"Okay, Sean from 'Say Anything' through to 'Basic Instinct,' get off the movie kick, and say what you have to say."

"That's a lyric from a song in 'Once.'"

"Sean."

"Gina."

"My patience is expiring."

"Are you free for dinner tonight?"

"What happened too fast, firm, and boldly? Try again."

"Are you free for breakfast?"

"Better."

"My place or yours?"

"Mine. I'll alert security. Alice will probably let you in if I give her fair warning."

Alice was at the desk, and she buzzed me in, watching me with the definitive hairy eyeball.

There weren't many words. There was urgency. It was a collision of needs, a crush of passion. Afterward, we lay beside each other. I couldn't control myself. I was laughing out loud.

Gina started laughing too. "What are you laughing about Sean?"

"Fast and firm," I replied.

"Boldly," she said, then we both laughed as she folded into my arms. Then we started up again. Slower, longer.

We were lying there catching our breath afterward when she started laughing again.

"What?"

"Rule Britannia!"

"Screw you."

"You just did."

We both laughed. Gina laid her head on my chest. Everything felt great. I might have nodded off for a few minutes.

"Where's my breakfast?" Gina asked.

"I'm a lover, not a short-order cook."

"Well, you better serve me up something, lover boy, or all of this is going off the menu."

"In that case I'm on kitchen duty immediately."

"Sean, is this something?"

Instantly, I had that male moment. I think it's instinctive. The thoughts about what to say. The quick joke, the calming platitude, the reassuring but trite gesture, all those male barricades to feelings, but I didn't go there. "Yes, this is something. Don't ask me for details. I don't know them yet, but you drove me to this moment, our moment, because you're something. Something substantive and grand. And Guy is expiring in your presence to become something better. With the hope that time with you is now centre stage."

"You had me at 'this is something.'" She lifted her head, kissed me, and then put her forefinger on my lips to quiet me. "Enough said, Sean. More than enough and more than good enough. Let's shower up and go out to a diner. I know a good one."

"Shower sex is usually good sex."

It was wet on wet, great sex, clean sex.

We arrived at GoHo's just before noon to find out Mo was just arriving for her shift. We waited for her over coffee.

Mo came toward my table, maybe *our* table now, in her typical full Mo bravado mode.

"What are you two having? Bangers and mash? Eggs over easy with sausage? You're both grinning like school kids, so either you just got laid or you won the lottery. By the way, GoHo's house rules, waitresses get a minimum fifteen-percent of all lottery winnings, but unfortunately, certain waitresses aren't allowed to do threesomes. Part of my faith thing, I think, although I really don't know for sure, as I haven't been practicing—my faith, that is, or threesomes, for that matter."

"You're hilarious," I replied, "and does your faith prohibit practicing threesomes or is it that you haven't been practicing threesomes? And just a wild stab in the dark here. You're not Mormon, are you?"

"We all know that I'm hilarious, Guy, and that I haven't been practicing threesomes or couplings, but I have been known to play solo from time to time. You know, just to keep my hand in my own business, so to speak. Now I know for sure you got laid, Guy, being so smiley and attempting to be witty. Gina, why oh why would you lower your standards so drastically?"

"Bad dry spell, Mo you know. Only oasis in the desert sort of thing."

"Tell me about dry spells. My nickname is Mojave."

We all laughed.

"Mo, my name is Sean."

"Really? No shit. Sean?"

"No, Mo, just Sean."

"Nice. Sensitive but still a manly moniker."

"We need two GoHo's Grandad specials, eggs easy over, rye toast, sausage not ham, and more coffee."

Pivot. Gone.

I couldn't read the meaning of the look on Mo's face prior to her trademark departure.

Gina caught Mo's look too. "You know, Mo has or had a thing for you."

I'm sure I looked a little dumbfounded as I responded. "No, I don't think so. We're just friends. She's kind to everyone."

Gina shook her head. "Sean, you're special to her, as is Lisa and that football guy."

"Smackin' Mackin you mean."

"Yep, that's the one. I bet if you asked Mo who her favourite customers were, the three of you would be on the Mo podium. The 'Mo-dium.' Medal winners."

I didn't know what to say, and a slightly awkward moment of silence fell across our table. As I thought of the meaning of me thinking in terms of "our" table, I looked across at Gina and smiled—from ear to ear, I'm sure.

"Something amusing you, Sean? Like your popularity with all these women in GoHo's, or are you just smitten with me?"

"Smitten? Absolutely!"

"Anything else?"

"Yep, just this bewildering wonderful sense that this, you and I, is right, is grand."

"Grand? The inner Brit in you keeps surfacing. I feel the same and very free and giddy. It's not just the post-coitus high, is it?"

"How clinical of you! No, there's nothing fleeting or temporary about how I'm feeling. The intimacy might have been a bit, well, I won't lie to myself here, a significant build-up of longing and passion that I've been accumulating during this space and time between us. At least I think I have."

"Sean, let's not dissect this. Just let it be and become what it becomes, but I have an immediate long-term hope."

"What's that?"

"I hope this becomes an annual event—our expiration-date anniversary."

"That sounds grand."

Mo arrived with our food. "Look at you two! The after-sex glow over the Granddad's special. No walk of shame for you two. Almost feel I should give

Guy—I mean Sean—the senior's discount. You didn't hurt the old guy, did you Gina?"

"I think he'll be okay. Ask him tomorrow."

Once again, a round of laughter.

Pivot. Gone.

"Will this become our expiry-day anniversary meal?" I asked. "The Grandad's special? The name lacks a certain romantic zest and fervour."

"Well, if we have a morning like this morning on this anniversary, we'll need a lot of nourishment," Gina replied.

We smiled, ate, and stared at each other, mostly in a happy silence.

Sean in, Guy out. Left behind. No trailing hand.

During the run-up to my expiration date, my birthday, I had also mapped out my career trajectory. I wasn't by any means content or complacent. I had end-game goals both corporately and personally, and my relationship with Gina was at the centre of it all.

I would leave some things behind, not out of necessity or loss or failure but from a clear-headed choice. I didn't want to catch or dangle a trailing hand. I wanted to walk side by side. Despite some intriguing roads or diversions, I had chosen a path that would be meaningful, wonderful, and important.

Like Lisa.

CHAPTER 43

Lisa Forward

April 1–4, Massey Hall, sold out all four nights! No April fools around here, folks! Massey Hall! The site of Gordon Lightfoot's annual concerts and Neil Young's live recording! I love that album.

We booked a pre-tour show at the El Mocambo on March 27. I always liked that number. The Big M, Frank Mahovlich, number twenty-seven. I liked him even when he won Stanley Cups with the Leafs' archrivals, the Habs. I never saw him play, but my dad told me that he was fantastic. Funny, that's the one thing my dad loved that stuck with me. Maybe it had something to do with being a Canadian, that generation-to-generation passing down of love and loyalty to an original-six NHL team.

The El! The legendary venue held 350 patrons. The legendary antics of the Stones and the recording of four of their songs live at the El Mocambo. The Keith Richards drug bust. Twenty-five Mounties surrounding his bed. Really? The Stones said the four songs recorded at the El were "the heart and soul" of their *Love You Live* album. All this was coursing through my veins as we ramped up for "show" readiness. Our guest list had been carefully crafted.

We were in full-fledged rehearsals of everything. The lighting, the sound, the stage, the road crew, the tour bus—everything was coming into place. Except my essential wingman. The absolutely essential tour manager. The guiding light, the necessary anchor who would provide stability and a rudder to keep us on course as we set our sails was not yet in place. I was handling too much, but I couldn't let go. My last manager for a tour of this magnitude had been my ex-husband. That tour had been a disaster both artistically and financially. During that tour I was completely dependent on cocaine and alcohol. I had never intended to rip off Janis Joplin's voice, but by the end of the tour, that was all I had left, the difference being that Joplin's voice was real in its growling gravel and grit, and mine was just a guttural gasp for survival.

I needed to stay straight and remain focused on my music. I needed someone honest, trustworthy, organized, and great at connecting and building relationships. A good tour manager had to be a loveable but caring prick, alternately tough and soft as the situation dictated.

We finished rehearsal and a run-through staging at Massey Hall early on the evening of March 21. I cast off several invitations from band members and some of our technicians for dinner and walked the three or so miles to GoHo's. I thought Sean might be there, and it would be nice to see him. He was a good man but not likely to be my man. I felt that it had to be his choice, not mine.

The alone time on the walk felt good. I had to admit that the time alone at home at night in bed also felt good. Focus is strength, and was I ever focused. Laser beam Lisa! I felt incredibly strong. I was self-identifying, figuring out who I was, what had shaped me, and most importantly, who I wanted to become.

I had been dating white men for most of my life only because they hadn't been black men trying to be white. I hadn't been embracing my own blackness because my mother's blackness wasn't fully authentic. I didn't want to play black or play white. I wanted to play me. My music got me there. So often early in my career I heard people say, "But she sounds so white." People in my immediate musical circle would say, "You write lyrics and music that are so white." They were right. "You're right, you're right, you're bloody well right, and you know you got a right to say." Right, Supertramp?

I wrote, I write white, right?

"Me, I don't care anyway." Wrong, Supertramp, I did care. Deeply.

I couldn't say that my songs didn't sound white, but they sounded like me. They were of me. They came from me. All that was right.

The walk felt wonderful. I started humming "Blinded by the Light," as sung by Springsteen as I thought about the transition from creating to performing. Creating was crafting, structuring, layering, breaking down, adding on, and fine tuning. Creating the finished work was a nuanced sculpting with the help of collaborators.

Then I would perform. The physicality, the staging, the theatrics, the lights, the sound and movement. Like an ice skater or an ice dancer, I would be judged on technical merit and artistic impression. The audience, my fans, would have mostly bought into the technical merit of my songs before the concert. They would have listened to the singles multiple times on the radio, streaming, or maybe even on CD.

In the next month, they might see and hear me in a guest appearance on a talk show. I always found such performances stunted and limited in terms of movement, my movement anyway.

My songs didn't call for dancers. Choreography wasn't in my wheelhouse or what I thought best expressed or represented my music. The two backup singers and I would engage in some low-level symmetrical movement based on the feel of the music. I'd play guitar on fourteen songs and violin on eight songs out of the planned twenty-two song playlist. We envisioned the concert at just under two hours, hopefully with a couple of encores. Movement. My movement. It was my moment, and it was all about my movement, my forward momentum. My movement. My moment.

I asked for a plank, a narrow thirty-foot strip straight out into the heart of the audience. That wasn't quite possible at Massey Hall, but the staging would give that impression. For the first time I wanted to walk into the audience and have them surround me with only a thin lifeline back to my band. That worried me, but at the same time, it didn't worry me. How would I get from point A to point B? By moving from the heart of the stage to the heart of the audience. Then what would I do when I get there? I would walk the plank. Or more likely strut. Or maybe dance, shuffle, or boogie. The music would propel me however it chose, and that would be more than okay.

When I reached the end of the plank, I'd be there by myself, and the journey would become real. Really real.

All the rehearsals accounted for movement. Lighting, sound, mics, backdrop, stage construction, audience seating, everything was affected by the building of that plank.

Often in my music career I heard comments like, "You sure don't move out there like a black girl" or "For a black girl, you dance pretty white." They weren't intended to be mean or racist, just a comparative statement that was true. I was certainly more Linda Ronstadt than Tina Turner. When my sleepovers were with a bunch of suburban, middle-class white girls, the outcome was middle-class white girl dance moves. I never took any of those remarks as overt racism or stereotyping, but they were definitely accurate. They mostly came from fellow black musicians. I knew how I was going to move. It was going to be me. Like a teenage girl primping for the prom. I was practicing my moves in the mirror at home. My stage manager was worried about building a plank that I wasn't going to use, which would be expensive in terms of construction and takedown while at the same time taking out prime revenue-generating seating.

My movement? Watch me live!

My stage manager wasn't convinced. How could she be? She hadn't seen my bathroom and hallway mirror moves.

My moves weren't Beyoncé or Britney stuff. Not even close. That wasn't me or my music. Maybe a leg-over-leg crossover strut. Take that, Shania. More likely a full-forward stumble. A Joe Cocker stagger, limbs all akimbo. Some frenetic strumming of Etheridge-like playing. Who knows? It would all fall out in the moment, and it would be breathtakingly real and raw.

The door to GoHo's swung open as a couple emerged with sparks in their eyes and lustful intent in their thighs. *Oh, Lisa, such a romantic.* My booth was open, as it should have been. Wow, I was feeling good. Like I knew I would. The rush of creating, adapting, and evolving my music had never felt so full and intense. Life was loving me, or I was loving life.

GoHo's was an oasis for me, despite the clatter and clashing reverberations of competing conversations. I always derived comfort from the diner's familiarity. Sometimes, even in comfortable and familiar places, troubling things take place, like dropping Mackin. "There's a fumble on table ten and, oh no! She dropped him like a dirty napkin. Flag on the play. That's a flagrant personal foul! Fifteen yards for unsportsmanlike conduct. That's going to leave a mark."

Mo was headed my way. "Going solo tonight, are we Ms. Rock Star? No entourage?"

"I gave the staff the evening off."

"How gracious of you. Now order fast because this fine young waitperson is having that door hit her equally fine derriere in thirty minutes or less."

"The servant class has risen. What sparks your Mo-ness this evening, if I may ask?"

"Job interview tomorrow. Serious interview. Fourth go 'round."

"That's great. Fantastic! Congratulations."

"A little premature with the congrats, Lady Lisa, but thank you."

"Probably not premature, Mo. A fourth interview is job-offer time."

"You think?"

"Yes. Who's it with, and what's the job?"

"You know the soup guys, the guys with ties? The owner is one of their sons. The job is a general manager position, not an assistant and not a secretary or an administrator but a manager."

"That sounds fantastic! That's right in the sweet spot of your talent. I see you orchestrate the organized chaos of GoHo's every shift. You create and drive the whole environment of human interactions and production."

"Maybe, but it would be a huge change. They would be taking a gigantic leap of faith. It means changing from the chaos at GoHo's to coordinating the administration of four factories with over four hundred employees. That's not just a leap of faith; that's a moon shot of faith."

"Mo, a very important friend of mine once told me, when I was embarking into fashion with Mackin, 'competency travels well.' He was saying that about both Mackin and me. He was right, and I'm right about this and you."

"Thanks for the vote of confidence, Lisa. It means a lot. A nice little boost for my rocket shot to the moon."

"I'm not trying to be crass or pry, but how's the cash in this job? You do know this family and they're good people, but this is business."

"Nosebleed dollars for your humble serving class. Seventy-five thousand, four weeks of vacation, full benefit package, including dental, and a three-to-one match on all pension contributions."

"Well, that's not just good. That's great!"

"They say it's on the low side. They're quite honest about that. This job would normally go to someone internal, likely a veteran senior manager from one of the plants. Probably a white guy in his late forties or early fifties, and they would pay him one and a quarter. You gotta love their transparency."

"Yes, honesty and transparency can never be underrated or undervalued."

"They say—and I believe them—that everything in their company is about performance, teamwork, and building cohesiveness. They say salary will be fast-tracked to outcomes. Deliver and ascend."

"That's unbelievable, Mo! They've made their offer. Tomorrow is a test of your belief in yourself. This meeting isn't really an interview. It'll be all about your courage and competency for the moon shot. What you need for tomorrow is faith in yourself. The faith you've demonstrated day in and day out. Leaving your parents when pregnant, with your little sister in tow. Raising your daughter and sister while you ground it out here at GoHo's. Educating yourself in night classes, online courses, and Saturday morning classes. You don't have to acquire faith or search for faith. You're the walking, talking epitome of faith in yourself. You can do this standing on your head."

"Yes, but then my skirt would be over my head, and my fine derriere and exotic area would be blowing in the wind. Thank you very much, Mr. Bob Dylan."

"Mo, you're too much!"

"Order before I cry and ruin the façade of my strong general-manager competence."

"The western sandwich on whole wheat with fries and chocolate skimmed milk, if it's cold."

"All three cold or just the milk?"

Mo was on a journey. GoHo's wouldn't be the same. I knew about the Hood family's offer and their generosity—Mo had told me. I loved the feeling of forward movement for Mo, Mackin, and me. Forward to his past. What a bold move. What courage. Who knew? I didn't. I never thought to explore. How shallow of me. I bought the whole American university football star, CFL gladiator, sports broadcaster, humanitarian, philanthropist, and fashion maven. Well, sort of on the last one. I never probed deep into his origins or the source of his drive. I never even thought about his racial identity, his ethnicity, or his cultural background. I never asked what had shaped his character. He never volunteered much about his upbringing or his family in Mississippi except his love for his mother and the vacuum left by his dad's passing.

I loved his whole package. Not that package—okay, that package as well. I mean his composition, his demeanour, his attitude. Mackin was authentic and genuine, yet everything he was, was built on a false narrative. Well, not exactly false, just not revealed. Some media outlets had called him a "Fauxcasian," as in a false white person. That had come out as a sort of a counterbalance to the wave of "Pretendians" who had surfaced in recent years. The flood of white people in the arts, especially literature and music, as well as academics and politics, pretending to be Indian was stunning. White people seeing an advantage to claiming Indian status in the States or First Nations or some form of Indigenous status in Canada. How despicable and calculating. It was strange, complex stuff.

I wondered if he was seeing or needed a therapist. Probably not. And who would I be to suggest therapy? Not only was I a broken girl and woman, but I had also danced forever on the stage of pretense. I had broken his heart and spirit, at least for a bit. Maybe I was the bump on the road or more likely the pothole that took him off road and sent him careening to his past. Then again, maybe I was thinking too highly of my impact.

Full speed. Godspeed to you, Mackin. Forward to your future through the past, Marty McFly. Go deep. Discover. I wish you joy in that, my Mackin.

What a good man! I knew that instantly and intimately. I felt lucky and blessed for that. People judged him by the so-called false front he lived with for decades rather than challenging the comfort of their own biased, stereotypical grand illusion. I knew Mackin and I weren't meant to be. Our forward was separate and in reverse. Yet we had both embarked on the journey to self.

"Here you go. Comfort food of the highest order. You need comfort, Ms. Lisa? You sure look contemplative and self-absorbed."

"Before you accept that offer and sign the deal, Mo, give yourself twenty-four hours to think about it."

"Why? Should I negotiate? You think there's something better coming? You think the two Gordons deal is better for me? Why would I wait?"

"Just wait. Breathe. Smile. Enjoy the time to reflect on where you're heading. Savour. Reflect. Think. Then and only then should you commit."

"You didn't answer one of my questions."

"Not my job to answer those questions. That's up to you. You know you. You know your circumstances and options. You know what you need and want. You'll make the right choice. Just take the time."

"Okay. This is too much about me. Let's talk about you and Guy—I mean Sean."

"What about me and Sean? How do you know his name?"

"Shh...Can a girl join you for dinner? My shift ended ten minutes ago at eight, but I wanted to chat with you. Just some girl talk."

"One hundred percent. Get your fine derriere planted."

"Great. I had faith you would say yes. My cheeseburger, fries, and chocolate milk are waiting."

Mo sat down, and we took a few moments to settle in with our food before I popped the big question. "How do you know Guy's real name is Sean?"

"He told me today at noon at the start of my shift."

"Wait, Sean was in for lunch?"

"Well, they ordered the Grandad's special from the breakfast menu, but it was noon."

"Wait, *they?* Who were they? Work companions?"

"Just one companion and definitely not work related."

"Spit it out, Mo. Who and why?"

"Well, the *who* was the vivacious, curvaceous Gina. The *why?* I can only surmise and suggest to you that they just came from a session of finding intensive intimate knowledge of each other."

"As in carnal knowledge?"

"You nailed it, Jack Nicholson."

"Are you sure?"

"They were glowing like residents of Chernobyl without the radioactivity or hair loss."

"Wow, that is news. Good for them!"

"And how does that make you feel, Lisa? I mean, I thought you and Guy—I mean Sean—were heading for a bedding."

"I thought that was a possible outcome, Mo, no question. And thanks for being so indirect and tactful with the summary of my potential sex life."

Mo shrugged. "Sometimes blunt is good. Well, how's the news settling?"

"Actually, it's all okay. Honestly, I was just thinking that neither Sean nor Mackin were going to be the man for me."

"You know, probably a good ninety-five percent of the women who frequent GoHo's would be ecstatic with either or both of those men."

"You're not suggesting Mackin and Sean are a tag team and into three-ways, are you?"

"I'm shocked you could say such a thing. That's raunchy even for me!"

"Just lightening the mood, Mo. Knowing Mackin the way I do, and sensing Sean's makeup, I think ninety-nine percent of women would be lucky to partner with either of those guys. They're not perfect, but they're good, decent men."

"I agree. Sometimes it makes me sad that they don't see me that way."

"What do you mean by that?"

"That they don't see me as a partner, a companion, as a woman they can desire."

"I see all kinds of men respond to your banter and your personality. Their eyes trail you from the moment you turn and head off to spike their order at the counter and then all the way back."

"Really? You notice that?"

"They notice you, and you know it. Don't be coy."

"But not Mackin and Sean. Not men of their calibre."

"Of that calibre? You haven't fully discovered what calibre you're capable of partnering with. You certainly haven't settled in the short or the long term given all the 'come-ons' you've handled here."

"No, that's true. I'm not ready to seek, let alone settle. I need to find out what the forward Mo can be. In this launching out, what will the future Mo become? When I know who I can be then I'll know who I want to be with."

"Well said, Mo. It's similar to why I've taken the deep solo dive into my music. To find me, maybe the best of me, and who I can become. That's my forward march."

"I love that, Lisa. The forward march. Forward to who we'll become, and on that future field is where we'll find our companions."

"Exactly! Or not!"

We both laughed, then raised our milk glasses and toasted our forward selves.

"Mo, I have a thought."

"Another one? Busy night in that head of yours. So?"

"Wouldn't it be something if our forward paths were a journey we could take together?"

"You mean as partners? Not as, what's the colloquial term they've been using lately? As companions?"

"No, Mo, I don't row the boat that way. I mean going forward as business partners."

"How and in what world?"

"The world that's beginning very soon. But I need to think it through and construct this notion, this inspiration I'm having."

"Well, you have my full attention."

"After your interview tomorrow, can you please come directly to my office?"

"Okay."

"I'll have a very concrete alternative for you to consider."

"So, Ms. Lisa, another toast. A very simple toast. Forward."

"To forward!"

"One more thing. I just have to say."

"Let's have it, Mo, but if this is some of your grand humour, don't share it when I'm drinking my milk. There would be something wrong, like a crack in the universe, if a black girl snorted brown milk out her nose."

"Well, that's the sort of the thing that happens when you get into colours. Here we are, a black girl and a brown girl from very different stations in life, talking about moving forward, and that feels incredibly right and good. So maybe there is a tiny crack in the universe that's moving us forward at the same time."

CHAPTER 44

Sean's Path

Everything felt so solid and substantial. Gina and I were moving rapidly into the journey of each other. The flow and feeling of our relationship seemed so natural. I didn't realize what a guard I'd put up. Now I felt carefree. Work was good, incredibly good. My approach was transforming from seriously serious to just serious, down a notch. All matters were no longer consequential, were not the singular determinants of outcomes, and all were not worth addressing or breaking a mental sweat over. It was not natural for me to let go like that. Being seriously serious was hard work and once established as my "go to" approach a hundred percent of the time, it was hard to throttle back. But I was. People had noticed the slow transformation. Those closest to me in terms of knowing my pace and normal volume of work could see it wasn't easy for me not to be me. They had nicknamed me "Captain Serious," like Jonathan Toews, the captain of the Chicago Blackhawks. I took that as a compliment, as Toews had captained the Hawks to three Stanley Cups before he was thirty. Even while not being me, I was still as serious as the sunrise about rising every day and getting it done.

I was going out for dinner and drinks, which I never do, with a group of peers. We were all at roughly the same level on the corporate totem pole. We were also roughly the same age, and among the five of us, two were females. We had pre-dinner cocktails and free-flowing wine with the meal. The mood was celebratory. We had just wrapped up and signed off on the year-end financials and the annual report. We had enjoyed a very good year. Bonuses and stock options would be significant, and with the financials signed off, we all knew our individual and collective compensation would be just short of staggering.

Someone commented that they didn't realize I could be this much fun. I replied that I used to be more fun. That made everybody quiet, and I could see and feel that they were thinking about the way I handled my wife dropping me. I said I always thought the humour on *Saturday Night Live* and *Second City TV* was great. Then my wife discovered Monty Python, and the humour was knocked out of me. And then I smiled. A real smile. And I laughed.

They were taken aback for more than a moment. Then one of the women, who was in a red-wine fog and had turned off her sensitivity filter, spoke up. "Didn't your wife leave you for a Brit?" She was an uncannily straight woman in her lack of sobriety, full of candor.

"Yes, she did, and that's the point. Brits aren't really that funny." I laughed again. The whole table caught on and laughed along with me.

"You know we've been calling you 'Captain Serious' behind your back," someone said. "I knew that" I replied. "I took it as a compliment, being compared to Johnathan Toews, 'Captain Serious' of the Blackhawks and three-time Stanley Cup winner. Just like how my group has been kicking your collective asses for the last three years plus."

Then they started jabbing back. They had great wit, except for "Red-Wine Woman," who was just trying to keep track of who was ribbing who.

Later, I mentioned how happy I was that they hadn't called me Captain Obvious. Red-Wine Woman asked me why. Another unintentionally great straight line.

"Well, I think that's obvious, my dear."

The dinner and the evening went well, but I was wondering how the following night would unfold. Lisa had invited me to a private concert at her condo two days before her launch event at El Mocambo. She'd left an invite at GoHo's for Gina and me for the launch at the El.

I was on a good path toward feeling whole again. Content but not complacent. Work and Gina deserved my full engagement. Gina deserved the best of me.

I deserved the best for me.

CHAPTER 45

Convergence

The fourth interview, as Lisa had surmised, was the job offer. The meeting was great. The opportunity seemed fantastic, but I still asked for twenty-four hours to think things through. They were gracious in understanding and accepting my request. Then I headed straight for Lisa's.

Lisa was awaiting my arrival.

"Mo, my dear. Your life is about to change dramatically."

"Yes, Lisa my dear, it is."

We both chuckled.

"This is a huge decision and a huge step forward. This new position is well out of your previous comfort zone."

"Absolutely. It's daunting, challenging, and intimidating, yet at the same time, dazzling, stimulating and enticing. I'm so ready. I believe in myself. I know I can do this."

"Absolutely, Mo. I believe you can. I believe you're ready, and I know you'll succeed."

"So, you wanted to see me after the interview to give me a confidence boost? Your sequencing is out of order."

"No, my sequencing is perfect. I wanted to hear your confidence and belief in yourself prior to what I have to say."

"Okay, so is this the part where you say that this position is a stretch too far or requires more than confidence and bravado? Which, by the way, I refer to as 'Mo-vado.' You know, my version of 'bravado.'"

"No, Mo. This is the part where I say I want you to consider an alternative offer because of your Mo-vado."

"An alternative offer? To do what? For whom?"

"I need a tour manager. The position is about building and maintaining relationships and dealing with a wide variety of people and character types. From absolute sleazeballs to narcissistic assholes to extremely sensitive musical talents and prima donna promoters. The job requires the organization and the orchestration of a thousand moving parts. A tour manager makes hundreds of decisions in a day from the minutiae to the monstrous with far reaching implications for all aspects of the tour.

"There is very little calm on tour. The tour manager sits in the eye of the storm and remains calm while everything spins around them in the vortex that moves the tour from show to show and from town to town. The tour manager must land the vortex because when the tornado, that a tour truly is, touches down on stage, the landing must be damn near perfect night after night after night. The tour manager is the symphony conductor who accomplishes all that."

"Let me get this straight. You're offering me something in that maelstrom? Like the travel component or what?"

"No, the whole thing. The whole constantly fucked-up, beautiful thing. All the nuts, all the bolts, and all the king's men and his horses. Because a tour is Humpty Dumpty pissed to the gills and falling off the wall all the damn time, and the tour manager puts him back together again every damn time."

"Okay, I can envision myself in that general management role for four factories. That has some order. But a tour? The way you describe Mr. Humpty Dumpty, isn't that, by definition, chaos?"

"Absolutely chaotic and beautiful and enthralling and fulfilling! A tour is complex. The variables are staggering and dynamic. Managing that, moving the icebergs out of the way of the *Titanic* and letting the band play on, that's the job, and I believe you can do it."

"Lisa, thank you sincerely, but that would be out of my league."

"It would be if you didn't have a great mentor with you who also has a plan to train you, although there will be an occasional baptism by fire."

"Who's this mentor?"

"Me."

"You? But you must perform, and you have to focus on the music."

"I want this tour to be as close to perfect as possible. The reality is that tours are hot messes. The tour starts in less than a month. I haven't hired anyone yet. I've been managing short spring and summer tours for the last fifteen to twenty years for myself and some of the performers I've produced. I was going to manage this on my own too. Then last night I had the revelation that this tour could be managed by the marvelous Ms. Mo."

"You really think so?"

"We would be working hand in hand. We start with four nights at Massey Hall. It's a luxury to work through all the staging aspects in one venue over four nights. Massey is a killer, though. It's an intricate, intimate venue. The planning must be meticulous. If an artist is magnificent at Massey, the tour sells out instantaneously. I want to be magnificent. I can train you on all the aspects for Massey. I know that old boy well, as do many of our crew, our extended family. Our road crew and equipment crews are second to none. Good people I've worked with for what seems like all my life.

"Well, why do you need me? Won't I just slow you down? Why do you need anyone?"

"First, I only surround myself with people I trust, and I believe in. You qualify on both counts. Second, there's a twelve to sixteen-hour period before each show when I need to disappear into the music. The stage, the lights, the sound, the rehearsal, the band, getting inside myself, getting ready to bring down the house."

"You're serious. You believe this can work? That I can do this?"

"One hundred percent, Mo, under my excellent tutelage. Massey will let us learn and get us ready. Fifty concerts in one hundred nights from coast to coast. If the tour catches fire, we can add ten to twelve more nights."

"Then this job is short term? The duration of the tour? A hundred nights?"

"No. It will lead to a full-time engagement with substantially higher pay and bonuses, based on performance, than your current offer. We might need to tweak the benefits a bit, but the health coverage will be almost equal to what you've been offered."

"What's the long-term engagement?"

"General manager for my holding company, LL Enterprises. Hell no, let's make that vice president."

"When would I start?"

"Tomorrow."

And there you go. Two paths intersecting. Convergence. Brown and black. No holding back.

CHAPTER 46

Divergence

The call wasn't unexpected. It provided more than a tingle of excitement. The private concert Lisa wanted to perform. She felt she owed me another personal moment with her music, that somehow, I was an integral part of her personal and musical journey.

I arrived right at 8:00. The door opened, and my first impression was that she was radiant, glowing from within. Our small talk was minimal and a bit awkward. Lisa asked me about Gina, and I stumbled through my answer, flustered and evasive. I don't know why because my mind was clear on Gina and my personal path. My thinking was fogged with old thoughts that maybe Lisa and I could have become something. Well, that path had been crossed and left behind.

"Sit right where you were last time, Sean. Your scotch is poured. I just need to add the rocks."

"Thank you."

"No need to be so stiff and formal. Relax. This won't hurt—much!" Lisa laughed at her own humour.

"Okay, I was worried that the scotch was for numbing. Will you play the same songs?"

"Actually, I won't play either one. I'm going to play you 'Wanted Man' and then one we just finished that I believe you'll really like. It is called 'The Maybe Song, Getting To Good.'"

"What happened to 'Immolate'? That was a powerful, agonizing, and searing beast of a number. And 'Lost and Longing' was heart rendering."

"You remembered?"

"Hard to forget those songs—or that night." My head bowed slightly in response to those memories circulating in the air between us.

"'Immolate' is too dark, too hard, too black, and too hurtful for the rest of the album. It'll come out someday, though."

"I'm glad. That song was a train wreck of emotional damage. I think it needs the light of day."

"It is, and it will. 'Lost and Longing' made the cut. I think you'll identify with these two songs, and maybe they'll move you. I hope they do—in a good way.

They're a little melancholy, but you and I have been to melancholy and back, if not worse places on our personal paths. I may play these two songs acoustically on the tour from time to time. So, this a great tune-up."

"Well, I feel privileged to be your audience of one."

"Thank you, Sean. Here we go."

The songs were beautiful. People were going to cry at Lisa's concerts. They were unbelievable symphonies of emotion that captured longing and love in the lyrics. The music was plaintive and revealing, inviting listeners onto the emotional tilt-a-whirl of love, longing, and looming loss. The loss a person felt when the ride ended, or they lost their ticket or their way or they fell off. I wanted to wrap my arms around these songs and embrace them.

And Lisa! When I felt my eyes welling, I sipped my scotch.

When Lisa finished, I was awestruck, silent and drained.

"Well?"

"You need to get a tissue company to sponsor your tour. There will be puddles of tears on the floor at every concert."

"You think so?"

"People are going to love these songs. They're going to hum them and sing along at your concert. They'll be compelled to sing the choruses. You're going to emotionally move men and women of all ages and descriptions."

"You believe they're that powerful?"

I choked up a little, trying to hide the catch in my throat and the tear in my eye with a solid belt of my scotch. "Lisa, these songs are overwhelming and emotionally powerful. People will be mush."

"Hearing you in particular say that that means the world to me. Thank you."

I drained my scotch and stood up. Tears started to flow as I said the only appropriate thing I could think to say. "Lisa, we're not fucking."

"I know." We both smiled at the exchange, but we didn't laugh.

"I have to go."

"I know."

And I left. The elevator ride was filled with strong emotions once again, but I made it home and poured a Jack Jacks, four fingers.

Ah Lisa, our paths crossed, and now they diverge.

I sat down and called Gina.

"How was your private concert?"

"Gina, I love you."

"I know, Sean, and I love you too." We chatted a bit and then made plans for the El Mocambo concert.

My thoughts were filled with Lisa's music and lyrics. I smiled because I was a wanted man, and I was getting too good. No maybes!

I deserved that path.

CHAPTER 47

Emergence

The invitation arrived by mail. The address was the tribal office. In my culture and identity dive, I had shut off my cell phone, email, and all social media. I had gone dark to find my light. Lisa's pre-tour launch was scheduled for the El Mocambo on March 27. It was somehow poetic, ironic, and maybe cruel that the night Lisa was launching, I would be launching myself into the deepest part of my cultural immersion. Cruel because our individual leaps of faith were happening symmetrically but not in sync. At one time I believed we both felt that momentous occasions would be shared, not separate.

The phone call I made to Lisa was short. I said I wouldn't be coming, but I wished her extreme success, enjoyment, and fulfillment. She cried and said she was sorry for being so cruel. I told her not to worry, that she had helped me set myself on a hard course to myself. It's strange how my origin path came about almost directly from the end of a relationship. Something was born when something died, or is that too clumsy or a too convenient a cliché?

I submerged myself in my culture. The conversations I overheard growing up in a white-dominated town about the Choctaw, "those people," were derogatory at best and unbridled, vehement racism at worst.

The Choctaw were the punchline in all the jokes and were often the communal punching bags around the local bars. In some ways, they still are. There was one bar called Cowboys and Indians, and it was just like a bad Western movie. The fighting was bad, with some occasional knife play, but mostly fists, boots, and furniture. The owner had the wisdom to remove all the tables and chairs and build a partition wall down the centre of the bar. On the side that was the exterior wall, the cowboys congregated with their drinks of choice—long-neck beer and whisky shots. There used to be windows along that wall. The repetitive breaking of those windows by bottles, chairs, and the odd human being getting chucked through them made window replacement a prohibitive expense. The boarding up of the windows made the bar look even more foreboding and instilled the sense that one was entering a dark and perhaps sinister place. It was all of that according to local legend and court records, which bore witness to the maelstrom of malevolence that took place within.

On the inside wall, the Indians drank the same long-neck beers and smuggled in pints of whisky that they passed around. The smuggling of the whisky into the bar in their boots and jean jackets made no sense, as they then drank the whisky openly. They just weren't going to pay two bucks per shot. The unwritten rule was if anyone snuck whisky in, they had to drink it. That was one of several myths that defined Cowboys and Indians. That was the Indian side of the myth. The cowboy side of the myth was whisky couldn't be served to Indians because they couldn't handle it.

The Indians would argue and insist that they were being financially prudent. They didn't make "cowboy money!" This was true because the Indians faced a wage gap between them and white people of at least two to three bucks an hour for the same job. In simple Cowboys and Indians bar math, that wage differential justified the astute financial decision to bring in their own whisky to even out the prejudicial economic wage differential.

The partition was just a thin wall that barely separated the Cowboys from the Indians. People had been tossed through that wall. When the bar was full, some patrons from both sides would stand in the narrow corridor at the start of the partition, in the so-called foyer area. It was referred to as "No Man's Land" or the "Combat Zone."

When the service was slow on their side—or more likely, when they were looking for trouble—the cowboys had to walk through the Combat Zone to order drinks. That usually occurred when a white guy had consumed a few belts of liquid courage and thought he was tougher than he was. Even then they only came into the zone of blood and guts in groups of three or four. The foyer also became known as the gauntlet. Blood spilled there often.

The owner was a brilliant businessman. In addition to building the wall and adding the partition, which allowed every patron to have their back to a wall, he replaced the tables and chairs with barstools. The propensity for barstools to be used as weapons led to his next redesign. No barstools and then no windows, additional side panels on both sides of the partition that extended four to six feet into the floor space. He created more standing room and wall space for more patrons to have their backs shielded, protected to a degree. Brilliant. His patrons, both cowboys and Indians, were hard-working oil, farm, construction, and factory workers. Many worked alongside one another. There was, however, none of that commingling nonsense in the interior of the Cowboys and Indians bar.

Cowboys were killed there once or twice a year. Indians lost an eye or a finger or a spleen or some other internal part four or five times a year. The cowboys always claimed the dead had been jumped by a raiding party. The Indians claimed they had been gouged, bitten, and knifed by guys who didn't fight fair, who didn't fight like real men. Who knew the truth? Nobody! Especially not the white police or the Indian band constables. Nobody testified ever. People grew up learning the Choctaw were savage, drunken killers. As for the cowboys, they were just hard-working men, blowing off a little steam, or so the papers, radio, and TV proclaimed. All the media was white owned, so who was going to argue? The Choctaw's side of the story never saw the light of day.

Cowboys and Indians was a fertile battleground for hatred.

My parents stayed within the white lines. Drove straight and stayed focused. My dad never ventured into that bar or any bar, for that matter.

Choctaw culture is rich. By the time I left in June for my camps and my broadcasting job, I would have learned the Choctaw ways. I'd be able to speak a little of our language, and I hoped to be grounded on my path as a Choctaw being.

In the first month and a half I learned things on the surface of my heritage, and I looked forward to the deeper meanings and understandings. I met a Choctaw woman, a healer who was broken herself and then returned to our culture. She didn't start off being kind to me. She called me out for my three-plus decades of convenient denial, so I could advance. Mocked my time as a Fauxcasian. She spoke the truth about my life because the Choctaw didn't countenance pretense or self-perpetuating prejudice. They spoke transparently, directly, and truthfully. She warned me that returning to Choctaw culture would be full of shame and pain for me. It was for her. She said all this with strength and grace.

I would come to being Choctaw through her teachings and those of others. I hoped to emerge with Choctaw grace and pride and maybe with her. I hoped our paths would merge.

CHAPTER 48

All Good in Indian Territory

Vice president of operations and tour manager. I was going places, both physically and professionally. It was stunning and elevating.

What about faith? Faith in myself? I did believe in myself. My faith in myself was grounded in what I'd done. Or, more correctly, what *we* had done—my sister, my daughter, and me. But what about our abandoned faith? What about being a Muslim woman whose family immigrated from India? What about that? My parents couldn't cope with the integration of their race and their faith. They hid in the bottle. They fought it by abusing themselves and their daughters, and in the process, they lost themselves.

Delta Dawn and I had speculated on our father's death. Death by Smirnov and snow plow. How original! What had he been thinking? If he was having any rational thoughts at all. Was it suicide? Had he just given up trying to bridge two cultures? Working at jobs far below his training and education, had he abandoned his faith, or had his faith abandoned him? Or was the transition of culture, status, and religion just too much at once? And how had all that turned him into a predator? Hunting his own daughters. We could never answer any of these questions with any degree of satisfaction or closure.

Delta Dawn and I just ran away. Survival was our religion, our belief rooted in each other. That was and is our faith. We had been to the temple three times, with my daughter, our little troop of three. All we seemed to need for so long was faith in each other. Did we need more?

The opening to faith, to our people's beliefs, was a tumble into some sort of grace. Whether we would embrace this faith, these beliefs, or not was hard to say. But it didn't matter at that moment. What mattered was the realization that closing down or shutting off parts of who I was didn't work.

My path wasn't as epic as Smackin' Mackin's. Everything he did was epic. His move to his Native self was courageous. My move to my Native self wasn't newsworthy and wasn't deemed courageous. It wasn't epic, and it wasn't subject to public scrutiny and critique. My move was epic, courageous, honest, and self-scrutinized, but just by me. All of this was by me, for me, for us, and it was good. Learning where we came from, whether good, bad, or just different was important. So many colours and shades in self-discovery.

Imagine my sister's life with the name Delta Dawn Savinder. How did that work on a daily basis, in our society, for anyone? Named after a country and a western song by alcoholic Muslim parents. Carrying that family history and name was a burden. Yet she picked a path and rose. Remarkable.

I looked ahead to the tour and penciled three temples to visit. We would see how the paths travelled.

Imagine GoHo's as the meeting place for two Indians, Mackin and Mo. One brown and one red. Or as was mentioned behind our backs, one dot and one feather. Despite those prejudices, our paths were to us and for us. All good in Indian territory.

One of Lisa's songs, which was getting some play on the radio, came to mind.

Song #10 "Find a Path"

This is some serious stuff
Striving, reaching for what
Find a path, pick a lane

Feel your heart
Follow your brain
Find a path, pick a lane

I just want to play
Can you play along?
Just me being me and you being you

For an hour or two
That's all we need
Just me being me and you being you

It's so damn hard
Figuring out what to do
Find a path, pick our lane

I think I have an answer
I think I have my way
Find my path, find my lane.

I just wanna play
I wanna play with you
Just me being me and you being you

Be Red Rover, call me over
I wanna be with you.
Find our path, find our lane

Be my four-leaf Clover
The good luck in our game of chance
Just me being me and you being you

The lane is narrow, the ditch is near
On the path we'll stumble
But will find our path, find our lane

CHAPTER 49

Lisa and Mo Unleashed

July 1, Canada Day, an outdoor concert on the front lawn at the Parliament Buildings in Ottawa. Day ninety-two of the one-hundred-day tour, which had been extended until July 25, ending in Charlottetown. We would have played sixty-eight times in one hundred and sixteen days. I wasn't tired, and neither was Mo. We both believed we were just hitting our stride.

Mo was mowing it down. When she got even close to going under water, she asked for help. No shame in that because out on tour, pride came before huge falls. Decisions often required instantaneous responses that were sequenced into a cascading series of actions that built the foundations of success for every show and the next five shows after that. Mo rose to the challenges as she mowed them down.

For me, it was something grand! Live performances were always a mixture of anxiety and excitement. The more we played, the more the intensity and pure adrenaline rush of performing took over, especially as Mo became more front and centre. Mo had become the epicentre of the whole carnival.

I was singing every song with conviction and clarity of soul and passion. I was playing and singing *me* in every song. My songs from almost thirty years ago felt fresh and vital because it was me singing me. Even cover songs were resonating with my passion.

The plank. I owned it. I skipped, danced, strutted, swaggered, and romped into the audience. I sat or stood at the edge of the plank and did a couple of acoustic numbers. My emotions hung in the air out there on the plank. The smiles, the grimaces, the breaths that came out as sighs, and the mist in my eyes were all unconscious expressions of me. Out on the plank. Me being me. Leaving behind any pretense, any false images, and any shred of self-deception. Me being me. Never once did I feel lonely out there, walking the plank. I was in front of a few thousand friends who I know were there because they cared for what they heard, felt, and saw, both now and then. What they were getting was an unfiltered, unadulterated version of Lisa. They could see, feel, and hear the real me. Collectively, they had my back.

At last, I had left all that other shit behind.

There wasn't even a hint of a trailing hand.

Sex! I had to teach Mo that concerts and shows smelled like sex. The air was filled with hormones and testosterone. I thought that tour was going to make a lot of babies. Almost every review of the show mentioned that the connection with the audience was intimate and passionate, from the sing-a-longs to the rhythmic swaying with hands in the air to the pin-drop cone of silence during the acoustic numbers. I believe an audience knows when an artist has let down their guard, their own walls of delusion, self-deception, self-promotion, or whatever form that wall takes.

Mo had to know that anybody could get laid on tour. Back in the day, some bad boys in the band had a woman in a few different cities and towns. Many of those women who were allegedly in their late teens and early twenties back then came to the shows, hoping to reconnect. I assume some did.

The issue wasn't whether a person could get laid. It was how a person conducted and controlled themselves. Mo had to be a leader and set the tone. Were we professionals or teenagers on an extended spring break? Mo kept us professional, although I'm sure she was tempted. More than once men and women showed more than passing attention and intention. Once they got over the shock that a five-foot-two Indian Muslim woman was running the show, Mo became an exotic figure. I picked her a full wardrobe for the tour. Her frenetic life on tour as the continuous calm in the eye of the storm required kinetic and mental motion.

Mo was constantly in motion. She cut her own distinct character, and her silhouette was stamped all over the tour. As far as sex, I think Mo was practicing abstinence. Maybe not by choice. More as an outcome of the frenetic pace the tour manager had to keep. She didn't have time or space for that kind of frivolity. We had the Gretzky imperative of needing time and space arising as a lesson once again. People need time and space to get their wild thing on. Mo didn't have either one.

CHAPTER 50

Mo in Mo World

Lisa was more energetic after opening night at Massey Hall than before it. As for me, I was too busy to be tired. I'd been overwhelmed multiple times, but Lisa was always there with a lifeline to prevent me from drowning. The realization that I could do the job wasn't like a light that just came on. It was a slow, gradual process. My ability to pivot wasn't only physical. It was mental, and I was good at it. Multitasking is the wrong word. A more accurate description is systemic sequential processing, acting and reacting, or simpler yet, being in the moment. In Ottawa I was totally on top of the game, of my game.

Mo in the world. Okay, maybe just across Canada with a couple of dips into the States. Still, it was Mo launching into the world.

I felt good, like it was my manifest destiny. Woman-fest destiny! Whatever!

What did faith have to do with it? That's an interesting question. One I kept asking myself. Working that way in a rambling, multi-faceted project with so many intricate moving and connected parts seemed to be my space, my niche. People still looked stunned when they met Maurinder Savinder for the first time, especially if they hadn't talked to me on the phone. First, from my name, they thought I would be a man. Second, they assumed it wasn't my first rodeo. Third, they made a whole bunch of stereotypical assumptions—lesbian, terrorist, and a hijab-shedding bitch.

Okay, they missed on two out of three. I was a bitch, but only when necessary.

The way Lisa manoeuvred through all the attention of being a rock star was amazing. Not only were her performances striking, but they were also sensual. Men wanted her, and women wanted to be her. To tell the truth, the reverse was true as well. Some women wanted her, and some men wanted to be her. The shows had a palpable sensual aura. Lisa told the audiences that one song was channeled from her teen years, growing up like a rich white child in the suburbs. She warned the audience that her dance moves would probably look like that, and they did.

Toward the end of the concert, she introduced a song, saying she had become a grown-ass black woman with the best coloured-girl boogie they'd ever placed their lustful eyes on. Then she sang and danced like a clearly-not-choreographed soul queen. All of it was real and authentic, and the women in the audience mimicked her moves.

For the last few dates on the tour, we had two T-shirts printed that read "a rich suburban white girl" on the front and "a grown-ass black woman" on the back. On the front and back were silhouettes that epitomized Lisa dancing in those respective modes with the words "dance like" emblazoned above the silhouette. The T-shirts sold out every show. Lisa's dancing had crossed a racial divide with her self-deprecating humour, which was captured on the T-shirt.

All the merchandise was selling out. The CD was selling like crazy too. "Wanted Man," "Getting to Good," and "Old Miseries" were all crossover hits. Topping the charts on the country stations was totally unexpected. They weren't beer-drinking songs, but they were about loss and love. "Old Miseries," now that was a good whisky-drinking song. I was so proud of my part in inspiring it.

Lisa wasn't having it, as she pronounced from time to time—sex, that is. She told me at the outset that abstinence was her game plan. She also told me with the energy I was spinning up, I should go fuck the socks off someone. I loved the lascivious, loin-locking, lust-loaded image in that visual. Occasionally, when some man was hitting on me hard, I whispered to Lisa. "Tell him to be careful, or I'll fuck his socks off." We giggled like rich suburban white girls from the valley—that is, the Don Valley or Humber Valley.

CHAPTER 51

Mackin Making Something Good

I texted Lisa and Mo several times to congratulate them on the tour. Their responses were warm, friendly, and short, but it was clear they were both thrilled with the tour.

My sports camp was two hours away from Ottawa. I left the camp just after lunch on Sunday. The concert was on Sunday night. Before I left, I called a special lunch with the Choctaw kids. We talked about their roles, their thoughts, their feelings and their experience up to that point. They were reserve kids, selected to work in the summer, far from home. There were twelve in all, two more than I originally planned. I should have brought twenty, but we needed proof of concept that the experience could make a long-term difference. Twelve participants allowed us to concentrate on the young Choctaw warriors and guide them. They were tough kids. Talented too. Some were athletic like the two Jimmys. Others had great but untapped academic ability. Some had innate but misguided leadership strength.

A tribe of fifteen-to-eighteen-year-olds with a lot of bad habits, some with chips the size of a cement block on their shoulders. At their core they all had the stuff of good men in them. Choctaw men. I never talked to them about their role as counsellors at the camp being an opportunity for growth and an expansion of their horizons. We talked about the character that we saw emerging in their trust and growing confidence and in how they carried themselves with integrity and decency among their Choctaw brothers. We also talked about the culture of that tribe, their tribe of twelve. About being judged on their character, performance, and behaviour. We talked about what they could become individually and collectively. To that point in their lives, both outside and to a degree on the reserve, they had largely been judged on the sole fact that they were Choctaw. Such judgments were laced with hateful stereotypes and the high bar of low expectations.

Their two-week training period was physically and mentally exhausting. I had always planned to let them have that weekend off. The campers arrived on Monday. I'd be there to greet them with my tribe. It feels good, giving back and learning more about myself than I thought possible. My hope was to help guide those young men to be strong, decent, courageous warriors for the Choctaw people.

CHAPTER 52

Closing in on Serenity

It was Gina's idea. Turned out neither of us had ever been to Ottawa for Canada Day. The fact that Lisa was scheduled to play "the lawn" in front of the Parliament Buildings, after our decision to go to Ottawa had already been made, added a new dimension to our long weekend get-away. Then the invitation to attend the concert arrived from the tour manager, Ms. Maurinder Savinder. Our Mo!

Gina and I were celebrating our four-month anniversary with our first vacation together. A trial run, so to speak for our planned August hiking adventure on the east coast. We were good together. I had pulled myself together.

We got to the Parliament Buildings early, walked the grounds, and enjoyed the magnificent views of the Ottawa River. We felt a surge of Canadian pride. Then we meandered down to the Byward Market, and I had haggis with scotch poured on it. Gina chose fish and chips with a crisp chardonnay. We talked about everything and nothing. Our conversation included dissecting the shortcomings of the current Liberal government, the wonder of multiculturalism, the bewilderment of creating haggis as an act of necessity, Gina's fingernail colour, and my surprisingly patriotic boxers.

The concert was set for eight, and we strolled back up to the lawn in front of the Centre Block, arriving just after seven. The lawn was filling up already. We were coming in from the East Block side when I saw Mo on the edge of the stage. I was genuinely excited to see her. Gina and I wove our way to the edge of the barricades until we were a good seventy feet from the stage where Mo was standing. Like a starstruck schoolboy, I called her name. She heard me, squinted into the crowd, then started her Mo walk. Just like at GoHo's while carrying five plates, she wove through security, roadies, and technicians without breaking her stride.

"Gina, has this man kidnapped you, or are you actually here of your own free will?"

"Well, Mo, how can a girl say no to an all-expenses-paid trip to Ottawa? I just keep my headphones on, so I don't have to listen to him talk."

I just smiled. "Let me know when you two are done masking your blatant affection for me."

With that Mo reached over the barricade between us and hugged Gina and me. Despite how close I felt to Mo, we had never hugged before. The three of us chatted about the tour. Gina and I asked question after question. Mo responded with her brash wit, which was set on full throttle. Her eyes danced and sparkled. She laughed and rolled her eyes. Her expressions told stories that her words couldn't match. She was clearly in her element and swimming with the elephants in an enormous undertaking. Without a hint of braggadocio or ego, she conveyed that she was the master of a three-ring circus. The elephants swam where and when she told them to swim. Mo was pure joy.

"So, how's the boss lady?" I asked.

"An absolute bitch, but then again, so am I! Fabulous, actually! She's going to make you sway, dance, smile, sing, and maybe cry a little—or maybe more than a little."

"She did that at the El Mocambo and when we saw her on the fourth night at Massey," Gina said. I nodded in agreement.

"Yeah, but out here on Canada Day she is totally immersed. Lisa is pumped to take this whole thing to another level. You're going to see that. Her singing and playing are so revealing. This is now a tour of raw, passionate transparency, intimacy, and confidence. Lisa is Lisa. She is more of her true self than even she could imagine. Whatever Lisa was before, that girl is in her rear-view mirror. You know that saying? Elvis has left the building. Well, Lisa has left Lisa."

Mo's words were powerful. Mo was speaking Lisa's truth, the truth that Lisa set out to find.

"What about you, Mo?" I asked. "Have you found Mo out here? You're lit up and alive with energy zipping out of you like lightning bolts."

"This feels like some sort of destiny. In this world, I feel like Mo Balboa, Rocky's smarter, better looking, younger sister. I'm crapping thunder and farting lightning, or something like that."

I laughed. "I think Stallone could sue you for butchering that classic line."

"He wouldn't dare. Mo knows shows. I've learned how to run a tour, how to manage this complex, rolling, intricate animal. I'm thriving in this environment. I haven't totally left myself behind, like Lisa, but this Mo has left her imposed limits behind, way behind. They're not even visible in the rear-view mirror. I've just caught up to who I can be. Well, I gotta go. The show doesn't go or flow without Mo! See you right here at the side of the stage after the show." She laughed and then hugged us both again.

Pivot. Gone.

Gina and I hugged each other.

"You know, Sean, I'm ecstatic for both of them. And before you say anything, I'm ecstatic for us. Now kiss me like a good Canadian boy should kiss his girl on Canada Day in Ottawa."

I did as instructed, because that's what good Canadian boys do.

Gina and I ambled to a spot about thirty feet back from the barricades, almost directly at centre stage. I was thinking about voyages, journeys, paths, whatever we call making our way to ourselves. Mostly, I was thinking about my own journey to get to that spot. Gina in my arms, love in my heart, content, happy, and centred. My ex-wife and I were climbing a thrilling, challenging, and rewarding corporate and cultural ladder. We were climbing together, and I thought we were still ascending when she declared we had plateaued. Well, actually, according to her, I had hit my personal plateau.

We wouldn't be planting the triumphant flag of corporate success at the peak together. From the point where she jettisoned me, I tumbled down more than a bit. Then some inner safety rope of character, some piton of inner strength, provided an anchoring point for me. At least I stood secure in a space of my own and on my own. My ascension restarted, and I had enough self-confidence to gain traction and climb. I looked deep into my capabilities, but more importantly, I looked inward. I looked at who I was and what I wanted. And I found it.

Gina made me decide who I wanted to become, a man of ambition coupled with compassion and wanting a companion. Turned out that for most of my life, having someone to love, trust, and come home to fulfilled my paramount desire. So, maybe I was stuck on one of Maslow's lower rungs. No, fuck that! Knowing what I wanted and reaching for it, that had to be self-actualization. Maybe it was, and maybe it wasn't I don't care because what I had at that moment more than filled all my levels of need.

I pulled Gina closer and whispered in her ear. "I love you."

That guy, that guy back there, was the epitome of a pure power-couple ascension. He was gone. Maybe he was never real. It seems a lot of us were using the rear-view mirror reflectively.

So, Mo, pivot in your new milieu, I thought. Every decision you make is like an order spiked at GoHo's. Done and done and serving it up like a son of a gun. Lisa, Lisa, Lisa. Dance, play and sing about your soul to your soul for your soul. And remember, and this is important, we're not fucking!

I smiled again and pulled Gina closer. How I got there seemed surreal, but I felt serene.

CHAPTER 53

Mackin Stage Left

I didn't think I would be so well recognized. Getting recognized started as a small avalanche with one head turning and a murmured "Isn't that. . .?" Then a teenage boy asked me to autograph his Red Blacks jersey. That team didn't even exist when I was in the league.

A small crowd formed, and then a man led me to his mother, who was in a wheelchair pressed up against the barricades in front of the stage. She was wearing an Argos jersey with my name and number on the back. She told me she had the jersey for over twenty years. As I chatted with her and signed her jersey, a flock of media photographers saw the minor commotion and headed our way. Before I could disappear, the photographers were upon us. I walked up to the stage from the East Block, purposely going behind the media trucks so I could avoid them. I didn't think the media would all be congregating pre-show at the eastern corner of the stage. The pack that gathered was fairly large for the spontaneous photo op and their ranks swelled just opposite the audience side of the barricades.

My longtime fan—Jean was her name, proud grandma and great-grandma—was reveling in the attention. When the reporters asked her questions, she kept telling them what a good and good-looking young man I was and how I was still her football hero. She also said if she were a few years younger, she would be, as her great grandkids said, "knocking boots with me." I knew right then that Jean and I would be on newsfeeds and in papers across the country.

Mo must have noticed the flow of media away from where they had been marshalled in a staging area to the right of the stage. She made her way over, and when she recognized me, she plunged through the crowd. I heard her call my name, and we made eye contact and were instantly beaming at each other.

"Mackin get over here."

"What do you mean?"

"Climb over the barricade."

"What?"

"You heard me, Smackin' Mackin. Get your athletic ass over here. You're with me." She motioned to the two security sides of beef beside her. "If this old man needs help, boys, boys give him a hand."

"I'm pretty sure I can handle this on my own," I replied.

When I cleared the barrier, Mo gave me a hug. We had never hugged before.

"Come on, stud. Here's your VIP pass. You're watching from the stage with me, Mo, tour manager extraordinaire!"

"Okay, Mo. If you say so."

"I do, so let's go. Get that backfield in motion."

I was in tow with the two security monsters who could have been linemen. It never occurred to Mo to ask me if I wanted to be on stage, and I wasn't sure I wanted to be. I didn't know if I was ready for a close encounter with Lisa. I caught up to Mo and told her the same.

"Good point, Mackin. Strong, smart, and sensitive. You should do Old Spice commercials. You know, Lisa might not be ready for a close encounter of the Smackin' Mackin kind. We'll hide you on the side of the stage. Lisa won't see you until the encore, but you'll see her. Be prepared to be blown away."

So, that was how I made it to the stage. A profoundly changed man from the one that Lisa had loved and left. I was trembling at the thought of just seeing Lisa. When she came on stage, my breath didn't catch. It stopped! Lisa was breathtaking. She wasn't more beautiful physically, but she was beatific, shining from within. I was standing on the left side of the stage, obscured from Lisa's view by various pieces of equipment. I could see her perfectly, though.

As the concert began, I was totally absorbed. I cried during some songs, especially the acoustic versions of "Getting to Good," "Wanted Man," and "Old Miseries." Lisa was more than good. The thousands of people spilling out from the lawn to the streets were enthralled. The CBC was broadcasting the concert live across the country. There I was in her moment of absolute ascendancy and triumph, basking with everyone else in her being her. On the side of the stage, there I stood, Lisa's last significant lover. On the side stage of her life, forever Smackin' Mackin, the now-engaged former first man of Lisa. My engagement wouldn't be the first thing I tell her. It would be the second.

Lisa didn't see me until she came to the side of the stage to talk to Mo before the encore. "Mackin!" she said, then hugged me hard. She felt good, and when she broke her clinch, she was beaming up at me.

"Mackin, you came! Thank you, thank you, thank you. I wanted you to hear me, to see me in this setting."

"How could I resist?" I spoke. "This is the only free concert on your tour."

We both laughed and then looked hard and long at each other.

"Mackin, you're celebrating with us tonight, right?"

"Absolutely, for a little while. I need to be back at camp tonight. I lead the six-a.m. run and workout."

"That figures. The dedicated hard-working man on a mission. Smackin' Mackin!"

"And you, Lisa? What I saw out there was you being you. So, mission accomplished?"

"For the most part, yes. Absolutely! It feels brilliant and sparkles with an energy, a life source."

"Well, you look and sound vibrant."

"Thanks, Mackin. Well, I gotta go! The big finale awaits."

Out she strutted to her world, a world she'd made for herself. She was gorgeous. Radiant! Whatever you call someone who has reached a point of personal awareness and fulfillment. I felt no longing for her as I watched her cradle the audience into her world. I just felt happiness for Lisa. She was magnificent!

And I was becoming me.

CHAPTER 54

Sean Summarizes

Mo's text arrived just before Lisa started her encore. "Meet me at the barricade where we saw each other. You two are coming to the after-party."

The show was phenomenal. It wasn't like Lisa was playing to the audience; it was the audience playing to Lisa, if that makes any sense. She was beguiling, bewitching, beyond belief. She wasn't the woman who had straddled me just a few months ago. She was someone straddling her own world as she rode through our world. "Powerful" is such an absurdly inadequate word to describe her performance. The crowd melted during her acoustic songs. She was singing from her soul. The sense of need, want, love, love lost, and uncertainty wavered in the air with her voice. There wasn't a person in the audience who didn't feel the pain of loss in "Old Miseries," the hope embedded in every chord and lyric of the "Maybe Song," or the agony and longing in the anthem to love of "Wanted Man." If someone wasn't in love at the start of the concert, they almost certainly were after.

As one of the encore songs, she did a rocked-up version of "Wanted Man." The crowd went crazy. Lisa owned the night.

At the end of the encore, Mo came roaring off the stage with her two behemoths in tow. They pulled the barricades open, and Gina and I slipped through. As the big boys clanked the barriers back together behind us, Mo led us to the left side of the stage. Al Mackin was there. The man who had shaken the sports establishment and other cultural pillars on both sides of the longest unprotected border in the world with just three words: "I am Choctaw."

When Mackin made that announcement, it was one of most undetected, unexpected, and powerful "coming out" pronouncements ever. Mackin showed a flare for the dramatic and then went dark. Speculation about what he was doing and whether he would ever return were rampant for weeks after the announcement. Nothing. Crickets. Mackin just went dark.

Mo asked if Mackin and I had ever met. "Sort of," we both mumbled. Mo made introductions all around, including Gina. Then we slipped into a moment of seemingly awkward silence. I was feeling awkward because we were Lisa's ex-lover and Lisa's ex-wannabe lover. At least I was feeling awkward. I'm not sure if Mackin was feeling anything like that or if he was even marginally cognizant of my ex-wannabe status.

The silence was shattered as Lisa bounded over to us and went straight to Mackin with a ferocious hug and kiss on the cheek." Smackin' Mackin picks the lovely Lisa's concert for his coming out of his coming-out celebration. Wahoo!"

Before anybody could say anything, Lisa loosened her grip on Mackin and focused her gaze on me. Her eyes were on fire, full of life. "Sean, formerly Guy, launches his out-of-town romance with the gorgeous Gina at my concert. Wahoo!"

Without stopping, she hugged us both, then turned her attention to Mo. "And we're all gathered to bask in the magnificent moment of her Mo-ness being the best damn tour manager ever! Rocking it all in glorious organizational and staging splendour on Parliament Hill on Canada Day! Mo, you're our royalty of rock, our sovereign of song, and to you, my liege, I pledge my gratitude, loyalty, and allegiance forever."

Mo doesn't waver or hesitate in her response. "Remember how we promised we weren't going to be theatrical, dramatic, or over the top on this tour? Good! You're nodding. That indicates you have the solemnity of that promise entrenched in your head. So, knock off the flowery bullshit, and keep it real."

Everyone laughed at the exchange. Their care, love, and appreciation for each other was obvious. We chatted at a fever pitch for fifteen to twenty minutes. Then Lisa was hailed and pulled to set up for a live CBC interview. Mo received a text telling her that initial indications were that it was the most watched Canada Day show since the Tragically Hip, ten or twelve years earlier. Mackin informed us that he had to get going anyway, what with the two-hour drive and 5:30 a.m. wake-up call. We all said our goodbyes. Then Mackin asked Lisa if he could have two minutes alone, and they wandered a little farther down the stage. I thought it was Mackin's moment to launch his effort to bring them back together.

I thoroughly enjoyed the chatter between Gina and Mo as Mo told one of many stories about her tour experiences. I gazed over Mo's head to the conversation taking place downstage between Mackin and Lisa. After a few minutes, Lisa put her hands on Mackin's massive shoulders. Both their chests were heaving from deep breaths. Lisa stood on her toes and leaned in. The kiss was soft and tender and lingered a moment beyond momentary. That kiss was much more than a momentary memory. It had the magic of some deep truths, meaning, and love.

Then Lisa loosened her arms, pivoted, and turned away. Not a Mo-quality pivot but still sharp and precise. Snap. Gone. It was all unfolding in a slow arabesque.

Off her toes and onto the soles of her feet, hoping they found the floor, so they were grounded, and she could push off and move in a direction, a path that was both charted and broken at once.

Mackin stood in a somber silence. His hands trailed down her arms to her hands as Lisa turned to leave. Mackin looked torn between loss and gain, if any expression can emote those contrary conditions. Then his face slid into confusion. He lowered his head, shook it in a barely visible movement, and then raised his eyes. They caught my gaze. Smackin' Mackin, that gorilla of the gridiron, winced in recognition of some sort of shared understanding. He nodded and then he turned, ensuring he was anchored and stable before his slow departure. He took long, purposeful strides in the opposite direction of Lisa. There was no hesitation. I wanted to shout at him. "Turn around, you damn fool! She's worth it. More than worth it. Swallow your pride. Shrug off whatever it is. Whatever she says, go to her!" But I didn't call out. My mouth opened, but by then Mackin had left the stage. Had left Lisa.

I would have called out, except I also saw Lisa's face. As their embrace dissolved in the dragging of hands over arms, registered on that face was the grace of wishing someone well and meaning it. Then in the following moment, as she turned away from facing the reality of what had just transpired, the meaning of it all must hit her heart, and that understanding was etched indelibly on her lovely visage. The registering and resonating were deep within her. A hard slap of reality, deep and cold. Lisa's shoulders quivered during her turn, and her eyes were covered with a wet mist. I didn't know who had left whom, but the departure hurt my heart. I wondered what it had done to theirs.

Mo and Gina chatted on as I stood transfixed by exits. Stage left. Stage right. Whatever door of heartbreak led into that night.

Mo's phone was on fire with texts. She tried to stay focused on us, but that was impossible. Members of her tour team were hovering just out of reach. She apologized and said we were welcome to attend the after-party at the Chateau Laurier, but she and Lisa wouldn't be there for at least an hour, maybe longer. Mo said the prime minister would be there, though.

Lisa had a string of interviews to do, and Mo had received three concert proposals from three large, prominent promoters in fantastic venues. Lisa had knocked it off the charts, and Mo had to go! She laughed and said that even the PM had to wait for her now.

Gina and I were happy to wander out into the crowd. The fireworks would be starting soon.

Journeys. They start. They end. Somewhere in between we experience many things. The start and the end seemed to stand out. Four of us had encountered each other at GoHo's so many months ago. Two of the four, Lisa and Mackin, didn't even know they were part of the encounter. Gina, of course, came along later. Close encounters of the hearts.

Then we all journeyed to Ottawa on different paths and different trajectories with different thoughts in our heads and in our hearts. Different versions of who we were. Isn't that always the way with us humans? I don't know. This isn't my field of expertise. Ask a former waitress like Mo, they know this stuff. They probably have the insights to tell us all something about the human condition and the journey.

The four of us. Close encounters of the GoHo's kind. Close but moving apart. Journeys beginning and ending with departures and sometimes with a trailing hand, but not this time. Not for any of us.

CHAPTER 55

What I Know (Maybe)

GoHo's is the same. There are some swings in the composition of the diner's crowd, depending on time of day, what team is playing, and what's going on in the city.

At the same time, GoHo's isn't the same. No Mo. No sassy brashness. No pivot, gone. No power table with the multi-talented Lisa and her lover, Smackin' Mackin.

Gina and I drop in every couple of weeks for some comfort food or after a movie or a show. We have a couple of Stormwatch at the high top. It's still our table, hopefully for a long time to come.

Seems so long ago that I witnessed the Lisa and Smackin' Mackin exit, bewildered by their respective body language and words. At that moment, I was still bewildered by my wife's exit, and Mo was just a bewildering source of humour, accommodation, efficiency, and, even if unspoken, understanding and compassion. It was in her eyes, her humour, her pivot.

What have I learned? What does this ramble and rumble and roar and rip of our intermingling amount to?

What I know about myself is this. We've all heard that military recruiting line: "Be all you can be." Similar recruiting vocabulary comes from universities, colleges, and technical schools. All that external, goal-oriented praise about you reaching your true potential. It's all bullshit. Those institutions need bodies to fill spaces. It isn't about you. It's a marketing line meant to entice you to spin in and become asset collateral.

What have I, Sean, call me Guy, learned? I've learned that being Guy allowed me to distance myself from Sean from time to time. Guy could sit at his high-top table and watch the world flow by. He could indulge in conjecture and speculate about the humanity parading into or passing by GoHo's windows. The parade of human behaviour and interactions for Guy to dissect and analyze. For him to empathize with, identify with, stare at in wonder, judge, assume, or not judge, imagine, rationalize, and quietly watch. Sometimes in wide-eyed wonder.

This allowed Guy not to be fully self-absorbed in the sadness of Sean. To escape from his grief of loss. Not just loss of love but loss of self-worth, self-confidence, and self-esteem. Those losses pile up on themselves. Sadness doesn't come in waves; it piles on. It gang tackles.

So, Sean, what did you learn?

What I learned is to be who I truly am. Learning what I need to be. Not all I can be but all I *need* to be. That's my essence, being me. It isn't about reaching some definition of potential. Some rung on the corporate ladder. Measuring up to some external assessment of what I can be. It's my understanding what I truly need to do to be me. That's all I need. I need to be me. In finding that I have found a soft inner space where I care for and covet me. This isn't self-absorption or a position of retreat or cowering away from striving. This is my gooey part that everything sticks to and flows from. It's my life syrup that sustains and strengthens because it's my core stuff. The stuff where the intellectual foundation and emotional framing determine how I will embrace life. Yep, my own register and measure of emotional intellect. The way I see and score my emotional intellect only for me. It's that sticky fibre of caring that binds me to all aspects of my world. Some belief that the soft inner space is soft as in weak. In reality, at least my reality, it is the strong, vibrant glue of self that has the strength to bind me and guide me to the world in the way that I need to stick. Stick not stuck.

I believe this is what we call inner strength. I need to be what I need to be. If I can understand that, embrace that, then I can attach to the world as my true self.

What falls aside with this core of self-determined soul is the self-indulgence of pretense, arrogance, narcissism, and false representation of self. This is not a naïve or "Kumbaya" view of the world. It's my grounding. My reactions to the external world are grounded in this self-understanding. My responses and reactions are guided accordingly, but they're never blind or absurdly believing that my need to be a self-determined person matches the realities of the real world.

My message? It could probably be perceived as a contrived, convenient, comfortable, contortionist's approach to the world. I can see that perception. That my thoughts are all some type of gobbledy-gook. If that perception of me provides someone some comfort, so be it. You be you. I'll be me.

So, my message? I care to be, really care to be, the me I need to be because if I can be that then I can be me for you. I guarantee that you can trust, rely on, and love that me. Hopefully, it's good, really good, for you to have this me in your life. Finding yourself for yourself is about getting to the you of you. I know, gobbledy-gook. Finding it, being it. It's hard to get there and even harder to stay there. All I can do is try. So, I try.

CHAPTER 56

A Question of Faith

I loved working at GoHo's. I loved the nature of the work. The study of people, the interactions. The adaptation to the needs, behaviours, conditions, and manner of others. The spectrum of customers, the mood rainbow, the prism of self that was reflected in the GoHo's faulty neon window lights.

The efficiency of the operation, the flow, the order, the organization and all the variants. The ability to react and recover when a stick was poked in the wheel.

From waitress to tour manager to VP. From pregnant teenager to mother to university degree to a career. My journey is full of joy. My journey is full of faith. And what about faith?

The religious faith I abandoned. Or do I, with a self-centred perspective, view this relationship with my faith as the faith that abandoned me? The shattered faith a daughter should be able to trust and have with her father. The broken faith of a young lover. Do I wallow in the pity pit of my faith that abandoned, shattered, and broke? No, that's not for me. That's a no-go for Mo.

My religion, my Muslim roots. Does faith come to us, or do we come to faith? Does it matter? Does my possible self, my future self, include my religious faith? I'm not sure. I study and poke at my faith with curiosity and openness. Is it a gateway to me? I don't know. We'll see.

I do know that my faith and skin tone come with an attached prejudice against me. This angers me, and I won't run from the perpetrators of those biases. That's their weakness and illness, not mine. I can't let that darkness enter or influence my faith. My faith is a faith in me. The faith that I can do the necessary things, the necessary work to overcome. To overcome being a pregnant teen. To overcome that my own father was going to sexually abuse me. To overcome any sense or thought of being entitled to play the victim. That is always a tempting justification to utilize for stopping myself. I'm a victim. That play gets me nowhere. That play stops me before I start. To overcome the doubts about being capable and competent enough to raise my baby sister and my baby. To overcome the racism and stereotyping I encountered at the diner, on the street, and in other encounters. Encounters with institutions who somehow knew what the well-being of my baby and sister should be better than I did. That generic, institutional bias that is based on my circumstance conveniently covered and categorized by a blanket of idealized norms.

No one can overcome all that horse shit without faith. Not the faith of my religion or any religion, for that matter. The faith of facing every day with faith in myself. That's what I screw my courage to every single day. That's the makeup of hope that I apply to my face and mind every day. I paint myself, steel myself, with my faith in myself.

At some points in my life my faith leads me to light. Not religious light, the light of accomplishing things. Little things like feeding my family and big things like getting a degree. Maybe I have those two reversed in terms of what's big or little.

I always had a belief in myself, a faith. Okay maybe at times it wasn't really faith. It was something darker. Desperation. At times desperation replaced faith and shoved faith to the side. I desperately kept going. What kept me going? What kept the pilot light on? Faith. Centred at my core in an unbelievable knot that secured me, anchored me, grounded me in a way that enabled me to move forward.

Faith in myself is my critical-core mass. The light in me, my pilot light, is my faith in faith.

I go forward with more faith in myself than ever. I have learned that faith begets faith. The process of belief in myself can grow exponentially. The more I believe in myself, the more battles I fight and win, the more my core faith grows. When my faith gets shaken, I latch on to that faith for strength, then faith births faith.

Faith in self-defines me. I'm blessed with that faith. Faith, I have believed in and given myself. Religious faith is not attached. If that type of faith does come to me, it will come as an independent faith that I will choose as an addition to my core faith in myself.

CHAPTER 57

I Am Choctaw

I am Choctaw.

I had no clue saying those three words out loud would have so much meaning attached to them. In one moment, I felt liberated and excited to begin a journey. The next moment I was anxious about the can of worms I had opened and the criticism and questions that would rain down on me.

Why? Why now? My mother's urging? Losing Lisa?

I was wondering mostly. Wondering what the essence of my heritage meant. What it could mean to me. This was the path I needed to take to myself.

The criticism is loud, incessant, and painful. The charges of being a denier of my people, culture, and heritage leave a mark. The charge of living a life based on deceit. Being a Fauxcasian? I mean, seriously, who ever heard that term until my revelation? The charge of being a hypocrite, a traitor, a turncoat, a coward. The criticism comes from all corners. The most painful comes from within the Choctaw people. But I've earned their criticism and perspective concerning my character.

I have decided to address the harshness and severity of the criticism by my actions, not words.

I am Choctaw. Now I need to embrace being Choctaw. Not for the Choctaw people but for me. If I embrace being who I am and what I am for myself, good can come from that. First, I need to feel good about who I am. Understand and respect who I am and where I come from.

No one can be as critical of my long, albeit passive, covering of my roots as I can. There were many opportunities when the limelight was shining on me, when I had a podium through celebrity, to announce my heritage. Why now? I never denied being Choctaw. I was never asked, but neither did I volunteer my heritage.

By announcing I am Choctaw, I changed my world. I shed a thick skin of image, of my established identity, and of my person. My whole public persona is now under the microscope. I'm being viewed differently from a plethora of perspectives. This coming out is solely motivated by me wanting to come to myself. Coming to who I am.

The mirage of who I was, how did that happen? How was it assumed I was a white man? That was the norm, and my looks and last name allowed that character to be created. My failure to reveal to myself and the world led to the big reveal after decades of image and persona layering.

The frames of the world, the streaming of my surface into the convenient river of whitewashing, happened with my silent, conspiratorial consent. It doesn't matter now how it happened or how I will be treated, vilified, or castigated. That external stuff is inconsequential. All that truly matters is that I find myself and what I strayed from. That what I find becomes a part of me or all of me and from there I go forward. My own "truth and reconciliation."

So, in I went. That's the why. As I come out of learning, I don't have some profound knowledge or sense of nobility. I come out humble and grateful, appreciative of my people's legacy and heritage. It's not an attitude of being better than any other race, culture, belief system, or religion. I come out with love and respect for who the Choctaw were, are, and can be. I embrace being part of my culture's past, present, and future. We, like any other people, have faults in our ways and our behaviours from time to time. And like most people, we have our strengths, faith, beliefs, traditions, values, and integrity. We intend good for all peoples, animals, the planet, and the wide world. With all these lessons, I go forward, blessed.

My feet are on the ground. I'm stable in who I am. I am Choctaw. In that lies my being and how I will meet the world.

CHAPTER 58

For Me, For Now

What's that line from "Closing Time" by Semisonic? "Every new beginning comes from some other beginning's end." I love that song.

I shut out and shut down Mackin, and at the end of the tour, what do I have? No Mackin. No Sean. No man. But I have me.

How much baggage do we all carry? What an overworked excuse of a cliché. We carry what we decide to carry; nothing more, nothing less. So, all I did was unpack. Another cliché. In my head, I sound like bad lines from the back room edits of *What About Bob?*

I didn't unpack. I freakin' moved into my own head, heart, and soul. Did I cut through layers? I don't know. At times I felt like I was replaying old home videos with a sharp, intuitive, insightful perspective on all the roles that people were playing. The actors and actresses were dynamic, vibrant, and real, except for me. I was alternately looking at myself as a victim, a pawn, a player, a bad ass, and a perpetrator. It was an out-of-body experience. I made myself angry at myself, sad for myself, happy with myself, and on and on. Mostly, I was puzzled by myself. The obvious facts and realities of much of my past I only bumped up against or brushed off as I lived through them. Why?

Why didn't I have the ability to stand my ground and say my piece? My out was convenient. No, not the booze, the drugs, the partying, the screwing, or all the crazy nonsense. I was an artist, a talent. So, I played to the tragic soul, the escapism of the misunderstood creative being. What a fuckin' con artist I was. I conned myself and probably no one else.

What have I discovered? Acceptance. Accepting who I was at times in my life, wrestling those parts of me into some semblance of understanding. There is, surprisingly, at the end of this match, this tussle with self, very little bitterness, resentment, or anger. Either towards others or at myself. I've learned that life is a chaotic, stewing pot, where everyone brings something of themselves to throw into the potluck recipe. Life unfolds with the ingredients provided by others for my evolving recipe of self. I came out well, tasty. Appetizing in my mind's eye. A worthwhile concoction of good intent and meaning with an occasional stray spice thrown in.

With time and striving, the dish can come out more than okay. Tasty. The music and the tour served me up to me and anybody who cared to listen, sing, dance, sway, and swim along.

My music is the taste of me that I give you all.

For me, for Lisa, at the end of the day, this is me, born a rich, entitled white girl to black parents. My apologies to Steve Martin and fans of the movie *The Jerk*. I've emptied my own well, bucket by bucket, and the water is now good to drink and share.

Lisa leaving Lisa to begin Lisa. The journey summed up in that lyric about new beginnings rise from endings of other beginnings.

Now I'm Lisa. That makes me smile. I know this Lisa isn't yesterday's Lisa or tomorrow's Lisa. The same as everybody else, every day the very you of that day can and will change, adapt, layer, evolve, progress, regress, undress, go to bed. Get up, get dressed, get going. How freakin' wonderful!

No pat answers, no mapped, trapped, or graphed trajectory. Just staying with the me within me and moving forward to the one I'll become. That's exciting and comforting and real.

That song lyric about endings and beginnings is from Semisonic. I love the chorus of that song answering the question about 'knowing who you want to take you home.'

I know who I want to take me home. Me, myself, I!

Who's taking Lisa home? Just me. Lisa taking Lisa home. That's something. Something very good.

For now.

CHAPTER 59

GoHo's Coalition of Colour

I was walking home alone past GoHo's when I saw Lisa sitting in her booth. Alone. I almost went inside to say hello, but a cold December wind was sweeping me home to Gina.

Lisa didn't see me, but I still smiled at her as the wind and my momentum combined to blow me past. We had talked several times at GoHo's over the last three months, after her tour ended. Just as I had talked with Mo and Mackin when I crossed paths with them at the diner. We were all good.

The three of them all seemed to shine with an inner glow. I knew enough about their journeys over the last year and a bit to know they had reason to beam.

Mackin had courageously addressed his heritage and confronted his critics with a demeanour of quiet resolve and strength. Mackin was becoming known as the epitome of class. He never countered his critics; he simply acknowledged their perspective and stayed the course. He was contributing a meaningful investment of time, effort, influence, and resources to what he believed, and he was conducting himself with dignity. The stories in the media described him as a stoic warrior for his causes and people. A Choctaw rising.

Mackin was just that, a stoic, smiling warrior. Mackin was also married with a child on the way, with his Choctaw wife and partner. His foundation had exploded with benefactors.

Mo is a testament to self-belief. Her journey has just been chronicled in a national newspaper article and a business magazine. Mo is becoming an icon as a self-made woman who has overcome adversity with a smiling grace, fierce independence, uncommon wit, and an adept, agile, intelligent business acumen. As the spotlight shines on Mo, she never discusses or depicts her rise as anything unusual or special.

When the media and the public express awe regarding what she has overcome, Mo just shrugs and says there was nothing else but to do what had to be done. What single mothers must do every day. She apologizes when she is asked what her strength is or what character trait allows her to rise. She also apologizes for not having a grand response and for sounding like such a trite cliché. Her answer is always the same. "Faith. Faith in myself. Sorry, but that's the only explanation I have. Mainly and simply because at times that's all I had. I had my daughter, my sister, and, of course, the Gordons' care. That was more than enough."

Mo is managing four tours under a separate company set up by Lisa, the Gordons, and Mo. She owns forty percent and will be crisscrossing North America, except for two months in Europe, with Lisa and the band. She is also overseeing other aspects of Lisa's various projects and work. Mo was brought in to discuss how the MLF product line could be integrated and adapted to all the concert clothing merchandise. The MLF brand was tagged on all four touring concerts and Lisa's concert merchandise. Mo joked that MLF now also stands for "Mo's Line of Fashion."

Go, Mo!

And what about Lisa? Well, she's a woman on fire. She has a new clothing line launching in the spring, new music being written, and new acts under contract. Maybe a budding romance with her drummer, her bass player, a retired NHLer, an RCMP officer, or an astronaut. Lisa is so central in the media's eye that if she shows up in the vicinity of a single eligible man of stature, they are romantically linked. Lisa only talks to me about loving her life and her music. Mostly, she talks about her joy for others, including Gina and me.

Me? I still like to eavesdrop on conversations at GoHo's, mostly with Gina. My ex-wife would call it "settling." I turned down the opportunity to do a six-month stint in Europe. I call it bliss.

There's a lot of stuff in a lot of rearview mirrors. You can check those mirrors endlessly. Check over your shoulder, turn around, and confront the past, or you can leave it all behind. You can pass GoHo's and smile.

I look back on it all. I refer to the four of us as Goho's Coalition of Colour. How we travelled parallel but very different paths to ourselves, our better lives. There are no trailing hands in our coalition. If there were trailing hands, those hands would be waiting to catch other hands. To hold other hands, to steady them, to help them along a path leading to themselves. There would be no missing the grasp of those hands.

I love how Mo makes me laugh. She tells the story of her exasperation in trying to explain Indians after reading the children's book *Ten Little Indians* to her sister.

Delta Dawn would ask when they got their feathers. Mo would explain about Indians of the feathered variety and Indians of the dot variety. Delta Dawn wasn't having it and could never quite grasp the need for a difference or separation between the two types of Indians because, after all, they were all Indians. Mo liked and accepted the wisdom in that. Because, after all, we're just human beings, and the four folks put together in GoHo's diner certainly demonstrate that individually and collectively. Black, red, brown, and white. In a diner where we learned that parts or our lives were screwed over, and somehow, we still emerged into our own light as we all left Lisa in our own way.

Song #11 "Leaving Lisa"

My starts have been false
I'm back at the line
Coming from behind
Leaving has to be timed

Time to leave, time to go
The heave and the ho
The emotional roll

Rock back on my heel
Then up on my toe
Loaded to spring
The race to I don't know

Time to leave, time to go
The heave and the ho
The emotional toll

Been training for goodbye
Leaving time is long overdue
Leaving her miseries
Leaving her sorrows too

Time to leave, time to go
the heave and the ho
Of the heart and soul

Racing down a new track
No sense in looking back
Not losing myself this time
Finding my grace by the finish line

Time to leave, time to go
The heave and the ho
Love lost and brought low

Leaving Lisa's not easy
No walk in the park
Driving down my own lane
And out of my dark

Time to leave, time to go
The heave and the ho
Finding Lisa 2.0

CHAPTER 60

Table Scraps from the Diner

Lisa

Some songs didn't make the cut for *Leaving Lisa*. As a prime example, "Immolate" just didn't fit the tone, the vibe, or anything else about the album. It's a song about self-destruction, and that wasn't where I was headed in my deep dive. It belonged to the four demons, and they weren't going to be the focus of my record or of my life. They were to be left.

One song, however, I just loved, but I didn't know how it fit. Most of *Leaving Lisa* is about why, and this song is about avoiding the why. It is about what. "What" got left in the studio, for now.

Guy/Sean

I look at Mo, Mackin, and Lisa and realize how vanilla my upbringing was. Just two good parents working to better themselves and provide a good life for their families. My siblings and I were normal and well-adjusted, just going through life in the suburbs. School, church, sports, kick the can, and neighborhood friends. Following a trajectory that wasn't really mapped, just seemed laid out that way. Go to college or university, get a job, get a girl, get married, have kids, have a career. There was never anything grandiose about it all; it just was what it was. A straight, clear line.

Nothing to worry too much about. Nothing to fear, and nothing to hide. It just all rolled out and happened. Everything went so well for so long and then it didn't. I was ill-prepared for adversity, but there's something in vanilla that's grounding, at least for me. Never too high, never too low. Just a guy who goes with the flow.

But now I want to feel more. More of everything. I'll take things that make my life "go bump in the night" if they come. And they will. Because I can rise. I can go off course, out of line, and come back. I can walk a crooked mile and maybe travel that path with a knowing smile.

Because I know that vanilla is a spice, and I have that.

Song Outtake from *Leaving Lisa* "What"

Please don't tell me why
You know that will make me or both of us cry
Me cuz I know "why" is the prelude to "goodbye"
You cuz you always choke when you lie

I just need a what
Something, some cause, that makes clear
How this will end with a thud
Some fact, some perceptible flaw
Like my bent nose or my weak jaw

Why? Don't even try
Your reasons won't rise, won't fly
Your story won't sell, won't go down well
"Whys" are just made to hurt like hell

The why can be drawn out and long winded
And once spoke never rescinded
Your why could be short and curt
You think abrupt will lessen the hurt

No, please just give me a fact
Don't worry about tact
Give me something real to attack
Put something heavy on my back

Why? My God, don't even try
There's nothing from you that I'll buy
There are no tears left for me to cry
My heart is done; my eyes are dry

I just want to hear a for instance
What I did that created this distance
What part of me creates resistance
Give me real, give me substance

No why. Never. There's nothing in why

Just what

Wa-wa-wa-wa-what

What, what, what, what, what

(In repeating "what," voice moves from a broken whisper to a primal scream, like Daltrey or Downie, and ends with the slowly whispered last line.)

Please don't make me cry.

ACKNOWLEDGEMENTS

Have you ever encountered a great storyteller? You know the type of person who could capture a room with a tale no matter the topic or the audience. That person who could draw you in and grab your attention, because they were genuine, had an authentic voice and a sparkle to their words. I have known a few.

The inspirational story telling of my high school hockey coach Brian Pounder stands out. Punch told stories of his youth, hockey and most importantly principles to live by.

The women in my family tell the same story at the same time only completely differently so at the end you don't know fact from fiction. My advice, in their presence, is to lean heavily to the fictional end of the account. When they spin their tales, I often ask them who is listening as they talk over each other. They all respond "nobody" but they advise me to never let that get in the way of a good story.

My friends Mark Dufresne, Mike Watson, Perrin Beatty and David Paterson can tell stories about the corporate world, politics, professionalism and personal journeys that are always enthralling, often humorous, passionate and without a doubt meaningful. I always learn something when I listen to these 'Four Horsemen of Words and Wisdom.'

There are many others, but there is one individual who still resonates in my heart and head as a great storyteller. My dearly departed buddy Dixon MacKinnon, friend to all and mentor to many. Dixon would charge people for his stories. A buck a person was his going rate. He once charged our eleven- year-old son and eight-year-old daughter for his entertaining story on how to boil shrimp. His motto could have been, 'If you have ears, then you pay up, my dears.' Dixon would tell a story about being 'hoodwinked' out of $300 dollars. His goal was to tell the story for one buck at a time until he recovered his losses. The story telling of 'The Lincoln Tunnel Boom Box Episode' I am sure ended as a profit center for Dick.

We all have stories of our heritage, our upbringing, our trials and tribulations that occur in our everyday lives. I have learned from occasionally listening and eavesdropping that all our journeys are important, vital and interesting. It's this stuff of life that inspires the creation of Mo, Guy, Lisa and Smackin' Mackin'. I sincerely hope you enjoy the main characters of Leaving Lisa as you listen in to their conversations at GoHo's diner.

I love the four of them, but then again, I am biased.

I want to acknowledge the talent of David Paterson, who took the raw lyrics from Lisa's compositions and created beautiful music for five of the songs, that I hope to share with you. Barb Thorson and Don Kletke took David's music and created a beautiful version of 'Cut in Half' and I thank them for their artistry. Hopefully we will be producing a few more songs from David, Barb and Don.

Sincerely,
Michael

BOOKS BY MICHAEL MCMULLEN

Scarred **2019**

Published in 2019, *Scarred* had limited distribution and became a top ten best seller in the Winnipeg market. SCARRED is the first in the 'Newspaper Crew' series, followed by *Garbage Boy – The High Bar of Low Expectations* in 2024 and the third installment arriving in 2026.

Scarred tracked the path of Scarface aka Garbage Boy and his mother over a decade as they struggle to ascend in the face of adversity. The boy faces the everyday battle of being an easy target for the local gangs and tough guys. The mother struggles to overcome the desertion of her husband and a brutal rape while doing the best she can for her three children.

They 'make do and get by' while lifting themselves up in the face of social class stigma amid the swirling cultural shifts of the late 60's and early 70's.

Scarface is accompanied by an eclectic group of companions, including his close friends Bogeyman and Scarecrow and his bosses Mister and Stone Pony. The underdog story involves an unresolved suspicious death and mayhem on the horizon. Scarface and his mom are 'persons of interest' in the death.

The humble bedside prayers of the mother go largely unanswered as the pair weaves their way through abandonment and abuse to find some sort of ascension.

Garbage Boy – The High Bar of Low Expectations **2024**

Garbage Boy has had it rough his entire life. His deadbeat dad deserted the family and his mom's abusive boyfriend is a menacing presence. His family's low rung on the social ladder makes him an object of ridicule and abuse in his small town. That all begins to change when Garbage Boy begins working for Mister and Stone Pony, two mysterious men who enlist his aid in their growing sanitation enterprise. Who thought that picking up garbage would be a road to redemption, never mind riches?

Garbage Boy's situation and status improve remarkably and everything is going well until he and his associates encounter a cocktail of chaos. Mister and Stone Pony's entrepreneurial ventures sparked a looming drug war with the Mayhem Motorcycle gang. Garbage Boy is engulfed in this swirl of conflict which is further inflamed by his own old grudges with local gang members. The escalating conflict threatens everything that Garbage Boy has gained…and then some.

UPCOMING RELEASES

The Last Flight of the Orioles Fall 2026

Childhood friends Jimmie and Mikie remained linked throughout their lives despite the very different paths they followed. One remained in their hometown, studied hard, worked hard, followed a straight-line career path and married the girl he first dated. The other not so much. They come together throughout their adult lives sporadically but always at crucial crossroads in their divergent paths.

The story is charged with emotion as Jimmie often feels forgotten by his friend and that their friendship exists or is on occasion revived only at the convenience of Mikie. They are both products of a culture that repressed men expressing emotions towards each other. Jimmie craves the affection and warmth of his close friend. Mikie on the other hand finds that need at best is an afterthought. The toxic masculinity that dominated their upbringing remains a barrier to a truly loving relationship and a full appreciation of their best friend. That is until the end, when these two Orioles embark on their last flight together.

The Last Flight of The Orioles is an emotional laden trip through time. Full of humour, reflection and the honest perspective of the needs and deeds of two men, who knew each other from day one but didn't really know each other until the end of days.

Lost and Found: The Shot Gunning of Mrs. D Fall 2026/ Spring 2027

'Lost and Found' the third book in the 'Newspaper Crew' chronicles, following *Scarred & Garbage Boy -The High Bar of Low Expectations*

Death brings closure. Or does it? Garbage Boy is gone but not forgotten. Closure remains elusive. In 'Lost and Found' the main characters stumble forward blanketed by the searing pain of loss. Some don't seek healing; some seek revenge or something even more tangible. Whatever they have lost or found along the way there will be no clear resolution until the exact fate of Garbage Boy is clear. They need a 'body' to close the chapter, make that two bodies.

The cocktail of chaos that enveloped Garbage Boy continues to be shaken and stirred. Mister and Stone Pony continue to grow the legitimate parts of their burgeoning business empire while forced into an unexpected alliance in the drug trade they are trying to exit. Scores need to be settled with the Mayhem Motorcycle gang, or do they?

There seems to be a lull before the storm. The entry of Mrs. D and her big time, greasy lawyer husband signals the start of another maelstrom of good intent and bad outcomes or is that bad intent and good outcomes? Depends on your perspective and which end of Mrs. D's shot gunning ways you are facing.

New characters enter the mix, new partners embrace each other tentatively and nothing is crystal clear. Spring thaws float both renewal and sorrows to the surface. The spectre of turbulence stirs just as the nightcrawlers do in the Worm Moon of March.

Does anything get resolved or do the characters just move from chaos to chaos, existing, between lost and found?

ABOUT THE AUTHOR

Michael McMullen has travelled widely and engaged with a wide spectrum of society. His work has often required building teams and working intensely with individuals in difficult situations. He has made presentations in front of large groups from university classes of 300+ students to business conference presentations of over 1,000. Through this he learned that a good story is like a good presentation; you have to attract and hold an audience with your words. He is the author of two other books, *SCARRED* and *Garbage Boy: The High Bar of Low Expectations*. Michael lives in LaSalle, Manitoba with his wife. Readers can find him on Facebook: Michael McMullen Author Page https://www.facebook.com/michael/mcwrites Author's Page Facebook, his website: www.michaelmcmullenbooks.com, on LinkedIn: Michael McMullen Author or on Instagram: michael mcwrites.

Printed in Canada